THE MOMENT OF TRUTH

Joanna

She seized her dream of money and success. A nightmarish moment revealed the terrible price she paid.

Dean

He devoted the best years of his life to one unwavering love. In a single moment, it was shattered forever.

Sara

She thought hers was the perfect marriage. Until she discovered her husband found his perfection . . . somewhere else.

ALAN EBERT

AVON BOOKS
A division of
The Hearst Corporation
105 Madison Avenue
New York, New York 10016

Published by arrangement with the author
Library of Congress Catalog Card Number: 86-8522
ISBN: 0-380-89855-1

Published in hardcover by William Morrow and Company, Inc.; for information address Avon Books.

First Avon Books Printing: July 1988

Printed in the U.S.A.

K-R 10 9 8 7 6 5 4 3 2 1

For Arline Ebert Greer,
my friend and sister

ACKNOWLEDGMENTS

The author wishes to thank

Elaine Winner for her honesty, enthusiasm, encouragement and love;

Nancy Evans Bush, executive director, IANDS, for her assistance, intelligence, humor, friendship and humanity;

Barbara Harris for sharing;

Blanche Meyerson for her guidance and her very being;

Kevin Meaney for his research assistance;

Walter Meade for his encouragement and support;

Richard Whitney of Linden & Deutsch for his legal expertise;

Pat Golbitz of William Morrow for her editorial talents and her understanding and caring;

Kathy Robbins for who as well as what she is in my life—friend and agent.

ONE

"WE must stop meeting like this," Joanna whispered as his face moved close to hers. She could feel his breath as his fingers played upon her cheeks and forehead. It was warm and moist, and it reminded her of Reynolds. She wondered how Reynolds would feel if he could see his friend and colleague doing to her what he, Reynolds Bennett, was known throughout Beverly Hills to do best.

"I'm cheating on my husband and I don't care," she said as her eyes stared into his. They were beautiful eyes, clear and blue. Like Reynolds's.

"Don't talk now," he commanded, his voice throaty and urgent.

The needle plunged and probed, moving under and about her "misery lines," those two deep crevices that began just under her nose and moved downward toward her mouth. The pain was minor and considered a fair exchange for the removal of those incriminating signs of aging. The needle was extracted and then plunged again, this time between her eyes where other damages had collected. The procedure would last eight minutes, a fair exchange, thought Joanna, for the five to six months of promised wrinkleless existence. The miracle of collagen.

"I think you're enjoying this," she said as his hands were again upon her face, patting those areas where he had injected the fibrous protein. He was like an artist putting his finishing touches on his work. Only he left no signature, no mark at all, as there was no knife to leave telltale scars. Her brilliant reconstructive surgeon. Years ago, he had been a plastic surgeon. But no more. Not since the word plastic had come to mean something else, something quite negative.

"So am I gorgeous?" Joanna asked. "Is it the face I think I had twenty years ago?"

"Shut up, Joanna, and let it set. It's a damn good thing you didn't see Reynolds professionally. He'd have strangled you. And I'm tempted," he added as he helped her to her feet. "By the way, why didn't Reynolds do this work for you?"

"Donald, you're dear but naïve. In Beverly Hills and Hollywood, where youth runs as wild as rumors, a woman must maintain the illusion if not the reality of youth and beauty," Joanna replied teasingly.

"Your illusion should hold for a half-year—give or take a month or two in either direction," he said as she slipped into the black velvet suit jacket she had removed for the procedure. "But don't hesitate to make an appointment if deterioration occurs sooner than expected."

"What charming phraseology . . . *deterioration.* I feel like the Acropolis—about to collapse in ruins. Either that or I'll wake up one morning to find my face around my knees," Joanna added.

"Don't worry. We can always lift it," said Donald reassuringly.

Joanna patted his cheek and was out of the office, down the fire stairs—a sure way to avoid others—in seconds. The Isuzu was parked a discreet distance from Lasky Drive, where many of the rich and famous had their nips and tucks in the privacy of their doctors' offices. Reynolds, too, had his office here, a pale cream and burgundy suite whose decor she had selected. Joanna wondered how Reynolds would feel about her collagen injections. Since she doubted he would notice, she dismissed the thought.

The morning was unusually cool for early September and Joanna was shivering by the time she slipped behind the wheel of the car. A glance into the rearview mirror revealed the promised red dots, measlelike, on her face. Donald said they would disappear in four hours. Makeup could then be applied. Which meant by the time she presented herself at Ma Maison for lunch with this year's

Sean Penn, a brilliant actor with an aversion to the press, she could look her old—no, her new—self.

She turned her face from left to right, examining its every detail. From either profile it was strong yet soft, and she really did look years younger than her age. She and Reynolds were a matching set with their blond hair and blue eyes. The difference between them was their noses. Hers was naturally small and it defied her heritage, while his was more in keeping with their Semitic ancestry.

She turned onto La Cienega where Stone and Bennett Public Relations was located. It would be a long day, culminating at dinner with Stacey. Joanna groaned at the thought and silently prayed that her daughter would be in a communicative mood and not her usual sullen self. It continued to amaze Joanna how men liked that sullen look on their California blond beauties, particularly when they were only seventeen. If only colleges would be as willing to accept Stacey as were most men. At the moment the outlook wasn't promising, unless Stacey's senior year at the Westlake School was unlike her others. Please God, let that be, or Reynolds and I will lose our minds wondering what to do with Stace for the next four years of her life, Joanna prayed.

Joanna was surprised to see Lilith's Cadillac parked in the garage of the small office building that housed their firm. At this hour Lilith was normally at home, preferring, she maintained, to breakfast with her family rather than to dine with them. At the end of the day, Lilith explained, she was so sick of talk that the last thing she wanted was to make or hear more of it. Particularly with children, even her own, as she was surrounded by children—Lilith's unique way of referring to their celebrated clients—throughout the day. If her children needed to talk, they had a father, grandparents and an MCI charge card.

As she entered the five-room suite Joanna could hear Lilith speaking on the phone, her voice loud and brusque as she hammered home some selling point to a reporter. Her door was open and Joanna noted, as she stood in the doorway, that Lilith's desk looked as if an entire day—and an exhausting one at that—had already passed.

"Hello, world," Joanna called. "The Tiffany of public

relations has arrived. Or, as *Los Angeles Magazine* also said when describing her as one of the movers and shakers behind the Hollywood scene, '*the* class act of flack,' " Joanna added as she moved on to her own China-blue and gray domain. Her desk was clean except for the two letters awaiting her signature. She knew what they were, although she was not sure whether she would send them. But then, she wasn't sure why she had written them.

The picture of Reynolds on her glass-top desk smiled enigmatically at her. Clients liked the picture. It spoke of stability and said that she was indeed what they had hired: a woman rather than a press agent. Another of their status symbols. Like their Porsches and Mercedeses. Not a bad scam for a girl from East Thirty-fifth Street, a graduate of Brooklyn College whose only goal—realized—had been to obtain her "M.R.S." with a B.A. being incidental.

"The Tiffany of public relations indeed," sniffed Lilith as she barged into Joanna's office without knocking.

"You're just upset because they excluded you," offered Joanna. "But think of it this way, Lil. If I am the Tiffany's to public relations, then certainly you're the K mart."

"And up yours, too," said Lilith as she plopped her considerable girth onto the loveseat to the side of Joanna's desk. "Look at the hour. Why have you come to do battle early?"

"Lilith, it's a job, not a war. A very nice job," replied Joanna as she twitched yesterday's roses into yet another floral arrangement.

"It's a war, baby. Them against us. We're surrounded by enemies, and what the hell have you done to your face?"

"There'll be nothing wrong with my face once you get yours out of it," said Joanna.

"Oh, shit. You're doing collagen," Lilith exclaimed.

"You make it sound like cocaine, for God's sake," laughed Joanna.

"You know, when I was turning forty, I had been in analysis ten years and was just getting my head together when my ass fell down. It was then I said, fuck it. I'll grow old ungracefully but happy."

"Well, you certainly have achieved your goal. At least half of it," said Joanna merrily.

That had been ten years ago, Joanna remembered—1975. She remembered because she was turning thirty at the same time the women's movement was coming of age. No longer was it enough to be the wife of and hostess for a noted plastic surgeon—they were still plastic then, like most of Beverly Hills—a chairperson for several socially oriented fundraisers, who could only claim the title of Mrs. among her accomplishments. She needed expression, and there was horsey, vulgar but brilliant Lilith Stone doing the press relations for one of the glitzy occasions with which Joanna had been involved. Each had been impressed with the other. Within a week Lilith had offered Joanna immediate position and power in exchange for the cachet and contacts Joanna had as Mrs. Dr. Reynolds Bennett. The fact that Joanna had then known nothing about press agentry disturbed her more than Lilith, who had knowingly maintained it wasn't what but who you knew in the Hollywood press, be it print or television.

"Lilith, how did you really feel when you turned forty?" Joanna asked casually as she again glanced at the two letters on her desk awaiting signature. Each said the same to two people who somehow had managed over the years to become one in Joanna's mind. Sara and Dean, her friends from childhood, all of Thirty-fifth Street, all the same age and sharing September birthdays. She hadn't seen either in years.

"Listen, kid, if you think forty sucks, wait till you hit the big five-o and you have that goddamn layout of Joan Collins in *Playboy* to tell you how a woman that age can look. Although why we think some broad with a small waist and big boobs that don't fall to her knees is beautiful is beyond me. Let me tell you, the way I hate Raquel Welch is nothing in comparison to the way I hate that broad."

As Lilith continued to speak, Joanna played with her own feelings about age. They were connected in some way to the letters she had written to Sara and Dean. Yet she didn't know how. A picture of Reynolds's face as he had looked four years ago on the morning of his fortieth birthday flashed into her mind—pensive gloom. She had tried to understand his expression. His face was speaking, but in the silence she could not hear the unspoken words. Just as she could not now hear her unspoken but somewhere known reasons as to why she wanted to see two people with whom she had exchanged nothing more meaningful than a handful of letters over the past years.

"Joanna," Lilith interrupted, "if the onslaught and ravages of age are making you bonkers, let me suggest either crisis intervention therapy or a young man. Frankly, I'd opt for the stud because in the long run that costs a helluva lot less, and unlike therapy, you can feel the difference in your life immediately. Boy, can you ever."

"You're filth. You know that, don't you? Filth, but fun," said Joanna. "Well, I thank you for the sage advice, and I'm sure both Helen Gurley Brown and Marilyn Chambers would applaud your counsel, but neither, I'm afraid, is the answer for me. I mean, really. What woman married for eighteen-going-on-nineteen of her soon-to-be forty years wouldn't be somewhat disconcerted by the passage of time? Even if the pieces of her life are all in place."

The phone ringing on her desk startled Joanna. Lilith answered with a crisp: "Who the hell is reaching out to touch at this hour of the morning? Dammit, Barney . . . what the hell is so fucking important that you'd call at eight-ten and on Joanna's private line? What? Listen, bee's dick, couldn't that have waited until we open at nine-thirty? Christ, but you investigative reporters are a pain. Listen, Reardon, why in hell would you want to attend this press conference? If you and your goddamn peep show are planning some exposé on my sweet little rockstar-turned-gospel-singer, I'll call every guy she ever fucked—and that's half of Cleveland—to break your balls . . . if you still have them at your age."

Lilith laughed at the response. "Do you want to speak to the 'Tiffany' of this operation, or is the fact that we know you're attending our press party supposed to make our day? Good! She says hello. Only she says it in French. You know how those Tiffany types are.

"Shithead," said Lilith as she placed the phone in its cradle. "I trust that guy about as much as I trust Mike

Wallace and Geraldo Rivera combined, and that's not much at all. Why he comes to our events is beyond me, particularly a breakfast press conference where there is no hard liquor. It makes me edgy."

"It's when he doesn't come that you should get edgy," Joanna replied. "The fact we can turn out the Barney Reardons at our events is what makes us what we are. And the clients love it. It makes them feel important, gives them something to tell their friends. *If* they have any."

"Christ, but I hate this business," groaned Lilith.

"But you love the living it affords you," countered Joanna.

"This is true. I'm a sellout. But only until I'm rich and can afford my own sensory-deprivation tank. Which reminds me. I have to go to the john."

As Lilith barreled out of the office, the sleeve of her tent dress caught Reynolds's picture sitting on the edge of Joanna's desk. It landed faceup on the carpet, where Reynolds continued to smile. As he always did. As well he should, thought Joanna. He was the man who had achieved all he had desired. Golf and tennis games with the rich and celebrated, a boat at the marina, two cars—one for sport, the other for elegance—a pool man who actually showed up at the house with the same regularity as their famous Japanese gardener and a reputation that now exceeded that of his famous retired father's. From whom he had inherited the business. There was no doubt the Prince of Washington Heights had lived up to her fantasies.

As she replaced the picture on her desk, Joanna thought how he would not remember her birthday. He would be contrite and would buy her something extravagant to pay for his guilt. They would then dine out at Spago's or the latest in place. A pleasant evening and another year would pass. She had nothing to complain about. Certainly she had a lot more than Sara did, with her little life in that little town married to that tight little mind of a sphinxlike man. And Dean . . . Lord only knew what kind of life he had now. Men like that seldom led satisfying or rewarding existences. But they had made their choices, as she had made hers. And wasn't she to be envied and admired? Perhaps that's what she wanted them to see.

Quickly, without further thought, Joanna proofread the letters before her. After signing each, she wrote a memo to her secretary asking that luncheon reservations for three be made for Saturday, September 28—Tavern on the Green, the Crystal Room only. With the ''only'' underlined three times.

I simply do not understand why some women hate doing laundry, Sara said aloud as she sorted socks, separated the whites from the colors, and searched for missing buttons and broken zippers. Her hands and her mind were busy. She would stay busy. Otherwise she would have to deal with Joanna's letter.

As she unrolled Robert's sweat socks, Sara's hands trembled lightly. She shook them hard, as if to castigate their independent anxiety, and then stuffed and closed the laundry bag. It was after all just a letter and she did have several options. She could ignore it, and then when Joanna called she could always lie and say it had never arrived. That excuse had worked with others before. Or she could accept and then on the appointed day claim one of the children was ill. That always worked, but had she used it before with Dean?

Damn Joanna and damn the film festival that was bringing her to New York. Why couldn't Joanna and the past stay buried? Of course, Sara reasoned, you could always do the mature thing and just decline. But what reason would you give? Mature people don't have to give reasons, she told herself. Well, that lets you out, doesn't it?

On the steps leading to the basement laundry, Sara felt the first of the palpitations. Her body broke out in a sweat that was both hot and cold. Dammit, Sara, you are not at gunpoint here, she reminded herself. You do not have to do anything or go anywhere you don't choose. Stop doing this to yourself.

As the laundry bag slipped from her hands and tumbled to the basement floor, Sara sat on the steps, reassuring herself that it was nothing more than anxiety and that nobody ever died from it.

There's always a first time, she told herself.

Isolate the fear. Enter the tunnel. No matter how dark, there's always a light at the end.

Sometimes there's just another tunnel.

Sara Schell, stop this, she demanded. Nothing's wrong. Your husband is but minutes away at the university, your children are safe in their school and you are safe in your own home. The past is nothing to fear. You are not the girl you once were.

The girl she once was. . . . Again Sara's hands began to shake. The tunnel was proving endless. The hell with the laundry, Sara decided. She would reverse her day, just be spontaneous for a change. The marketing first; laundry later. Of course Dana and Naomi would be disappointed. They looked forward to shopping with their mama every afternoon after school. It was their time together, that time when Sara would enter her daughters' world and share their lives. She, more than the girls, looked forward to that hour. Well, tomorrow things would be as usual, and tonight she would discuss Joanna's letter with Stefan. He, with his logical chemistry professor's mind, would know exactly what she should do. Not like her. She felt first and thought later.

Sara mounted the steps to the hallway that separated the rear of the house and its sun-drenched kitchen from the front, where the living and dining rooms were on either side of the house. In the living room she sat in the window seat overlooking what was not quite a lawn and the four-foot terra-cotta brick wall that separated the eighty-seven-year-old colonial from the world beyond. Which was largely that of other faculty wives and their children. It had been the wall that distinguished the house from the others in the Gray Farms community of Princeton. It had also been the wall that made Sara want this house more than any of the others she and Stefan saw.

Stefan was not as enthusiastic. The house was to be his gift to himself for having obtained tenure ten years ago. He objected to the indisputable fact that the house was badly in need of repairs. She argued what house in their price range would not be, and insisted that very little was in need of immediate attention. Very little had ever received it. She rationalized the decay by adding a child rather than something mundane like a new boiler or kitchen every few years. And why then repair a house when there are growing children around who will only destroy it?

She convinced Stefan with her enthusiasm. Yes, the house was frayed around the edges, but it was home. A wonderful happy home filled with their two boys and two girls. She was content. Stefan was happy. He had both his home and his teaching and research projects, about which she had little understanding other than they gave his life—and therefore her own—meaning. She was the wife of an admired Princeton professor, the much-published Dr. Stefan Schell. She liked that identity.

Sara's eyes fastened on the piano that had been Stefan's from childhood. Out of tune, it was also out of touch, as none of her children were musically inclined. Even with its yellowed keys, the piano was Sara's favorite piece in her home. It lent stability. It was grand, like a Grand should be. She had made it the focal point of the room. On top of the lace shawl she placed over it were pictures of the family, but most important, of the children. They surrounded the photograph of her and Stefan, taken on their wedding day fifteen years ago. She looked happy. None of the strain she had felt was evident.

Stefan looked as he often did: like Abraham Lincoln. Tall, slender, with deep, penetrating eyes that drew as much attention as his manicured beard, he was one of very few men who looked comfortable in formal wear. Sara remembered how his eyes had steadied her as she walked down the aisle, shaky from the medication she was still taking. With every step she reminded herself that he loved her. And then, miracle of miracles, before God and their respective families he promised to take her in sickness and in health, to love, honor, cherish and protect—what wonderful words!—till death did they part.

Her mother was alive then. There was no picture of her on the piano, but her face and its expression that blamed the world was etched in Sara's mind. That day she had been happy, had thought for a moment there was indeed a God. Her Sara was married. The bad times were over.

She died within the year, and although an argument could have been made that her mother was dead or dying for most of her life, Sara nonetheless felt it was her problems that sent her mother to an early grave.

Again Sara looked at the bride in the picture. For the first time in her life she had been beautiful. Her chestnut hair was swept back from her face, outlining its sharp edges and angles. The severity was striking. In her tight-bodiced but flowing wedding gown, no one noticed that she was flat-chested. She wore only lip gloss and eye liner to heighten her large, almond-shaped eyes. She also wore heels, huge three-inchers, to lengthen her already long line. And still Stefan towered over her. Another wonderful feeling.

Stefan had liked her body then, she remembered. Not as passionately as some others, but Stefan wasn't like others. And now, so many years later, they were older, and passion was replaced by other things far more important. Like friendship. Like family. They didn't often sleep together anymore. Stefan used the den so as not to be disturbed by her snoring and not to disturb her with his late-into-the-night reading of periodicals and journals for which he had no time during the day. She understood. The times they were together, Sara relished awakening with him near, feeling his warmth as he lay next to her. But sometimes feelings were awakened within her that were reminders of other times . . . misspent. She quelled them, lulling herself with the firm belief that what she shared with Stefan was what every woman really wanted.

Quickly Sara walked toward the kitchen and her car keys. Best to do the marketing now, she reasoned, before further damage could be done with further recollections. She would buy something special for dessert. For the children, the source of her light. Joanna had but one, and Dean, of course, none. Sara wondered about that. A life without children must hardly be a life at all, or one hardly worth living, she decided. Children were life. Children were like the wall around the house. They kept the love in and the world at a safe distance.

She would not go to the lunch in New York, Sara decided. The girl Joanna and Dean knew as Sara, like their friendship, didn't exist anymore. No lunch. No New York. Even if Stefan drove her into the city and waited for her, she could not go. Stefan of course would argue that she could, and if he pushed as he had so many times in the past, she would undoubtedly prove him right. But she didn't want to be pushed down memory lane even if it was to see Joanna. God, but she had loved her so once!

The car keys were atop Joanna's letter on the kitchen counter. As Sara reached for them, her eye caught the proposed date for Joanna's lunch. She began to laugh. September 28. How wonderful! The laughter turned to tears of relief. She didn't have to go to the supermarket now. There was indeed a light at the end of the tunnel. She, Sara Schell, didn't have to go anywhere on that date, least of all to New York, because she truly had a prior commitment. Joanna had chosen the same Saturday as the one now designated for their son Evan's bar mitzvah. And how was that for an excuse that couldn't be questioned, and one not even she had used before!

They were lying spoon fashion in the king-sized bed. Dean's eyes were closed and his face was buried in equal parts of neck and hair.

"What are you thinking about?"

"A bar mitzvah," Dean replied as he rolled onto his back, "and I'm damned if I can understand how Joanna's luncheon reunion of the Thirty-fifth-Street Three has suddenly turned into a religious experience in New Jersey. It just doesn't add up. Sara didn't invite me to her first son's bar mitzvah."

"Oh, yes, she did. Last spring. And you declined."

"I remember. Last year's model was named Robert; this year's, Evan. I sent a wallet."

"The hell you did. *I* sent a wallet. In your name. And you're welcome."

"Now why would I ask you to do something like that for me?" Dean asked. "And why didn't I go?"

"You were pissed . . . something about Sara in the past always having some kind of excuse when you wanted to see her. I thought it was bullshit then. I think it's bullshit now."

Dean looked at the man who had risen from the bed and was now stretching to his full height as he looked out the bedroom window onto Ninety-second Street. The body was lean and hard, and the man looked much like the blue-eyed, straw-blond boy Dean had met eight years ago in a conventional Village bar. He still looked twenty-seven. Which was aggravating, Dean thought, watching Chris jerk himself into his jockstrap; he did nothing but jog three times a week. Not like Dean, who had to struggle to maintain his weight and body with almost daily workouts at the Y. But then he was five years older, almost forty, not a comforting thought for anyone and least of all for an actor.

"So why do you think it's bullshit?" Dean asked as he watched Chris lace up his running shoes.

Chris shrugged. "You tell me. Do you want to go this year?"

Dean thought and finally had to admit: "Yes and no. I haven't seen Joanna in years, and although Sara's just across the river, neither of us has made an attempt to see the other."

"Knowing how you hate foreign travel and the trouble you have with the currency, what's the big surprise?"

"Great, Chris. I'm trying to talk and you're doing shtik. Help, for Chrissake."

"OK, I'm helping," Chris said as he sat beside Dean on the bed. "What are you afraid of?"

Dean bristled. "Why do you always think I'm afraid of something?"

"Cut the crap. This is me, remember?" Chris said as he stood abruptly, slapping a visored hat with wings attached at the sides on his head. "We both know if you weren't dodging something, you'd go."

"I hate that dumb hat," Dean said. "If the medical profession ever saw you wearing it, they'd drum you out of the corps."

"If they didn't dump me when I wore you on my arm to the AMA dinner last fall, I think they'd forgive this hat. As though I give a shit. And that's the difference, Dean. I don't give a shit, and you do when you shouldn't. You don't want to go to that bar mitzvah because you're still hiding in the closet."

"Well, let's face it, Chris. We might not go over very big in suburbia," Dean said.

"Are you kidding? We'd be terrific," Chris replied as he began running in place, a ritual of his warm-up exercises. "And if you're worried about your macho image, you big Italian stud, I'll let you lead when we're dancing."

"And I bet you would," Dean said, shaking his head at the prospect.

"Damn straight I would. And if you only had balls as big as your dick, you would, too," Chris countered. "Because then you wouldn't give a damn who knew you're gay."

"Sometimes I think you know me too well," Dean moaned.

"Don't complain. Just remember all the years when no one wanted to know you except in the biblical sense. And be grateful."

He remembered. Too well he remembered. The years before Chris spent in bars and baths and other sexual battlefields where oral but not verbal skills were prized. Talk disturbed and dislodged the fantasy, ruined the image, particularly his, as he had been such a definite type with his dark, brooding face and his muscular body. For years he had been cast in a role as the strong, dominant male, and over the years he had found the role less bothersome to play than to resist the typecasting. Until he went stale and something within refused to respond each time he took center stage to play someone else's vision of him as a leading man. More and more there had been the difficulty of getting up for a performance.

But there had been none of that with Chris, who had demanded honesty by his own honesty. He didn't chit or chat but spoke in earnest. About politics, social issues and himself, his *real* self. No one did those things in a gay bar.

Dean looked at Chris. "Do you know how disconcerting it is trying to hold a civilized conversation with a man who is not only running in place but wearing a hat with wings attached to it? I can't tell if you're coming or going."

"You never had any trouble telling when I was coming before."

"Swell. Now he adds some filth to what I hoped would be a mature conversation," Dean said, annoyed.

"Come on, Dean. Cut the shit and face up," Chris said, his voice hard. "Why do you give a goddamn whether they know or not that you're a homosexual? Chances are they've put it together by now anyway. And damn, it doesn't bother me that they're heterosexuals. Live and let live, I say. After all, they're just people. Hell. It doesn't even bother me that my mother married one. He's not such a bad guy, even if he does like *Monday Night Football* and beer."

"Too bad he doesn't share that enthusiasm for you and your Monday night preferences," Dean said, knowing he was going for a low blow.

"Listen, Dean. That's his problem, and I refuse to make it mine," Chris replied softly. "My dad does the best he can do. Remember, Lawrence, Kansas, is Middle America. They think and feel differently than New Yorkers. But you, you live in the big city. You should be long over your homosexual paranoia."

"Give me a break," Dean said. "Just because I'm from the city doesn't mean I didn't get my share of the shit. Remember, my father turned me out of his life when he discovered I was gay. And my brother barely remembers I'm alive. And what about your wife? You haven't forgotten how well she took it when she discovered shortly after you did that you preferred men to women."

Chris sighed. "Barbara didn't 'discover' it, Dean. I told her. And there's a big difference. I *came out* and told her. That she couldn't handle it was understandable. Shit. It wasn't all that easy for me. It was not what I was supposed to be or do. But it was who I was . . . who I am. I had no choice. Barbara did. She's really not a bad person, Dean. Just unenlightened. But what was I about to ask before you jumped all over me? Yes . . . is there something else going on that makes you reluctant to attend the bar mitzvah?"

"Do you think you could stop bouncing up and down like that?" Dean asked. "It's making me nuts. If you're going to talk, talk. If you're going to run, run."

Chris continued to run in place, looking at Dean patiently.

"All right," Dean said, resigned to Chris's stubbornness. "It's what I think is called an identity crisis. I'm feeling like nerd city . . . a zero."

Chris stopped running.

"I mean . . . who the hell am I?" Dean continued. "What do I tell Joanna and Sara if we go to New Jersey? Hi, guys. This is my husband, Chris. He's a doctor and I'm a housewife."

"I hate that kind of talk," Chris said angrily. "I'm not your husband; you're not my wife. We're lovers."

"You know what I'm saying," Dean argued. "Dammit, Chris, I'm soon to be forty fucking years old. Half my life is over, which is a damn sobering thought. I'm not young anymore. You can't apply 'promising' to someone my age. The simple truth is I'm an actor who hasn't acted in years, who hasn't even tried to act in years. I'm nothing."

"Not to me you're not," Chris said defiantly.

"Chris, you mean well, but that doesn't help. It really doesn't," Dean repeated with a sigh. "It's not enough for the moment that we love each other. That's not what this is about. Actually, you're not the right person for me to be discussing this with. Hell. You're part of the problem."

"Then I'm going to continue my running," Chris said as he began his in-place motions again, his face reflecting anger but also concern.

Dean entered the bathroom for his usual hot-to-cold shower. He had not meant to offend Chris and was surprised at the resentment that had crept into his words, particularly since their eight-year relationship had finally given some meaning and direction to his life. And the home they built, a wonderful, old and yet new brownstone, bought but not yet paid for with Chris's earnings as a pediatrician. They found the building four years ago after many months of search. It was beaten up and in disrepair, abandoned by its owner and seemingly by life itself. Dean nurtured it, building from within to without with his hands, heart and a talent that spanned the generations in the Di Nardo family. Four years of his life were consumed by the renovation. Now he managed the top two rented floor-through apartments, as well as Dr. Christopher Langdon's life above his ground-floor office.

It had never seemed a mistake to make Chris the focus of his life eight years ago. Then, Dean remembered, as he soaped first one side of his body and then the other, it was the only sensible decision due to Barbara, *Mrs.* Langdon, who wanted her pound of flesh and extracted it each month in the form of a check that covered her expenses. Which Chris paid to her, not because of sexual guilt—or so he insisted—but because he felt guilty about what his newfound sexuality did to Barbara and their marriage. After all, Chris had explained, Barbara dropped out of college in her junior year to support him through medical school. She gave up her ambitions, her plans for a career.

Big fucking deal, thought Dean. And what about the ambitions and the career he had given up in order to support Chris through years made difficult . . . no, impossible, by Barbara's demands for creature comforts and revenge? Too clearly he remembered the state of Chris's health when he was working extra shifts at Montefiore Hospital, moonlighting at others, just so he could "honor" what he thought of as a commitment to Barbara.

Yet, Dean recalled, he personally had not minded all that much about the existence of Barbara Clarkson Langdon. Not only was she a world away in Kansas City, but there was something about being so totally loved that made jealousy absurd. Barbara was never competition or threat. Just an annoyance for the financial chunk she took each month, a chunk she now wanted to increase due to inflation. Still, Dean decided, if anyone were truly responsible for his being nothing, it was Barbara, as she had caused him to take on Chris's financial burdens and thus negate himself.

Bullshit! Dean admitted as he rubbed himself dry and commenced to shave. Barbara had been a welcome burden. What he viewed as her greed freed him from endless auditions that produced endless rejection. He was as beaten up and abandoned as their building when he decided—and *he* decided—that Chris's career was more important than his own. The carpentry work not only gave him an income but relief from the rejections and the nagging doubts that those rejections fostered about his talent.

And so, Dean remembered as he slapped his face with a light aftershave lotion, what was only to be a few months of temporary adjustments became years. Problems failed to exist because he denied their existence. It felt right, good, until Joanna's letter, followed shortly thereafter by Sara's invitation. Now he was suddenly resentful, even angry, at himself and Chris, although he wasn't certain why. Only one thing was clear: He was turning forty and he was not what he had planned to be or what others thought he would be. Of course that could still change, but it would mean new pictures, a search for an agent, making the rounds again. It would also mean spending less time taking care of the house, of Chris, of their life together, and more time taking care of himself. And that would take a courage he wasn't certain he had.

Chris was munching on a granola bar as he continued to jog in place when Dean re-entered the bedroom. "I only hung around to say if you decide you want me on your arm in New Jersey, I'm ready. I even got my passport renewed just last month," he said.

And he was gone, down the stairs of the duplex and into the hallway of their second-floor landing. Despite the carpeting installed throughout the stairwells, Dean could hear Chris as he thundered down the remaining flight of their five-story brownstone. The front door opened and closed. From the window, Dean watched as a man, looking more like Mercury with that dumb winged hat on his head than he did a pediatrician, ran up Ninety-second Street, across Lexington Avenue toward the park. The sight made Dean smile.

He kissed her lightly, patted her outer thigh and rolled away.

"So how'd we do?" Joanna asked. "Did we win?"

Reynolds looked at her dumbly.

"The race," she explained. "Surely we must have been in some kind of competition. Didn't you set a new world's record this morning for man's fastest orgasm?"

He was up on his feet, bobbing up and down fighter-style. "It's not the quantity but the quality of time," he said, smiling. His expression said he was content. His morning ritual had begun. As he walked to his usual spot before the open windows Joanna said: "You know, you have a great ass."

He was stretched out on the floor, in the beginning of his one hundred situps, when he grunted: "It's the tennis. You should try it. In fact, you should get on the floor with me right now and exercise."

"Listen, stud. If I get on the floor with you right now it won't be for the kind of exercise you're talking about," Joanna replied.

Reynolds laughed but otherwise did not acknowledge her innuendo. As far as he was concerned, that part of their morning was complete. Next were the pushups, to be followed by his bath and breakfast. Joanna watched from the bed, admiring his endurance and the washboard stomach that rippled with his every exertion. There was no doubt her husband was a hunk, as sexy at forty-four as the boy almost half his age who exercised her at the office three times a week. She was never surprised anymore when rumors rebounded that he was having an affair. Years ago she had dismissed the gossip as nothing more than that. Everyone's sex life was a matter of conjecture in Beverly Hills. Joanna could not remember when what she had thought was not possible suddenly became probable. She also could not remember exactly when she had decided the affairs were meaningless. After all, this was Beverly Hills and not Brooklyn. Here the very word "faithful" was an antiquity.

As she lay on the bed, Joanna suddenly observed that Reynolds made love almost exactly as he did his push-ups—in a quick, rapid-fire succession of motions. He actually looked better at it than he was. She should get up, Joanna thought, start the coffee and then shower. As she wrapped herself in a silk robe from Robinson's, Joanna found that her body had not recovered from the attack Reynolds had mounted minutes ago. Trembling, she stood in the hallway trying to identify the sounds coming from Stacey's room. When they grew louder, Joanna, alarmed, burst through Stacey's door and saw Stacey in her bathroom, sitting on the floor, bent over the bowl and vomiting. Joanna rushed to her, placing a hand on her daughter's shoulder. When the spasms stopped, Stacey stood and began washing her face.

"I wish you'd knock first," she said, her voice between a whine and an accusation.

"But you were sick," Joanna said. "Seems to me you've been sick a lot lately. Must be some kind of bug in your system."

"R-i-g-h-t!" Stacey replied as she turned and gave Joanna a look that blended contempt with amusement. "Some kind of bug," she reiterated.

Joanna looked at Stacey. Her blond hair was thrown about her head, unkempt and wild, and Joanna could not tell if it were by style or happenstance. Her skin was pasty, but her body seemed lusher, fuller, despite Stacey's impossibly tiny waist. Joanna's words were spoken before she was aware she had thought. "Are you pregnant?" she asked.

"Just a little," Stacey replied. "Maybe two months."

When Joanna stiffened, Stacey laughed. "Lighten up, Mom. It won't inconvenience you. One of the girls is coming with me after school on Friday to take care of it. So forget it."

"But what about the pills?" Joanna asked, dumbfounded.

"They're not infallible. Also, you have to take them, and I forget," Stacey said matter-of-factly.

"Stacey, some things you can't forget. That's why we put you on the pill. Because you'd forget your diaphragm."

"Mother, I already told you. I don't like to premeditate sex. I just like it to happen."

"A fact of which I am all too aware," Joanna said, her sarcasm not lost on Stacey.

"Mother, don't make this into some tragedy. It's just an abortion. I know lots of girls my age who have had them."

"I can't tell you how much better that makes me feel," Joanna replied drily. "Things were so much easier in my day when sex was still somewhat of a taboo and not as matter-of-fact as it seems to be today."

"Tell me you were a virgin when you married, Mother," said Stacey derisively.

"Damn close. I was twenty when I became sexually active with your father. Not fifteen."

"So I was more advanced than you," Stacey said with a shrug of her shoulders. "Please, this is no big deal so don't make it into one," she added as she brushed her hair, an act that softened Joanna considerably.

"Stacey, it is a big deal. I think we should talk to your father," Joanna said. "He should know of a doctor."

"Mom, I told you, I have a doctor. So back off. I'm a big girl."

"You are still my daughter, Stacey."

"A fact neither of us can deny or forget," sighed Stacey. "No matter how hard we try."

"Now what is that supposed to mean?" Joanna asked, annoyed. "God, but I wish these years when I'm the one dressed in black while you're the one in white would just pass. They're a bore."

"Then forget it. Go. I need to dress for school," said Stacey as she rummaged through her closet looking for something presentable to wear to the exclusive and fashionable Westlake School.

"Tell me. How do you expect to pay for this doctor you intend to see on Friday?" Joanna asked.

"I don't," Stacey said as she picked her way through blouses and sweaters. "I thought I'd send the bill to Dad at his office. Of course I could always use the money Grandfather gave me last year for Christmas."

"That money was for your trip to Europe to be taken upon graduation and before entering college next fall," Joanna reminded her.

"*If* I graduate and *if* I decide to go to college," Stacey replied. "Now please. Let me finish my dressing."

She had been dismissed, and as she stood in the hallway Joanna felt her anger rising. Stacey had always been a problem despite all their efforts. The best schools, clothes, a car, trips, a diaphragm at fifteen when she asked for it. Reynolds would have to speak with her. She could not have Stacey seeing just any doctor for such a procedure. No daughter of hers would be the victim of some butcher's botchery, the news of which would travel the entire Beverly Hills circuit within minutes of Stacey's arrival at some local hospital.

"I could use a shot of vodka in this," Joanna said when Reynolds handed orange juice to her as she entered the kitchen. "What a way to start the day."

There was no response as Reynolds continued to speed-read through the *Los Angeles Times.*

"And thank you very much for asking what's wrong," added Joanna peevishly. "It does so help to know I'm not alone in the problem, particularly when the problem involves your daughter."

"I'm listening," Reynolds said as he turned his attention to the sports page.

"She's pregnant," Joanna said, watching the newspaper to see if its reader would react. "She and her friends are planning a 'coming-out' party this Friday," she added when Reynolds remained silent. "I want you to stop it. I want you to find the best doctor but make sure he's not in Los Angeles. The last thing I need is to have this made public by some 'confidential source.' God, but the lack of privacy in this town can be suffocating."

She waited for a reaction, some show of anger or concern. There was none.

"Reynolds, we are talking about your daughter. She's pregnant and about to have an abortion. Certainly that is more important than the upcoming Rams season," Joanna said angrily.

"I see no need to become hysterical, Joanna," Reynolds said calmly. "I'm aware . . . I'm concerned. I'll take care of it."

"And how are you going to take care of ensuring this doesn't happen again?" asked Joanna.

"I don't suppose there are any convents for Jewish girls," Reynolds said as he poured himself another cup of coffee.

"I don't think that or this situation is funny," Joanna replied, her annoyance showing.

"I'll talk to her, Jo," Reynolds said softly, "but I think we had better face facts. Stacey is not a kid anymore but a hot-to-trot young woman. We've done our job. We've outfitted her with the tools. Now it's up to her to use them.''

''I suppose so,'' said Joanna, suddenly feeling tired and yet relieved.

''We can't change the facts, Jo, but we can accept them. She's pregnant. She needs an abortion. I'll arrange for the best doctor available. *Not* in L.A.'' When Joanna continued to look grim, Reynolds added: ''At least look at the bright side. Her plumbing works.''

She sat stunned, hurt, her face burning as if it had been slapped. He had wanted another child, a son in particular, but she had been unable to give him one. After Stacey, she had suffered a series of miscarriages that eventually resulted in a hysterectomy. She had only been thirty-two.

''Reyn, I need to talk to you about New York,'' Joanna said, deciding the subject of Stacey had been exhausted for the moment.

''Tonight,'' Reynolds said as he gulped down his coffee. ''I have an early nose job this morning.''

''We're not home tonight. You're at your father's and I have a screening.''

''This weekend then,'' said Reynolds as he rushed from the kitchen to complete his dressing.

The weekend then it would be, Joanna decided. A little poolside chat at Caesar's Palace. At some celebrity pro-am tournament that she was not only representing but in which Reynolds would play. He would be happy. Give him a golf club or a tennis racket, throw in a celebrity or two and his life was complete. If only Sara had a golf course in her backyard and a Kennedy for a neighbor, convincing Reynolds would be easy.

''Is that all you're going to eat?'' Joanna asked as Stacey entered the kitchen and brewed a cup of tea.

Waving a soda cracker in Joanna's direction, Stacey replied: ''This is all I can handle.''

''Listen, Stacey, I spoke with your father, and he is going to arrange for you to be cared for by a top doctor. Now don't give me that look. I'll feel a lot better knowing you're in the hands of someone your father knows or who he has at least researched. Anyway, we'll have it done the weekend after next—we're going to Vegas this Friday.''

When Stacey shot her a look Joanna added: "You're welcome to come with us."

Stacey put down her tea. Through clenched teeth, she said slowly, bitterly: "You must be kidding. You expect me to walk around feeling this kind of sick for another ten days so the two of you can play in Vegas? Forget it. Sometimes I don't believe you. The answer is no. I'm going for my abortion Friday."

"Stacey, another week at this stage of your pregnancy won't make any difference," Joanna protested.

"To whom, Mother? You? Well, guess what? It matters to me. A lot. And if that inconveniences you in some way, then butt out."

"It's my job, Stacey. The tournament . . ."

But Stacey was gone, leaving Joanna alone with her thoughts and the *Los Angeles Times.* She opted for the *Times,* wondering if the exclusive story and the three-column items she had sent to their three entertainment columnists had been used. She felt much better when she saw that they had.

TWO

ENCIRCLING Sara on the carpet were half a dozen lists, each concerned with a different aspect of the bar mitzvah. The one currently in her hand was divided between what Michele Caterers (''Elegance Without Extravagance'') would provide and what she and her mother-in-law would cook for the at-home buffet.

''Did you make your barber's appointment?''

The answer to Sara's question was part grunt and half groan and came from a place Sara knew to be other than the here-and-now of her living room. As usual, Stefan was preoccupied, lost in his research, dedicated to a project that made little sense to her. Why Stefan or anyone would want to define the structure of water defied her imagination. She could not grasp what the ramifications of such a discovery would be and therefore dismissed it as a subject of interest to anyone but Stefan and those others at Princeton who assisted in the project. Yet Stefan's research pleasured her. His work made her feel important.

Sara was on her feet heading toward the stairs even before the clock on the mantel struck ten. At the top of the second-floor landing, she knocked twice at the boys' bedroom door and entered when they didn't respond. Both Robert and Evan were in bed, staring at the television that divided the room into two separate but equal parts—or war zones as they sometimes happened to be. Neither noted her presence as each remained glued to the gyrations of the undulating unkempt blonde who was singing about her being, or not being, a virgin. The blatant sexuality of the video disturbed Sara.

''Guys, it's past ten. I want you both in bed,'' Sara said.

"We are in bed," Evan protested.

"Don't be smart," cautioned Sara.

"He wouldn't know how," Robert interjected.

A pillow in the face greeted his response.

"None of that," said Sara before the battle could begin. "Tomorrow's a school day. Bedtime . . . now!" She turned off the TV and the light in two swift movements. In the darkened room she stooped to kiss first one and then the other of her boys before she backed out the door. Across the hall, all was quiet in the girls' room. Peering in through the partially opened door, Sara saw Dana hidden by the tent she habitually made of her blanket, and Naomi asleep on the floor, where she once again had fallen from the bed. Gently Sara lifted her eight-year-old, careful not to wake her as she deposited her between Andy Panda and Raggedy Ann on the bed. As she studied her girls from the doorway, Sara felt a familiar longing and heard the familiar contentious voice that argued: "You are too old to have another child."

As though for the first time, Sara weighed the pros and cons of those words while fixing Stefan another cup of coffee in the kitchen. She knew his feelings on the subject but did not understand them. A child would not tie her down at this stage of her life, as he maintained. A child would be another tie, which was far different, she argued. But Stefan had remained resistant.

He was still involved in his journals when Sara wordlessly handed him his coffee and returned to her lists. Of the forty-six people invited, thirty-eight had accepted. She looked at the names: Richard Wein, Mark Rosenberg, Nicholas Fern, Denise Wolfe. Not one face emerged to make a picture. All were associates of Stefan. All were immersed in water. For a moment Sara wondered if any of the faceless names were single. After all, Ina would be there. With Josh and Sharon. Sara wondered if the children would threaten an available man. The hazards of divorce. Sara shuddered at her sister's condition.

The preparations for Evan's bar mitzvah pleased Sara. Although her own Judaism had been ignored until her children were born, she now found that her religion provided yet another sense of solidarity, of togetherness, of family.

It centered her, and whereas Stefan found religious ritual ridiculous, she found it comforting. The bar mitzvah, however, was not without its difficulties. She wondered what Stefan would say when he learned she had guessed incorrectly.

Sara looked up from her lists at Stefan. She noted the tiredness, the lines that now seemed so recently etched on his face, and again wondered if he wasn't well. But he had denied that possibility once before and maintained he was just stressed from curriculum overload. Too many classes, too many projects and too many conventions for a man who had just passed the half-century mark. She urged him to cut down, particularly on the out-of-town trips. She hated those weekends without him, hated being alone even if Stefan insisted being in a house with four children could hardly qualify as being alone.

"Stefan, I guessed wrong," Sara began slowly. "I never thought they would accept the invitation, but both Joanna and Dean will be attending," she added, her voice contrite. "I really am surprised," she quickly continued. "Lord knows over the years how many times Joanna may have been in New York and she never called. Now she's traveling to Princeton. It feels strange. Yet," Sara mused, "I'm rather glad. I must admit I'm curious after all these years. I don't know if I ever explained how close we once were. When I think of my childhood, the first person I think of isn't my mother . . . or Ina, but Joanna."

"You're not anxious about them coming?" Stefan said from behind his journal.

"A little. No," Sara corrected. "A lot. Both she and Dean are almost like strangers now after so many years. I don't know what they'll expect to find, but I'm glad that they're coming here. It gives me a chance to show off."

He was looking at her oddly.

"You know," she explained, "you, the kids, the house. It's a lot."

"I'm sure, given what you've told me about Joanna, that she has a house to put this to shame and a business even I have heard about. I don't think she'll be too envious, Sara."

She suddenly felt chilled. Inviting them had been a mistake after all.

"What about the other man, Dean's friend? Is he also attending?" Stefan asked.

"Yes. I mean, I suppose so. Why do you ask?"

"I don't know how I feel about my children being exposed to homosexuals. I don't want Robert or Evan to think the relationship between these two men is an acceptable alternate lifestyle. At least not for them. Now please understand me, Sara. I'm not opposed to their relationship. That is solely their business. It only becomes mine when it affects my children."

Sara stared at Stefan, looking for a clue to his statements in his eyes. She saw none. Not hostility, not fear. His reaction, she decided, was pure Stefan: intellectual rather than emotional. Yet she was annoyed. She wanted to argue but couldn't when she realized that she, too, felt homosexuality was not an acceptable lifestyle for her children. In admitting this, she was bothered by what felt like a judgment of Dean, someone who had not judged her when she had felt so judged by others. Dean had supported her throughout her illness. He was one of few who knew the terror she experienced just leaving the house or answering the telephone. Although he did not understand her fear of the outdoors, her crying jags and the days she could only bathe and dress herself, he never ridiculed or minimized her discomfort. It was with Dean that she took her first walk. It was with Dean that she rode her first bus. He had had to hold her hand both times, so great had been her fear at being alone in the world.

Neither she nor her family ever used the word *breakdown.* She hated it and was appalled by all the ramifications attached to its meaning. But she had indeed broken down. On a subway car, trembling and crying, all under the scrutiny of late-night riders, one of whom finally thought to call a transit policeman. For a time a sanitarium was considered, but her mother intervened at her request. She could not go, would not, knowing for certain that once in, she would never come out. And so her mother went with her twice a week to the psychiatrist on Eastern Parkway. Her mother sat with her in the back of a taxi, holding her hand as Sara held on for dear life. And after the sessions, when she was too distraught to speak, her mother would hold and comfort her, pretending the driver of the taxi wasn't there. Once Sara had thought to open the back door as the cab sped down Flatbush Avenue, the idea of flinging herself recklessly into the onrushing traffic suddenly appealing. Only the presence of her mother prevented her. After that the doctor prescribed Valium for her anxiety, Elavil for her depression and Placidyl for sleep. Still her heart pounded, as if seeking to burst free and flee the scene of the crimes she felt she had committed.

She had told no one other than Dean the reasons for her breakdown. Only they weren't the reasons, her psychiatrist maintained, but the symptoms. The reasons were locked in her unconscious, and it was their job in analysis to root out those reasons and free her. The excessive behavior, as he called it, the "acting out" was simply a release for her anxieties, and anxieties were a cover for any number of emotions a person might find threatening. As was promiscuity.

Dean had understood. How and why only became evident when he shared a self that had existed but remained hidden, at least from her, since he was seventeen. She didn't think to be shocked or mindful of his homosexuality then. Her own behavior made his seem neither unusual nor bizarre. His own sexual patterns were not all that far removed from hers. Which was why he could feel her pain. It was like his own, the reasons for which also lay buried in his unconscious.

"Sara, I hope you know I have nothing against Dean personally," Stefan was saying, recapturing her attention. "I know your history with him, and I assure you I will treat him and his friend as I would any of our guests. I was only expressing a concern . . . for the children and also to a lesser extent for you."

She nodded. Yes, a concern . . . for her. She remembered that concern, as she had felt it, as they stood under the *chupah* the day of her wedding. She remembered his eyes as they steadied and then anchored her. In their dark green gaze she knew who she was, and that was more calming than either her therapy or the drugs she was taking. And so she had stopped both.

The clock chimed eleven. Almost nervously Sara collected her lists. Casually she asked as she rose: "Will you be joining me soon?"

She had tried to keep her voice light, nondemanding, unconcerned. It was by now a well-practiced bedtime ritual. She tried not to look at him, to only faintly hear but not react to his response when he said: "I don't think so. I still have some work to finish."

Again, ever so offhandedly, she said: "If you change your mind, I'll be up awhile." Her hand brushed through his hair as she passed his chair. She was on the stairs when she heard him say: "I'll try, Sara."

Flushed, Sara could feel the warmth already filling her face and body. Her skin was tingling and she felt lightheaded, dizzy from sensations that made her feel like a girl. She was happy. She had every reason to be, she decided.

"Smoke, man? I've got good smoke, good weed. The best."

Dean pushed past the drug peddler standing at the entrance of the subway, ignoring his open hand in which rested some loose joints and a packet that could have been either cocaine or heroin. As he stood on the corner of Broadway and Seventh Avenue he looked about, trying to understand the excitement he had felt as a child whenever he had exited the subway from Brooklyn and had stood here, at the "crossroads of the world." But he couldn't. Even with the sun rising, the area was ugly and worn. To the west were the usuals, those who did their assorted sex and drug business under the marquees of the movie theaters that lined Forty-second Street. To the east were the pushers of another kind, those who hawked junk or merchandise that had conveniently fallen from a truck. And to the north, where he was headed, were the theaters, many of them closed, feeling the effects of spiraling costs in a world of downward creative endeavors.

Undoubtedly the area had always been shabby, but to a child and then boy and then young man from the Flatbush reaches of Brooklyn, it hadn't been apparent. At least it was alive and so far removed from the living deaths he saw about him. His father never came to the city; his mother only at Christmas when she took him and his brother Tony to see the Christmas show at the Music Hall. His parents' lives had revolved around the television set. In that tube they saw life, but they never lived it. His mother was dead now, long ago buried in a cemetery in Queens and in the recesses of his mind. He had remained in that house, on that street, helping her to die from her cancer just as he had spent his early years helping her to live. When she was gone, so was he. He seldom returned, uncomfortable with his father's discomfort with his sexuality.

The theater district was quiet. As were his reactions. In recent years Dean had avoided this part of town, avoided the theater in general, protecting himself from the pain and the anger he felt whenever he viewed an actor in a role he knew he could have played. And when the award season arrived he never watched the Tonys or the Oscars; each actor's victory was his own defeat. But this morning there was no anger. He was both nervous and excited, feeling more purposeful than he had in years.

He had not told Chris because he was not certain he would or could go—until this morning when he knew he must. His need for self-respect had propelled him, conquering his fear. Temporarily. Secretly he had prepared his audition pieces, monologues different from the others he had prepared in the past because these were for older men, fathers and husbands, not boys.

Despite the early-morning hour there was a crowd waiting for the doors of Actors Equity on Forty-sixth Street to open, to be the first of hundreds to sign up for the various auditions that would begin in the building at nine-thirty. As Dean surveyed the crowd he observed how everything and yet nothing had changed. The same pretty boys and girls, the same optimistic feelings, only these were new hopefuls who just happened to resemble the old. And the old were in evidence, too. They were quiet, withdrawn, saving their energies for the producers rather than playing for the crowd about them. And they all played to and for one another, testing their magnetism and appeal, hoping if they could incite and excite, they might be able to seduce where it counted: onstage. Dean knew that game and had played it often and well. This morning, nervous, unsure, he wanted to play it again, wanted to search the crowd until he found that acceptance in another's eyes, that proof that he was still desirable. Until Chris that was how he had lived his life, at auditions, and in bars and baths that were really nothing more than auditions of another kind. Only there he always won the role.

He had always hated these "cattle calls," as they were referred to in the trade. Only if they were actually that, they would have been kinder; the ASPCA and the Humane Society would have demanded better treatment. But actors were cattle, herded here and there in roundups that sometimes produced, as they had for him, two seasons of stock in New London and three showcases. One of the showcases actually got to Broadway for three whole nights, making him a card-carrying member of all the trade unions. Proof indeed that he was an actor. One of thousands.

He had never forgotten those three nights on a stage. In the real world of Brooklyn, where he felt he never belonged, he was a stranger, uncomfortable in clothes that fit but didn't suit him. Onstage, on Broadway, he was home, no longer a misfit but part of a family. It was why he had left home, left college to live in slums and tenements where you had more locks on the door than you had food in your refrigerator. To be an actor. That, the work, was all that mattered. Even the lack of it had been important. It bolstered one's identity. It just had become so difficult, the opportunities so rare, the successes so infrequent. He had found that without the opportunities to use your craft, it doesn't die but you do . . . a little. Chris should have pushed him, Dean thought. Chris should have demanded that he at least try.

Enough! Dean decided. He needed nothing at this time to distract his attention, least of all an increasing anger toward Chris for injustices that might be as imagined as they were real. Still, the persistent doubt that Chris had minimized his work nagged him.

"With that look on your face I hope you're auditioning for *Dracula.*"

The girl was pretty, twenty-five at most, and Dean knew she didn't give a damn about the look on his face but was using it to flirt, to parry with her increasing anxiety as the hour grew later and thus the line she was also on nearer to its destination.

"I'm here for the Chekhov plays," Dean said.

"It figures. You look very Russian with that haunted expression," she replied. "Just stay out of the auditions for the Neil Simon comedies and you should do fine."

He would have answered, but suddenly the line moved. He moved with it, aware that it was his decision, as well as his feet, that was taking him back into the past and out of a present that had suddenly become uncomfortable.

It was dishonest. It was ludicrous. But best of all, thought Joanna as she surveyed the crowd in the Maisonette at the Beverly Hills Hotel, it was a job well done. The press was there in force to hear her client, Lileen Lavery, dedicate her life to Jesus. Hers was actually an old, tired story among rockers, particularly former disco queens known as "sirens of sleaze," but Stone and Bennett Public Relations had fashioned a new twist. This day Lileen, basically to save her ass from public condemnation, was announcing the formation of a foundation bearing her name that would assist unwed teenage mothers with drug problems. It was a chapter out of the singer's own book; that chapter provided today's press conference and, if Joanna knew Hollywood, next season's Movie-of-the-Week. Lileen's life had everything made for sweeps week: sex, drugs, a breakdown and—if you could believe her publicity, which Joanna could not since she and Lilith had invented it—a resurrection. Lileen, drug-free, was saved. Praise God and hallelujah!

Joanna could not look at the buffet table, where breakfast was being served. Her stomach was still in her kitchen, trying to recover from the early-morning skirmishes with both Reynolds and Stacey. Like this event, it was ludicrous. Under any circumstances she was too young to be a grandmother. As reporters elbowed their way to the soft scrambled eggs served with a dollop of Beluga caviar, toast points, English jam and freshly squeezed orange juice liberally spiked with *the* name in Champagne, Joanna mingled with her guests, nodding here, smiling there, playing her created role of the perfect hostess. Nearby, Lilith was servicing the client, a beautiful, dark-skinned woman Joanna found dumb, selfish and often mean. But she was a name in her industry, a multi-Grammy award winner with a record company that paid for her public relations, including the tab for this press conference and all the glory that the Beverly Hills Hotel staff could supply.

Joanna had purposely chosen the Maisonette. Charming and elegant, it was in perfect contrast to Lileen. Its sliding-glass doors, adjustable to make the room any desired size, overlooked the tennis courts and the swimming pool, where a major portion of the entertainment industry sank or swam without ever entering the water. The Maisonette, with its couches and wing-backed chairs facing the fireplace, was not unlike the living room in her rambling Cape Cod house on North Canon Drive. Very understated and considered quite chic. Like the Valentino cream-colored crepe suit she had chosen to wear this morning. Joanna knew it would be startling in comparison to the rug Lilith had thrown about herself and the Frederick's of Hollywood ensemble Lileen was sporting.

"I'm so glad the pages of *Vogue* could do without you this morning," Lilith whispered as she sidled over to where Joanna was standing.

"Where's Lileen?" Joanna asked, remembering the days when they had to take turns watching their client before she shot up and shot off her mouth.

"The john. The dumb broad. I introduce her to *Newsweek,* and before I can get her out of there she's into this heavy rap on the causes of famine in East Eopia. I thought I'd die. After she left I kept trying to smooth things. If he bought it, the *Newsweek* noodnik now thinks the famine was worse in the eastern sections of that country than the others."

Joanna was laughing.

"Go ahead, laugh. Disaster is approaching. A client is about to make a fool of herself and of us, and you think it's funny. God, what am I doing here? Certainly in Your infinite wisdom You had a better plan for Your daughter than to administer to some drug-crazed nympho with leather lungs."

"How is she going to handle the press conference?" Joanna asked, recalling all too well the hours of tutoring in which they had engaged yesterday.

"She says she has memorized all the responses. A good thing we kept them monosyllabic or down to five easy words," said Lilith. "If she stumbles I'll jump in. You stay by the doors. Writers never leave a press conference if you're at the entrance. But whatever you do don't look at me. If I see that look on your face I'll break up. Now go. Mingle. Spread your charm or your legs. Anything that will save this account will be appreciated."

Joanna watched as Lilith circulated among the rock press, grubby-looking children who put down the Establishment as they wolfed down the caviar and Champagne. They loved Lilith's rough humor but treated her as if she were some goddess who had come down from the hills of Beverly to bestow blessings on the less fortunate. Joanna knew she was better with the "majors"—*Time, Newsweek, Life*. She appreciated their boredom. After all, there were no new stories. Just new names to tell them. A little tickle here, a nudge there, usually got her the coverage she wanted. She was equally successful with television. Both *Entertainment Tonight* and *Show Biz Today* were mush. They were helpful without ever being hurting. And Barney Reardon, no matter how skeptical, wasn't about to hurt her either. Joanna was less sure about *60 Minutes,* which had surprised both her and Lilith by attending.

Lilith was signaling for attention, clanking her jewelry like a drum. It brought laughs and the attention of the press. They continued to laugh as Lilith did her quasi-Joan Rivers routine, a warm-up for Lileen, who was certain to pose as terribly sincere. Joanna went over the drill. Lileen had been warned: Say nothing controversial. No matter what the "Good Book" said.

Lileen appeared at Lilith's side, looking more like a walking video than a girl about to fund a nonprofit foundation. The questions began. About drugs, sex and inevitably about reconciling her new religious beliefs with her former identity—that of a purveyor of sex, as seen, heard and discovered in gay discos across America. Joanna waited for the response she and Lilith had prepared: We are all God's children, and it is between man and his Maker to know what is right and what is wrong. Judge not lest ye be judged.

Lileen smiled and as she held her Bible to her breast bit the hand that had initially fed her. She damned the practice of homosexuality and homosexuals. Their souls are sick. The reporter from *The Advocate* booed loudly. Lileen was not deterred. On a roll, she debunked feminism as the tool of a "bunch of dykes, the anti-Christs in this God-fearing country."

At least no one was bored, thought Joanna as all hell broke out in the room. Lileen had taken a page from other famous rock stars who had gone God instead of gold. Only she was now writing a new chapter. The gospel according to Lileen Lavery. And others would read and believe it. Which only proved to Joanna how a little religion in the hands of the wrong people was as lethal a weapon as any in the nuclear stockpile.

As questions were thrown about the room like beanballs, Joanna's mind drifted to familiar but also unpleasant religious memories. Her parents were what was known as "High-Holy-Days Jews," those who attended services only on the three most solemn days in the Jewish year. And that, it seemed, entitled them to berate and judge all others whose lifestyles were different from their own. In their minds *they* were the Chosen People. Certainly more chosen than the neighbors who didn't keep a kosher home, and infinitely more chosen than the *goyim* on the street. Judgmental and hypocritical, her parents had nonetheless been comfortable with their "God bless" and "God knows" and "if God is good." Only they were unaware that they were niggardly, uncomfortable people who also used their own translations to define God. Neither knew how to be nice to one another, to themselves or to their children. They were mean-spirited, which made her father one of the borough's most feared grade-school principals. Even her mother had hated to do substitute teaching under his rule. Still, when duty in the form of the board of education called, she would heed the call and mother her second- and third-grade little ones with the same dispassion with which she mothered her own.

Lileen was now weeping, repenting her "wicked ways," but no, she would not reveal the name of the man who had fathered her out-of-wedlock child. But he was both heathen and hell, Lileen maintained. She praised God for mercy, for taking her from the depths to which she had fallen and elevating her to where she could now save others. Whether they wanted to be saved or not, thought Joanna. Still not unlike her parents.

They had foisted her bas mitzvah on her. She had been uninterested. But they had insisted. For themselves, the relatives and the neighbors. The event had finally taken place at the Kingsway Jewish Community Center, but the real event, the one that truly counted in the eyes of the to-be-impressed, was the smorgasbord held hours later at the house. A veritable feast followed by a marathon of Mah-Jongg and pinochle games. No wonder she had grown up neither knowing nor caring if there was indeed a God. Like Reynolds, she was mainly agnostic, which was why they hadn't pressed any formal religion on Stacey. Today Joanna was more than just glad they hadn't. She was embarrassed more for God, if He existed, than for herself or Lilith. And regarding God, He either existed or He didn't. And if He did exist Joanna's only hope was that He wasn't in the Maisonette at this moment listening to Lileen's horseshit. And if He were in attendance Joanna hoped He had the good sense to try the caviar.

Laughter broke Joanna's mood. Lilith was brandishing a finger as she stood beside a now-rattled Lileen. Lilith was fielding an irate writer's questions, making it clear he should give up his turn at the plate before he got beaned. Other questions came flying at the podium, some quite hostile, others asked in the guise of humor. And all because Lileen had simply said Jews would not go to heaven because they do not accept Christ as their Savior.

Lilith took charge. For every curve a reporter threw, she delivered a hit. When the man objected, he was victimized by Lilith's legendary mouth, which caused the assemblage to laugh, thus breaking the tension. Soon they were forgetting, at least for the moment, that many had been seriously offended.

Joanna was restless, anxious now for the press conference to be over. Her job was done, and she had the tension in her neck and shoulders to prove it. She ached for the release that would come soon. She again surveyed the room. *People* magazine was looking snide, *Us* earnest and *Rolling Stone* aghast. Associated Press looked amused, but that could have been from the steady supply of orange blossoms with which the lady had plied herself. Joanna knew she would have to dictate the story to the reporter later. Not the first time she had engaged in such a service.

Enough! Lilith finally ordered. A few of the reporters applauded. Still others hooted derisively. Most just looked relieved that the conference was over. A few pocketed the leftover sweet rolls on the buffet table as they departed. It was time to say her good-byes, thought Joanna as she moved quickly to smooth and smile among the departing guests, taking an arm here and a hand there, bidding a hurried good-bye to the Cable News Network, reminding their sour faces that they had promised to do a feature. Barney Reardon was leaving, a noncommittal look on his face. Marilyn Beck looked less than thrilled. Considerably less. Shirley Eder was smiling, whispering through clenched teeth that she would see Joanna later at lunch in the Polo Lounge. Lilith was pushing Lileen toward the exit, where a limousine was waiting to take them to a *Good Morning America* taping.

Joanna floated through the dispersing crowd, touching all with either a smile or a hand. When the room was empty she stretched languorously, trying to move the knots that had now collected in her back. In the lobby, she searched for the ladies' room for relief and repairs. When her hair was finally stroked into obedience, Joanna strode to the bank of elevators that would take her to the fifth floor. The car was empty. Had it been occupied by anyone she had known, she would have chatted about the press conference, making it seem she was in the hotel solely on business.

The room number was memorized. It was the same

room number for any hotel they would visit, be it the Century, the Beverly Wilshire or the Hyatt. She used her key to enter and, without speaking a word, began to unwind as Barney Reardon began to undress her, one hand on her breast, her nipple, her thigh, as the other unbuttoned or pulled whatever was holding her from him. His lips were buried in her hair and then her neck. He bit her ear as his fingers fondled and softly pinched her nipples. She could feel him straining against her, his largeness an indication of his arousal. His mouth pressed on hers and his tongue entered, probing and inquisitive. She soon lay naked on the bed looking up as he stood over her, masturbating as his eyes roamed and made love to every part of her body. Then he slowly lowered himself onto her, placing his hardness between her breasts and holding it there until he began to move slowly up . . . and then down . . . higher and then lower . . . closer to the two centers of her existence that he wished to probe. As he did, Joanna could feel the tension leave her body much as she did.

An hour later, refreshed and tranquil, Joanna closed the door on that once-in-a-while, when-schedules-permit-and-the-need-is-great aspect of her life and rode the elevator to the lobby and the Polo Lounge, where she found Shirley Eder amusing herself with a cross-the-tables conversation with Lana Turner.

THREE

DANA was in one end of the tub, Naomi, the other, as Sara gently washed the legs of both. The girls were all pink and chatty, humming snatches of songs heard on the radio in between the exchange of gossip about other children. Their banter always included her. She was part of her children's worlds and was pleased that she knew each child they named. She also knew their teachers, the ones who were lenient and the ones who were not. There was actually very little Sara didn't know about her children's lives. They had no secrets.

For Sara this was a wonderful time of day. Although the girls often protested they were old enough to take their own baths, Sara hated to give up the nightly ritual that gave her so much comfort. There was little comfort this night, however. Once she put her little girls to bed, she was to be forced out . . . from Princeton . . . to New York. Sara breathed deeply, yearning to submerge herself between her children in the world of bubbles and giggles in the bathtub. She did not want to leave her home. Let Stefan and the other department heads celebrate their grants without her.

He would be at her side. He had promised that he would never be farther away than the place to her left at the dinner table. His hand would be there to reassure, even to hold.

She really shouldn't go, she silently argued. Evan was fighting a cold and was apprehensive about his bar mitzvah, now just a week away. And poor Robert was experiencing such pangs of jealousy. The attention that had been his a year ago now belonged to his brother. Robert needed her encouragement. Now more than ever. A young person of fourteen rather than a young boy. But he was still too young to be the sole baby-sitter for the family. She had told Stefan that, but he had assured her they would be home by eleven, midnight at the latest. And the boys never went to bed much before that hour on a Friday night.

But suppose Evan's cold grew worse?

What if Dana had an asthma attack, Naomi, a nightmare?

What then?

She was needed at home, Sara decided as she wrapped her girls in towels and then clutched them to her. No matter what Stefan said.

Joanna found Reynolds in their bath, the lights dimmed, wine cooling in a nearby ice bucket and a Barry Manilow cassette crooning from the tape deck in their adjoining bedroom. His dreamlike state said clearly: Do not disturb. Joanna had to. With Stacey's abortion having occupied the previous weekend, the trip to Caesar's Palace and the talk he had promised had never materialized. It was now or never.

As Joanna fought her way through the conflicting aromas of Caswell-Massey and Colombian Gold to sit on the edge of the oversized pink marble tub, Reynolds acknowledged her presence by offering her a toke from the rolled cigarette in his hand. Joanna dragged deeply, holding it in her lungs, before washing down the drug with a healthy gulp of Reynolds's favorite California chablis.

Almost matter-of-factly she said: "Reyn, I would really like it if you came with me to New York next weekend."

"Ma nish tanah?" asked Reynolds with the few Hebrew words he knew, those from the Passover service that asked: Why this night as opposed to all others?

"Well, it's been years since we spent autumn in New York, and the fall is so special in Manhattan. And there *is* the film festival," continued Joanna, her voice soft and seductive.

"Joanna, you're working the film festival. What am I supposed to do while you're pimping for one of your producers? And don't say sit through the program," said

Reynolds as he filled his lungs with the last of the joint. "Christ. With the shit they've shown there over the past few years they could put both Sominex and Nytol out of business."

"Reyn, the truth is I would really like you to be with me at the bar mitzvah."

A groan followed by the submergence of a blond head under soapy water was Joanna's response.

"Oh, come on, Reynolds. An old friend of mine has invited us to her son's bar mitzvah, and it will look strange if I go alone," Joanna argued.

"How come it will look strange this time and it didn't all the other times you went places alone?" Reynolds asked.

"This is different, Reynolds, and you know it."

"But why is it, Joanna? Explain to me."

"Because a onetime friend of mine, maybe my closest friend, is . . ."

"Bullshit. It has nothing to do with Sara, and you know it," Reynolds interrupted.

"I want to show you off," Joanna said abruptly.

"Shit, Joanna! I don't want to do this. I promised Merv I'd play in his tournament, and besides, I've nothing in common with Stefan, and Sara's cookie-about-to-crumble act is a fucking bore."

"You haven't seen them in years. Sara may have changed. And you're not being very compassionate," Joanna protested.

"Spare me your Mother Teresa number. You weren't Johnny-on-the-spot for Sara all those years. When Dean told you about her breakdown, you decided since you weren't supposed to know, you didn't. So don't talk about my lack of compassion."

"That was years ago, Reynolds. Have you any idea how painful it was for me to know Sara was suffering so while I was here three thousand miles away? Besides, Sara had Dean. He was wonderful with her. But that's Dean. He just naturally takes care of people."

"It's a pity he's gay," said Reynolds. "He could have made some nice girl very happy."

"So he's made some nice guy happy. What's the difference?'' Joanna asked. ''You know, when I was a little girl I used to dream I would grow up and marry Dean and live happily ever after.''

''Obviously a fairy tale,'' said Reynolds, chuckling at his play on words.

''I hate humor like that,'' Joanna snapped.

''Oh, come on, it was just a joke so don't make it into a gay-rights issue. Now what's really going on with you? What's at the bottom of this big deal you're making about my going with you?'' Reynolds asked as he added more hot water to the tub.

''I'm not certain,'' Joanna replied as she stood and began to pace the marble bathroom floor. ''Maybe it has to do with turning forty.''

''Shit! When is that? Do you want a party?'' asked Reynolds as he drained the remaining wine in his glass.

''It was, Reynolds. Yesterday. And the only thing I want,'' Joanna added, hoping the guilt Reynolds was now experiencing would work in her favor, ''is for you to come with me to New York. To show you off, my successful husband.''

''Bullshit. It's to show *you* off to your friends,'' replied Reynolds, his voice slurred. ''To show them how well you've done.''

''What the hell is that supposed to mean?'' Joanna asked angrily.

''Next you'll be asking me to make a pilgrimage to see your mother in that zoo she's in on Long Island,'' Reynolds continued, his eyes drooping.

Joanna stormed out of the bathroom, slamming the door with a force that made the pictures on the bedroom wall shake. He had read her mind. She had considered visiting her mother. But not alone. Never that. Masochistic she was not. Her mother would have to live—if that's what she did—another year without her. Besides, she didn't know her own daughter when she was there. Better therefore to leave her care to those trained to deal with the horror of her Alzheimer's disease. She couldn't cope with it any more than she could cope with her mother when she had truly been alive. And hadn't their relationship really died long before her mother's brain had?

Reynolds entered the bedroom wrapped in his terrycloth robe. ''Sorry,'' he said.

''Forget it,'' Joanna snapped. ''And forget about New York. Lord knows I wouldn't want to interfere with your tennis or any other *game* you might be playing,'' she added snidely.

''I'll go, Joanna, OK?''

And he was gone, disappearing as the bathroom door closed behind him and on what was about to be an unpleasant conversation one or both would have greatly regretted.

Dean was sprawled on the sofa when Chris's key turned in the lock. His eyes remained shut as Chris's casual ''Hi'' announced he was home. He could feel Chris moving across the room toward him and then stop as he saw the eight-by-ten glossies spread about the coffee table. Dean heard him riffle through them. Tense, he waited for Chris's reaction.

''They're great,'' Chris enthused. Dean opened his eyes to find Chris looking first at him and then at the pictures. ''You know you've gotten better-looking as you've gotten older. Nicer-looking,'' Chris said. ''I mean . . . you look nice, whereas when you were younger you looked a lot of things, but nice wasn't one of them.''

A silence ensued before Chris asked the anticipated question. ''When did you decide to have new pictures made?''

What was he hearing in Chris's voice? Dean couldn't tell. ''A couple of weeks ago,'' he answered.

More silence before Chris finally asked as he again thumbed through the pictures: ''You going to fill me in?''

''I guess I owe you that since you're paying for the pictures.''

''What the hell is eating you, Dean?''

''Lots of things. It's been a tough day, a rough couple of weeks, and I'm pissed by the ball-busting fact that I don't earn my own money, that I'm dependent on you for every dime. It makes me feel like shit.''

''Dean, if you want a salary for the work you do around here, say so. I'll put you on the books. God knows, considering how much you handle, you come cheap at any price. So name yours. Now would you tell me what the fuck is really going on?''

Dean was up from the sofa, padding around the room barefooted, trying to decide what hurt more—his head or some part of him that couldn't be labeled, only felt. As he searched for an answer to Chris's question, Chris asked: ''Why didn't you tell me about the pictures?''

The moment was awkward until Dean spoke his truth. ''I wasn't sure how you would take it.'' When Chris's face registered a lack of understanding, Dean added: ''I wasn't sure you'd be very enthusiastic or encouraging. In fact, I thought you'd be down on the idea.''

''What else?'' Chris asked, his face having turned from in-all-day pallor to beet-red.

''That you'd try to talk me out of it, that you'd be selfish, even threatened.''

''That's a helluva lot of shit to have piled up,'' said Chris as he sat down heavily on the sofa. ''I'm beginning to think I may need a lawyer since you seem to have your case all prepared and are acting like judge and jury. Not to mention the injured party. And I'm still not sure of the charges. Maybe I need a postponement until I can get my brief together.''

When Dean remained silent, Chris exploded: ''Dammit, Dean, I hate it when you do this, when you save things up, nurture them in your mind and then dump them on me. It gets us in trouble.''

Dean remembered. The last time a similar thing occurred was when they had bought the building four years ago and Chris was busy, very busy, too busy establishing his practice. Dean had felt ignored. He was alone all day and for much of the night in a building Chris said was theirs but which Chris paid for, at least in part. It was to Chris the bank loaned money. It was Chris who had the mortgage payments to meet. No matter that their lawyer, at Chris's insistence, had arranged joint tenancy, which made him Chris's legal partner in the building. That hadn't mattered. What mattered then was that Chris was gone all day at work and then, given his exhaustion, gone all night.

Which was the rationale Dean had used when he became involved in afternoon liaisons with a computer programmer. In his mind, the affair was Chris's fault, and so he could be angry with him. It was not unlike the anger he was feeling now.

The computer programmer had given him gonorrhea. He gave it unknowingly to Chris, who gave him hell upon his discovery and also refused any responsibility for Dean's actions. Which had made Dean angrier as he knew Chris was right. Which didn't make the anger any less. He had solved it—or perhaps Chris had with his dictum: "You want to fuck around? Fine. But do it in someone else's life. Not mine. You can't have it both ways." And then they had talked. From it came the resolution.

"I've been auditioning," Dean began. "I started a couple of weeks ago. At first I didn't tell you because I didn't want to admit to myself that's what I was doing. I was easing into it. Only you never *ease* into it because the fuckers never make it *easy.* Auditioning still sucks. Nothing has changed. You take a number and you wait. If you're lucky they let you read, usually to a group imitating the deaf, the dumb and the blind. They know only two phrases: 'Thank you' and '. . . next!' So why do I do it? Because I need something that's me, that's mine and mine alone. Something that says Dean Di Nardo. I mean . . . you have your fulfillment; where is mine?"

He didn't wait for an answer but proceeded as Chris watched, his face reacting to each of Dean's statements. "Today I went to see Howie Krieger, my old agent. Guess what? He's become big-time. I couldn't get past his secretary, who told me to make an appointment. When I tried Krieger relayed that I'd be best off seeing his colleague down the street. Well, this so-called 'colleague' turned out to be a Maurie Freissan. He's a not-very-pretty vision of what happens to the Howie Kriegers when they haven't made it by the time they reach forty. Like me. The poor slob was delighted to see me, said I was the perfect type for the new market that is 'eating up' older men. He meant me. I'm now an older man. He pumped my hand when I left, said: 'We'll be in touch.' I don't know who he meant by 'we' unless he counts his answering machine as an employee."

Chris rose from the sofa. When he tried to approach Dean his hand was shrugged from Dean's shoulder as Dean pulled away.

"No. Just wait," said Dean. "After all, you wanted to know what's going on. Now I'm telling you. I spent lunchtime addressing and stuffing envelopes with pictures of that face you just described as 'nice.' I sent them to fifty casting directors and producers, hoping it was nice enough for them to maybe give me a call. And guess what? I discovered in one of the casting guides that the new producer of *Where the Rainbow Ends* is Ralph Kayne. He was the unit manager the two summers I did stock at New London. We slept together . . . I think. It's hard to be certain as there were so many of us acting like kids playing in a sandbox. Only we used a bed. Anyway, will he remember me? I both hope so and hope not because I'm not sure what he will choose to remember."

They sat facing one another, Chris on the sofa and Dean opposite him in the Eames chair. The silence was broken when Chris said softly: "Dean, where the hell are we if after all of these years we don't let one another in?"

"I'm sorry. I just couldn't," Dean said quietly. "I was too caught up in my own anger."

"I think some of your anger is justified," Chris began. "I'm not thrilled you're out there banging your head on those same walls again."

"Chris, it's *my* head!" Dean exclaimed.

"But when you get hurt, I get hurt. Dammit, Dean, how do you think I feel when you come home all messed up because some asshole wouldn't let you read because he didn't think you were the right type? What do you think evenings are like when one of us waits for a callback from an audition that never comes?"

"You never had to live with any of that," Dean protested.

"The hell I didn't! Where do you think I was during the first six months we were together?" Chris replied. "Shit. You've forgotten. Well, I haven't. I remember your being out on the street all day trying to get any kind of acting job and getting nowhere. I remember because you'd bring all that shit home with you. Do you know how I felt seeing you all twisted and bent out of shape? Well, now you know."

Dean sat semi-stunned in his chair, unable to move or respond. Why had his memory insisted that he had stopped auditioning as soon as he met Chris? Now he remembered it hadn't been that way at all. He had stopped gradually and then completely when finances had become an issue.

"You should have pushed me, Chris, forced me out the door no matter what your feelings about acting," Dean said finally. "You should have been more supportive."

"Why? For what?" asked Chris angrily. "To see you hurt even more? Dean, I was so damn glad that you were out of that rat race. It was killing you."

"Not being in it has killed me," Dean replied, equally angry.

"Dammit, Dean. Tell me you weren't glad to get out of acting," Chris demanded.

"You're damn right I was. OK? Satisfied? I was angry and hurt, but I wasn't in any worse shape than you were during your residency at Montefiore Hospital when they ran you ragged all day and into the night. In case you've forgotten, how often did you want to quit when you saw too many half-assed doctors practicing half-assed medicine? And on babies! But you hung in. That's the difference, Chris. I'm forty years old and I didn't hang in. I threw it all away while my lover stood by and watched."

"I wasn't aware that's how you felt about what we've got going together . . . didn't realize you considered all of this," said Chris as his arm gestured about the house, "throwing *it* all away."

"Listen, Chris. I love this house, loved laying every goddamn brick, tile and you in it. This house, our home, is my rock. I did it for us, for me. It's what I have to show for my life, and God knows it's my only form of self-expression. Chris, get off you and this house. This isn't about you. This is my scene."

"And what am I, a supporting player?" Chris asked.

"You should have been," Dean replied, his eyes now locked with Chris's.

"I guess I thought just building this place . . . us . . .

was enough of a life for you,'' said Chris, looking sadder than Dean could ever recall.

''That's the problem, Chris. It was,'' Dean replied softly. ''It became a safe little nest, a cocoon. But look at me, Chris. I'm middle-aged, and who and what am I?''

''The person I love most in the world . . . the one who makes my life work.''

''Chris, I shouldn't be about making your life work but my own happen. We're two men living together. One of us has made his life happen while the other, me, hasn't accomplished a damn thing.''

''I think making another person happy is one helluvan accomplishment. I also think building this place is also an accomplishment. It should give you some sense of pride.''

''Chris, we've been over that. Talk to me straight. Didn't you like having me here?'' asked Dean, his voice tight with the tension he was now about to release. ''Wasn't it comfortable for you knowing I was always here, taking care of you, of us, putting us before me, putting you before me? Chris, if I had been you, I wouldn't have wanted that boat rocked either.''

He had said it, voiced his angriest thoughts. Now he waited to see how Chris would receive them. In his typical fashion, Chris thought a long time before speaking.

''You're right,'' he said simply. ''I was comfortable, safe, too. It was a way of holding on to you. Keeping you safe was keeping me safe at the same time. OK, so what now? Do you want a divorce?''

Dean laughed. ''No, I'm exhausted. I want dinner. And I want you to cook it. I also want you to know I'm using and abusing you. I know what's gone down has really been my responsibility and not yours. I just need to lay some of the shit somewhere and you're the one who's closest.''

They looked at each other from opposite ends of the coffee table. ''Chris, I've got to try again,'' Dean said.

''I can see that,'' Chris replied. ''One question: Are you any good?''

''Oh shit! I keep forgetting you've never seen me act. Chris, I'm more than good, I'm real good.''

''Well, then,'' said Chris as he rose from the couch, ''I say let's go for it. I also say tonight, to preserve what's left of our precious male egos, we order in Chinese food. You get the menu and I'll dial. Or I'll get the menu and you dial. Or we get the menu together and then take turns dialing a digit."

"Why don't we just tear off our clothes and go to bed instead?" asked Dean as he moved toward Chris.

"I always said man does not live by egg roll alone," said Chris as he began to unbutton his shirt.

As they approached the Lincoln Tunnel, the Friday night traffic heavy, Sara sat close to Stefan, her eyes fixed on the toll booths. Ahead lay the enclosure, that gaping hole that she often feared would cave in, drowning her with the waters of the Hudson River. On the other side of that gaping hole was Manhattan, where there were other waters, deep waters, in which she once had really drowned.

She would not panic. She would breathe deeply and concentrate on nothing. No thoughts, no memories. She moved closer to Stefan. Her hand covered his on the steering wheel. Another minute, he promised. But in another minute they would be in the heart of Times Square. People, noise, confusion.

It came at her in unrelenting waves of sound and motion, of drunks weaving in and out of traffic, seeking to wipe their windshield, hopeful of the dollar they might earn not for their efforts but for their disappearance. On the corner of Eighth Avenue and Forty-second Street, an evangelist was shouting of Jesus and salvation, while diagonally across the street a marquee promised "Live Girls, Live Sex Acts." Sara closed her eyes to obliterate the madness. She thought of her home and her children in bed. She grew calmer, and then the car turned east on Fiftieth Street.

She hadn't asked where the dinner was taking place. That it was in the city was horror enough. She never dreamed it would be at the Tower Suite in the Time & Life Building. When Stefan told her, she should have immediately known the trip wasn't possible. She should have run past the wall and into her house. It would not have been the first faculty function she missed. Stefan's associates knew she had young children who required care.

They knew because Stefan told them the many times Sara remained at home rather than force herself into a world she found frightening.

They would be there in minutes, Sara realized, unless—please, God!—traffic remained at a standstill. She needed more time to remind herself it was only a building and that she, not it, contained the bad memories. Remember the fun, a voice advised. But it was exactly the "fun" she didn't want to remember.

Yes, the job in the research department had been fun. More than that . . . exciting, even thrilling. It was exposure to people and a life outside Brooklyn. And Brooklyn was where she was supposed to be, teaching in some grade school. Her mother had wanted that. She thought she had too, until she read and then answered the advertisement in the Sunday *Times*.

She did not know what to wear to a job in Manhattan. She had nothing suitable, as she had never followed style, thinking her thin body could never support whatever fashion was dictating. But she had eyes. She saw what attracted the men at the office. With her first paychecks she wandered through Bloomingdale's and wandered out, dazed by her boldness. She had purchased hip-huggers, mini-skirts, poor-boy sweaters and boots. She changed her hairstyle, stopped making it "do things" and simply parted it in the center, allowing it to fall smoothly on either side of her head.

As though she had not been in the company's employ for several weeks, she was noticed. Suddenly she was asked out, asked in, asked where she had never been asked before.

Her mother was not pleased with her or her new life. Arguments raged about her being late for dinner or not being for dinner at all. Names like the Ground Floor and Hurley's did not impress her mother, who only wanted to know why Sara's dates didn't bring her home or call on weekends.

Sara never explained. What her mother didn't know wouldn't hurt her. And if she herself didn't understand, what matter? No one needed to understand in the sixties. That was the point. Understanding was out, feeling was in, and she was feeling. Finally, she was liked. Finally, she was desired. She was constantly on the edge of excitement, often toppling over into it with any number of the men she met at Time/Life or at the various parties to which the research staff was invited. She had actually met Stefan at one of those parties. Not that she remembered. What mattered was that he did.

Her lifestyle was no different from the girls' with whom she worked. They, too, were popular. They, too, went out, often with the same men. But whereas they gossiped, compared performances and endowments, not Sara. She couldn't possibly share what was now making her life so totally brilliant. Finally, she had color. Finally, she was a woman.

All the parking lots were filled. Stefan apologized as he finally gained entry to the one by the Ziegfeld Theatre. It would be a four-block walk to their destination. She felt him lead her from the car, her last refuge, as he handed the ignition keys to the attendant.

"Do I look all right?" she asked stupidly.

"Fine," Stefan replied.

She knew he lied. The black jersey dress was eight years old, bought when her body was the same weight but thinner. She now bulged at the waist and just above her pelvis. She had never noticed before. And her hair had lost its sheen, muddied as it now was with its strands of gray. I'm a mother and not a model, Sara told herself as she clung to Stefan's arm. They were walking past the Hilton Hotel. She had been at the Hilton her first time; across the street at the Warwick others. And down the street at what was once the Americana more times than she could remember. She remembered herself in all the situations: hopeful, yearning, romantic. She could never remember them. They tended to blend into one male face that remained indistinct. She heard snatches of words she wanted to forget as they were never the words she had wanted to hear in the first place. They were not of love but commands and complaints. If she did *that* with one of his friends, why wouldn't she do *it* with him? And finally she did it because she couldn't stand his displeasure.

She had been at the Hilton that last time. He had opened

the door to his room and she was immediately confused. There was another couple in his bed. Obviously a mistake. Only it wasn't. She felt humiliated. Whoever he was didn't care. He simply shrugged and said: "If it's not your thing, OK." He was taking off his clothes to join those whose thing it was when she left. No one noticed. No one cared. She wasn't even offered cab fare.

Now they were passing the very same subway entrance into which she had stumbled that night. The stairs had smelled of urine and beer. She had vomited. She stood on the platform waiting for a train and shaking as though it were the dead of winter. She was trying to understand through the terrible confusion in her head. If he liked her, why did he need the others?

The train arrived and when she was seated, huddled in a corner of the car near the door, she asked herself: If you like him, why do you need the others . . . so many others? Because it is the sixties, she replied. Because I'm looking for something. Love . . . and I've found it. Over and over again.

She had laughed. Loud, raucous peals of laughter. Her answers were funny . . . ridiculous . . . senseless. God, were they funny. The people who shied away from her were ridiculous. As were those gathered about her on the train. And the police . . . her mother . . . all funny. All senseless. Nothing had made sense. Not for months. Not until Stefan, a man from her past but with whom she had no past, had called.

He was with her now as they entered the Time & Life Building, moving toward the elevators and the Tower Suite. He was guiding her, his hand firmly grasping her by the elbow. Sara wondered what she would do if he took his hand away. It was a thought she had had many times before.

FOUR

"JESUS, Joanna, you'd think you were meeting an old lover the way you're carrying on."

The man in bed was right, but then Dean was an old lover of sorts, the first to hold her hand when they walked to school and the first to hold her in male arms even if it was only when they were dancing. Again Joanna twisted and turned in the mirror. The beige silk was perfect. She reached for the matching bolero jacket as the house phone rang.

"He's downstairs waiting," Reynolds said groggily as he hung up the phone and rolled over in the queen-sized bed. Joanna grabbed her purse and at the door reminded: "Be ready by eleven-thirty. It will take at least ninety minutes to drive to Princeton." Reynolds grunted. Joanna knew as soon as she left he'd be out until a previously arranged wake-up call roused him.

She was nervous without knowing exactly why. In the hallway mirror by the elevators she again checked her hair and makeup, wondering if she had changed much over the years. It was exactly nine since she last saw Dean at that awkward lunch at the Café des Artistes. She was full of her new life as the public relations executive, and he was sullen, uncommunicative, with seemingly nothing to say even when he did speak. The lunch had never been repeated, despite her fairly frequent visits to the city. It just seemed more of an inconvenience than her time or interests allowed. The occasional letter, the Christmas and birthday cards, had been quite sufficient.

Dean waited by his car, wondering who Joanna would be this time. He saw her before she saw him, emerging from the Helmsley Palace like a racehorse from the starting gate. She moved elegantly, looked beautiful and bore little resemblance to the fresh-faced, chubby-cheeked girl he had once known. This woman's face was a mask, uncluttered by any signs of aging or feeling. He wondered if she would once again "make conversation," meaningless talk about famous people he only knew by name. But as she walked toward him smiling, her hand extended in greeting, as her cheek brushed his, their bodies momentarily touching in an almost-hug, she rekindled something he couldn't quite define. Smiling, Dean suddenly felt quite glad he had decided to accompany Joanna on her sentimental journey.

From the moment they drove across the Manhattan Bridge onto Flatbush Avenue in Brooklyn, Joanna felt the changes. The Paramount and Fox theaters, places where she and Sara had all but swooned to the music of Frankie Valli and the Four Seasons, Bobby Rydell and the Shirelles, were gone. So was the neighborhood, once a miniature version of what people thought of as Times Square. The movie palaces and once-elegant department stores were replaced by discount houses where *se habla español.* There was no style, only shabbiness, and Joanna felt distant, removed, a stranger in a once familiar part of town.

She brightened at Church Avenue, remembering the evenings she and Sara would spend at Garfield's, a cafeteria that was the fifties equivalent of a singles bar. They had all but drowned in coffee that junior semester, waiting for a senior from Erasmus or Midwood High to notice them. Once one did and Joanna had necked with him in a nearby park, leaving a horrified Sara who had called her "fast," which for those days, Joanna now realized, she might very well have been.

She chatted amiably, unaware that her recollections were serving as just one more barrier between them. When they reached the intersection where Nostrand and Flatbush avenues convened, she grew silent, as Dean drove through the Brooklyn College campus. She was remembering how much like a cocoon the environment had been. Her eyes were searching first Boylan and then Ingersol halls when she said: "I was happy here and would have been content to remain forever."

Dean looked at her oddly, and Joanna shrugged as she explained. "I felt so ill equipped to handle life then. There we three were: Sara, the brain; you, the talent; and me . . . I hardly knew what I was. Sara with her smarts could have been anything. But then she worked on her grades while I worked on my tan. Even then it was obvious I was a perfect candidate for Southern California success," Joanna said, laughing. "Thank God a Reynolds came along to rescue me. The Jewish prince, a soon-to-be doctor. And that in my family's eyes saw me graduate with honors."

He was surprised. He had never imagined Joanna ever felt ill equipped to handle anything. It was he who hid throughout his college days until he couldn't hide anymore, he who was afraid of living a life he wanted but that terrified him, having heard for so many years that it was wrong . . . "sick."

He had been an outsider at college, the different one with different dreams of personal and professional success. For the two years he remained on campus he anguished that the boys who attracted Joanna were the same who attracted him. He was alienated and alone until he found those places where boys, similar to those he had coveted, thought of him as he thought of them.

They were parked now on Bedford Avenue, across from an ivy-covered building. He hadn't enjoyed James Madison High School any more than he had liked college, feeling even then different from other boys his age. But he excelled on the swimming team and frequently dated to avoid the suspicion of the jocks and the girls who pursued him.

"If I were all that fast, or at least as fast as Sara thought, how come she and I went stag to the junior prom?" Joanna mused as she stared at the columns of what was meant to be a Georgian-style building. "I made her lead, of course. I thought that looked better to the boys who also came stag. How I used to bully that girl," she said, laughing.

But then her expression changed, and when she spoke her words were barely audible.

"I loved her, you know. Sara was always so grounded, while my concerns were to be pretty and popular, the object of men's mad desires." Again Joanna grew silent, and when she spoke, Dean was surprised by her words. "It's such a terrible time in a kid's life. Such confusion and doubt. We all knew how we didn't want to be—which was like our parents—but we didn't know how to be another way. At least you always had a dream, always wanted to be an actor."

They had come to the public school on Quentin Road, and Joanna was stunned by how much smaller it was than she remembered. She was looking up at the windows of P.S. 222 when she said: "You know, I actually remember the day you moved to Thirty-fifth Street and the first day you came to school."

Dean looked at her disbelievingly. He had been only five after all.

"A woman always remembers the great moments in her life," Joanna explained, a smile on her face. "I watched them unload the van that moved you on a Saturday morning. Your brother, Tony, saw Sara and me staring and gave us the finger."

"That's Tony," said Dean wryly. "He still gives people the finger. Only now he does it legally, under the jurisdiction of the American Bar Association."

"You came late to your first afternoon in class," Joanna recalled. "They seated you at our table—we had tables then, not desks—and you put your head down and went to sleep. Talk about rejection. I was crushed. What you did, of course, was considered terribly babylike among five-year-olds who had long outgrown the need for afternoon naps. It was almost as bad as peeing in one's pants."

"For which, if I remember correctly, you took class honors," Dean said, laughing suddenly at the memory. "And you always denied it. You would stand in the middle of your puddle with a 'Who, me?' expression on your face and then swear it wasn't yours."

"At least I didn't blame it on Sara, and believe me, I was tempted," Joanna said, amused. "But this recollection is not about my bladder problem but unrequited love—mine for you. Do you remember Lois Greenberg? She was tall, thin and had long, black, lustrous hair—which I bet she dyed even then—and you had this monstrous crush on her."

Dean remembered. "I called her Low-Ass and I was always yanking her hair. I don't think she loved either a lot."

"Oh yes she did, the hussy," Joanna protested. "She just pretended not to. And I, martyr and good neighbor and friend that I was, taught you how to kiss so that if and when Lois ever succumbed to your dark, swarthy ten-year-old good looks, you'd be ready."

"But you had me practice on Sara," Dean said.

"She needed it more than me," Joanna explained. "And I just bet yours were the only lips to touch hers until Stefan's."

Dean looked at Joanna, annoyed that she still knew nothing about what had once been Sara's life and wondered how that was possible. Easy, he decided. As with so many other things, Joanna had never asked.

"You'll be pleased to know I don't make puddles anymore," Joanna said as they began to drive.

"And despite your and Sara's efforts, I turned out to be a really terrific kisser."

"I am sincerely and genuinely glad," Joanna replied with mock seriousness. "In fact, you've relieved me of a great worry I've carried all these years."

They looked at each other and smiled, the earlier tension between them dissipated. They were sharing the warmth of childhood memories without any of the responsibilities of adult friendship.

"I feel like Alex Haley searching for my roots," Joanna said as she stared out the window at the gardens dotting Avenue P. "I really do appreciate your making this trip, particularly when we have the long drive to Princeton later," she said, continuing to watch the houses and the streets pass by. "I don't know why it felt so important to me to do this. I guess a part of me feels all this is still home,'' Joanna explained. ''Maybe the first place you lived, where you grew up, is always home in your mind.''

Not so, thought Dean. The only place that was home to him was where he was living now. There, love was unconditional; acceptance, total.

Joanna's eyes were on the Circle, the oval island that made two lanes of Kings Highway, directly off of which was Thirty-fifth Street. Even before they turned the corner, she could see the semi-attached house where she once had lived. It looked exactly the same. Parked in the car before it, Joanna stared at the house's brick walls as if trying to see within. Suddenly she was out of the car and up the steps, ringing the doorbell. A woman with a child clutching her jeans leg appeared in the doorway. She listened to Joanna speak and then opened the door. Dean watched as Joanna entered hesitantly.

Dean walked up the tree-lined street as he had so many other times in the distant past. All was familiar without a familiar face emerging from the row of houses. New neighborhood children were playing touch football. Only the language had changed, rougher now than the game. He watched, unaware of the passage of time until he felt Joanna's arm hook through his own. Together, they watched the game in progress.

''That was very strange,'' Joanna said softly. Dean knew she was referring to her impromptu visit to her house. ''It's no longer my home. The dusty-rose walls and carpeting are now a blah beige. The flocked wallpaper in the dining room is now wood-paneled. The smells in the kitchen are unfamiliar. And my father isn't sitting in his favorite chair hidden by a newspaper, with my mother nearby engrossed in correcting test papers or essays.''

He felt her arm, and her body tightened before she spoke again. ''I went through my entire childhood hoping my father would look up from his paper and my mother from her grading just to notice that I was there. Me, this little girl who wasn't and couldn't be a giant like them.'' Joanna caught her breath. She wondered if that's how Stacey ever felt.

They watched as one of the children caught and then dropped a long pass from the ''quarterback''—a boxlike girl who knew every four-letter word to express her disapproval of the fumble. Joanna laughed. "Shades of Trudy Kaufman. You do remember Trudy, don't you?"

"One does not easily forget a Trudy Kaufman," Dean replied. "Godzilla with a football. What a mean little thing she was."

"Do you remember the brawl I had with her?" Joanna asked, beginning to laugh.

He remembered. Two of Trudy's passes had been intercepted, so she proceeded to beat up on the receiver, who happened to be Sara, recruited into the game when flu or weather had claimed everyone else. Joanna had taken one look at Sara's bloody nose and had flown at Trudy in a flurry of arms, legs, hair and nails. Minutes later, torn and tattered, Trudy had drifted home, leaving Joanna the victor, despite her never once having opened her eyes while doing battle.

"I always meant to ask how it felt to be a legend in your own lifetime," Dean said.

"Some legend," Joanna replied. "When the dust cleared, I was holding half of Trudy's hair in my hand, crying. Not that I was hurt. But I had peed in my pants again and I was afraid my mother would kill me. Sara helped me hide my underpants in her backyard, and unless the new tenants are gardeners, those pants are buried somewhere under three feet of sod."

Joanna and Dean both jumped as not one but two identical-looking little boys bounded out the front door of the two-story shingled house that once had been Sara Rosen's. Joanna and Dean each was thinking of all the years when Sara's mother was alive and no one had been allowed to use any door to the house except the back door. Now even the draperies were drawn, and from the street one could see into the living room—unheard of during their childhood, when Mrs. Rosen had kept the blinds closed and the furniture covered by sheets until company came, which was almost never. The Rosens' lives revolved around the kitchen, where Mrs. Rosen lived much as she had in Minsk: waiting to flee at the slightest sound of Cossacks storming up Thirty-fifth Street in their never-ending quest to kill Jews.

"With all the time I spent in this house, I never once saw the bedrooms, never once just hung out in Sara's room the way we hung out in mine," Joanna said. "Mrs. Rosen made the upstairs off limits. It was like a Brontë novel. Somewhere in that great upstairs was a Mrs. Danvers hiding a body. Probably Mr. Rosen's, now that I think of it."

Dean barely remembered the man who had disappeared when Sara was ten, leaving more money than anyone suspected he or his "rag business" was worth. It was not something Sara ever discussed.

"Her mother didn't have an easy life," Joanna recalled. "And she didn't make it any easier the way she closed the draperies and the shades to shut out the world. Still, I used to love to visit. Her kitchen had real warmth. I had more meals there than at my home. And she fed me as though I were one of her own, which, considering the amount of time I spent in that house, she may very well mistakenly have thought I was."

They continued to walk, passing the Gurson and the Kameron houses. Stanley and Willy, the two most popular and therefore rejecting boys on the block.

"Do you ever wonder about all the people we knew back when?" Joanna asked. "Wonder what happened to them; how their lives turned out?"

He didn't. They were buried with so much else from his past.

"I'd like to see them again," Joanna mused.

"I'm sure all of Thirty-fifth Street would be impressed as hell with Stone and Bennett Public Relations, the clients you represent, your lifestyle. Shit. I doubt if Trudy or Stanley or Willy could compete with that," Dean said coldly.

She looked at him oddly, drawing away both physically and emotionally. "I fail to understand why my success should make you angry," Joanna stated. "Unless it's because you have so little of your own. You have no right to dislike me for what I am just because you aren't any of those things."

They were staring at each other, strangers once again. Dean shrugged. "You're right, Joanna. I am jealous. Which is probably exactly what you want me to be. Undoubtedly Sara and I must be uncomfortable reminders for you. After all, if you hadn't met Reynolds, you might be just like us . . . nothing."

She flinched, recognizing the truth in his words. "Well at least I went out and got what I wanted. And I didn't fall apart in the process."

They walked on, each nursing his own hurt and the anger that had collected for years.

"I don't understand any of this. Not really," Joanna said, near tears. "We were all so close once. Inseparable. And then we were all in other places, in other lives and with different friends. Only I never made other friends like you and Sara."

"We were never all that close, Joanna," Dean said, his voice, like his manner, aloof. "There were always things you never knew or cared to know about me. And Sara, too. And I couldn't tell you. You know why? Because you never really wanted to know anything that didn't directly apply to you. And that hasn't changed, Joanna. You're self-involved. You don't think to ask about others. You weren't comfortable with Sara's illness and you certainly were never comfortable with me."

"Because *you're* not," Joanna said angrily, standing now before what was once the Di Nardo home. "You're so damn guarded. As if you had some awful secret that I didn't already know. Wise up, Dean. I knew it all years ago. I just didn't ask because you didn't tell. And a person stops asking when she picks up the kind of signals you were giving out. If you had once let me in, Dean, I would have felt trusted. Like a friend."

He heard, although he was not happy with her words. How could he explain that fear prevented him from letting her in, from trusting? "It would have hurt too much if you had judged and walked away," he finally said. "Like the people who lived in this house," he added, nodding in the direction of the Di Nardo home. "In case you didn't know it, Joanna, my family wasn't exactly warm and nurturing, at least not where I or my differences were concerned."

Joanna noted the look on Dean's face and for a moment she thought he might pick up the garbage can at the curb and hurl it through the living room's picture window. She suddenly felt the urge to touch Dean, shield him, although she did not know from what exactly.

His voice was near a whisper when he spoke again. "Jo, if you wanted in, you could have had in. Just by asking. But you didn't. It was like . . . if you don't ask, and if we don't discuss it, then it doesn't exist. Face up, Jo, my being gay bothers you."

"Not as much as I now suspect it bothers you," Joanna replied. "What a load you've just dumped. How do you ask something of a supposed *close* friend when his every unspoken gesture says, 'Butt out.' It wasn't me in the closet, Dean, but you. I only learned about Chris through little things Sara would say. And you still haven't told me one damn thing about who you really are."

Dean looked at her, seeing something new.

"You never told me, Dean," Joanna said, her voice pained. "And I would have understood. I really would have, Dean. Because I loved you."

He turned to face her squarely. With his eyes on hers Dean said: "Joanna, I live with a man, have for eight years. It's a marriage, much like any other. Good times, bad times and the rest in between. I love him. And better still, he loves me."

Joanna put her hand on Dean's arm. As they walked back to where the car was parked, she said: "I'm happy for you, Dean. And I'm glad you told me. I can accept your life a lot better feeling you accept it, too."

Sara sat between Stefan and Ina, her hand in Stefan's where it rested lightly on his knee, her eyes on the *bima*, where Evan was soon to read that portion of the Torah that would complete his rite of passage to Jewish manhood. Sara looked at Ina, who turned and smiled, caught in the moment as her son Joshua prepared for his *alleyah*, that honor reserved during the bar mitzvah ceremony for those men nearest the celebrating family.

As the prayer continued before the open ark, the voices of the congregation raised in Sabbath songs of praise and thanksgiving, Sara, too, sang to a God she felt had been merciful and kind. Her life, as anyone at Temple Micah could see, was good. She wished Joanna and Dean were there to see that. This, not the reception, is what she had wanted to show them. Surrounded by family, she, Sara Schell née Rosen, had made that family possible. She had devoted her life to them, and woe to those who thought motherhood was a lesser accomplishment than a career. It *was* a career, and she had never felt denied or unfulfilled. There is no greater fulfillment than children. They were her. They were of her. Her imprint was in all of them. Let others like Joanna find their fulfillment in other market-places. She knew where hers was to be found.

Sara's arm slipped about Ina's shoulders. Her sister was alone in the world with her son and daughter; a part-time mother and a full-time employee at a job in Manhattan that did nothing more for Ina than supplement the child support Arthur sent monthly. Her sister was forty-five, not quite old but not exactly young. Hers was not an easy life.

Stefan was rising, moving solemnly toward the *bima.* His would be the first *alleyah* awarded. As he climbed the few stairs to where his son and rabbi waited before the open Torah, Sarah felt a flush of pride. Stefan looked elegant, stunning. She watched his face as he gazed at Evan with pure love. It was a look Sara had seen Stefan give all of his children from time to time. She turned in her seat to see if other women in the congregation saw what she did when she looked at Stefan. From the looks on their upturned faces Sara knew they felt the strength, the inner security and the confidence that so much was the man.

Stefan's voice, normally deep and resonant, was barely audible as he struggled with the Hebrew words. She had begged him to practice, but he had refused, insisting the day was Evan's and not his, so why should he be concerned with something he normally was not. But he was wrong, Sara thought. The day belonged to all of them. The bar mitzvah was as significant a moment in her life as it was in Evan's. Perhaps more so as she understood the tradition. That was what Stefan denied. The specialness of continuation, of belonging to a heritage that was thousands of years old.

She had felt that specialness from the moment her eyes had opened that morning. Stefan was lying next to her, and she was as surprised as she was delighted, since he was unexpected. He felt warm and was not unresponsive to her touch. He awakened slowly, became aroused as she initiated their togetherness. When she felt the moment was right she moved closer to him, as close as she could, side by side, until they were almost one. She felt wonderfully small against him and he huge within her as she buried herself in his chest. Together they rocked, cradlelike, in a steady pace. Until it stopped. But then Stefan often had problems sustaining and even maintaining. It didn't matter. The morning was special. *It* had been special. Comparisons to others were destructive. Besides, she never wanted to be that out of control again. Heights of passion had once reduced her to the depths of despair, she reminded herself. What she had now was all she needed.

Tears filled Sara's eyes as she watched her "men" on the *bima,* Stefan's hand resting lightly on Evan's shoulder. From where she was sitting Sara could feel its strength, yet its lightness. That hand had been there for her many times . . . from the beginning.

She was remembering. The house in Brooklyn . . . the days of nothingness . . . his phone call. Her psychiatrist had urged her to accept his dinner invitation, to resume living. He had also urged her to say nothing of her past. She hadn't. Except that she had suffered a breakdown. Yes, she had used that word. He had been solicitous, even impressed, as if her mental instability was some sign of extreme sensitivity to be coddled and nurtured. She invented a romance, one that had been bitterly disappointing. He had accepted that, too, and instead of feeling jealous seemed quite content knowing another had found her desirable. He offered salvation. He married her, taking her far away from her past and into a new life in Princeton. A safe life, one without subways and tunnels except for those that sometimes surfaced in her mind.

The service was over. Her son had been bar-mitzvahed. The congregation was singing "Adon Olam," the closing Sabbath hymn to God. Joyfully, gratefully, Sara sang along.

Joanna was surprised. She, the public relations person, the one *paid* to enter lions' dens and do battle, was afraid, intimidated actually, by just the thought of entering a nondescript brick house in Princeton. She had expected Sara and Stefan to be at the door, but there was no one, just guests milling about the house and spilling out into the backyard. She spilled with them, seeking a familiar face among the hats and hairstyles more indigenous to Princeton than Beverly Hills.

She saw Stefan first, head and shoulders above the others, looking much as she had remembered him: solid and imposing. When the crowd semi-parted, she saw Sara. The gray dress was ill-fitting and without style, despite the rose that grew from her side at the waist. It did not compliment, nor was it complimented by, the orchid corsage pinned to her shoulder.

Their eyes locked. Sara looked away and then back again before she began walking, a smile creasing her face as she drew nearer. Suddenly they were standing before one another, nervous smiles on their faces. Sara giggled. Joanna laughed. They hugged, holding one another until embarrassment and reason pulled them apart. Joanna was surprised by the jealousy she felt when Sara greeted Dean in no less an effusive manner. She noted Sara's embarrassment with Chris and her hesitancy with Reynolds, and the way she clung to Stefan, who clung to his pompous pose. After the initial pleasantries Stefan disappeared, taking Sara, who promised Joanna she would return as soon as she had greeted the other guests.

Joanna drifted to the buffet table, suddenly hungry. Its offerings were far different from those she had seen at recent lawn parties in Beverly Hills, where the lawn chairs didn't smell, as these here did, of Coppertone and baby oil. There pretty umbrellas dotted the manicured lawns. Here there were only mosquitoes and sun for unwelcome covering and pockmarked crab grass in which to catch one's heels. As she nibbled at the *pâté*, which proved to be chicken livers and not *foie gras*, Joanna watched as Sara played the hostess, making the rounds, glued to Stefan's side. Not only was the dress unbecoming, but the hair needed something, thought Joanna, like a style and a rinse, anything that might change and color the drabness, which was Sara's overall effect. She looks her age, Joanna decided. Every day of it and then some.

And just maybe she doesn't give a damn, Joanna reasoned. Just maybe looking her age doesn't offend her. Maybe her identity isn't tied up in how she looks. It never was, so why should it be now? Maybe she's decided to grow old with grace not being a factor. What business is that of yours? Why should what Sara is or isn't offend or threaten you? What is it you want?

Joanna answered her own questions. Before this day ends and another begins, I want to see Sara's bedroom.

Sara was putting faces to names as Stefan's associates bunched together as if they didn't see enough of one another at the university. Richard Wein surprised her. She had imagined him as short and fat rather than tall and lean. He was not wearing a wedding band, which meant she should seat him later near Ina. A Mark Rosenberg, also from the university, was talking to her, but Sara wasn't listening. Even as she made some inane response, her eyes were following Joanna. As she accepted Dr. Wolfe's congratulations—she was a fellow in Stefan's department—Sara measured Joanna's appearance. Once again Joanna made her feel inadequate. She was stylish, although too thin, too drawn, Sara decided. But compelling. You could not overlook her presence. She supposed some might even term Joanna beautiful.

Thank you, Sara murmured as the Wolfe woman exited, commenting on what a lovely party it was. Still more guests were introduced, but Sara only half heard as she watched Joanna take a napkin from a waiter's passing tray and wipe the lawn chair nearest where she was standing. Seated, she looked like a queen on her throne, observing. Near her, Sara noted, Chris stood, engrossed in a conversation that produced easy laughter among people who but moments ago had been uncomfortable strangers. Like Joanna, he seemed too perfect to Sara, too handsome with his face full of gleaming white teeth and eyes much too blue for a man.

She drifted over toward Ina, wrapped around Dean, holding on to his arm as if she feared he might slip out of her life again. They had always liked each other, Sara remembered. Dean looks older, Sara thought, not at all the boy but a man who seems strained, as though his shirt collar is too tight, preventing him from quick turns to see what menace might be lurking in the corners of the garden. He saw her staring and looked away, just as she herself turned, heeding the call of some other guest on the other side of the lawn.

Joanna was nursing a drink and a headache, the latter brought on by the former, as she never drank Champagne, and certainly not this quality of Champagne. She feigned interest as she stood with Reynolds, listening to him dispense his considerable charm. She could see that the women were charmed, particularly when he explained how he was much like an Oriental in philosophy; he believed in "saving face." Only he got paid for doing so. Surreptitiously Joanna checked her watch. She had been waiting and then waiting some more for Sara, who had promised to return for a chat. But Sara continued to float in and out of crowds, beginning to droop like the orchid now swan-diving from her shoulder, several of its petals amputated due to the crush of well-wishers. Once Joanna had caught her eye, and Sara had made some kind of gesture that Joanna had interpreted as: "in just a minute." The minute had passed, along with many others.

Joanna drifted into the house, feeling at odds with herself and the party. She wondered how soon she could leave without appearing rude. To judge from Sara's attitude, not soon enough. Sara's little girls were sitting on the living room floor playing some kind of board game with other children. They were pretty, something Joanna had not expected. Both had Stefan's strong features and dark coloring, but what made each pretty was Sara . . . her softness. Although the features were not the same, Sara was there in their faces. The girls looked nice. Yes, nice, as Sara had looked when they were young.

Joanna thought of Stacey. Her daughter had always been beautiful, always the source of much comment from strangers, but had she ever looked nice? Joanna couldn't remember, and that she couldn't, upset her. A mother should know if her daughter looked nice. The girls were laughing. Little laughs from little girls. Had Stacey ever laughed like that?

Dammit! Where is that woman, Joanna demanded, as her eyes searched the room for Sara. And then she relaxed. She even laughed as she wondered why she was pushing for this talk when she hadn't the vaguest idea what they would talk about.

Dean wrapped his arms about the waist of the woman standing at the kitchen counter. His mouth pressed to her ear, he whispered: "We have to stop meeting like this." Sara turned from the platter of canapés she was preparing—much to the dismay of Michele Caterers—to face the man who was holding her securely. Suddenly, through the facial lines that had never been there, she recognized the boy. Impulsively she hugged him. He laughed.

"You did good," Dean said. "It's a terrific party."

She wanted to cry. She had been so worried wondering what he and Joanna would think, certain each was accustomed to something far more elegant. She pushed a cheese puff into his mouth and then led him to Stefan's den, the one place where she knew they could be alone. Once there, the ease of the moment evaporated and the room was heavy with the past.

"I'm glad you came," Sara said, as she thought otherwise.

Dean looked about him, thinking how much he disliked the room's austerity, its lack of warmth despite its row upon row of book-lined shelves. With its dark leather chairs and couch, its heavy draperies, it felt oppressive. Much like Stefan.

"So how are you?" Sara asked when Dean didn't reply.

"I'm fine," he answered, turning toward her. "I'm trying to get reestablished professionally, making my comeback, you might say, only I've really nothing to come back from. I never had much success, so no one is exactly clamoring for my services. You know," he continued awkwardly, "that I put my career on hold several years ago."

"No. How would I?" Sara replied, not meaning to

sound as she felt: injured. "I just thought you gave it up as you matured."

"Acting is not a kid's game, Sara," Dean said.

"I'm sorry," Sara replied, embarrassed. "I only meant I've always thought of acting as something you dream of doing when you're very young. Didn't we all want at one time to be Elizabeth Taylor and Rock Hudson?"

"That's not what acting is. You're talking about ego and fantasy. I'm talking about a profession," Dean said angrily.

"Dean, please. Don't be angry. I don't know what I'm saying. I'm nervous. Your being here is making me nervous."

"Then why did you invite me?"

"Why did you come?" Sara asked, wanting Dean's answer before she could consider answering his question.

"Curiosity," Dean replied as he shrugged. "I wanted to see how your life turned out. I was nervous too, nervous about what you'd think and how I would appear to you after so many years."

She laughed. "Everything you just said are words that have been in my head and on my lips. It's all Joanna's fault. I felt so trapped by her invitation. Yet there was a part of me that wanted to see both of you, and the truth is, now that I'm looking at you and we are talking, I'm glad you're here. I mean that," Sara added as she suddenly felt choked by tears.

Dean smiled. "So how are you really, S.R.?"

She looked at him, not knowing whether to laugh or give in to the tears. He hadn't called her by her initials in years, something he had always done, much to her delight, as it made her seem important. "I'm OK," she said with some conviction. "There are still some days when I think it would be kinder if Stefan took me out in back and shot me as you would a wounded horse, but . . . they're just days. They pass. I know their limits, know just how bad they'll get and just how bad I'll get with them. But mainly life is good. As my mother and yours would have said in the old days: I married well. Stefan is wonderful. The kids are great."

"But what about you?" Dean persisted.

"That is about me, Dean. If you were married or had children you would understand that."

"I am married, Sara. That's why I do understand. All too well."

"Haven't you realized yet, Dean, that nobody gets it all? I at least have more than most. A home, a family. I've learned to make the most of what I do have and less of what I don't. And what did you mean when you said you were married?"

Dean hesitated, uncertain whether he wished to or could explain what he had said much too glibly. Sara's life was limited, provincial, and so much time had passed between them that he wasn't certain he wanted to or could trust her with his most intimate feelings. "Joanna and I went to Brooklyn this morning," he said, changing the subject. "To Thirty-fifth Street. It hasn't changed very much."

Thinking, Dean was unaware that Sara's expression made it clear she did not understand why he or Joanna would want to do such a thing.

"It hasn't changed or even aged much, Sara," Dean continued. "But we have, and that surprised me. I realized this morning no matter how I feel, I'm not twenty or even thirty anymore. I really am forty."

"If you had kids, you'd have no doubts," said Sara, laughing. "Nothing makes you feel your age or ages you faster than children. You just can't think of yourself as a child or even as being young when you have kids of your own."

"I could be a parent," said Dean thoughtfully. "I could act that role. But it's hard to act the adult when some part of you is still a child."

"Which part is that?" asked Sara.

"The one that feels denied, the one that feels angry about having lost something precious—although I don't know what it is," Dean replied.

"Why did you stop calling?" Sara asked suddenly.

Dean was startled by her question. "I just didn't feel welcome, as if my calls weren't anything but an intrusion. Stefan obviously wanted to be to you what I once was. You wanted that too. Which was only right. But you made no room for me. My presence seemed to embarrass you, as if I were some reminder of things you wanted to forget. I understood that part of it. What I didn't understand was your trying to forget me along with everything else in your past. I just assumed you couldn't handle who I was, and frankly I couldn't handle who you were becoming. It wasn't Sara to me."

"It wasn't you but an entire world I wanted to leave behind," Sara explained. "I regret you got left in the process. But perhaps it was necessary for me to survive. Then, too," she added, reaching back into her recollection for clarity, "the world you chose to live in struck me as being rooted in fantasy rather than reality. And I needed to remain rooted, grounded in everything that was real. Otherwise I worried I'd go over the edge again."

"Do you still worry about that?" Dean asked.

Sara laughed, although there was no smile on her face. "Anyone who has ever had a breakdown worries about that," she replied. "It's always there, hanging on your shoulders, to frighten and embarrass you. I often pretend I'm like other people. You remind me that I'm not. And I've never been able to forget how good you were to me. That, too, is a problem. The debt feels insurmountable. And it is. There is nothing I could ever do to repay you."

"You owe me nothing," Dean said. "It never occurred to me that you did. Had the situation been reversed, and it could have been, you would have done the same for me."

"But the situation wasn't reversed. You didn't crack. I was the cripple."

"Your judgment of yourself is far worse than what mine or anyone else's could be. For Chrissake, Sara, go easy. You didn't commit any crime."

Joanna was sitting at the piano, looking at the yellowed keys with disgust. The afternoon had been a shambles. She had been ignored by Sara and deserted by Reynolds, who fled at the drop of the most casual invitations to several sets of doubles at the Princeton Racquet Club. And in Stefan's borrowed clothes. Not that she could blame Reynolds. At this point if someone, *anyone,* threw her a life preserver, she, too, would grab it. Rude or not.

He was punishing her, Joanna decided, for being dragged to a bar mitzvah in New Jersey, when she was being punished enough by her very ignored presence here. She didn't need his added rejection. Amazing that Sara could still be busy. How obvious need she make it to show her disinterest, and in such a tacky fashion? But then Sara never was a hostess.

" 'Chopsticks' or 'Heart and Soul'?" Chris asked as he sat next to Joanna, cracking his knuckles before placing his hands on the keyboard.

"Neither I nor this piano can handle either anymore," said Joanna. "It's out of tune and I'm out of practice."

"It's too bad they've let a great old instrument like this go," said Chris as he played a few chords that were blatantly dissonant through no fault of his.

"It's too bad they've let a great old house like this go," said Joanna as her eyes searched the cracked ceiling and rain-stained walls.

"They could use Dean out here for a day," said Chris as he followed Joanna's eyes.

"A month is more like it," Joanna replied.

"I couldn't spare him," said Chris.

It was such a simple declaration of need that Joanna was startled. "I gather Dean is good at fixing things," she said finally.

"He designed and built our brownstone. It may not be featured anytime soon in *Architectural Digest*, but it's pretty impressive, particularly for someone without formal training. It's even impressive for someone with training."

"He takes after his father," Joanna said, remembering how handy Mr. Di Nardo had been with his hands.

"No, he doesn't. He really doesn't. Not at all," said Chris as he stared at Dean talking with Ina while Stefan observed.

"Can I get you two anything?"

It was Sara, looking weary and strained. She was biting her bottom lip, a gesture Joanna found familiar.

"Why don't you just sit and relax," said Chris as he stood, leaving Sara the seat next to Joanna on the piano bench. Sara looked as if she were about to be caged with a lion. If Chris noticed, he said nothing.

"We were just talking about how Dean built their brownstone," said Joanna. "Chris was saying that Dean is quite the talented architect."

"Perhaps that's what he should be then," said Sara, not thinking.

"He already has a profession," said Chris gently. "He may not as yet be successful, but it's just a matter of time and contacts. One he has plenty of; the other he has none."

Joanna cringed, thinking Chris was about to ask that she open doors for Dean. It was a thought not new to Joanna, and one, she was certain, that had always been in Dean's mind. But she and Lilith had a cardinal rule: Never intrude on clients or contacts, as both like to have favors done for them but not the reverse.

"Joanna, certainly you must know people who could help Dean."

It was Sara who had spoken. Sara, the woman who had said nothing to her all afternoon, had finally said words on which Joanna wished she would choke.

"If Dean came to Los Angeles, could you do anything for him?" Sara persisted.

"Why am I going to Los Angeles?" asked Dean as he came upon the group in conversation.

"I was asking Joanna if she had contacts to help you there," Sara explained.

Joanna and Dean looked at one another, forced to confront an issue that had remained unspoken between them for years. Joanna smiled, looking directly at Dean as she spoke. He was handsome, not unusual for Hollywood, but forty and unknown. Not a terrific combination.

"I could arrange for several casting people to see you. There are also several producers who would do me that courtesy. Of course it's more difficult with agents. They want to see you in something before they'll discuss representation. You'll of course need pictures. . . ."

"He has that. New ones. They're good," said Chris.

"And an up-to-date résumé. Plus clothes. Appearance is important these days. The scruffy-looking actor is a thing of the past," Joanna continued.

"Between us two we have one wardrobe," Chris replied. "We should go."

It was the "we" that bothered Sara. Joanna was speaking to Dean. Didn't Chris realize that?

There was a long silence that Sara did not understand, broken when Dean finally asked: "What are the chances, Joanna?"

She shrugged, knowing they were not good, that time was working against him unless he had great undiscovered talent. Still, it wasn't impossible. He might not become a star, but he might find enough work to at least make him eligible for twenty-six weeks of unemployment. "It's worth a shot," she replied. "You know the score. It isn't any easier in Los Angeles than it is in New York. If anything, it's worse."

"He handles the rejection better than I do," Chris said. "It kills me when people don't return his calls or give him a shot at auditioning."

Would you just shut up, dammit? Just keep your unsolicited comments to yourself, Sara thought, screaming to herself.

"It's damn frustrating to sit by and watch the rejection. And to be helpless. To be unable to do a damn thing about it. I'm not used to that as a doctor," Chris added.

Sara looked at the man standing near her. His expression bothered her. She looked at Dean and could see that he, too, was embarrassed. Then she looked at Chris again, at Dean, and again at Chris. All within seconds. And she finally had the answer to a question she had asked earlier. She now knew what Dean had meant when he said he was married.

Ina was calling. Thank God, thought Sara, thinking she could now extricate herself. It wasn't Sara Ina was seeking, but Chris. He left, a small favor, leaving her sandwiched between Joanna and Dean on the piano bench. "I hear you went to Brooklyn this morning," Sara said, turning toward Joanna.

"Yes, we visited old haunts. I'm sorry you weren't there," Joanna replied.

"There's enough old haunts with the three of us sitting

at this piano without my having to leave Princeton,'' Sara replied.

They were surprised by her remark, mainly because it was true. ''Music is what separates man from beast. Do you remember who said that?'' Sara asked.

''Twisted Sister?'' Dean replied.

Joanna giggled. ''No, fool. Miss McDonald in the seventh grade. Music appreciation. The most fearsome woman I ever saw. All those breasts, a girth like Dom De Luise and the face of a bulldog wearing lipstick. She used to swing her baton like a cudgel.''

''I think she was the world's first dominatrix,'' said Dean.

''First what?'' asked Sara.

''One of those funny S-and-M ladies with whips and chains who beat up on their lovers. Can't you just see her in black stockings and a garter belt with a little leather cap on her head?'' Dean replied.

Joanna laughed, although Sara's expression made it clear she did not think it funny. ''She hit me once,'' she said suddenly. ''With that baton. All because I couldn't identify 'Country Gardens' when she played it.''

''I remember that,'' said Joanna. ''Your mother came to school the following day.''

''Yes, my mother, the woman who went absolutely nowhere ever. All five feet two of her came to do battle with Miss McDonald. And won. I was never hit again. Unfortunately, I still can't identify 'Country Gardens,' '' Sara added, smiling.

''Which only proves you have intrinsically good musical taste,'' said Joanna. ''God, when I think what used to teach children in those days!''

''Do you remember the time Trudy Kaufman hit her back?'' Dean asked. ''Gave her a bloody nose.''

''I'm sure that story was apocryphal,'' said Joanna.

''Trudy never denied it,'' Sara insisted.

''Would you? It enhanced her image,'' Joanna replied.

''What do you think ever happened to Trudy?'' Dean asked.

''She served as a tank in the Vietnam War,'' said Joanna

without skipping a beat, "and is rumored to be the real Hulk Hogan."

Dean and Sara laughed.

"The class wit strikes again," Dean said.

"Class shit is more like it," said Sara. "I was just remembering how you used to drag me places. The dances, the sorority meetings, the bars where we were under age and very frightened."

"Fess up, Sara. You loved it. And if I hadn't dragged you, you wouldn't have gone," Joanna replied.

"That's exactly right," Sara said, suddenly serious.

"Well," mused Joanna, "see what I did for you?"

"It wasn't for me, Joanna," Sara replied calmly. "It was for you. You needed a date, a companion to get you through the door. I never wanted to go to any of those places. I went to make you happy."

"But you would have had no life if we hadn't gone," Joanna protested.

"No, Jo, *you* would have had no life," Sara corrected. "I had a life. It just wasn't the life you thought I should have. For years you led me down the garden path, and I like a fool followed. Then you took off, abandoning me."

The moment was awkward, stripped as it suddenly was of humor. Without word or explanation, Dean rose from his end of the bench and left, leaving Joanna and Sara alone. They sat awkwardly side by side, finding it impossible to speak.

Joanna laughed. "Life's little ironies. Here I've been waiting all afternoon to speak with you, and now that you're here it's suddenly hard to think of a thing to say."

"Oh, for God's sake, Joanna, what do you expect?" Sara asked. "We haven't seen each other in years—and I imagine there's all sorts of feelings about that—and you expect us to pick up where we left off? I hardly think so."

"You needn't be so snappish about it, Sara."

"I've had a hard day. I'm tense . . . nervous. I've not only had a bar mitzvah to contend with, but you and Dean. It hasn't been easy."

"I'm sorry we've been such a strain," said Joanna. "Perhaps you shouldn't have invited us."

"Perhaps I shouldn't have," Sara agreed.

Joanna rose, but Sara's hand on hers stopped her. "You did abandon me," she said. Joanna sat.

"I felt suffocated, as though I were strangling," Joanna explained. "I couldn't breathe. I felt so responsible for you. I always had. When Reynolds and I moved to California, I even felt we should take you with us."

"I felt that, too," Sara replied. "But then I made my own life. Only I made a mess of it."

"And I felt responsible for that, too, felt had I been there, none of it would have happened."

"Do you know what happened?" Sara asked, alarmed.

"Only that you had a breakdown. That's all Dean would tell me," Joanna said. "That was enough. I cried for days, but I couldn't face it or you. I'm just not any good at dealing with anyone's pain. I don't know why. I seem to pretend it's not there, and soon enough it isn't."

"I never forgave you for not being there when I was ill," said Sara softly.

"And I never forgave you for being ill," Joanna countered. "I felt you did it just to hurt me, to get even for no longer being your mother, father, sister and brother."

"Those are roles you assumed. I never asked," Sara protested.

"In subtle ways you did," Joanna argued.

"This really isn't the time to discuss all of this," Sara said, suddenly flustered. "I have guests."

"Sara, you started, now finish," Joanna insisted. "Don't run out on me."

"The way you once ran out on me?" Sara asked.

"Dammit, Sara. If you needed me so much, why didn't you pick up the phone and call. You also shut me out."

"Shut *you* out?" Sara laughed, her voice shrill. "You *were* out. I couldn't broadcast my breakdown to a stranger."

"And since when is a best friend a stranger?" Joanna asked.

"When she makes herself that. When she marries and moves, not just physically but in every way possible," Sara replied.

Joanna shook her head even though she knew Sara's words were true.

"When I got ill," Sara continued softly, "I wanted to call you but couldn't. I felt you had somehow violated our friendship . . . my trust. I felt alone."

"But you had Dean and your mother," Joanna said.

"They weren't you. Nobody can ever be your best girl friend but your best girl friend. And that was you."

"Sara, I just couldn't do it. I was too afraid. I hardly could carry myself, so how could I ever have thought I could carry you?"

Sara laughed without humor. "Funny, I just never thought of you as being afraid. Dean and I used to call you Joanna the Fearless."

"Well, it wasn't true. I had bogeymen of my own. There were many nights I searched under the bed and in closets before I could fall asleep. Today I know better. I just don't look . . . ever, and that applies to everything in my life. I just leap and maybe remember to look later. And I don't question things too closely because I just might find answers that tell me nothing I need or want to know. And *voilà!* Look at me. It works," said Joanna, smiling.

"What was in *your* closet and under *your* bed?" Sara asked softly.

"Fear. Just plain fear. Mainly that I couldn't measure up. When I met Reynolds the fear intensified. He was a powerful man. More so even now. He commands attention, particularly that of women. He's wonderfully attractive . . . sexy. He's accomplished and he has a natural élan that sets him apart. His parents raised him to be a little prince, and I had to teach myself how to be his consort. It wasn't easy. I knew no more of fashion and taste than you. I made myself over. Quite successfully it would seem. But I was always afraid of being drawn back to the girl I was when I married. Perhaps that's why I came today: to prove that I'm not. And I'm not," Joanna concluded with finality.

"No, you're not," Sara agreed as she lay her hand on Joanna's. "You're a beautiful woman who exudes confidence, quite the princess . . . no, queen. I guess the difference is: I'm no longer your loyal subject. I have my own kingdom, my own prince. I suppose there will always be a bogeyman, but Stefan and the kids keep me far from his reach."

"Sara, I'm sorry if I hurt you," Joanna said as she held Sara's hand in her own. "I never meant to." She was about to say more, to ask about Stefan and the children when suddenly the lights dimmed. Dean was pushed toward the piano by Ina as Chris, his face lit by forty burning candles, entered the room with a tiered cake singing happy birthday. While Stefan observed, his pipe filling the air with a sweet-smelling smoke.

As Chris approached, Joanna searched for the still absent Reynolds, Sara beckoned to Stefan to come closer and Dean looked away from the face filled with love that gazed at him over mounds of whipped cream and pink roses. Someone yelled, "Speech," but suddenly shy, not one of the celebrants could think of a thing to say.

They were inching their way into the city, one of the many cars caught in late Saturday night traffic, en route to discos and parties that first began long after the crush of theatergoers had ended. As she leaned into the cushioned backseat of the Pontiac, Joanna felt no sense of urgency to return to the city and the present. She was drifting through the day, remembering, reliving moments of Brooklyn and Princeton and time spent with Dean and Sara.

Reynolds stirred, shifted in his corner of the car and returned to sleep, his mind seemingly uncluttered by anything more meaningful than three sets of victorious tennis. He had returned from the courts shortly after the cake had been served, his half-smile that was almost a grin and his eyes that shone a bit too brightly making it clear to Joanna that he had been "smoking." Still, he had been charming, making conversation with Sara, with Dean, even inviting all to Los Angeles, where he would show them the city. They had been charmed. As people often were by Reynolds.

The same could not be said of Stefan, who had observed as they talked, his pipe more in his mouth than words. He had made her uncomfortable, acting more as a monitoring parent than peer. Yet Sara didn't seem to notice. Strangely, she had seemed at her most relaxed, participating frequently in a conversation that was exclusionary to those who hadn't been part of the childhood spent on Thirty-fifth Street. Somehow Chris had managed to include himself, obviously aware through Dean of the childhood experiences that had united them. He was amusing and attractive, thought Joanna. From the backseat, she stared at the head of the man sitting directly in front of her. Chris's hair was naturally streaked with strands of blond, the exact color of which she had so desperately sought to duplicate over the years. It looked soft, and Joanna had to resist an impulse to run her hand through it. She wondered if men ever made such affectionate gestures when they were alone with one another.

As he fought the merging traffic on the turnpike, Dean fought an impulse to push Chris's hand from his thigh, where it had rested lightly for the past few minutes. Repeated glances in the rearview mirror assured Dean that Reynolds was asleep and thus oblivious and that Joanna couldn't possibly see the intimate gesture. Still Dean was uncomfortable. Often he had argued with Chris about his open display of affection. Not that Chris ever flaunted his homosexuality, but he certainly didn't deny it when it came to Dean. Chris thought it appropriate, and although Dean could not argue that it wasn't, he still felt his feelings—whether or not they negated who he was and who they were as a couple—should be respected.

The car radio was turned to WLTW, and Dean could feel more than hear Chris humming along with the lush background music. Occasionally, the fingers on his thigh tapped in rhythm to the bass beat that underscored that of the violins. Dean turned from the traffic to look at Chris briefly. His eyes were closed, and with a half-smile on his lips he looked like a contented child about to fall asleep after a full day. Chris was like most doctors, Dean thought. He slept wherever and whenever, a survival technique learned during internship.

Although he had planned to take the Lincoln Tunnel into midtown Manhattan, Dean decided the Holland Tunnel would be faster, as little of the Saturday night traffic was going that far downtown. Exit fourteen was just ahead. As he edged into the right lane and the turnoff, Chris's hand slipped from his thigh. Dean's emotions were mixed when he realized that Chris, snoring ever so lightly, was not now about to put the hand back.

Joanna was staring at the interior of the Holland Tunnel, trying to remember when she had last been in it. As a child, on those rare Sunday outings when the family would drive to visit her father's mother, they drove through this very same tunnel, and she in her innocence had thought once they left the tiled tubelike interior that did funny things to her ears, they would be in Holland and she would see windmills and tulips and children in wooden shoes. It never happened. But then, she thought, surprised by the feeling that threatened to overwhelm her, there had been so few windmills and tulips in her childhood.

She wondered if Stacey had windmills. She didn't know. She remembered Sara asking that afternoon: ''How is Stacey?'' and she, echoing the question as she silently wondered . . . how is Stacey? She had said fine, not knowing if that was true, nagged by a sudden dread that it wasn't. She had immediately dismissed both the question and the dread, but now it was there, in this tunnel, confronting her.

Joanna turned from the window. Tomorrow, she reassured herself, she had a press conference luncheon with the producer whose bomb had detonated at the opening of the film festival Friday evening. Tomorrow night she would be on a plane. She hated planes. They frightened her. The next day, provided the plane didn't crash, she would be in her office, in her life, home again.

She could not explain the tears that were suddenly trickling down her cheeks. It must be exhaustion, she decided as she reached into her handbag to find two Anacin tablets for her headache. It had been a difficult day.

As they drove out of the tunnel, Joanna felt the downtown Wall Street high-rises hovering about her. As a child their shadows on the evening skyline had seemed like menacing monsters, terrifying her as their car drove through their midst. Thirty years later Joanna was again relieved when the car turned toward the West Side Highway. New Jersey was now on the other side of the river. Sara was again physically distanced from her life. Mileage separated them. And lifestyles. Yet Sara seemed closer somehow than she had ever been.

The car was speeding through lower Manhattan as Joanna thought of three relationships built around the adventure of growing up. How different each of the three was. Hers, of course, was the most different and obviously the most enviable. She was the success. Of the three, she was the Tiffany's. Yet they each had something, and she had felt something for each.

They had driven past the Christopher Street pier and the Westbeth Housing Project, past the Ganesvoort Meat Market, when Joanna saw it out of the corner of her eye. She knew what was about to happen, could feel it although all feeling had left her body. She wanted to call out, to warn of the car approaching out of control, disobeying all traffic signals as it tore across the highway, its headlights blinding. Joanna heard the crunch of metal, the shrieking, shattering of glass and the screams. Horrible screams. Terrifying. From the car. Her car. Her.

She saw the blood spreading in the roadway like an oil slick and the people running to pull bodies from the wreckage before the fire could cause an explosion. She saw a headless body in the street with its head near and yet so far. Then she saw herself through the people hovering about her. And from her great height overlooking the destruction, Joanna heard the sirens of the emergency medical service approaching almost as fast as the blackness people called death. As she sank into it Joanna thought: "But I never got to see Sara's bedroom."

FIVE

BILLOWY clouds drifted over and enveloped Sara, numbing her mind and body. She burrowed more deeply into her bed, knowing soon, with just a flick of the remote-control button, she would remove the flashing images of the late-night news from her TV set. Sleep would be welcome, earned, too, Sara thought as the tension of the day continued to dissipate with the advent of sleep. She had managed a bar mitzvah and a reunion. Enough for one day. For a year, she laughed, as her eyes opened and closed and then opened again, caught suddenly by the picture on the television screen.

A remote from the scene of some awful accident. Not suitable to watch before bedtime. The crowd was still there, staring at the cordoned-off area, the bloodstains and the wreckage.

Sara shuddered and wondered if Stefan would join her later. She imagined him there in bed, making the warmth warmer. Just knowing he was in the house gave her a cozy feeling. She liked having Stefan near. She wasn't like Joanna, who obviously felt secure whether Reynolds was with her or on some tennis court miles away. But that was Joanna's life and it had little to do with hers, thought Sara.

The newscaster seemed so far off that she wasn't sure she had heard him correctly. Names, familiar names . . . Dr. Reynolds Bennett, his wife, Joanna. Dr. Christopher Langdon and Dean Di Nardo. One dead . . . decapitated, the others taken in critical condition to . . .

The clouds lifted. The warmth evaporated into chilling cold. A dream, Sara thought as her hands clutched the remote-control button. But the story had changed, and Sara found herself watching the weekly Lotto drawings until she was awake and aware. Then she began to shake. She shook all the way down the stairs into the living room, where she thought she would find Stefan. But like the sleep that had come but moments ago, Stefan, too, was gone.

She searched the den, then the kitchen. A check of the driveway proved the car was gone. There is nothing to do but wait, thought Sara as she sat huddled in the window seat in the living room overlooking the wall surrounding the house. Stefan will be home in a minute, she assured herself.

An hour later, Sara shivered and drew the comforter she had taken from their bed more tightly about her. The house was still; the only noise was the questions in her head that produced fear but no answers. The telephone sat in Sara's lap, as did their address book. Twice she had been through the listings looking for someone to call, someone who might have an answer, *the* answer. She could think of no one. Of course there was a simple explanation, she reasoned, so simple that it couldn't enter her mind to arrest any of the questions that whirled there in a bumpy flight of confusion.

I will not allow my imagination to run away with itself, Sara insisted, without considering where it might go. She recounted the safe possibilities. Stefan had taken a hurried drive to replenish a dwindling tobacco supply . . . had gone for the early edition of the morning paper or fresh rolls, yes, fresh rolls, for Sunday morning's breakfast.

None takes this long, thought Sara as she slid out of the window seat after checking the clock on the mantel. Trembling, Sara, wrapped in her comforter, again climbed the stairs to the bedrooms to peer in at her children. They were still there, asleep in beds big enough for just one or she would have lain next to Naomi or Dana. Again she smoothed the wisps of hair from her daughters' faces, adjusted their covers and checked the window to see that it was open enough but not too much before she moved on to the boys' room to do the same.

A car pulled into the driveway. Its door opened and closed gently. She heard feet crunching on gravel. A key turned in the kitchen door lock. Another opening, another quiet closing.

I will not call out. I will not act like some hysterical woman, Sara told herself. I will go downstairs and act like a reasonable person. I will find out exactly what happened and then laugh at my insanity. She was at the foot of the stairs before she realized, face to face with Stefan as he came from the kitchen. He seemed startled by her appearance.

"Where were you?" she asked, her voice sounding strange, even foreign to her. But please God, let it not sound accusing or desperate, she prayed.

"I'm surprised you're up at this hour," Stefan replied. "This is the middle of the night for you," he said, his tone light and almost bantering.

"Where were you?" she repeated, trying to mimic his tone.

"What do you mean?" Stefan asked as he moved past her into the living room.

Sara followed, wanting to scream. "I mean where were you?" she asked, wishing she wouldn't harp so at him. She had flicked on a light and was looking into the face of a man she didn't know. It was strained and the corners of his mouth were twitching.

"You were asleep when I looked in on you. As you often are when I check at that hour," he began.

Yes, so? thought Sara. She used the TV for just such a purpose. As company to fall asleep. Often her only company. "Where were you?" she asked, this time aware her voice was shrill despite her attempts not to be that kind of woman, the type who drives her husband away with needless fears.

"I went for a drive," Stefan said. "I do that sometimes when you're asleep. To clear my head. To think about what I've just read. To relax me."

Had he not added the last, she might never have been so foolish to have said: "You hate to drive. You've always hated to drive. Because you don't find it relaxing."

His face fell apart. In pieces. She wanted to rush and help him reassemble it, but he spoke first. "Sara," he began, his voice calm and reassuring although Sara could see he was neither. Suddenly Sara felt afraid, more so as she watched him struggle with words. For a moment she thought she really should drop the conversation, turn her back and pretend neither it nor Stefan's absence had happened. There was no need to pursue this unless she wanted to know the truth, and she didn't. She really didn't.

He told her anyway.

"I've been seeing someone."

She didn't hear him.

"I'm sorry. I never meant for you to find out," he added.

Sara looked without seeing or hearing but was faintly aware there was a man standing in front of her. She didn't know who this stranger in her hallway in the middle of the night was.

"Who is she?" she heard someone ask and wondered how anyone could have the nerve to ask such a question at a time like this.

"It doesn't matter," he replied. "Just someone. I've decided not to see her anymore."

Thank God, she thought. "But why?" she asked, amazed that anyone could be so dumb to ask such a question. What difference? Didn't he say he wouldn't see her again? Why invite trouble? Why ask why?

"Because she wanted us to marry," Stefan answered.

Marry? But you're already married, she thought. "There's been an accident," she said. "A terrible accident. With Joanna and Dean. Somebody's dead, but I don't know who."

He was looking at her oddly.

"Doesn't she know you're married?" some crazy woman asked, despite Sara's pleadings that she not.

"Yes, she does," he replied. "Sara, what's this about an accident?"

"Is she crazy? Doesn't she know you have children? Who is this lunatic? Stefan, I'm frightened. I don't know who was decapitated, who to call. Does she love you? Do you love her? When did all this happen?"

"Yes."

She heard his voice. It was anguished. Yes, he said. But yes to what? To which question? Don't ask, she commanded. The less you ask, the less you'll know . . . the less you'll have to forgive and forget.

"I think we had better talk," she said as she again took her place on the window seat. This time, no matter how tightly she wrapped herself in her comforter, Sara felt cold.

From the dilated pupil that was not reactive to light, to the discolorations at the base of her skull, Dr. Sidney Reese had deduced that the patient had a blood clot applying pressure to the brain. A CAT scan would verify it, and as attendants wheeled his charge out of the trauma center for the one X ray the total emergency environment could not provide, Reese affixed Joanna Bennett's chart to the gurney. That she had no broken bones or internal injuries was a miracle considering the car in which she had been riding had been totally demolished.

But the true miracle, thought Reese, was the passenger found walking dazed at the site of the accident with only slivers of glass protruding from his face and hands to prove he had been in the crash. Suffering from shock, the man would have nothing more than his emotions to deal with when he was released from the hospital.

The patient now before him was not so lucky, thought Reese. He was about to undergo exploratory surgery to locate the source of his internal bleeding, which could be major or minor depending on the extent of his injuries and which organ, if any, was involved. The man might live or he might die. The issue was of little interest to the doctor, who, once he had done his job as expertly as possible, prided himself on emotional distance.

The phone call was neither interruptive nor surprising to Reese. The caller informed him that the doctor's preliminary diagnosis had been correct. The scan had shown that the patient, Joanna Bennett, had indeed suffered a skull fracture across the miningeal artery. Blood was accumulating rapidly in the epidural space, and extreme pressure was being exerted by a blood clot on the brain. If the patient was not to die, a likely possibility considering her condition, that pressure had to be removed immediately. The patient, the caller added, was currently being prepared for emergency surgery.

She could feel the sense of urgency in the room, its green-robed and masked occupants moving in robotlike precision. She tried to speak, found her voice, but no one heard.

Her blood pressure is dropping, Doctor.
I'm not getting any pulse.
Proceed with the craniotomy.

She heard no more, the words growing fainter as she floated from the room, her speed accelerating as she was swept higher and higher into a tunnel, so long and so dark that it seemed endless. She felt as much as heard music not quite like any other she had ever experienced as she hurtled through the darkness. She was surprised at how unafraid she felt. There was no pain and no anxiety. Colors, vivid, almost electric and pulsating, flew by her consciousness. A meadow of green, a sea of blue, flowers of such shape and size and vibrancy, and faces, familiar faces, beckoning. With love. Her father. And there beyond, in the distance, just a pinpoint of white at first, was seemingly her destination. A light that grew into an enormous Being of amber and gold with awesome flashes of silver.

She gasped. She cried. Never had she felt such warmth. She rested in Its glow, clothed herself in It, absorbing as she was absorbed in It. Within her was a feeling she had long suspected was there but hiding . . . joy. Unmitigated, unbridled joy. Born of love. The most unconditional, all-encompassing love she had ever known. She breathed deeply, feeling a peacefulness, a serenity, a completion that seemed so natural even if it was so new to her. She reveled in the glow, feeling at last she knew who she was and what she was meant to be. As if she had come home.

Only she wasn't being allowed to stay. It was not yet her time. She pleaded. But if she were heard, there was no response except for the wind that then howled through the tunnel from which she had come and through which she was now returning.

Joanna's eyes fluttered open. Slowly she took in her surroundings. Unfamiliar but not strange. She whimpered. This wasn't where she wanted to be. White flashed in and out of her vision. A nurse not seeing she was awake. She wanted Reynolds. She yearned for Stacey. But there was no one in the room except Reynolds as he had been when she had first met him at a "smoker." He looked so young, this medical student prince from Washington Heights.

Where was he now? she wondered. Her question puzzled her. Did she mean where was Reynolds at this moment or where was that Reynolds of that moment? She couldn't think. She could only feel. That she had lost that Reynolds forever.

Tears splashed on her cheeks. She turned to the other side of the room. A vase of flowers—from whom? she wondered—on the bureau. Their brightness was even more blinding than the white of the nurse's uniform. A remembrance, vague but trying to surface. Of other flowers, other colors. Of unimaginable brightness. It rushed back to her, color upon color, love upon love. Gone. Lost. Taken from her. Her tears turned to sobs.

She called out for Reynolds. But there was no Reynolds. How often over the past years had she called and had he not been there? she wondered. And Stacey, how often had she called and had she, her mother, not been there?

A nurse entered, looked at Joanna, looked again, and began pressing buttons. Another nurse arrived, a doctor, still another doctor. But no Reynolds. No Stacey. Nothing that felt like home.

"I do not want to be sitting here," thought Sara as she huddled into her comforter. Stefan is home and that's all that matters. Let well enough alone. But the lines on Stefan's face she had thought these many months were the product of overwork said things were not well and there was little to let be.

Sara looked at the man whose face had been familiar and comforting until a few hours ago. She was horrified and frightened. His pain seemed worse than hers. She wanted to comfort him, tell him everything was all right, that life would go on as before, but she couldn't. She wished someone could tell her the very same things she wanted to tell Stefan, but she knew no one could.

"What did you say about Joanna and Dean?" he asked as he looked everywhere but at her.

The question revived the horror she had felt, first at hearing the news and then at realizing he wasn't in the house. "An accident," she mumbled. "Someone has been killed," she continued, feeling that someone was her. "I don't know who to call or what to do," she again anguished, listening to her voice and wondering about which tragedy she was speaking.

"Who is she?"

Her question was direct and simple.

"It doesn't matter," Stefan replied, his voice weary. "It's over."

"It matters to me," Sara said loudly, the intensity of her voice surprising her. "Who is she?" she demanded.

"Just someone I've known for a while," he answered.

"A while? How long is a while?" Sara asked, her voice hard, sounding ugly even to her as she imagined one of his students, someone young, probably blond, undoubtedly slim.

"Sara, it just doesn't matter," Stefan pleaded. "She'll leave Princeton. It's no better for her than for me this way."

Watching Stefan caused her to feel something stirring within that made her want to scream. His pain was causing her guilt. She was feeling bad because he was hurting.

"How did this happen?" Sara asked, not realizing she verbalized what she was thinking. "I don't understand. I'm your wife. What does she give you that I don't? How could you live such a lie?" Thoughts entered Sara's head that twisted at the core of her being. He had said he often looked in on her at night. For what reason? To what purpose? "Did you often leave here at night when I was asleep to see her? And where do you see her? At your office, her apartment? Both? Does her family know? Oh, my God," said Sara, thinking of the worst. "Could you lose your job if she told anyone? Dammit, Stefan, who is she?" Sara cried out.

"Stop, Sara. You'll wake the children," Stefan said, concerned.

"I'll wake the children?" echoed Sara. "Oh, my. Wouldn't that be awful. Well, maybe I should wake them. Maybe I should call them down here right now and tell them their father is running around with some girl from school, running around and running out on them."

"Sara, please. You're being hysterical."

"Oh, I'm so sorry, Stefan. Tell me," said Sara as she slid out of the window seat and stood before him, "how should I be—calm, forgiving and feeling that this is just another tunnel and that the light at the end will soon appear?"

"I told you, Sara, it's over. What more do you want? What more can I say?" Stefan pleaded.

"Something . . . anything, dammit, that will help me to understand," said Sara. "Stefan, you say I'm the winner. Tell me why then do I feel like I've lost everything?"

"Sara, it will be all right. I just need some time to adjust."

"*You* need some time to adjust?" Sara mocked, wanting to laugh at the incongruity. "What about me? What about my adjustment?"

"We'll make it," Stefan said.

"But why? Why us—why me and you and not you and her?"

"Because we have a family. We *are* a family. It will be all right, Sara. It will," Stefan reiterated.

She wanted to believe it. She would believe it, she decided. If not today, then tomorrow, or next month. Next year, for sure.

His eyes fluttered open and then closed as he was again drawn into that netherworld in which pain was distant and yet near. He heard a voice coaxing him into the bright white of the antiseptic room and a world he didn't feel ready to enter. He had seen it earlier, awakening from a nonrestful sleep before falling back into this other world of silence, a world where nurses didn't hover, ambulances didn't scream and questions to which he had no answers weren't asked.

Awake now despite his efforts, he felt the fingers on his pulse. He looked past the white of the sleeve into the face of the young girl with the dishwater-blond hair piled under her nurse's cap. She smiled and said the doctor would soon be by to see him.

Chris . . . she meant Chris, he thought gratefully.

The sheets were soggy and as he turned to relieve his body ache, the pain stunned him. His cry brought the girl once again to his bedside. She explained the surgery, the incision down his middle that had allowed the doctors to explore for internal injuries and to suture the broken blood vessels. He was a lucky man, she chirped. His ribs . . . well, let the doctor tell him about that, she said, smiling.

Where is Chris? he asked. Dr. Langdon, he explained when her face didn't register recognition.

His case, she said, was being handled by Dr. Rotchstein.

He knew no Dr. Rotchstein. He wanted Chris. Where was he? he demanded in a voice so weak it carried no clout.

She didn't know a Chris or a Dr. Langdon, the nurse said patiently, but if he was expecting someone, there was a man who had been waiting for some time to see him. Should she fetch him?

Yes, he replied impatiently, relieved that he wasn't alone in a hospital room for reasons he couldn't quite remember. A bar mitzvah . . . Sara and Joanna . . . a hand, Chris's hand, on his thigh . . . Joanna screaming. Something had happened to Joanna. And then there was nothing left to remember. The screen in his mind went blank.

"Dean?"

"Chris?" he replied, smiling as he opened his eyes. But it wasn't Chris. Squinting, he brought the familiar face into sharper focus.

"It's me, Dean," the voice said tentatively.

He knew both face and voice now. What he didn't know was why his brother was here.

"How are you doing?" he heard Tony ask in a more conciliatory tone than he had heard from him in years. "Are you in pain?"

He didn't know. Things were registering too slowly for him to feel above or below the numbness.

"Tony, what happened? What am I doing here? And where's Chris?" he asked, his tongue thick, his mind refusing to activate.

"There was an accident, Dean. A car hit yours as you were coming off the West Side Highway."

Joanna's screams. They made sense now.

"But you're all right," Tony was quick to assure. "Nothing serious. A cracked rib, some bad bruises. When the incision heals, you'll be out of here. Could be in a week."

Dean looked at the man who had not looked so kindly at him since they were both kids. "You're going to be all right," he heard Tony say, his voice surprisingly heavy with emotion. "Papa's outside. He wants to see you."

Dean laughed. "If Papa's here, this has to be heavy-duty stuff. You haven't got a priest waiting out there to deliver last rites, do you?"

Tony didn't smile, let alone laugh.

"What's up, Tony?" Dean asked. "Is there something you're not telling me? I do have all my arms and legs, don't I?" Dean asked as he dragged his hands through a quick check of all his parts.

Tony turned away. When he again faced Dean, his expression immediately dispelled any and all of Dean's numbness. "Is it Chris?" Dean asked. "How bad is he?" Dean demanded, his voice rising with his fears.

"He's dead, Dean. He was killed instantly. Dean, he felt no pain. For God's sake, Dean, you can't get off the bed. Dean! Nurse? Nurse!"

He felt himself slipping, falling into another time and place. He struggled, fighting to remain rooted, but he wasn't strong enough. He cried out just one more time before hands held him to the bed. He heard the name he called, but with every ounce of strength he could muster, he resisted the knowledge that the person would never, could never, answer again.

The pile of dirty laundry sat in the basket waiting to be sorted as Sara sorted through her own dirty laundry, those thoughts that refused to be quieted. Throughout the weekend she had known she would hate Monday, dreading it with every passing hour. Stefan would leave the house, leave her and return to his other world, the one to which she had no access. She could only imagine what would happen there, only think her dirty thoughts as she sifted her dirty laundry.

Sara kicked at the clothes basket, spilling clothes over the basement floor. Her rage was preferable to her grief, which seemed without bottom or sides. Rage made her feel powerful and not as impotent as she suspected she really was.

He had said he would not leave, yet she disbelieved him. His pain gave her no reason to do otherwise. And that pain, so evident in his entire manner, pained her the most. He wasn't entitled to it. How dare he confront her with it, make her see how painful this decision was for him. But he had made his decision. The affair was over. Why then did some piece feel missing and why did she need to have it?

Sara checked the clock. Nearing eleven. He will have been at school three hours now, time enough to have someone young and slim change his mind again. Time enough for many things, none of which did Sara wish to consider. Despite all their talking over the weekend, she was not satisfied. She doubted if she ever would be again. Something had been taken, ripped from her, that could not be replaced. It was more than trust, more than security. It was indefinable, which was what made it all the more irreplaceable.

One question gnawed as it remained unasked and thus unanswered. She would ask it now. She would call and demand to see him. It wasn't enough, not for her, for Stefan to say he wouldn't see *her* again. It wasn't satisfying to hear Stefan say he would stay because she was his wife and this was his family. She needed to hear more, and she needed to hear if he could say it.

Sara was shaking. She had been ticketed en route to the university, stopped and summoned for driving through a traffic signal when she had been someplace in her mind rather than on the road. It was her first violation in fifteen years of driving. But then it was the first time she had felt so violated in as many years of marriage.

She would forgive him. He had made a mistake. They would talk . . . again. She would listen . . . again. She would try to understand. She would ask what she needed to know and hope his response would be what she needed to hear.

He had not been able to come home when she had asked and so had reluctantly agreed to her coming to his office. She had never been there before; he never had suggested she come and she had never thought to enter his world, which she viewed as both foreign and private.

It was more cubicle than office, a windowless four-wall enclosure lined with shelves and books. The desk was old, scratched and stained, piled with papers that looked to Sara to be exams. He half rose when she knocked and entered, his smile more solicitous than welcoming and thus adding to her discomfort. She wanted to ask if anything was new or if anything had changed since he had left home that morning.

"You never said you loved me," she blurted before reason could censor. Couldn't she at least have managed a hello-how-are-you? she asked some other self that wouldn't respond. "You told me you were staying," she continued, speaking into a startled face. "You mentioned things about family, about my being your wife, but you never said you loved me."

She stood there trembling, needing to hear—and afraid she wouldn't—words that would change her reality. Stefan remained seated, never moving toward her as she so much hoped he would.

"Did you reach the hospital?" he asked.

"Dammit, don't do that," Sara yelled. "Yes, I reached the hospital, but that's all I reached. No calls are being put through yet. Now answer me, Stefan. Answer me," she pleaded.

"Of course I love you, Sara," he said softly.

The emptiness remained. Something did not compute. "Are you sure we are what you want?" she asked, not trusting herself to ask the question uppermost in her mind.

Stefan nodded.

Ask, Sara, she prodded. Ask him if *you* are what he really wants. Ask why, if he loves you, is there a her? Also ask why he looks so awful and if he would be happier elsewhere . . . with someone else. But she didn't. She asked and said nothing, her courage suddenly gone. She was at the door, wondering why she had come and thinking it ridiculous that she had, when she heard him speak.

"Sara, I'm sorry you're hurt. I never meant that to happen. Never."

She opened the door and hurriedly left the building, passing any number of students who could have been *her*. On the drive home, the car hit a squirrel as it dashed across the highway. Sara never saw it. Not before or after.

Joanna's eyes found Stacey sitting on the edge of the bed. Reynolds, standing nearby, was staring, and Joanna could see that he, like Stacey, was wondering what madness would come next. But it wasn't madness and Joanna searched for some way to make them understand. She looked at Stacey and reached for her hand. She could feel it tense as she took it in her own, raised it first to her lips and then her cheek.

Stacey looked away, embarrassed by her mother's unusual display of affection. Although she had cried and clung to Joanna when she had first been allowed to visit, now, whenever Joanna tried to express what she was feeling—which was love—Stacey stiffened and withdrew.

Joanna was always touching. No matter who entered the room, doctor, intern or nurse, she touched, made physical contact in some way, delighting in the one-to-oneness. Now she squeezed Reynolds's hand, happy and grateful he was alive with only scabs and discolorations to mark his miraculous survival of the accident. She remembered how he had once loved to hold her hand. He was a boy then and she a girl. Now she felt a girl again, younger than she had ever been.

To make them understand was difficult, as often she had difficulty maintaining clarity of thought. Too many painkillers and mind-altering drugs had been introduced when doctors, told of her talk, became convinced she was hallucinating as many trauma patients did. But she never doubted her reason or sanity. She knew that where she had been and what she had seen was not a hallucination. The doctors did indeed drill a small hole in her head to perform the craniotomy, but a hole in the head did not necessarily mean one was crazy. She must make them understand that, and exactly what had happened. But as she turned her gaze to Reynolds and then Stacey, Joanna wondered how she could explain a feeling, one that began from within and radiated out, a feeling of total and complete love for who you and all others are. She couldn't, and that depressed her.

That wasn't all that depressed Joanna. Her depression often engulfed and then frightened her, given how it came in waves. It bolstered Reynolds's feeling that she was "troubled," in shock perhaps, or as the doctors had said when he had conferred with them: traumatized. She had tried to explain her depression, knowing it made sense to her but seemed crazy to others. She felt she had lost something precious while they wondered how losing one's life, dying, could ever be precious.

Because she had found life, she had explained. Life within the Light.

Reynolds had looked at her as if she were some strange stranger, and Stacey had laughed nervously.

She was depressed because she had wanted to remain within the love, within the Light. She couldn't tell them that, of course. How do you tell your family you prefer some other place to theirs? But that, too, wasn't true. Not totally. She had returned to this place, to this life, for them. There was unfinished business, errors to be corrected.

In her initial excitement at finding Reynolds alive, she had babbled about her experience. Alarmed, he had not truly listened but called in specialists who checked everything but her words. They then prescribed the drugs she didn't want but took to pacify Reynolds who, he explained, had been through his own ordeal. He really hadn't betrayed her, Joanna decided as she stroked Reynolds's hand. He just did not understand—her fault perhaps—and therefore did what he deemed best. She must try again, and again if necessary, to help them comprehend.

"Listen, you two," Joanna began, trying to make her tone light and cheery, "I know you think my brains got scrambled in the crash or that I now have not one but two holes in my head, but you must hear this. I am not in shock. Nor am I traumatized or hallucinating. I really did die. Not once but twice. And I witnessed my own death both times."

Stacey moved from the bed toward the door. "Listen, I'm going uptown to catch a flick. Maybe *Bambi* or *Pinocchio,* or even *Deep Throat*—anything to get out of this twilight zone," she said as she wrapped herself in a denim jacket.

"Stace, please," Joanna begged. "At least listen. Reyn, we're intelligent people. We've read about people who have had a near-death experience. We even discussed it, so why are you now negating it?"

"Jo, you're tired. You should rest."

"Stop patronizing me and answer my question, Reynolds."

"Because if you recall, Joanna, when we discussed it neither of us believed in it, although we agreed that people who had the experience did. We thought it interesting, but we never gave it much credence. After all, Jo, we both stopped believing in heaven and hell, angels and devils, long ago. We discarded all that mumbo jumbo for facts."

"Reyn, God is as real as the three of us sitting here," Joanna replied. "And I never said He didn't exist, just that I didn't know."

"And now you do," Stacey said, her voice reflecting her cynicism.

"Yes, Stace, I do," Joanna replied softly. "Because I've felt Him or It, or whatever that Presence was."

"Joanna, bear with me for a minute," Reynolds said, using his doctor voice as Stacey turned away from the bed. "You do agree you've had a terrible accident—blows to the head, brain surgery."

Joanna nodded.

"Then I ask you, Jo, isn't it possible you are imagining this happened or confusing it with hallucinations caused either by the blow to your head or the drugs they administered?''

''No,'' Joanna said flatly.

''Jo. Just consider it,'' Reynolds asked. ''Sleep on it.''

''I have slept on it, Reynolds, and that's how I know it wasn't the things you're suggesting. This was no dream. You wake up from a dream, and no matter how real that dream seems, you know, once awake, that it wasn't. This is real, Reyn. This happened. And it was exquisite. Oh, Reyn, the colors, the aromas. And the music. How you would have loved the music.''

''You're getting worked up, Jo, and you shouldn't,'' Reynolds said as his hand found the buzzer that would bring the nurse.

''Reyn, don't shut me out. Hear me,'' Joanna said as tears threatened to overwhelm her.

The nurse arrived. She looked at Reynolds and then at Joanna. After checking both her watch and the chart at the foot of Joanna's bed, she said: ''It's not yet time.'' Reynolds stood and very carefully enunciated his wishes. ''Then make it time, *Nurse.*'' The woman exited.

''Reyn, please. I don't need sedation,'' Joanna pleaded. ''I need you to listen. After the accident, I actually saw myself on the ground. Stacey . . . don't go. Listen to me. I was in the air, maybe thirty feet or so above the crowd. I didn't realize I was dead, but I must have been. I even saw myself being cradled and then lifted into the ambulance. I saw . . . Oh my God . . . I saw.''

''Joanna, stop. You're making yourself sick. Joanna, do you hear me? The doctors have all agreed that you can be out of here in a week if you just take your medication and rest. The headaches will stop, the nausea, too, if you just rest.''

But Joanna wasn't listening. She was seeing, her eyes open wide in horror. ''I saw . . . the head in the roadway.''

Reynolds was annoyed. He had withheld from Joanna any information that could be upsetting. He wondered who had told her—Sara, the nurses?

''Oh, my God, it was Chris,'' Joanna cried as she pulled back the covers and struggled to get off the bed. She had one foot on the floor when Reynolds grabbed her. "But I must see Dean," Joanna screamed. "He must feel awful. Let me go, Reynolds," Joanna cried as she struggled against Reynolds's hold. "He must feel so alone." She pushed against Reynolds, sobbing as she pummeled his chest. "I need to see Dean, dammit, and I need *you* to see and hear me."

But Reynolds couldn't do either. He was occupied watching the nurse administer the thirty milligrams of Valium that would shortly take Joanna out of her distress, and his, and into a world where both she and he could rest.

As he half watched the families "feuding" under the affectionate supervision of the game show host, Dean thought of his own family. They had stood about his bed, uncomfortable in their truce, not speaking, and then when they did, never mentioning the one thing he wanted and needed to talk about. Nothing had changed. In death as in life, Chris didn't exist for them. Nor then did his pain. He had asked them to leave. His father had not understood, and Dean had not explained.

Tony called daily, asking about his incision, his ribs, the lacerations, but never about his true injury. Tony offered his professional services when he understood his personal ones were insufficient. Tony tried, but he couldn't make that leap into Dean's reality, finding it much too threatening to his sense of maleness. And so he sent Janice, his wife, to comfort Dean, certain Dean would be more comfortable with a woman. The implicit statement in the gesture infuriated Dean.

He lived with anger constantly. It prevented him from sleeping as it prevented him from thinking or using his waking time to any purpose. He avoided contact, including the phone calls from Sara. Instead he watched television game shows where people won and lost. That he understood. That he could relate to. He would laugh and sob as contestants spun the wheel and won a fortune or suddenly found they had gone bankrupt.

When Sara called a third time he had listened as she spoke. Only she didn't speak but cried. He had not responded as he could not understand her grief. Chris had meant nothing to her. The intensity of Sara's distress annoyed him. He severed the conversation just as he severed himself from his reactions to her pain. He remained cut off, suspended, unable to feel anything but this heaviness that weighted down each hour of his waking day.

He had awakened from a fitful nap once to find Reynolds by his bed. He still was not certain whether Reynolds spoke or if it was a dream, but the words persisted. "You'll go on. You'll get out of here and live." Now, as he watched one family joyously defeat the other, Dean remembered the intensity with which Reynolds had spoken. Like a command or a commandment.

Joanna was a flight above him, her head still bandaged but her headaches gone, he had learned. The operation was a total success, its only telltale mark the half-dollar circle of baldness where she was shaved for the operation. He lay on his bed, staring at the ceiling, thinking of Joanna up there, while he was trapped below in a world he could not understand. There was no way he could comprehend Chris's death. The accident, yes. But the fact that Chris would not be there, would never be there again, that simply was incomprehensible. At any moment Dean felt Chris would walk through the door, bully him out of bed and out of his mood. If that failed, Chris would then seduce him into bed, knowing that with Dean sex was the one thing to which he could always relate even when he couldn't relate to himself.

Dean lay flat on the bed staring at a detergent commercial, trying to imagine not seeing Chris again. It wasn't possible. It wasn't even worth considering because it just wasn't real. Leave it. Move on to *Password* or the *$100,000 Pyramid.* Guess the actual retail value of the showcase. If the price was right you won. If it was too high you lost. Just like life.

A light knock, and the door opened gradually. Tricia Hill entered, smiling nervously. In one hand she held flowers, the kind of mums wrapped in waxy paper one buys at subway entrances. In the other she held a briefcase. "I thought you'd want to see the mail," she began hesitantly, her face tight and anguished. He nodded, a signal she could approach the bed. As she came closer Dean could see that the woman was fighting for composure.

"Some checks came in and I deposited them in Dr. Langdon's account. I also used some of the signed blank checks in the safe-deposit box to pay the month's mortgage and the bank loan. The light bills have not yet arrived. Nor have the tenants' rents, but it's early in the month yet. . . ." Her voice broke and she began to cry. She searched through her handbag for tissues, apologizing as she did.

"I'm so sorry, Dean. So sorry."

Her face was buried in her hands as she wept, and Dean found it strange observing the woman, so normally stiff and starched, in emotional disarray. Tricia Hill had been the perfect nurse and guardian of Chris's world below their own. No matter what the emergency she remained calm, a trained professional who served both her profession and her employer well. Just as he had run life above the ground-floor office for Chris, she had run it below, making sure bills were sent, bills were paid, and that books and schedules balanced. She was Chris's office wife, although old enough to be his mother.

She collected herself, asking about his health as her face searched his, asking questions she couldn't verbalize. She had known them as a couple, and although that had never been discussed, she had never given Dean reason to think she either judged or disapproved. Boundaries had been maintained. But on this day she silently sought to transgress. Her pain was stirring his own. He thanked her for her time and interest, took her proffered hand, held it a fraction longer than he previously might have and then made it clear by his words that he wished to be alone. Which he was. Nothing could ever change that. Even if he still didn't believe it.

He awoke later in a pitch-black room, one that matched his mood in sleep. As he lay sweating despite his chill, Dean tried to recall what had so disturbed him. Fighting against his mind's insistence to forget, the dream took focus.

He had been watching his mother's funeral and observing his silent grief as he approached her coffin. His sense of loss was physical, as if a hole existed where his stomach should be. He had approached the pine box warily, expecting some kind of retribution from the dead for his having survived.

The coffin had been empty. He had stared into it, feeling an even greater loss than he had previously known. At that point he had awakened, fearful and depressed. As he lay searching the darkness for some symbolic light to shed on his dream and thus his mood, Dean thought of Chris. As a dead person . . . a body. He had to be buried. There had to be a funeral, a closure to a life and to his grief. He hadn't thought of that, hadn't felt that necessity. He hadn't wanted to. As he succumbed again to the blackness Dean decided that in the morning he would make the arrangements.

Stefan was but inches away, yet Sara felt the distance was insurmountable. As she lay awake with too many thoughts for company Sara tried to focus on one, think it through to some resolution, but it slipped into the morass of confusion in her mind. No matter how often they talked, she had questions but no answers, at least none that Stefan could give.

Stefan moaned, shuddered and then was again silent in his sleep. He had taken to their bed since the weekend. The gesture did little other than to assure her of his physical presence. Their daily conversation was stilted, terribly pleasant, however, in its inconsequentia. She had lost her best friend. She felt cheated. Her marriage had been fraudulent. He wasn't, *they* weren't, what she had thought. His infidelity had changed everything.

Sara chastised herself. Enjoy the fact that he is here and not somewhere else and with someone else, she cautioned. Pick up the pieces. Pretend. Rebuild. So he made a mistake. What of your own, your many? Think of them. Think of how he saved you from them. You owe. Be grateful. Think of Dean. Think of Joanna. In the hospital and her husband leaves, returns home. What practice and which patient could be that important? No woman should be left in such a situation. No woman should be left. . . .

She would have to visit Joanna, Dean, too, of course. It would mean a trip to New York. Perhaps Monday when Stefan was attending a conference at the Omni Park Central. But he was spending the night. She could only drive in with him, but she would have to take the train back alone. She could, Sara told herself as the idea of traveling alone caused her to tremble. She could do that, she assured herself. She could, she insisted as the cold sweat appeared on her brow.

What could she say to Dean? His loss was even greater than her own. At least Stefan was alive, she thought as she turned onto her side in search of someplace where sleep would come. Only later, as she began to drift off, did Sara realize that her back was to Stefan and she was facing a wall. This time the wall, like the others she had created in her past, did not feel very protective.

As she strolled the length of the hospital corridor, nodding to passersby, Joanna thought of Dean and their phone call earlier that morning. She had felt his distress even though he hadn't spoken of it. Not a word. Not a cry. She worried. And then she had been distracted. By yet another doctor who wished to probe. This one took notes, tried to look nonjudgmental and closed his interview suggesting she contact any number of the universities studying psychic phenomena or Dr. Elizabeth Kübler-Ross, who had long been interested in those who *thought* they had had a near-death experience. She had thanked him for his time and said she would think about what he had said, wanting to add she hoped he would give her the same courtesy. A nurse followed the doctor, an elderly woman who slipped her a piece of paper with the word IANDS scrawled on it with an address. The International Association for Near Death Studies, she explained nervously. Call them, she suggested, and then disappeared, as though she had imparted some secret information that put her welfare in jeopardy.

As she faced the elevator Joanna realized she missed her family. She had left them at this very place a day ago, assuring them as they assured her that everything was fine. Which it was. She had hated their leaving. It was obvious they had not. Never before had Stacey seemed so anxious to return to school and Reynolds to "saving face." She said she understood, but she really didn't. It was terrible to be alone in a hospital. Again she thought of Dean. He was the most alone.

With the nurses busy, no one watched as she pressed the button calling for the elevator. When it arrived no one thought it strange when she entered, a patient in a robe covering a hospital gown. More people stared, probably wondering if the bruises on her face would heal or whether such a pretty woman would be permanently scarred. The doctors insisted she would not be, that she would be fine. In all ways. She could be released within days, with her only warning: to take things slow.

When Dean didn't answer her persistent knocking, Joanna opened the door to find him sitting in a chair, looking at her but aware only of the words he was hearing on the telephone. His face was ashen, and Joanna could feel the agitation in the room. She approached the chair and without thinking took Dean's free hand. She never heard him say good-bye to the caller because he never said it. He simply lowered the receiver and said in a grief-stricken voice: "They've buried Chris."

His eyes were blinking rapidly and Joanna squeezed his hand tightly, trying to infuse love into it.

"They've buried Chris," Dean repeated, his voice hushed. "They took him back to Kansas and buried him three days ago."

Joanna wedged herself into the chair beside Dean. She didn't speak; she listened.

"They didn't ask. They didn't tell. They just took."

His pain seared through her.

"They had no right. He was mine!"

He was sobbing now, his body folded in half, spasming from pain. Joanna wrapped herself around him, rocking his body as he allowed her to hold him. She crooned to him as he cried.

"His home is not in Kansas. It's here," he sobbed.

As she smoothed his hair, Joanna wanted to tell him that it didn't matter where Chris was buried because he was someplace else, someplace wonderful, and that Dean shouldn't mourn. But she didn't, knowing he wouldn't understand. So she held him, rocking him as she would a child, trying to understand how it would feel not only to lose the person you loved most in the world but the right to bury and mourn that person. Dean's anguish entered and passed through her, leaving her weak and hurting. Soon she, too, was crying, and as she held him the thought came to her.

"Dean, have a memorial service," she urged. "Do it for yourself. Invite Chris's friends and colleagues. But do it. Do what you would have done ordinarily. It's only right."

Dean looked at her, confused but then comprehending. Yes, he could do that, he said. The day he was discharged. He would call Campbell's now. Make the arrangements. Have a proper service. He had stopped crying. There was something to do, and it was only later when he allowed himself to feel what it was that Dean began to cry again.

SIX

THE hospital was up ahead. In a moment the car would stop, the door would open and she would be standing on a curb, alone in New York City for the first time since her marriage. Her husband would drive off to his conferences, confident, Sara hoped, that her confidence was real when of course it was not. But then she couldn't let him know she was afraid. Not now when she wanted him to think she didn't need him quite as much as he thought.

During the drive from Princeton Sara had sat rigidly on her side of the car, her seat belt buckled, wondering what had possessed Chris not to do likewise. She liked the feeling the belt provided, the security it offered. It was her only security at the moment. Yet she was lucky. Events had miraculously conspired to place Stefan in New York at his conferences the same day as Joanna's release from the hospital and Dean's memorial service for Chris. Thus she had a chauffeur and protector if only for part of the day. Although she had quietly asked—when every part of her yearned to beg—that he alter his schedule, Stefan maintained he could not. Conferences were scheduled without a break. He would not only be unable to attend the service, but he would not be there to collect her later. This meant she would need to find her own way to Penn Station and the train that would have her back in Princeton by five that evening.

"Are you all right?"

The question, normally one that would have pleased Sara because it showed Stefan's concern, today offended her. "Of course," she replied as she opened the door. She knew he thought she wasn't, and he was right, but she wasn't going to let him see that.

"Now remember. Just in case. Campbell's is on Madison and Eighty-first Street," she said through the open car-door window. "The service is at one."

"If you have problems later, call for a cab from Campbell's," Stefan replied.

"I'll manage," Sara said quietly. "People do get in and out of taxis in New York every day," she added as she nodded a good-bye and turned toward the hospital. People do, but you don't, she thought, her legs wobbling unsteadily as she mounted the few stairs to the entrance. From the corner of her eye she watched as Stefan's car disappeared up the street toward Sixth Avenue and the uptown drive to the Omni Park Central. She was alone, frightened, cold and yet far too warm in a wool suit more suitable for December than early October.

The hospital was vast, with corridors that seemed like labyrinths. Banks of elevators went east and west, forcing Sara to the information desk. Once directed, she walked slowly, dreading that moment when she would face Joanna, fearful of what she might feel and worst of all what she might say. She breathed deeply, strengthening her resolve to be cautious. When the elevator doors opened on Joanna's floor Sara felt a flush of nausea. She hurried to the ladies' room, where she found sanctuary in one of the stalls. The temptation to lock the door, to hide, to give in and cease pretending to bravery when none existed was tempting.

She would not do this, Sara decided. There would be no giving in. Her skirt was down and she up from the commode before she could think further. The cold water she splashed on her face at the sink reactivated her resolve. After a quick check of her makeup and hair, she was at Joanna's door. When there was no response to her knock Sara slipped into the room. Joanna's back was to her as she spoke on the telephone. Sara waited for some signal that said it was all right to enter further, but there was none. Joanna was engrossed, miles away, Sara presumed, when she heard the name *Stacey* spoken often and softly.

Sara's eyes toured the room. It was one continuous floral arrangement with its baskets of flowers. As she waited Sara fingered the accompanying cards, feeling foolish as she read . . . LILY TOMLIN, SALLY FIELD, LIZA MINNELLI and TOMMY LASORDA. One particularly splendid arrangement, complete with balloons, read: LOVE YOU, LILITH. Her own offering, sent from Princeton, seemed small and terribly insignificant in comparison. She pushed the now-wilting bouquet from the front to the back row where it would not be noticed.

It was just a small cry, a gasp actually, but it made Sara turn. Joanna was facing her, tears in her eyes, a smile cutting across her face. More than a smile, Sara decided. A beacon. She was unprepared for such a smile and for the rush across the room of the body that flung itself upon her, clinging and hugging. Sara pulled back from the embrace and stared into Joanna's face. The eyes, although misty, were bright blue and twinkling. Her face was a peculiar mixture of radiance and sadness. Joanna looked both older and younger. Holding her at arm's length, Sara surveyed Joanna as she might a museum painting, searching for any evidence of the trauma Joanna had just been through.

"What is it, Sara?" Joanna asked.

"It's nothing," Sara replied. "It's just . . . I didn't know what to expect. I was worried. But you look wonderful."

"But you don't," said Joanna softly. "No, it's not your hair or your dress," Joanna added as Sara's hands flew to both. "They're fine. It's you who's not. What's wrong?"

"Don't be silly," Sara said impatiently, pulling away from both Joanna's arms and her stare. "It's absolutely nothing," she protested. "Just nerves," she added awkwardly.

She felt Joanna's hand taking hers. She resented the familiarity. "Don't!" she said, her voice more whine than the command she had hoped for. "Please, Joanna," she protested.

"Let me."

Just two words, but with them Sara relaxed. "It's hard for me to travel," she said, admitting half of her truth. When Joanna looked confused, Sara added: "I don't travel alone. Not since I was ill." She felt ashamed and unable to look at Joanna, who was holding her hand, stroking it, like one would a little puppy. "I get flustered . . . frightened."

There was none of the feared laughter or ridicule. But there were tears, which surprised Sara.

"I know how that feels," Joanna said. "For the first time, I'm feeling very alone, and even if it's only for a few more days it's upsetting to me because it would not have been in the past."

Joanna was crying and Sara stood there stupidly, not knowing what to do. She had heard that patients were often depressed after surgery and not in control of their emotions. That explained Joanna, but what about her?

"I was talking to home, when you came in," Joanna explained. "They just seemed so very far away, so removed. Stacey doesn't want to hear anything about the accident."

"Joanna, it must have been terrible for her," Sara interjected, "almost losing both parents. Give her time."

"She seemed glad I've decided to listen to the doctors and remain in New York a few extra days before flying home," Joanna said softly.

"Do you want to stay with me?" Sara said almost too quickly.

"Thanks, but I'm staying with Dean," Joanna replied as she again hugged Sara. "He needs the company."

I do too, Sara wanted to scream.

"It's only for a few days, although Reynolds said to stay as long as necessary, that there was no rush. I can't think of a worse thing for him to have said," Joanna laughed. "Not exactly music to my ears."

The pain in Joanna's eyes was evident, and Sara turned from it, hoping therefore to turn from her own.

"He was really very concerned," Joanna was explaining. "He'll call our travel agent and have all the arrangements made for my return flight. Including a wheelchair to and from the boarding gate if I need one. Which I won't, of course. I really am quite fine. Which is why it was so unrealistic of me even to think he might fly in to get me. Particularly me, the woman who has traveled alone the world over on business."

And she was crying, again leaving Sara at odds as to action. "I'm glad you're here," Joanna said, the smile breaking through the tears. "Oh, don't look so alarmed, Sara. These mood swings of mine are predictable after surgery. I'm fine. Honestly."

They stood staring at one another until Joanna again flung herself into Sara's arms. "Oh, Sara, I do love you so."

Sara stood wooden, surprised by Joanna's declaration and therefore unable to respond, although every part of her wanted to relax into the warmth she was receiving, be it permanent or not. She patted Joanna on the shoulder as she again moved back and away. "I'm glad I'm here too, Jo. I wish I could have been here sooner, but I've had a few problems of my own."

The words slipped out. She tried to reclaim them by quickly adding: "It was a shock . . . your accident . . . death . . ."

"Sara, something's wrong. I can tell," said Joanna. "Are you sick?"

Sara laughed. "No sicker than usual, but I'll muddle through. I always have."

"Sara, I'd say you've done a helluva lot more than just muddle through your life."

"Would you, Joanna?" asked Sara, a half-smile on her face. "Well, you'd be wrong. Muddle is exactly what I do. Sara, the muddler. That's me. No, Joanna, please don't touch me like that," said Sara as Joanna stroked her hair. "I'm not your child. Stop. It bothers me."

"Sara, what's wrong?" Joanna asked as the women stood face to face.

"It's just nerves," Sara insisted. "I get this way when I'm frightened."

"Why are your frightened? You're not alone. You have me. You have Stefan. Sara, talk to me."

"We should be leaving," Sara said as she looked at her watch. "We're due at the funeral home in twenty minutes."

"Sara, I won't press," Joanna said as she put on her

suit jacket. "I just want you to know . . . some bonds are unbreakable. You're a part of me. Maybe it was that part I was looking for when I suggested we three lunch for our birthdays."

They were sitting in the backseat of the taxi when Joanna became aware of still more tears, chilled by the breeze flowing through the open window on her cheeks. She was as surprised as she was not upset. Quite the contrary. She was enthralled. Watching a city and its people on an autumn day suddenly seemed like the very best thing anyone could do. Sara's hand was resting in her own. They were like girls again, Joanna thought, little girls watching life pass by as they stared through open windows. Sara had not spoken since they had hailed the taxi downtown at the hospital, but in her silence Joanna had felt communication. Sara's distress showed in the biting of her lip and the hand that jerked spasmodically from time to time.

"Joanna, why did you come to the bar mitzvah?"

The question, like the voice that asked it, came from a far-off place. Joanna hesitated before answering. "To prove how complete my life was," she finally said. "Only I didn't know that. But then, what did I know? At the time of our birthdays I remember thinking half my life had passed, leaving some awful void that only death could fill. And, Sara, that's what happened. Death not only filled my life but made me a child again, a little girl playing in what feels like God's playground."

Joanna could feel Sara staring at her. She knew by the way Sara's hand had stiffened that she had not understood. "Listen, Sara, if I sound crazy to you, join the club. Charter members are Reynolds and Stacey. If I were you, or them, I, too, would think I'm some sort of crazy lady, or at least one who had suffered one bump on the head too many. Sara, there's no way to say this but to say it. I died twice after the accident."

It wasn't just Sara but the cab driver who was listening.

"I died and went some other place, heaven, perhaps, where I stood before this incredible light. Sara, I'm certain It was God. I can't imagine what else It could have been because He . . . It . . . made me feel as I never have in my life . . . totally loved. And perfect. Unflawed. There was no longer anything I had to prove to anyone. And it was so beautiful there, so unlike anything we know here on earth, that I didn't want to leave. I still want to go back, which makes me feel guilty toward Stace and Reynolds. But Sara, it was such a lovely, complete feeling."

Sara wasn't listening. Not any longer. But nor was she judging. She was simply thinking how ironic it was and *so* typical that Joanna had found her light just as her own had dimmed and Dean's had died.

The taxi stopped before Campbell's. When Joanna paid the driver she waited for Sara to open the door near the curb so they could both get out. But Sara remained rigid, her eyes open and reflecting fear. "I need a moment," she said as Joanna pushed her from the taxi. They stood outside the funeral home, Sara leaning against its wall, mopping her face with a handkerchief. "What do you think it's like to lose someone you love?" she asked, her voice strained.

"Awful," Joanna replied. "I can't think of anything worse than losing a mate, unless it's your child."

"Yes," said Sara as tears filled her eyes. "It's the worst possible loss. I just don't know how anyone survives it." She was shaking, trembling, holding on to Joanna's arm when she added: "I wonder how Dean will. Unless it's not the same thing with two men."

"Sara, I was with Dean. I heard. I saw. It's the same. Loss is loss. And it's not just Chris that Dean has lost, but their life together. He's alone, Sara. He has to start over again."

"And at forty that has to be so frightening," Sara said as she nibbled at her bottom lip.

Joanna encircled her with her arm, leading her into the funeral home, where they were directed to a small chapel on the first floor. When Sara balked at the doorway Joanna whispered: "You don't have to go in."

Sara took a deep breath, and as she pulled herself into a military posture she said: "Yes, I do. I must."

The chapel, with its lack of religious artifacts, was stark simplicity. The highly polished wooden pews shone under the soft lighting. Toward the front, just below the raised area on which the lectern stood, Dean sat alone. As she looked about the chapel Sara realized that, despite the late hour, it was sparsely filled with a dozen people at best. Was this all the family and friends? she wondered, experiencing an almost overwhelming sense of loneliness and loss. She rushed ahead of Joanna, down the aisle toward Dean. When she reached his pew he stood slowly, favoring the side where his rib still mended. Her hug was fierce. Sara tried to speak, the words taking shape in her mind, but her lips could produce no sound. Joanna stood with her hand on Sara's shoulder, anchoring and steadying her.

A stranger in formal attire approached. "I think we had best begin, Mr. Di Nardo," he said softly. Dean's eyes searched the chapel, found Tricia Hill just as she entered and seated herself. He then looked down and away as he answered: "Yes, begin." He sat between Joanna and Sara, his back and facial muscles rigid. He felt Joanna's hand slip into his, heard Sara's tremulous breathing and watched with unseeing eyes as another formally attired stranger approached the lectern. His notes were before him, prepared from a single discussion with the bereaved. It suddenly struck Dean as ludicrous that this stranger should be delivering Chris's eulogy. But there had been no one else, no member of the family, no friend, who had come forward. There had been no response whatsoever from Chris's family. They had been as silent and rejecting in death as they had been during Chris's life. His own family was also absent, as they had been through most of his life. And friends . . . somehow they had never had the time or the need to make any. Theirs had been an insulated and an isolated life, yet it had never felt that way, complete as they had been with one another. Still, he had thought people would attend—colleagues from the hospital with which Chris had been affiliated, doctors and nurses, students whom he had taught. Such was not the case.

This, too, is not real, Dean decided as the stranger droned on, his voice rising and falling dramatically as he eulogized the dead. Dean shut his eyes and his ears, withdrawing into a private world where only barely could he hear the stranger speak of loss, of a dedicated man and of the effect that man had had on those he loved. Sobs. Terrible, gut-wrenching sobs shook Dean's composure as they shook the austerity of the chapel. Whispers carried throughout, people wondering who the mourner in the wool suit was and what her relationship had been to the deceased. They were startled when she rose, made gestures to the man beside her, gestures that tried to explain why she couldn't stay, had to leave. She pushed past the bereaved and the woman sitting next to him. They heard as he called out her name, watched as the woman he called Sara ran down the aisle and out of the chapel, disappearing into the midday crowds on Madison Avenue.

Throughout, the stranger continued to eulogize just as Joanna continued to hold Dean's hand.

Traffic on Madison Avenue was moving slowly, hampered by the hour and the fact that it was Monday, the day of the week when nothing moved well in New York. Sara was walking and running, pushing by lunchtime strollers and shoppers, her eyes desperately searching for an empty taxi. The world was larger than she remembered and filled with twice as many people, all, she felt, staring at her as she darted in and out of the street, her arms flailing at nonexistent empty cabs. At Seventy-ninth Street one stopped, depositing its passenger at her feet. She stood there hesitating, not knowing where to go, except to Princeton, and doubtful whether the driver would take her that far and if he did whether she had sufficient money to pay for such a ride.

Sara continued walking, assuring herself she was fine and that she need only get to Penn Station, where trains must be departing for Princeton before three. If not she could wait, have lunch at a restaurant or call Ina. Of course. Call Ina. Wait at her office. Be with her. She found an unoccupied phone on the following corner. She knew the number by heart just as she knew the voice of the receptionist when she stated: "Feinberg and Kroog." She asked for Ina and waited as the receptionist rang through to that part of the office where the secretaries shared space and a view of Central Park that soothed the tempo of their work. Within seconds the voice Sara heard was no longer comforting in its familiarity as it announced that Mrs. Rivlin was at lunch. Could she return the call? Sara hung up, fighting to regain the control she had achieved just prior to dialing. A taxi deposited its passengers at a corner Sara was aimlessly crossing. This time she did not let it pass, but propelled herself into the backseat, wondering even as she did what she would respond when the driver asked her destination. Her mind raced. She couldn't face Penn Station, not its immensity, its strangeness and all its people. She needed someplace safe.

"The Omni Park Central, please," she said, the decision made as quickly as the idea came to her. She would use Stefan's room until two-thirty. She would rest for an hour, perhaps even doze, build her strength and resolve for the return home. Perhaps she could reach Ina and Ina could take part of the afternoon off. To drive her home. Maybe Stefan's conferences were dull, a speaker ill. Maybe he would be free . . . could drive her . . . them . . . back to the house. There were lots of possibilities, probably even more than she realized, Sara thought. She leaned her head against the upholstered cushion. Soon she would be resting in the same bed Stefan would be resting in that night. The thought was not as comforting as Sara had hoped it would be.

Joanna watched as the mourners filed past Dean out of the chapel. Only a few stopped, a woman Joanna had heard Dean identify as Chris's nurse and two of the building's tenants. The others left looking either confused or embarrassed, not knowing to whom they should be offering condolences. It was for them an awkward situation. Dean wasn't family. Nor was he husband or wife per se. He was lover, and for the average person there were no rules of etiquette to cover that situation, and so he and the situation were ignored as though neither existed.

She took his arm, standing by him until the last person had left the chapel. Standing next to him, he felt thin to her. When she looked at his face in the bright afternoon sun, she saw how much thinner he had become since the day of the bar mitzvah.

"Can you walk to the house?" Dean asked.

"Depends on how long a walk we're talking about," Joanna replied as she measured her strength.

"Before we turned forty I'd have guessed ten minutes," said Dean. "Now that we're old and infirm, twenty to twenty-five."

"Let's give it a shot," said Joanna as her hand gripped Dean by his bicep. "We can always ask a boy scout to help an old person across the street or hop a cab should we get tired, which I suspect I will, considering my sole exercise of late has been strolling hospital corridors."

"We could also stop for lunch," Dean offered.

She looked at him, suddenly realizing he was in no hurry to go home and understanding intuitively exactly why. She thought of her own home and was surprised by the anxiety her thought produced. She yearned for her family but now wondered if they shared that yearning. Dimly she heard Dean talking about Sara, speculating on the cause of her distress and worrying about her ability to deal with it. She responded vaguely, thinking of Stacey's distress—not that Stacey knew it was distress—but she did . . . suddenly. She couldn't speculate about Sara, Joanna realized, as Sara kept most things a secret, fearful of the world's condemnation if it knew a truth that probably only Sara viewed as being so terrible. "We'll call later," Joanna said. "She should be home by five."

But each found that Sara could not be so easily dismissed. She remained an unverbalized concern in their thoughts as they proceeded up Madison Avenue toward the Nineties. Joanna tried to shop the passing boutique windows but found she couldn't sustain an interest as Dean's silence distressed her. Tension built when they neared his neighborhood. Suddenly Joanna felt weak. "I need to put my feet up," she explained as she stepped into the street to hail a cab. As one slowed to where they stood, Joanna said to Dean: "You were right. Old age is a bitch."

She had closed her eyes, shutting out a city and a reality she did not want to face, drifting in some safer reality, when Sara felt a hand outstretched to take hers. The doorman at the hotel was assisting her. Now it was her body that rebelled. Tired, it ached to remain where it was. The expression on the taxi driver's face said that wasn't possible. She debarked, striding briskly into the hotel and to the front desk, where she asked for Dr. Stefan Schell's room number. Her face blanched when told they were not permitted to release that information but if she wished to reach Dr. Schell, she could try the house phone. She demanded to see the manager, assuming an assurance, an almost righteous indignation, that surprised her. When confronted by the hotel's authority, she produced her identification of credit cards of all kinds and demanded the room key without further delay. She was immediately obliged.

The room was dark when she entered, its shades and draperies drawn. The light switch responded noiselessly to her touch, revealing a standard hotel room, luxuriously furnished but nonetheless just a hotel room, the first, Sara realized, she had been in for many years. For a moment she tried to recall whether she had ever "slept" here when the hotel was called the Park Sheraton. Her memory failed as fatigue enveloped her. She must rest but not sleep. She must page Stefan, call Ina, find some way to get home, with someone. She must.

She lay on the bed shivering, not wanting to disturb its neatness by slipping under its covers. The obligatory extra blanket all hotels store in the closet would do fine, she decided. She found it atop the built-in shelves. As she raised her arms to reach it she brushed against Stefan's suit. As she brought the blanket down she thought how pretty was the aqua-blue color of the silk dress, how cooling and soft the cream-colored blouse. She fondled the linen skirt, liking its lightweight texture.

She closed the closet door and entered the bathroom. On the vanity, Mennen's men's deodorant, a Bic razor and Old Spice mingled with Soft & Dri and an assortment of Georgette Klinger products.

She was shaking as she walked to the closet, opened it and ripped the aqua-blue dress from its hanger to hold it against her body. It was short. Very short. She flung it to the floor, resisting an impulse to shred it with her hands. She looked at Stefan's gray suit hanging limply on its hanger. She raised her hand to strike it but was interrupted by a door opening. Stefan stood looking from her to the dress on the floor, hotel security at his side.

"It's all right," he said quietly to the man whose face remained impassive. "It *is* my wife."

Her handbag lay on the desk. She grabbed it and raced toward the door. She was almost past him when she remembered her shoes. Bolting back into the room, she found them by the bed. She had one on and the other off as she hobbled into the hallway with Stefan begging her to stop and listen. She pushed the button for the elevator as he reached for her.

She struck at him repeatedly with the shoe she held in her hand as the doors to the elevator opened and several startled passengers watched. She beat at him with the heel of her shoe, connecting twice before he could cover his face. The elevator doors closed. People pulled back, leaving her the bulk of the elevator's space. She wanted to scream at them, too. She dashed through the marble lobby into the street and into a cab.

"Where to, Cinderella?" the driver asked.

Sara looked from him to the shoe in her hand, trying to find a suitable answer. "Penn Station," she finally replied, not knowing what else to say and where else to go.

Ina? . . . It's me . . . Sara. . . . What do you mean I sound strange? It must be the connection. . . . What? . . . I'm at Penn Station. . . . No, Stefan is at his conference. . . . Of course I'm all right. . . . Don't be silly. It's just the connection. . . . Ina, I had a great idea. Wouldn't it be fun if you came out to Princeton with me for the evening? Just you and me. . . . Of course the kids are there, but I can send them off to their rooms. . . . We could rent a movie from the video store and . . . Well, I'd wait for you to finish work . . . wait here. . . . Ina, don't start. I'm fine, I tell you. . . . Can't Josh and Sharon make their own dinner? . . . For God's sake, Ina, they're not children. . . . I'm not yelling. No, listen, Ina. Forget it. . . . Ina, I'm fine . . . I'll call you later. . . . Good-bye.

She found another quarter in her handbag and dialed information, relieved to find they indeed had a listing for a Dean Di Nardo at the address given. Sara tried to memorize it but couldn't, her mind too frantic from the bludgeoning activity about her. Searching for a pen in her handbag, she dropped the phone just as she found one, losing her connection with the operator. Dialing information again, she repeated her request but found once she received the number, her fingers failed. She simply couldn't stop their shaking to slip a quarter into the slot. When she noticed two people waiting for the phone Sara hung up. She walked briskly along the edges of the crowd, startled each time the loudspeaker boomed an arrival or departure. Near the other end of the terminal she found an unoccupied phone and dialed, not prethinking what she would say when someone answered.

Dean . . . yes, it's me, Sara. . . . Oh, I'm just fine now. . . . I'm sorry about before. . . . I . . . Dean . . . can I stay overnight? Have you room? . . . What does it matter where Stefan is? For God's sake, Dean, I asked if I could stay overnight. . . . No, I don't want to talk to Joanna. I'm talking to you. . . . Dean . . . can't you understand? I just thought it would be fun if the three of us spent the night together. . . . Stop questioning me. . . . Never mind about the children. Let me worry about them. They're my children, after all.

She stared at the departure board, not hearing or responding to the voice on the telephone that persisted in its questioning. But she heard her own. They were her children, hers alone, and they expected her home by five. They would worry if she wasn't. She must make them dinner . . . couldn't possibly leave them alone in the house overnight.

Sara hung up the phone. The crowds had increased, but Sara, oblivious, walked through them toward the ticket counter. Asking for a ticket to Princeton, she paid for it with steady hands and then walked quickly to the boarding gate and the train that would take her to her home and children. All else simply no longer mattered. She couldn't and wouldn't allow it to.

* * *

Joanna's eyes fluttered open. The light seeping through the shaded windows created unfamiliar shadows, but through her confusion of whether it was day or night, the hospital or her bedroom in Beverly Hills, she remained calm. Searching with her hand for a lamp, she touched a cold, soggy sandwich, a reminder that she was at Dean's, sleeping in his bed.

Groggy, Joanna thought to turn over and return to sleep until her eye caught the time on the clock radio by the bed. Evening, not night. Dinner to be fixed. She thought of Dean, of Sara's phone call, and was immediately awake. Still somewhat unsteady, she slowly walked down the stairs, finding Dean sprawled on the sofa, his mouth open, an occasional snore breaking the silence. She hadn't noticed the room before, such had been her exhaustion when they finally reached the brownstone. It was a nice room, nothing lavish or elegant but comfortable. A combination of leathers and tweeds. She had been distressed by the sofa, which resembled an unmade bed with its rumpled sheets and pillows. Again, she understood without asking why Dean preferred to sleep there rather than in his bedroom.

As she looked at Dean's face reposed in sleep and remembered how distressed that face had been when they entered the brownstone, Joanna was reluctant to wake him. He had been agitated by Sara's phone call, concerned yet angry that she was sounding an alarm without telling where the fire was. She, however, had only been concerned, feeling from Sara's behavior throughout the morning that something was very wrong.

The phone rang just as she was searching the refrigerator for any kind of juice that would alleviate what felt, despite the early evening hour, decidedly like morning mouth. Lifting the receiver from its hook before the ringing could wake Dean, she whispered her greeting. The answering voice, calm and controlled, asked if by chance Sara was there. No, she replied. She had called earlier but was undoubtedly home by now, Joanna added as her eyes read six on the kitchen clock.

"No one answers," said the voice, maintaining its control. She assured him there was no reason to worry, that if something were wrong someone—a neighbor . . . one of the children—would have called him at the hotel. The voice sounded neither reassured nor panicked. It was only after the disconnection that Joanna realized the voice had no quality at all, and that, too, bothered her.

She dialed Sara's number, letting the phone ring a dozen times before she accepted what Stefan had just said. No one was home. Like Stefan, that worried her. A woman who calls from the train station somewhat frantic, or sounding that way, doesn't leave home once she finally reaches it. Why hadn't she thought to tell Stefan to call the moment after he reached Sara? Well, she would continue to call until Sara answered, no matter what the hour.

"Was that Sara?"

"No. It was Stefan," Joanna replied, surprised that despite her efforts Dean had been awakened. "Did anyone phone while I was asleep?" she asked.

"If they did I slept through it," Dean replied as he took steaks from the freezer. "Were you expecting Reynolds to call?" he asked as he began to scrub vegetables for a salad.

"Well, it is only three in the afternoon in Los Angeles. Working hours," Joanna explained. "I'm sure he'll call later. Can I help?" she asked as she watched Dean dry the lettuce leaves.

"Just by fixing me a drink. Some white wine on the rocks."

"It certainly was nice to sleep in a bed, in a bedroom actually, where I could rest without a parade of women in white marching in to tamper and tinker with my body," Joanna said as soon as they were seated in the living room.

"You'll get a good night's sleep there," Dean replied.

"I couldn't take your bed," she said.

"Take it, Joanna, and don't argue. I'm actually more comfortable down here," Dean said, the grief that had been absent in sleep now again etched deeply in his face. She looked at him, absorbing his pain as though it were her own, but could only say, "It will pass in time," words she hated as soon as they were uttered.

"I don't know," said Dean as he shook his head. "You

see, our bedroom was often where our lives met. I mean . . . because of Chris's schedule the bed was often the *only* place we met, communicated.''

She thought about her bed . . . their bed, in Beverly Hills. Where they slept without ever meeting. And their communication was one-sided. All his. It negated her even as it required her for his sexual satisfaction.

''Sharing a bed with someone is really sharing you, your life,'' Dean continued. ''It's hard to withdraw from someone who is there next to you. . . .''

Not so, Joanna thought. You can be next to and yet very far away. Very far indeed. As a means of protecting.

''Dean, maybe there are just too many memories here,'' Joanna said, thinking of her shock when they had entered the brownstone and she had seen Chris's shingle hanging on the door.

''I want the memories,'' Dean answered. ''This house represents the years of my life that made the most sense. My life had meaning here. Or I thought it did until your letter arrived. That caused an eye to open. You know, I accused Chris of standing in the way of my fulfillment. It was a lot of bullshit. I stood in my own way. Now acting seems meaningless. I lost what mattered. But I have the house. That mattered to Chris. It matters to me. We gave this house to one another. I could never sell it, if that's what you were suggesting before.''

''It was a dumb idea,'' Joanna said, ''although I think now would be a terrific time for you to come back with me to California. I'd phone around, see what could be set up. It would keep you busy, and that's not a bad idea right now.''

''I can't leave just yet, Joanna. I just wouldn't want to be that far away from Chris right now.''

Joanna understood. She didn't want to be as far away from Reynolds as she now felt herself to be. And still two more days and three nights to go.

Dean was seasoning the still-frozen steaks, preparing them for the microwave, when she remembered Sara. It was time to call again. If Sara was home, at least one of Joanna's fears could be alleviated.

* * *

The phone was ringing as Sara entered the house. Robert ran ahead to answer it. From the kitchen Sara heard him yell: "It's Joanna Bennett."

"Take a message and tell her I'll call back," Sara said as she hung her coat in the hall closet. She was helping Dana with her jacket when Robert called: "She says she needs to talk to you now for just a second."

Sara sighed. She did not want to talk to Joanna or anyone else for that matter. "Naomi, take Dana upstairs and get yourselves ready for your bath. I'll be up in a moment. Evan, no MTV until your homework is done. You, too, Robert."

Her sons' groans accompanied Sara into the kitchen, where the phone rested on the kitchen counter. She looked at it as if it were an instrument of torture. She should leave it there, walk away and bathe the girls, forget its existence, she thought.

"Joanna? Hi," she said as she grabbed the phone and immediately began talking. "Listen, please tell Dean how sorry I am about before. I was being silly. Or maybe just jealous of the two of you there having fun and me going back to Jersey."

"I was worried," Joanna said softly.

"Worried?" echoed Sara as though that were the silliest thing she had heard all day. "Once I got home I didn't feel like cooking so I took the kids for Chinese food."

"And the trip home?"

"Dull . . . uneventful. I don't know how people do it every day. And not just every day but twice a day! But I guess that's what makes me happy to be a housewife in Princeton while others commute to work in Manhattan."

"Sara, are you all right?"

Joanna's tone was seductive. Sara hesitated, yearning to yield. The moment passed when she heard Naomi call from upstairs: "Ma? We're ready."

"Gotta go, Jo. The girls are in the tub and they need me. I'll call you later," she added, knowing she wouldn't.

"Sara," Joanna said hurriedly, "Stefan called here earlier. He sounded concerned. Has he reached you yet? Maybe you should call him if he hasn't."

"Yes, I'll do that," said Sara seriously while wanting

to laugh. "I'll be sure to call Stefan and tell him everything is fine. Speak to you later," she added jauntily just before hanging up.

In the upstairs bathroom Sara found the girls sitting opposite one another in the tub. She slipped to her knees and began soaping first Dana, then Naomi, her hand gliding lovingly over their smooth bodies as her mind glided over the day's events. The girls' chatter was rhythmic and constant, much like the wheels of the train she had taken but hours ago. Lulling, soothing, she had concentrated on their sound, synchronizing her breathing to the click-clack. The landscape had disappeared as she stared out her window, seeing and feeling nothing until she became aware she was neither trembling nor sweating. Her heartbeat was regular. She was like any other traveler.

"Ma."

The voice was whining, complaining.

"You're rubbing too hard."

Sara looked from the washcloth in her hand to Dana's reddened back. Quickly she splashed sudsy water on it and made loving circles with her hand. "Better?" she asked, wondering why memories of a triumphant train ride should now be provoking anxiety. Her throat was closing and she had difficulty breathing. She felt faint. The ringing of the telephone brought blood back to her head. She yelled for Robert or Evan to answer it, but neither responded. Annoyed, she hastily dried her hands on a nearby towel and walked swiftly to the extension in her bedroom.

"Hello?" she said accusingly.

"Sara, it's Stefan."

She was surprised and disappointed. She had hoped he would follow her home, offer some explanation as he begged forgiveness. When he hadn't, she assumed she would never hear from him again.

"It's impossible for me to talk now," she heard him say. "But I will leave after the morning meeting."

She remained silent.

"Sara, are you there?"

Where would she be if not there? Where else had she been all these years?

"Sara, talk to me," his voice urged. She remained silent. ''Let me say good night to the kids,'' he said in defeat.

''No,'' she replied.

''What do you mean, no? Sara, I want to talk to the children.''

''You can't. You have no right,'' she answered, her voice flat.

''No right? I'm their father,'' he replied angrily.

''And just when did you remember that?'' she asked sarcastically.

''Sara, the kids have nothing to do with what's happening.''

''Ah, but they soon will,'' she said threateningly.

''Sara, I want to speak to my children.''

His voice was harsh in its demand. Sara considered his words and then replied, ''I'm sorry, Stefan, but I'll tell you what. I'll talk to them for you. After all, I have lots to talk to them about. Don't I, Stefan?''

''Sara.''

It was a one-word plea, and it caused Sara to wince before she hung up.

It had been easier during the night when she had lain alone and awake. Then she had confronted him, shamed him with his actions, refused his explanations and apologies. Then she had insisted she was no one's doormat, that she was finished. Out the door and into a new life. But now as Sara sat opposite Stefan at the kitchen table, watching his every move and expression for meaning, she wondered if she could leave him and the only life she had known for fifteen years. As she played with her fingers in her lap, she played with the one thought she had avoided through the night: that the decision had been made for her; that he had returned only to tell her it was over and *his* new life was beginning.

She had to find her resolve again, had to be firm in what she wanted, or she would lose everything. But what did she want? Sara wondered. Stefan . . . her family . . . together. . . . Their lives to remain intact . . . her self-respect . . . peace. And to strike him. To hurt him as she had never hurt anyone before. Revenge. She wanted that, too.

She composed herself and waited just as she had been waiting since his return a quarter-hour ago. He had put away his toiletries—a sign of his decision, perhaps; she wondered. He had then joined her in the kitchen, taking coffee, never speaking, although the slouch of his shoulders, the downward cast of his eyes and the pallor of his skin said much. She found she couldn't talk to him and suddenly searched her mind to recall what they had talked about these past years. Her mind tumbled about children's illnesses and report cards just before he said: "Sara, I don't know what to do."

His tone was anguished. She waited for more. None was forthcoming. Good God! Was he asking for her help? Did he expect she would help him reach a decision? "About what, specifically?" she asked.

"You . . . the kids."

"What do you want to do?" she asked, fearful of his response.

He shrugged. "I don't know," he said, his words barely audible. She waited and watched. What she saw was not possible. Tears were edging out of the corners of his eyes. They infuriated her. It was unacceptable behavior from Stefan. And who was he crying for? Which loss was he mourning? How dare he again make her feel sorry for him?

"Do you want a divorce?" she asked in spite of every warning she gave herself.

He did not respond.

"Well, you can't have it both ways," she said, her voice shrill. "I won't have it. I won't," she repeated, as much for her sake as his. "I can't live with it. I'm not even certain I can live with the fact that you lied to me. Or that I should. Obviously she is someone who means a great deal to you." She waited, hoping he would correct her assumption, admit it was just a middle-years fling or a midlife crisis. He didn't. Which prompted her to ask, again despite her own warnings: "Are you so in love with this girl?"

His answer took away more than her breath. "Yes."

Again she waited, but he said nothing more. Her heart was fluttering, her head about to burst. "And so you're thinking of giving up your family, your home, everything we've worked for, for this girl?"

"Stop calling her a girl, Sara. She's a mature woman."

She did not understand at first, thinking Stefan simply meant the girl was older than her years. "Who is she?" she demanded.

"I told you before, it doesn't matter," he replied.

"Doesn't matter?" she echoed. "Of course it matters. It matters greatly. To you, obviously, and so to me. I want to know who she is, dammit."

"Denise Wolfe," he replied softly.

She searched her memory. The name was familiar, but she could put no face with it. Then she saw it. First as just a name on a list of names. A guest list. For their son's bar mitzvah. Then she saw the face itself. At the reception. His colleague. He had brought her to *their* house. He had even introduced them.

"But she's short," Sara said stupidly. "And dumpy . . . my age." She felt frantic, suddenly more threatened by the fact that Denise Wolfe was indeed a mature woman and not some pretty young girl as she had imagined. Her mind was reeling. Stefan was leaving her for a woman who was certainly no younger or more attractive than she. It made no sense.

"Why?" she asked. "Why her?"

"Sara, I didn't plan this. It's something that just happpened two years ago."

"Two years ago?" she challenged. "You mean this has been going on under my nose for two years?" She was shaking, trying to gain some kind of control by holding on to the ends of the table.

"We stopped once. Or tried to. Because it wasn't fair to her."

"Wasn't fair to her?" Sara said. "How sad," she added sarcastically.

"It wasn't fair, Sara. Denise is only thirty-five. She has one bad marriage behind her. She would like to marry again, and I wasn't offering her anything."

"What are you offering this poor unfortunate woman now?" Sara asked.

"I don't know," Stefan replied helplessly.

"Why her, dammit? You haven't told me that yet. Why her? Do you know what you'd be throwing away if you leave?" she asked, burying her own question.

"Yes, I do," said Stefan. "If I leave I lose my family . . . my children. If I stay I lose a chance at living with some kind of hope . . . passion."

She did not want to hear any more. He was killing her. It was exactly as he said: He was in love with another woman. No. Not another. Another denotes two: Denise Wolfe and someone else. But in listening to his words, it was apparent there was no someone else here. At least not someone he was in love with.

"If you leave, Stefan, I want you to know I'll take everything and in particular the children. I doubt if they'll ever want to see you again."

He was looking at her oddly, much the way she had been looking at him minutes ago, trying to determine who this person was speaking to him in such a fashion.

"Maybe I should go to a hotel for a week or so. Just until I can think clearly and make a decision."

"No! No week or two away from the house," snapped Sara. "I'm not putting my children through that kind of anxiety. The minute you pack a bag you're gone. For good. No . . . I'm not up to telling my kids that Mommy and Daddy need some time apart. Frankly I'd be a lot more comfortable telling them their father has been cheating. On them and me."

Stefan had risen from his chair. "Sara, don't make me hate you," he pleaded.

"You don't know what hate is," she hissed.

"I'm sorry," Stefan said as he turned toward her. "I don't know what to say or do. I need time. I'm frightened."

As he left the room and the house for his afternoon classes at Princeton, Sara thought: Stefan, frightened? That was no more possible than the few tears she thought she had seen trickling down his cheeks moments ago.

* * *

He was watching her pack, knowing that once she left, the house and he would be empty again. He watched as she folded her dressing gown and placed it neatly next to the carefully wrapped and rewrapped gifts. Little "things" she had found when they browsed through artsy little stores on Madison Avenue. A cameo brooch for Stacey, antique gold cuff links for Reynolds. She delighted herself with her "treasures" and, like a child, could barely keep her secret when she spoke with her family that evening. Again they had been distant and shy, and she had felt stifled at not being able to express her love and her joy that she would soon be with them again.

This afternoon she would be on a plane. Dean knew she would leave some part of her with him just as she was taking some part of him with her. He felt sad, sadder than he had since the day he first returned from the hospital to find that Chris really wasn't there, not physically. It wasn't that Joanna had filled a space but a need. She not only talked but listened. They shared their discomforts and fears; she, her joy.

"I still think you're crazy," Dean said as she closed the lid on the suitcase. "It's too much traveling for someone just out of the hospital."

"All I'm doing is sitting in the backseat of a limo, and if you look out the window at the size of that mother, you'll see it could be divided into four apartments—two of them duplexes," Joanna replied.

"At least call and tell Sara you're coming," Dean argued.

"She'll just tell me again not to come, and I'm going," Joanna said firmly. "Something is wrong with that girl, and I can't return to California without knowing what it is."

"Joanna, it just doesn't make sense. Two weeks ago Sara was someone you hadn't seen or thought about in years."

"The same is true of you. So?" Joanna replied. "Things change. Or haven't you noticed?"

"But it's almost two hours to Princeton. From Princeton to the Philadelphia airport it's at least half an hour. Plus the time in the air. Jo, you're pushing yourself. You could get sick."

"And then what, die?" asked Joanna, her voice mocking as she looked at Dean affectionately.

"I don't understand how you can make so light of death when you came so close to it," Dean said as he helped Joanna carry her suitcases down to the main floor.

"That's exactly why I can," Joanna replied. "It was not only a nice place to visit, but I wouldn't mind living there. Not at all."

"Then why do you think you came back?" asked Dean. "Supposedly, from what I've read, people who come back from an NDE do so for a very specific reason."

"Mine were Reynolds and Stacey, particularly Stacey," Joanna said as her eyes brimmed with tears. "I owe her something. I think it's me."

"Do you have your airline ticket?" he asked.

She checked her purse. The ticket was next to her wallet. She had everything, including a sadness she knew she would not leave behind. She would miss Dean, the house and the comfort she had found in both.

"It seems of late I'm forever leaving places where I want to stay," she said, fighting to contain her emotions. "You'll be fine, you know," she added as she slipped into her heels. "It will be tough for a while, but don't make it any more difficult than it has to be by locking yourself away in this house. Do things. Work at your career. Actually I still think you should pack up and come to Los Angeles."

"I'll miss you, too," he said suddenly, smiling when she least expected.

Joanna slipped into his arms, clinging to Dean much as she had when they were young and he had been the brother she had never had. She felt his hand brushing away wisps of hair from her face. "Dean," Joanna began, struggling to verbalize what had not yet been realized in her mind. "There is no death. I saw that . . . felt it. There is only life and more life. Chris is all right, Dean. He's happy. Take comfort in that."

He pushed away, asking: "I don't understand, Joanna. What is it exactly that I'm supposed to take comfort in? I lost the first person in my life who loved me as I am, without qualifications. Where's the sense, Joanna, the rhyme and reason?"

She knew. The answers had all been there, she suddenly remembered, at the moment of meeting the Light. It had all been so clear, so obvious and so simple. Now that clarity was gone. Her frustration took the form of tears. She felt his touch before she heard him say: "Joanna, I wish I had your faith. It would help . . . a lot."

She hugged him, holding him longer and in a deeper, yet less complicated way than she had ever held any man. She could feel him in total and not in part. It made her feel as she had never felt before with a man . . . complete. "I'll call as soon as I'm home and settled," she said, shaken.

"Do you have your medication?" he asked, not knowing how else to express his concern.

"Don't worry, Dean. I'm fine. But do take care of yourself," she said as she picked up the heavier of her two suitcases, leaving him with his still-healing rib to manage the lighter. At the curb, as the limousine driver held open the door, she turned, smiled and was about to step into the car when Dean reached out and touched her cheek.

As the limousine pulled away Joanna felt his was the loveliest gesture any man had ever made toward her.

That Sara might not be at home was a possibility.

It was nearing two when Joanna recognized the house. Nicer than she remembered, it was the kind of old-fashioned country home that a tended lawn and some big bright azaleas and rhododendrons would make beautiful rather than promising. The wall surrounding the house, its intent so clear, thought Joanna, needed only ivy to soften that intention. There was a car in the driveway, a sure sign that someone was home. Joanna told the driver to wait until she returned unless she ran past the allotted time it would take to reach the airport in Philadelphia. Then he should call her.

As she walked up the driveway, Joanna realized the windows were shut and the draperies drawn on the ground floor. It was too familiar, like a house Sara had left long ago in Brooklyn. Joanna shuddered as she rang the doorbell. She shuddered again when Sara stood there looking surprised, confused and upset, her face worn and her shoulders rounded. "I'm starving," Joanna said as she entered without being asked. She walked directly to the kitchen, followed by Sara, who motioned her to the table as she opened the refrigerator. As Sara began beating eggs and melting cheese, Joanna looked about. Nothing in the kitchen was out of place or dirty. The cabinets, like the floor, were gleaming, as were the top of the range and the refrigerator door. The neatness of the room disturbed Joanna. Kitchens were not meant to be that clean. Her attention turned to Sara, bent over the stove, fixing an omelette. Her shoulders were hunched and slightly heaving. Something told Joanna to leave Sara be for the moment, not to intrude on tears that were silently speaking of grief.

"Can you talk about it?" Joanna asked when Sara placed the omelette before her on a plate garnished with sliced tomato and cucumber strips.

"It would be a lot easier if you said hello, how are you, first. It would also be easier if you had been around the last fifteen years or so," Sara said, but without anger or bitterness.

"I'm here now," Joanna said. "By choice and not from guilt. And how are you?"

"Terrible, thank you for asking. And you? Seen God again, perhaps?" Sara asked as she stirred her coffee, making slow circles with her spoon as a child might. "I'm sorry. I'm being a bitch," she said as she looked up with concern at Joanna. *"Are* you well . . . does anything hurt?"

"Nothing physical," Joanna replied, surprising herself with her reply. "Dean sends his love."

"I let him down. I feel awful about that," Sara said. "I wanted so much to give him something, but . . ." Her voice failed. Again she lowered her head, and Joanna could feel Sara's distress. "It's so hard to talk about, Jo. It's so personal, and I'm so ashamed . . . embarrassed. It feels like one more instance of my lifelong battle with ineptitude."

"Sara, there were many things you were when we were growing up, but inept was never one of them. In case you've forgotten, you were in the honor society in high school and on the dean's list in college. You did a helluva merengue and a great twist. No, you were never inept. Not in the important things that I just mentioned."

"How about boys?" Sara asked.

"You were inept," Joanna said seriously. "So nobody's perfect. Now what's up?" Joanna reached across the table for Sara's hand.

"I never thought this could happen to me, yet it's happened," Sara said, biting her upper lip.

"What, Sara? What's happened?" asked Joanna patiently.

Sara hesitated and then whispered: "Stefan is . . . unfaithful."

"Many husbands are," said Joanna, not thinking.

"As are many wives, I'm sure," Sara replied. "Are you condoning their actions?" she asked.

Joanna thought, Was she? She didn't know. Why didn't she know, she wondered, her mind suddenly moving into places she had not been aware she had been avoiding. Why had she been so complacent about Reynolds's affairs? How did she really feel about them . . . and her own? She was barely hearing when Sara continued.

"And the woman is nothing. She's a little younger but not particularly pretty or even attractive. I just don't understand."

Nor did she, Joanna realized. Barney Reardon was also neither particularly "pretty" or attractive.

"Why then?" asked Sara just as Joanna was asking the same question to herself.

"Maybe because she pays attention to him," Joanna replied, her mind retracing all the times neither she nor Reynolds had paid attention to the other. "Maybe because in some deep, inner way, Stefan is lonely and this woman makes him feel admired, needed."

"And are you implying I don't do these things for Stefan?" Sara asked, her voice shrill.

Joanna was startled, suddenly aware that her musings had hurt more than helped Sara.

"Well, let me tell you, I do. I admire him. I need him. He's a brilliant, accomplished man. Until recently he was my best friend, and I thought I was his. I thought we were a couple unto ourselves. Our children came first. The kids adore Stefan. He listens to them. How many fathers actually do that? How many really get involved in their children's lives?"

"Not many," said Joanna sadly, "and I suppose the same could be said about mothers."

"Not this mother," Sara snapped. "My children . . . my family . . . came first."

She was crying, this time not bowing her head to hide the tears that streamed down her face. "Joanna, he's been seeing her for two years. That makes my life a lie for two years. Do you know how that hurts! Almost as much as the possibility that he might leave me for her."

"Doesn't he know? Don't you know?" asked Joanna, horrified.

"I don't know anything. I'm such a fool I thought I was happy, that *we* were happy all these years. Now I discover we weren't or that he wasn't, and that it has all been lies. I feel as if my entire marriage, my history, has been plundered and raped. And I don't understand. I don't know why he's seeing her."

Any more than she knew why Reynolds saw other women, Joanna suddenly realized. Or why they had separate lives that came together only superficially and perhaps stayed together for only superficial reasons. The last frightened her.

"Do you ask? What does he say?" Joanna pursued.

"He doesn't, except for mumbling something about passion. Which is a laugh," said Sara bitterly. "There are many things Stefan knows, but passion isn't one of them. Don't look at me that way. You're thinking, what could I possibly know about passion? Plenty. Too much, actually, although there's been precious little of late. Well, I've told him. He can't have it both ways. He can't be here and go there. I won't stand for it. I won't."

"Maybe there's something he's not getting here that you can give him," said Joanna, thinking of what she might have denied Reynolds.

"Like what?" Sara asked defiantly. "I give all I have. I wish he would only take what I offer. But he doesn't. Oh, well, nobody gets it all. We all settle, particularly when most things are good. But dammit! I don't know what this woman has. I only know she exists and gives Stefan something that makes me feel inept. I'm not pretty. I'm not glamorous. I'm not a professional. I'm not you. I'm only the woman he married, and suddenly that's not enough."

She was sobbing now, but before Joanna could reach her Sara was washing the luncheon dishes, scrubbing the sink and sponging the kitchen counter. The flurry of activity made Joanna think of her own. The five, sometimes six days a week at the office. The many nights of working late. Why? What was she avoiding with her own version of scrubbing and polishing? Underneath her "Tiffany" exterior, she, too, was only the woman he had married.

Joanna came to where Sara was standing at the sink and from behind laced her arms about Sara's waist. Sara relaxed, softly crying as Joanna's shoulder supported her head. "You're not alone, Sara," Joanna crooned.

"You're wrong, Joanna. I am. I've always known that. In sickness, in death and when your marriage is going down the drain, you're alone."

"I just meant I'm here if you need me," Joanna replied. "We even have room for you at the house. And Dean is just across the river. He'll need to feel needed now, and frankly, Sara, so do I."

They stood silent for a while, each dwelling on her own thoughts. "What are you going to do?" Joanna asked finally.

"I don't know. I guess I won't know until Stefan knows what he wants," Sara answered.

"Do you think that's wise?" Joanna asked, concerned.

"Wise? No. But all that's possible at the moment? Yes," Sara answered.

The excitement had begun to build when the captain announced they were flying over the Grand Canyon, its outlines distinct even from the height of 33,000 feet. Within the hour they would be landing in Los Angeles and she would be home, a thought that sent shivers throughout her body. She was nervous, not about the landing, which normally would have been uppermost in her mind, but about home . . . Reynolds and Stacey.

Joanna was a reluctant air traveler at best, but this trip she had felt no fear. Soon she would be with her family. She would hold them in her gaze and in her arms. If things between them were not perfect, they at least were.

Her stomach knotted at the announcement of landing in twenty minutes. She thought about her appearance. The suit was appropriate for travel, but its businesslike manner was not the way she wanted to look for Reynolds. Her makeup . . . she wasn't wearing any, she remembered. Her compact revealed a face that did not look tired despite others' fears that she was attempting too much too soon.

She applied eye liner, freshened her lipstick and ran a brush through her hair before reclining her seat and closing her eyes in a last effort to calm herself. She had missed them, more than she would have had there not been an accident. Truly she had been born again, and she wasn't even a Christian, she thought, and then laughed.

"There will be a wheelchair waiting, Mrs. Bennett," the stewardess said softly as she knelt next to Joanna, discretion her intent.

"Oh, I don't think I'll need it. But thank you," Joanna replied.

"It's a very long walk from the landing gate to the terminal. Even with the moving sidewalk it's exhausting," the girl advised.

"We'll see," said Joanna. "But I do think I'm just fine," she added as she patted the girl's hand. Her eyes again closed, and Joanna drifted to that moment of meeting, rehearsing what she would say, enjoying how she would feel when he touched her. She could feel him. As she inhaled, she could smell his aroma, his skin after a shower, before a bath, during lovemaking.

When the plane touched down, she burst into tears, surprising herself and others in the first-class cabin with her emotion. Soon she was laughing, little giggles that she tried to suppress by placing her hands over her mouth. She thought of something Lilith had once said—how she only cried at weddings, funerals, takeoffs and landings—and laughed again. Lilith delighted her even if the prospect of returning to active duty on their battlefields did not.

Joanna remained seated as passengers lined up to deplane, each now rushing as she had once done to exit, to be first at the baggage claim, first at the taxi stand. Control of one's life regained. She stood, smoothed her skirt, fitted her jacket and walked slowly toward the exit door. Smiles from the stewardesses; smiles returned. She resisted the urge to hug the one who had taken such good care of her, knowing her gesture would be misconstrued.

Her nervousness increased with each step. Just a few more yards through the tunnel and she would emerge into the lounge. She was already searching for the blond head that usually stood above the others, seeking to connect with the blue eyes that had once wooed her from across a crowded room at a college smoker.

Panic. He wasn't there. She checked her watch. The plane was not early. Nor were they more than the customary ten minutes late.

"Mom?"

The voice was tentative, like that of a child afraid of waking its parents from a nap. Joanna turned. An apparition, blond, beautiful. Her daughter in shorts, a tattered sweat shirt and a piece of filmy gauze plunked upon her head in some semblance of a bow. She looked frightened and shy. Joanna uttered a little cry and then swept Stacey into her arms, repeating her name as she alternately hugged and kissed her.

Stacey pulled away, embarrassed and uncomfortable with Joanna's outburst of affection. "But you look so wonderful," Joanna said as if needing to explain her feelings. "And I'm surprised. I never expected you. Where's your father?" she asked, thinking Reynolds must be double-parked at the terminal entrance in order to make things easier for her.

"He couldn't make it. Now don't get upset, Mom, he tried." Stacey saw the disappointed look on Joanna's face. "But he couldn't reschedule some committee meeting at the hospital. Really, he was in a bind. They're planning some kind of tribute to Grandfather, and Dad had to go. Anyway, you're looking good, Mom," Stacey said as they began their journey on the moving sidewalk that would take them to the baggage claim. Joanna felt empty, hungry for the first time since lunch with Sara, so many hours and a continent ago. Work is work, she told herself. They had always had that agreement between them. There were also emergencies and necessities in work. That, too, they had understood. But somehow not today. She again looked at Stacey, touched her hair gently and was plunged still more deeply into a settling depression when Stacey gently pushed her hand away. A shock. A picture worth a thousand words. Only as they waited for the luggage it became apparent to Joanna that Stacey didn't have a thousand words in her. At least not for her, her mother.

"How is school?" Joanna asked as they walked to the parking field, each sharing the weight of one particularly heavy suitcase, their hands touching where they both gripped its handle.

Stacey's face said it all. "It's school. Not much better or worse than it's been. Only now there's an end in sight. Less than a year and I'm free."

"To do what?" Joanna asked.

"I'm thinking of going into acting," Stacey said.

She wasn't surprised. Somehow she had expected that Stacey might one day confuse looks with talent. Many California girls did, thinking the stares they received when their shorts were too short were indications of their star potential.

"I'm thinking of having some test pictures made during Christmas break," Stacey continued. "Dad thought you would know of some photographers who might be looking for a subject. That way I'd get the photos free."

It was all happening too fast. For the first time since the operation Joanna was experiencing both the dizziness and the nausea the doctors had forecast.

"Mom, are you all right?" Stacey's voice was more frightened than concerned.

Joanna steadied herself. The question she asked she hadn't contemplated. "Will your father be home when we arrive?"

"Mom, open your eyes. Look!" Stacey urged.

They were standing by a silver Mercedes, so new that its paint shimmered in the final rays of the diminishing sunset. The upholstery was a deep, rich cordovan, a glint of red to its purplish brown. She did not understand. Stacey took her by the hand to the rear of the car and pointed to the license plate, which read: "Joanna."

"It's yours, Mom," Stacey squealed. "Dad bought it for you. A welcome-home present. Isn't it super? Wait until you feel it. You'll never want to drive your Isuzu again. Not that you could. Dad sold it when he bought this. It cost a fortune. Tape deck, telephone, the works. Neat, huh?"

She was appalled. The car and its plates offended her. She could never be one of those who announced their arrival and the fact that they had arrived professionally and financially by wearing her name on her license plate. That wasn't her style. She wanted to cry, so deep was her loneliness. He had meant so well, but it was so wrong.

* * *

She lay next to him, feeling his warmth, listening to his every breath. Familiar moments of marriage. In the dark she reached for his hand, remembering how in the early days of their courtship they would lie partially clothed in bed for hours, just holding hands, until the day of their engagement, when she trusted them to do more. Even then, after their lovemaking, she was left with a feeling that she had done little other than give him something valuable.

His hand did not return her pressure when she squeezed. "Reynolds," she called softly.

"Jo, you're tired, you should rest," he whispered.

"Don't be afraid, Reynolds. I'm all right. You can love me. I won't break."

"Rest, Jo. It's been a long day," he replied as he turned on his side. "Maybe in the morning."

But in the morning, as she lay waiting and wanting, she wondered why he was still hesitating. Didn't he know she was well or must she prove that to him? She kissed his face, her mouth moving from his eyes to the sides of his cheeks, his lips and his chin.

He remained still.

Her tongue flicked from his ear to his neck and down to his nipples, for him always an erogenous zone. He stirred as her hand roamed his pelvic area, touching, caressing. She was giving him pleasure with her hand and her mouth, making love to him.

And he was atop her, not waiting but assuming her readiness. His excitement was enormous. He entered slowly, and then feeling her wetness he plunged, throttling her with his motion. A steady, throbbing pulsation that ended moments later with his release and her frustration.

SEVEN

DEAN was nervous. For the first time in three weeks he was leaving the house for a reason other than groceries. Ralph Kayne had called, and the producer of *At the Rainbow's End* had suggested lunch. But for what reason? Dean wondered. Professional or personal? From the picture and résumé he had sent, Kayne knew what was on his mind, but he had no idea what thoughts were passing through Kayne's head. He hoped they were of business and not pleasure.

Although he was expecting it, the doorbell startled Dean. When he opened the door Tricia Hill stood stiff and starched in her gray suit and ruffled blouse that climbed halfway up her neck. She declined his offer of coffee, preferring to get to the matter at hand. Settling herself on the sofa, she withdrew a yellow-lined pad from her briefcase and placed it on the coffee table. The large, legible longhand was readable even from a short distance. When she began talking, Dean's instincts told him not to listen. Her voice was devoid of emotion as she slowly and carefully took him from point to point, issue to problem, repeating the names of accountants and lawyers should he need assistance.

Dean's mind wandered, finding it impossible to discuss Chris solely in terms of dollars and cents. Dimly he heard her say the will had been probated—at the request of Chris's parents—and the building, of course, was his; the Joint Tenancy With Right Of Survivorship ensured that. He had also been named the sole beneficiary of Chris's estate, which was nonexistent considering the mortgage and home-improvement loans still to be paid.

He remembered how they had fought when the idea of a house first arose. He couldn't see being so encumbered with mortgages and loans, but Chris had wanted a place of their own. That seductive phrase . . . a place of their *own* . . . had been the deciding factor. And so for two additional years after they had agreed upon purchasing a place, they continued to live in their walk-up hovel so that Chris could save enough for a down payment. Then they had walked the streets, looking at many brownstones before buying this one, Dean remembered. It was all but abandoned, run-down and ramshackle, and thus priced at a bargain two hundred thousand dollars. The home-improvement loan, received only when Chris had offered the house as collateral, had been near that. Then, the sums they had been dealing with felt like play money. Dean had expected that any day Chris would announce they were buying Boardwalk and Park Place. It was no more real today now that the house was worth, according to an outside appraiser, approximately a million dollars.

"Unfortunately," Tricia Hill was saying, "the income currently generated by the building is not enough to carry it. If you're to live here rent-free, and if the building is to pay for itself, you must immediately lease the ground floor, either to another doctor, or, if the space is divided and remodeled to suit, to one or even two tenants."

He looked and saw that she had everything itemized. Overwhelmed, he wished she would stop and that Chris would begin. To take over. As he always had. But she continued with her sparkling efficiency. "I've placed ads in all the key newspapers. Space like this is at a premium, you know. In fact, I've already arranged for a Dr. Robert Feingersh to look at the space on Thursday. You won't forget, will you?" she asked, concerned. He would not, he promised, although his mind rebelled at the thought of some other doctor practicing in Chris's office.

Dean watched as she thumbed through her notes, making sure she had not been guilty of some oversight. Soon she would be gone, and yet another link to Chris, he realized, would be severed. She handed him the notes, placing them first in a large manila envelope. They were now his reference guide, his map to that part of Chris's world he had never entered.

"If you need any further assistance, don't hesitate to call," she said as she stood, smoothing the folds of her skirt as she did. "Well, I'd best be going. I have several interviews this morning. It's nice to have someplace to go. When I'm not working I feel so displaced, as if I don't belong anywhere."

She laughed nervously, and Dean understood that she, too, was frightened. "Tricia, thanks for everything," he said as he took her hand. It was cold and unresponsive. She did not wish to be disturbed. She looked about the room and said as she crossed it and walked to the door: "He was a nice man. And a very good doctor," she added, almost as an afterthought. She wished him luck; he bid her likewise. And she was gone, making him aware once again of the emptiness surrounding him. He stared at the manila envelope on the table, thinking not of its contents but of Tricia Hill and what it must be like to be middle-aged, unemployed and alone. He wondered if she had dealt with the possibility that she might always be alone. Had he? His circumstances were not much different from hers. Except that he owned a building, a place that was his, a statement that he belonged somewhere and proof that he had once belonged with and to another.

Sara had understood this when they had talked recently. Houses hold identities, theirs and your own, she had said almost vehemently. A lifetime had been lived within the four walls of her house and its foundation was strong, she had mused. Its history could support through any storm. From Joanna, Dean knew which storm Sara was referring to, and he ached for her. Her pain, unspoken, was therefore even more painful to him. He had been particularly touched and yet anguished when she had offered to meet him in the city for lunch. He knew how difficult that would be for her and understood it was her way of saying she cared. But he had declined, not wanting to see her or anyone else. Which was why he had not left the house for anything other than necessities until today.

His nervousness returned. He was due at lunch within the hour. He would be, as Joanna had suggested, aggressive. He would ask for work as an extra if necessary, anything that would make him feel like a working professional. Later he would make the rounds of commercial agents. There was no reason his armpits couldn't sell deodorant as well as any other actor. He had decided he must work, even if it meant visiting Los Angeles and letting Joanna pimp for him.

Later, as the taxi drove him through Central Park to the West Side television studio where *At the Rainbow's End* taped, Dean both blessed and cursed Joanna for having urged him to follow up his picture and résumé to Ralph Kayne. He had been embarrassed, as it felt like begging, but Kayne had been warm, almost too warm and effusive, in his greeting. And when the producer suggested lunch, Dean wondered what exactly the man had in mind.

He thought about Joanna. Despite the changes she had made in her life, she did not sound happy. She was now leaving her office as close to six as possible, insisting her time was needed at home. Only home, if his perception was correct, didn't need her as much as she seemed to need them. Reynolds was always running here and there, doing this and that. Nonstop. Stacey, too, was more visitor than resident, and somehow it didn't seem strange when Joanna spoke of loneliness despite living in a full house.

As he stepped from the taxi Dean became aware of the people milling about in front of the studio, many of them eyeing him curiously. "Are you anybody?" one asked, an autograph album held in a ready-to-strike hand. "Not yet," he replied humorously, "but I've got hopes." The fan moved back into the assembled group, a look of annoyance on her face.

After checking his name on a list, the receptionist at the entrance handed him his identification tag. The security guard beckoned him through the heavy steel fire door, pointing up the stairs to the second-floor offices where he was expected. The hallway was bustling with cast members running toward dressing rooms and makeup. Another assistant took him into Kayne's office, the first on the left, and Dean was surprised by its strictly requisitioned-from-supply furnishings. A metal desk and two heavy metal chairs upholstered in the kind of imitation leather meant to last a lifetime sat on some nondescript Astroturf-like carpeting. A desk lamp with a burnt brown shade didn't help the dim light of the room. On the wall were signed and framed pictures of the stars and guest stars of the series. They were the only personal touches in the room.

The tall, well-built man who suddenly entered was Ralph Kayne. Almost twenty years later, his eyes still took in more with a single assessment than what most people saw when they looked at themselves in the mirror. Now he was looking at Dean with unabashed interest.

They were sitting in a booth, their prospective client sandwiched between them, pretending indifference to the stares of conjecture mixed with admiration and envy that carried across the room to where they were sitting.

Joanna hated the Polo Lounge and usually shunned it as she did other clichés of her business. But in Hollywood it was still *the* address for business, particularly at this end-of-the-day hour. As she glanced at their prey's face, Joanna knew Lilith had once again made the right choice. The child whose business they were wooing was pretending her much admired "cool." She was used to the admiration of twenty thousand shrieking young fans, but as the new goddess of rock in spike heels and spiky hair, she was unused to commanding the attention of network and studio heads who were part of the Polo Lounge's usual decor.

Lilith was comfortable. She could see that the child was no different from other rock stars they represented. She wanted respectability. And this child, despite her outrageous appearance, which had already brought the condemnation of several church groups, was frightened by her success and yet greedy for more.

Joanna felt on the outside looking in. She was uninterested and somewhat ashamed, wanting to tell the child whose business they were coveting to invest her money more wisely than in public relations. She avoided Lilith's eyes, knowing that she should soon, at the moment of sale, jump in for the kill. Perhaps the week she had spent at home might not have been enough for full recuperation, Joanna thought. Yet she had wanted to feel useful again, needed to leave behind the accident and the surgery and the phone calls from clients and contacts who wished to express their concern. She had thought her work would tranquilize, but it hadn't. She was no happier at the office than she was at home, although she continued to go to both places, where her charge and business cards insisted she belonged.

There was silence. In it Joanna could feel the attention at her table shifting from Lilith to her. She was on. She spoke softly but effectively, maintaining that it was not the quantity but the quality of the publicity they would obtain. A name in the paper placed solely for ego was meaningless, but that same name placed in that same newspaper with an item designed to sell either tickets or a producer—anything that furthered the *artist's* career—was meaningful and what public relations should be about.

It was the "artist" that always proved effective. Singers and actors alike, jugglers, too, Joanna assumed, loved to be called that. It legitimized them. And the other buzzword—the almighty *producer*—was the key that unlocked every child's dream—that of being a film star.

She watched the child's eyes as she spoke, finding that she was staring into greed and a youthful lust for power. Joanna stopped in midsentence, unable to find a finish for what suddenly felt decidedly like an act. Lilith concluded in her breezy, informal manner, suggesting that the girl "shop around," explaining that choosing a public relations agency should be like choosing shoes. A good fit is what mainly mattered. The ploy was the *pièce de résistance.* Few stars could stand being told to take their business elsewhere, *if* they preferred. It made them feel they were not as wanted as they fantasized. The child left, followed by a business manager. Only as he shook her hand did Joanna become fully aware the man had been sitting there the entire time. To him would fall the horror of haggling with Lilith over fees and expenses.

What was now for Lilith the thrill of victory felt like the agony of defeat to Joanna. They would get this account, of that she was certain, but why did they want it? That it would enhance their image and their bankbooks was suddenly not enough reason. The girl was this season's freak show in her leathers and lace. Given the way trends changed in pop music, she would be thought of as a clown in a year or two. They should be preparing her for that instead of nurturing the fantasy.

She was about to leave when she felt Lilith's hand on her arm staying her. "Let's have a drink. Just us kids. You tell me your dreams and I'll tell you mine." Joanna was silent. "OK," said Lilith, "I'll begin. In my dream I'm five foot eight, one hundred and twelve pounds. I have the most awful time keeping my weight up. My work at the Albert Schweitzer/Mother Teresa Institute is very rewarding. My husband looks like Mel Gibson and my children have yet to be born. Best of all I have a cleaning woman who actually shows up on the day she's expected and washes windows and floors. Now let's hear yours."

"I have two professions. I pet puppies and I pat ballplayers' buns when they come into the dugout after hitting a home run," Joanna began.

"You mean you do not own your own public relations agency?" Lilith interrupted.

"I most certainly do not," Joanna replied.

"Well, then, if as it seems neither of us, even in our fantasies, wants to do publicity, I think we have a problem. I could be wrong, but I don't think we can stay in business with both partners hating what they do."

Joanna sighed, settling herself more deeply into the booth, almost forgetting to smile and feign delight when Rona Barrett entered and acknowledged her. "I don't hate the business, Lil. It's just that it doesn't seem very important anymore."

Lilith gasped in mock horror. Her eyes rolled as she whispered: "My God, Joanna. Be still. Not in the Polo Lounge of all places. What do you want to do—start another Wall Street panic, only this time on Rodeo Drive? Not important? How dare you bring such a word to this discussion? Next you'll be using words like 'relevant' as if this was the sixties or something."

"I used to feel we performed a service. I used to think what we did was meaningful."

"It isn't?" Lilith again gasped. "Promise me, Joanna," she said in a conspiratorial whisper, "that you won't tell. Don't you realize such talk could topple an entire industry? Listen to this woman. *Important . . . meaningful.* People have been blacklisted in this town for using such words. Happily you're with me, Joanna. I'm your friend and I can be trusted. Because someone else might take this kind of information and misuse it, and you would never work in this town again."

"Lilith, is any of what I'm saying getting through?" Joanna asked.

"Much too loud and far too clear," Lilith replied. "Well, what the hell, I suppose if I had nearly died and was given another chance to live, I'd probably run off with Tom Selleck, and if he wasn't available, then with Benji. Yes, Joanna, you are getting through, and it's not helping my increasing anxiety. I understand you all too well. You're not anyplace that I haven't been. But I hang in. Because it's a job. Because I'm crass and commercial. I like to eat. I like comfort. I like all the things that money can buy, and the only way I know to make money is to work. So although it is true I hate our business, I don't hate myself for doing it."

"Nor do I," Joanna replied, "but I do hate aspects of the job. They're dumb and demeaning. I don't want to meet any more airplanes or fetch any more clients from their homes or hotels to an interview. They're adults. Let them find their own way."

"That's your first mistake. They are not adults but children," Lilith countered. "The Louis B. Mayers and Jack Warners made them children long ago . . . stunted their growth with their star systems. So what we now have are talented but spoiled children used to making demands and having them met. And if we don't meet them they will pick up their hot little properties and go where some other eager publicist stands ready to wipe their altered noses and their tight little asses. Those are the facts, ma'am. We either face them or give up the business."

"Or make new facts," Joanna replied.

"We'd starve to death if we did," Lilith said.

"No," Joanna argued. "There's always something to eat."

"You've got that wrong, m'dear. In this town, there is

always some*one* to eat. In this case: us. We'd be devoured by the sharks within weeks."

They sat with neither speaking until Lilith said: "What we need is to expand, hire some type who looks like and therefore we could dub 'vice-president.' We need an official plane greeter, handshaker, and master of charm, manners and manipulation. Someone who also just happens to be wildly attractive."

"I'll call the palace tomorrow. Perhaps Prince Charles is available," Joanna said.

"Well, he does have the contacts, although Lord knows he's shy of actual working experience," Lilith replied. "But then, look at how well you've done. Good. Call in the morning. Now before you race out of here, which you're obviously about to do, think about what I said. Maybe we should hire someone. Also," she said casually as Joanna signaled for the check, "I want to know if there is anything I can do for you."

Joanna sat back, silenced by Lilith's quiet question.

"I'm not blind, Joanna," Lilith continued. "I can see it's more than business that's bothering you. I just want you to know I'm here if you need me."

Joanna debated, knowing that the Polo Lounge was neither the time nor the place for an intimate discussion. She surprised herself by saying: "Nothing makes sense anymore, Lil. I can't seem to find myself or my place, and yet I know both are around here somewhere. I'm just . . . depressed. Actually, that's not altogether true, and that worries me. Sometimes I'm in this state of euphoria, feeling as I never have in my life. It's a state of oneness. Other times I feel lost. The mood swings frighten me, so much so that I've decided to see another neurologist next week. Perhaps there is some physiological reason for what I'm going through. Maybe there's been some damage to the central nervous system or the brain."

"I don't think this is about your brain, Joanna," Lilith said. "What's really going on? What's happening at home?"

"Nothing, and that, too, is part of the problem," Joanna replied as she rose. Lilith followed, waving to Ann-Margret as she passed her table. As they waited for the parking attendant to fetch their cars, Lilith pressed: "I don't see what could be wrong at home. Stacey is at that difficult stage—part child, part beast. But Reynolds, he so adores you. Do you know he consulted with me before he bought you the house in Malibu? Yes," Lilith said as she noted the surprised look on Joanna's face. "He wanted to know if you had ever expressed a preference for Palm Springs or perhaps even Laguna Beach. He was so like a child. So excited about surprising you."

"Well, he certainly did surprise me," Joanna said.

"You don't seem very happy about it," Lilith responded questioningly.

"Lilith, we'll hardly ever use the house. It's a lovely idea, but a waste. Reynolds prefers tournaments in Tahoe and Vegas, and there's not a surfboard between us. Although I'm sure Reynolds will buy one if he hasn't already. He's on one continuous buying spree, as I'm sure you've noticed," Joanna said as she pointed to her diamond-and-ruby earrings, and then the Mercedes that the attendant was driving into view.

"Yes, it's a tough life you have, Jo. Imagine. A husband who insists on buying you things. Any divorce-court judge would know instantly that's mental cruelty."

"He doesn't talk to me, dammit," Joanna snapped as she faced Lilith.

Lilith blanched. She took Joanna's hand, guiding her away from the onlookers and eavesdroppers. "Then talk to him," she whispered. "Tell him what you need. Men forget. Particularly after many years of marriage."

"He doesn't want to talk. He wants to have fun," Joanna said, tears forming in her eyes.

"Talk to him, Joanna. Talk and then talk some more. Reynolds will listen. The man adores you. It's so obvious how proud he is of you."

Lilith's car arrived. Joanna hesitated and then hugged her partner. "Thanks," she said. "I'll try." She looked at her Mercedes, trying to like it as she entered from the driver's side. She thought about Lilith's words as she sped away from the Beverly Hills Hotel. She wondered what it was that Reynolds adored, that made him proud. She began to shake as the answers suggested themselves to her.

He adored what she had become. Not *who* but *what.* He was proud of the image and was content to know only it and not what lay beneath it. He had bought the package, one she had so artfully created out of fear ten years ago when she intuitively knew she would be losing him if she didn't change. Her M.R.S. title had been in jeopardy. He was moving in circles in which she was a square. He was discovering what women had always known—that he was attractive. He had help in that discovery, but not from her.

Alone in the house on North Canon Drive with only motherhood to occupy her day, she had felt tucked away, a relic in an attic of someone's life, collecting age and dust, some stale reminder of his past, uninteresting and certainly less desirable than the women who came to his office. She had never consciously thought to create herself anew. Hers was a role into which she had slipped from the day Lilith suggested the partnership. She created the character from some place deep within. Her audience bought it. In that audience was Reynolds, and because of that she had found it impossible to come offstage. And so she remained in character.

She had thought his adoration was love. She had also confused his admiration with acceptance. Neither was true. Her head was pounding as she pulled into the driveway. In the house the phone was ringing persistently, and Joanna answered the intrusion with an almost defiant hello, as if daring the caller to say anything she didn't want to hear.

It was Dean, a Dean she only barely remembered from childhood. A Dean of enthusiasm and hope. Names came flying at her, but the only one she recognized was that of Ralph Kayne. Who had asked him to remove his shirt! She listened as he bubbled about an audition and an appraisal. By the director and casting director. There had been no lunch. No fond reminiscences of the past. Just that eye of Kayne's measuring him for a role.

Joanna listened, smiling as she realized Dean was reacting as any actor might.

He had suggested dinner sometime. Ralph Kayne had suggested dinner! And that bothered him. Did Kayne want him as an actor or just him?

And she had thought only women had such fears.

When the conversation ended Joanna was smiling, basking in Dean's excitement. Her mind drifted from New York to Princeton. She wished someone would ask Sara to remove her shirt so that some sense of her worth and desirability would be restored. Joanna ached for Sara. She did not understand how Sara could allow Stefan to remain in their house when he did not know if he wanted to remain in their marriage. And she was sleeping alone while he made up his mind. Only she wasn't sleeping but lying awake, wondering if he was slipping out of the den, out of the house, and out of her life and into the life of another woman.

She would call later, after dinner, Joanna decided, a dinner that was miraculously cooking if she could trust her sense of smell. The aroma that filled the house was familiar and yet strange. At the stairs leading to the bedrooms it was its strongest and sweetest. But it wasn't Friday, Joanna thought, once she identified the fragrance. Not the end of the week when Reynolds indulged in his bath, his wine and his pot. At the entrance to their bedroom Joanna saw Reynolds sprawled on the bed, no bath running, no wine cooling and no cigarette of any kind still an ember in a bedside ashtray. Instantly she turned toward Stacey's room. She knocked once and entered, not waiting for a reply. Stacey, too, was in bed, her eyes closed, her lips and fingers moving to whatever beat she heard on the Walkman radio plugged into her ears. As Joanna watched, Stacey sucked hard on the joint in her hand, drawing smoke deep into her lungs.

She was shocked, although some part of her knew she should not be. She had long suspected Stacey smoked and had hoped pot was the only drug she used. But to think it and then to know it were decidedly different things . . . suddenly.

Joanna approached the foot of Stacey's bed, tweaking her daughter's big toe to get her attention. She stood there awkwardly as Stacey opened an eye, acknowledged Joanna with a wave and then retreated behind closed lids to music playing so loudly Joanna could hear it through the earplugs hidden in Stacey's ears.

She took the toe again and pinched. Stacey attempted

to read her lips as the Walkman remained plugged in her ears, her expression one of mild annoyance. Finally she took one plug out and grimaced as she heard Joanna say: "I want to talk to you."

"Can't it wait, Mom? I've had a bitch of a day and I'm trying to cool out."

Joanna sat on the edge of the bed, aware that Stacey inched away as she did. "Stace, I really don't like the idea of you smoking pot," Joanna began.

"Oh, come on, Mom. What's the big deal? I've been smoking for years," Stacey replied, looking at Joanna as if she were insane.

"But not in this house . . . I hope," Joanna said, sounding foolish even to herself. "I guess I think there must be better ways for you to relax. What happened at school to upset you?"

"Give me a break, Mom, would you?" Stacey said. "What happened? she wants to know. School happened. It sucks. I hate it," she added as she replaced the plug in her ear and turned up the volume.

"Turn it off, Stacey, I'm talking to you," Joanna said.

Stacey did not respond.

With one yank the Walkman was in Joanna's hands. Stacey jerked up into a sitting position. "What's with you? That hurt," she said as she rubbed her ears.

"Look, Stacey, I'm not happy with your doing drugs of any kind," Joanna began.

"Mom, be real, for God's sake. Smoking pot is not doing drugs. It's harmless, not like if I were doing speed or smack or crack or even booze."

"Stacey, no one seems certain whether pot is or isn't harmless," Joanna argued. "There is some evidence that claims it causes chromosome damage, that it's harmful to brain cells and in particular to pregnant women."

"Mother, it's one lousy joint. No more or less than what Dad uses to clear cobwebs."

"Your father is a grown man. You're a child."

"Look again, Mom. You're gone a lot so you may not have noticed, but I'm almost eighteen. I haven't been a child or even a girl for a very long time."

"What's all the noise about?" asked Reynolds as he stood in the doorway, looking groggily at the situation.

"Mother is really taking it out there because I'm smoking," Stacey replied. "I think she's gone weird—or *weirder*—on us."

She looked at Reynolds to reprimand Stacey for her barely disguised hostility. Instead, she heard him say: "What's up, Jo?"

"I'm just concerned that Stacey is solving her bad day, or any other problem she might have, with drugs. I just think it would be better if she talked, if *we* talked."

"Jo, it's just a joint. It won't kill her."

She looked at him, trying to understand, to recognize his intent. "Well, it won't," he added, holding firm when he saw her expression.

"It's probably her spiritual experience," Stacey said sarcastically. "She's probably now heard God telling us all to go straight."

Again she waited for Reynolds to intervene, to tell his daughter that this time she had gone too far. Again Reynolds said nothing. But she did. "What else would you like to say about my so-called spiritual experience?"

"Face up, Mother. You got clobbered on the head. Your brains got momentarily scrambled. You hallucinated. Deal with it. But stop making us nuts. In case you haven't realized, ever since you came home we've all been walking on eggs around here. Why don't you just give it a rest and land . . . come back to reality."

She stared from Stacey to Reynolds, whose face remained expressionless. At the door Joanna turned and said: "Sorry to disappoint you, Stacey, but the fact is what I saw was reality. And it was better—far better—than any reality you might think you've found through the so-called benefits of some drug. And while we're on the subject, and since we all seemingly disagree, let me make it very clear that since I own this house and you live in it, I will no longer tolerate any further pot smoking. Not by you or anyone."

They were lying in bed, the tension of the evening still between them. As Reynolds tossed, Joanna turned. She had hoped for comfort but felt instead his condemnation.

"You're coming down too hard on Stacey. You have to lighten up," she heard him say over his turned-from-her shoulder.

"Reyn, do you think maybe we've been too light on Stacey all these years?" she asked.

"Even if that were true, Joanna, you won't change things by ramming home your point of view."

"But that wasn't what I was doing," Joanna interrupted, amazed at Reynolds's perception. "I was concerned."

"Not at her age," he continued as though he hadn't heard Joanna speak. "Not after what she's just been through. You forget, Jo. She almost lost us both. She's reacting."

"Reyn, the way Stacey is reacting often makes me feel she would have been happier had I died."

"Joanna!" he said, shocked and angered by Joanna's seemingly cavalier statement. "You should have seen her when she first saw you in that hospital bed, your head bandaged. She was frightened. She cried."

"And I'm frightened for her, Reynolds. I'm frightened that you don't understand. You're too permissive. You don't establish boundaries."

"For Chrissake, Jo. The kid smokes a joint now and then. Big deal."

"She also gets pregnant now and then and flunks classes and skips school," Joanna retorted.

"Let go, Jo," Reynolds said wearily. "Let her live. She's almost eighteen. So she's made a few mistakes. She'll probably make a helluva lot more. So what? As long as she's not hurting anyone and is having fun, what difference?"

"Reynolds," she replied, trying to control her emotions, "the difference is she may be hurting herself, and that hurts me. It should also hurt you."

"You're too intense, Joanna."

"Reynolds, don't make this about me. It's about our daughter. Despite her age she's just a little girl. So many of her actions prove that."

"Could you just relax, Jo? Christ! If you would just let

up on yourself maybe you'd let up on Stacey, quit hassling her.''

''And just exactly how am I doing that?'' Joanna asked, hurt now as well as angry.

''By imposing yourself on her. The girl hates school. Stop pushing it on her. And stop pushing college, too. Let her live her own life.''

''I'd be happy to,'' Joanna replied, ''if you could tell me how with no education and no skills—not to mention no goals that I can see except some half-baked interest in acting—she is supposed to live.''

She heard him sigh first and then respond. ''People just live, Jo, and they have a damn good time doing it. I wish you'd realize that. Honestly, I think nearly dying didn't teach you a damn thing.''

His words were spoken with such vehemence and anger that Joanna remained silent, playing with thoughts and words that might make Reynolds understand how much she had learned. Particularly about them, mainly about him. But could she explain, and if she did, would he understand that the sex he now wanted constantly wasn't to reaffirm their love but his presence on this earth? Would he feel anything if she told him that afterward she felt ravaged and alone?

She would tell him now, begin . . . somewhere, right here in bed where so many of their problems existed. She turned toward him, her thoughts a jumbled monologue. By the time she could order them, she heard his light snoring. She trembled, fighting back tears. With her finger she began to trace the lines that began at his nose and ended at the sides of his mouth. She touched the cleft in his chin. No face was as familiar to her. She loved the face, had from the first. It was strong yet soft, as beautiful as it was handsome. She had always assumed it mirrored the man who wore it.

She stared at Reynolds sleeping. Softly she whispered something else she had wanted to tell him ever since her return from New York. ''Reynolds, please listen. I'm not a Mercedes. I'm really not. I'm just an Isuzu, and it's all right with me.''

* * *

As signs announced the city limits of Princeton, Sara stole a look at the man sitting next to but not near her in the car. Sweat lined his upper lip, and his face was ashen and tight. Occasionally his hands shook as they clutched the steering wheel, his knuckles white from an internal pressure he was applying. He frightened her. This was not the Stefan she knew. She did not know who this man was. Had she ever? she wondered, thinking about his sleepless nights and the moans that permeated his rest when he did sleep.

The idea of the Sunday in New York had been Sara's. It had not only surprised Stefan and the children but her. She seldom suggested outings unless they were in the immediate area. But of late she felt pressed to change things, particularly herself. Stefan had been hesitant. He pleaded illness. She had refused to be sympathetic, both to his pain and her own. Her head was pounding, and her anxiety level increased rather than decreased as they neared home. There they would not have the relics and treasures of the Museum of Natural History to discuss. They would have only themselves and their own lives. Neither did well with that. Stefan maintained he needed time. She gave him that and an atmosphere much like their neighborhood library. At home they tiptoed about and around one another, polite and quiet. But she felt that if she brought up any aspects of the problem, Stefan would put his finger to his lips and go, "Ssshh."

Over the past three weeks Sara had considered options and solutions, allowing her mind to travel in formerly forbidden areas. She could leave Stefan, separate and even divorce. She would survive. But surviving wasn't living. But then living wasn't what she was currently doing in her marriage.

On good days she considered the possibility that Stefan would remain. But if he did, could their lives continue as if nothing had changed when everything had? Her marriage was damaged. A man she had thought was not only her husband but her best friend proved to be only the former, and that was in name only. Forgive and forget? She could do neither, she realized. Yet she could continue in the marriage because of what they had created together and because . . . because she was afraid of the future without him.

The kids were scrambling out of the car, rushing toward the house, anxious not to miss the opening minutes of some MTV special. As he walked in front of her, Sara saw Stefan as older, his posture more a question mark than his usual exclamation point. So often when she looked at Stefan now Sara felt fear knot in her stomach. She could not walk through that door, could not prepare another dinner, hold another inane dinner conversation. Not tonight. Not for the children's sake or her own.

"I don't want to cook," she said hurriedly as Stefan was about to enter the house. "Ask the kids if they want pizza or Chinese."

He didn't question her request. He seldom questioned anything anymore, acting as one who had lost his right to question or dissent. She waited by the car, thinking that any moment she might vomit. She began to tremble. "What, Sara?" she asked herself. "What?" Her breathing became labored as her chest tightened. It would explode, she feared. It would or she would.

It was fear. It was anger. It was fear of her anger. It was being out of control. It was being trapped. Yet she could see the exit sign. What she couldn't see was her taking it.

"Chinese," Stefan announced as he opened the door on his side of the car. She waited for him to lean across and open hers, but he didn't. She knew the conversation would be like that too. She must open it, pry it open if necessary, and it was necessary. She couldn't live like this another moment. She said words to the effect as soon as they had driven away from the house. He did not reply.

"I need to know where I am . . . where *you* are," she began. "I can't function any longer without some kind of communication. I need to know what you're thinking, what your plans are. I need to talk."

His face was ashen and his voice, when he spoke, was dead. Still its impact upon her was greater than if he had shouted.

"You always want to talk, Sara. You talk and you talk

whether or not anyone wants to listen or respond. You talk people to death. You even talk at the children, involving them in every one of your insecurities. You never stop. And you never see the stop signs on other people's faces. Because you don't look. Because you're always so damned involved with yourself, taking your own emotional pulse.''

He paused, fighting to breathe through his rage, but her shock was so great she couldn't interject, couldn't stop the flow of his pent-up feelings. He was staring through the windshield when he continued.

''Do you know what it's like to live with someone who thinks she's the only one in the world with needs?'' He was staring directly at her. ''When have you thought about me, Sara? What I might be feeling. It's always about you. When is it my turn?''

He was shouting, his face, like his voice, no longer dead but painfully alive. She was terrified, pleading that he watch the road, fearful that he might kill them both, and not unintentionally. ''You said I couldn't have it both ways, that it was either her or you. So I gave her up. Now what have I to look forward to? More years of passing time, of hopelessness. Awaiting death or grandchildren—whichever distraction comes first. Where's the passion, Sara? She made me feel passion, made me passionate. I was young again, alive. With you . . . how does a man feel passion with his own child? And that's what you are, Sara. That's what I got when I married, not a wife but a child, a responsibility.''

This wasn't Stefan, she told herself. Stefan doesn't speak in such a fashion, doesn't have such needs. He was just tired . . . distraught. He didn't know what he was saying. In the heat of the moment, she reasoned, people often say things they don't mean, things for which they're sorry they ever said later. He was overworked. The strain was too much. But he really should stop sobbing, Sara thought, particularly while he's driving. Besides, it doesn't suit him. He's not that kind of man. Talking had been a mistake.

He suddenly parked at the side of the road. Sara sat quietly, not stirring as her thoughts moved quickly through her head. His words came back at her. Replayed at a slower speed, she examined each sentence, each accusation, and this time felt something other than shock.

"You wanted the responsibility," she said, grinding out each word. "You were only too happy to take it. The responsibility and the control. You knew how I was when you married me. I never pretended. And because I talk so damn much, as you say, you always knew I hadn't changed. If I clung to you, just remember it was you who held out his hand. You needed me to be just as I was to complement just who you were."

"You were smothering, Sara," he said angrily. "You overwhelm people with your neediness. There's never been any room in our marriage for anything other than your anxieties."

"If you had asked, dammit, I'd have made room," she shouted. "But you never let me in. You never let anyone in. You pretend at being this perfect being, this tower of strength, and because you're so convincing we all believe you. Certainly I did. Maybe you let *her* in, but when did you do that for me?"

"You didn't want to hear, Sara. You wanted me to be a certain way, a way that was comforting and comfortable for you."

"And tell me it wasn't comforting and comfortable for you," Sara replied. "That's one responsibility I refuse to bear alone." She grew silent, fuming, clutching her handbag tightly, fearing if she didn't she might strike him with it. "And let me tell you about passion. Let me tell you of all the nights I waited for you, wanted you. Of all the times I had to take matters into my own hands, so to speak. Would you like to hear my fantasies? I do have them. I keep them locked away, buried. But you could have reached them. It might surprise you, Stefan, to know that at one time I was considered quite a hot number. You just didn't know how to light the flame. Good God. Even those nights when you were there in bed, how I wanted you, because you really weren't there at all. But I survived it. I told myself passion at my age is the least of things in a marriage. That it's just sex, not the stuff of which lasting relationships are made. Only now I hear it is. You have found *the* answer, *the* fountain of eternal youth, while poor me still deludes herself that a home, a family, a marriage are more important than passion."

"And that's enough for you for the rest of your life?"

She heard his question, heard the despair in his voice, and replied: "It was. Loving you made it enough."

Sara turned her head from Stefan toward the window. She wanted to go home, to her children and to the nightly bath with Dana and Naomi. She wanted to return to the life she had known for so long. It had been a good life. No matter what Stefan said. A good life for her, she realized. But what about him? The question was startling. What about *him?*

"What are you anxious about?" she asked, turning back to face Stefan.

"About death . . . dying . . . of life being over without my ever having really lived it. Of just going through the motions instead of living. Can you understand that?" he asked, looking pleadingly at her.

No, she couldn't. She wouldn't allow herself to. It wasn't a new but an old question, one she had asked of herself several times since the night of the accident. Yes, she wanted to reply. The thought had crossed her mind, but she had carefully and methodically crossed it out.

"We should get the food now," she said stiffly. "The children must be starving."

"What about you, Sara?" Stefan asked as he turned the key in the car's ignition. "Aren't you starving too?"

Sara lay still in her bed listening to the sound of her breathing. Despite the down comforter in which she was enveloped, she was cold. Her bed was cold. She clutched the pillow for warmth, comforted by the feel of something pressed to her. She turned on the light, hoping to dissipate the darkness. The room lightened, but not her mood. Stefan's words crawled in and out of her consciousness like a nasty bug one couldn't catch quickly enough to kill.

She hated his words, their accusations stabbing at her with both their truth and falsity. Yes, she often talked at him just as she often talked to herself, to allay an ever-present anxiety. But she had never thought she was the only one with needs. Her children always came first. She was a good mother, dammit, and a damn good wife. That's what her life had been about. If Stefan wasn't satisfied, then she had failed, and her living, even her life, had been in vain.

That conclusion tore at the structure of her being. She was down the steps and entering the den before she could think about what she was doing. Stefan was sitting in front of the television staring into a blank screen. For a moment she thought he was asleep, but the hand he extended to her said otherwise. She took it, confused, wondering what this offer was about and what price would go with it. She stood stupidly by his side, her hand resting in his, both watching a blank television. "Stefan," she began softly, "if you're so unhappy, why stay?"

He shrugged. "What about the children? What about you, if I go?" he asked.

She snatched her hand away. "I can manage on my own," she said angrily. "I don't need you to stay out of pity or guilt or some sense of duty."

"Perhaps I stay because this is where I should be . . . where I belong," he replied.

"Why?" she stormed. "You don't love me. You don't even like me."

His hand again extended toward hers, but this time she couldn't take it. "Sara, I do like you. I also love you. No matter what I said before, you're a good mother, a good person."

"But not a good wife, I gather," she said testily. "I lack something that your Miss or Ms. or Mrs. Wolfe has; something that makes you feel alive, young and not middle-aged and growing older each day. How nice for you. Tell me, does she have a brother who can do the same for me? Her ex-husband will also do just fine."

He was silent, his face gray and filled with such pain that it pained her. Still she could not stop. "What is it, Stefan? I'm waiting. I want to know exactly. Obviously she doesn't talk too much or have any great insecurities that make her cling to you. OK, I know what she hasn't but I'm in the dark as to what she has. Is it that she shares your interests, is a vital person and not some drab little woman who's tied down to kids and the boring chores of running a household? Is she a smart dresser as well as an interesting, exciting woman who's undoubtedly multiple orgasmic?"

"Yes," Stefan replied softly.

"Well, dammit, that's probably why her first marriage went down the drain," Sara snapped. "She was probably so damn busy being all those things that she had no time to be a wife and mother."

"Sara," his voice was pleading. "Please stop. I can't take any more."

"*You* can't take any more?" she asked derisively. "Poor baby. And how do you think I've felt these past weeks? All right, I know I haven't been easy to be married to," Sara said as she paced. "I'm anxious. I panic. But I must be some other things or why did you marry me?"

Her back turned from him, Sara waited for an answer. When none came she wheeled around, determined to defy herself and demand that he leave. But he was sitting in his chair, his back arched, a hand to his chest, his face locked in an anguished grimace. His eyes were pleading. Her answer was to rush to the phone and dial 911 for emergency service.

Stacey's foot was jiggling, a testimony to her nervousness. Joanna reached across from the driver's seat and patted Stacey's hand. It was cold to her touch. Joanna let her hand rest on Stacey's a moment longer than usual. Stacey did not react.

As they drove to the Beverly Wilshire Hotel, Joanna thought of their dinner earlier that week. They had not communicated, or Stacey hadn't, despite Joanna's attempts to if not tear down the wall between them, then at least put a chink in it. The wall had proven to be made of iron. Even the direct: "Stacey, why can't we talk?" spoken in frustration drew only a laconic and unconcerned reply of: "Out of practice, I guess." And when she had suggested that they get into practice, Stacey had simply shrugged and said: "OK, you begin."

She had, with a preamble that perhaps wasn't wise. "Stacey, you know I love you." Stacey's look stopped her immediately. The expression was a mixture of amusement and disbelief. "What is it, Stacey?" she had asked, needing clarification of the message so clear in Stacey's unspoken attitude.

"You say you love me," Stacey began. "I'm waiting for the 'but.' There must be a 'but,' some new thing, or old, that you're about to criticize."

"That wasn't what I was about to do at all," Joanna said, upset. "I was about to say: You know I love you, so why can't we be friends?"

"Because you're my mother," Stacey had answered, her meaning quite clear: that one relationship precluded the other. "Besides, friends I've already got."

She thought there was a snipe, even an insult, somewhere in that last remark, but she didn't pursue it. The evening droned on with more banter than talk. Still Joanna had been encouraged; some communication had taken place. When she asked if Stacey would like to participate in the mother/daughter fashion show luncheon for UNICEF, Stacey had become excited. Two of the participants had taken ill and they would be last-minute substitutes wearing, unfortunately, gowns already selected. But it would be fun, flouncing down a runway with Frances and Candice, Janet and Jamie Lee, all looking gorgeous and young enough to be sisters.

Only it wasn't fun, thought Joanna as they drove up Wilshire Boulevard. Not for Stacey anyway, who was now sickly green in color. She again reached across to squeeze Stacey's arm. "Don't worry, Stace. If you trip, I'll trip with you. We'll call it *fall* fashions and hope everyone laughs." Which Stacey did not. Joanna, too, was nervous, although she did not take her debut as a model seriously. But the mother in her wanted Stacey to shine. They were wearing Bob Mackie originals intended for the mother/daughter team who found it necessary to withdraw. Probably they had caught cold from the draft in the gowns, Joanna thought. At least her sequins came to the neck. Stacey's seemed to cover her neck and little else, something that had once made Cher famous but now made Joanna uncomfortable. It was a very mature dress, to be worn by a not-yet-mature woman.

They were descended upon, besieged, as soon as they

entered the makeshift dressing room; told they were late as hands took familiarities with their bodies, all but ripping clothes off their backs. A drink—sherry, Joanna thought—was pressed into their hands. She tried to refuse Stacey's, but suddenly Stacey was nowhere in sight, whisked away by Mackie himself into a private fitting room for last-minute adjustments.

The activity in the room was frenetic. Joanna watched it roar by her, remaining calm and inwardly amused. It was, after all, only a charity fashion show. None were professional models. No one's job was on the line. Still, Joanna knew if but one of the celebrity mothers showed a hint of bulge, she would be the evening's and the morning's news. Joanna laughed. It was vicious but harmless fun. She was having a good time and was glad she had decided to take Stacey from school for the day. They were both profiting from the experience. She needed similar time alone with Reynolds. Perhaps one of the many vacations he was planning was an answer, although how she could spare more than a long weekend away from the office, considering how much time she had already been away, was a question. Then, too, if they did go to Mexico or Hawaii, when would she deal with the home in Malibu, empty except for some magical bed Reynolds had bought that went up, down—did everything it seemed but the samba as it also dispensed heat and massage? Years ago they could have put a down payment on a small house for what the bed had cost.

People were fussing with her hair, having finished with her face, when she heard a roomful of women, cosmeticians and hairdressers gasp. It was a reaction usually reserved for the entrances of a Barbra Streisand or a Raquel Welch. Joanna's eyes did what her head, currently being ringed with pearls, could not: turned toward the room's object of attention.

At first she thought it was Bo Derek, so simple and perfect was the girl's beauty. But the expression, that there was expression, made it apparent this was some other full-bosomed, small-waisted, typically California-grown beauty. Not quite ripe and yet lush. Her hair was brushed back from her face, falling in gentle waves to her shoulders. The makeup, unobtrusive, accentuated the almond-shaped green eyes and a mouth that naturally turned in a pout. In what was not quite a dress and far less than a gown, the girl floated in seemingly nothing more than sequins and pearls.

Joanna began to cry. This girl was a beautiful woman who only bore some startling resemblance to the child she so long ago had held in her arms and who she wished she could hold again. And this beautiful woman was smiling at her shyly but so very proudly. What wonders have I and God created, Joanna thought as she returned Stacey's smile.

EIGHT

THEY were sitting in the lounge area waiting for more tests to be concluded. Although Stefan continued to suffer chest pains and blackouts, if the instruments attached to almost every part of his body were correct, there was nothing wrong with his heart. Ina was hovering, insisting as she argued that Sara take another bite of the sandwich she had prepared.

"I just think it would be a good idea if the children, or the girls at least, stayed with me for a few days," Ina persisted. "Think how much easier things would be for you."

At the moment Sara looked as if things would be easier if Ina just went away and left her alone. "The girls stay, the children stay," she said wearily. "We need to be together."

"But Sara, look at you. Dead on your feet. All that running back and forth between the house, the school and the hospital . . ."

"Ina, Sara's made her decision. She feels she can manage, so leave her be," said Dean.

Ina withdrew, an injured look on her face. Sara patted her hand. "I know you're just trying to help," she said consolingly. "But you can best do that by preparing a few meals and freezing them." Ina smiled, pleased she now had something she could do to alleviate some of Sara's burden. "I could also pick up the kids at school and bring them here if you think they'll be allowed to see Stefan."

"Bring them regardless," Sara replied wearily. "They should feel a part of what's happening."

Ina picked up her handbag and the debris from the lunch

she had prepared. She offered Sara another chance for another bite of either chicken salad or tuna before she folded the half-eaten sandwiches in their wrap and reluctantly put them with the rest of the garbage. "Well, if I'm to make dinner and pick up the kids I better get going. Will you still be here when I return?" she asked Dean.

"I doubt it," Dean replied as he checked his watch.

"Ina, just go. I'll be fine," said Sara, again patting Ina's hand. "I can manage."

Dean looked from sister to sister and saw that Sara could indeed manage; better than Ina, who was showing far more signs of stress and strain. From the moment he had entered the Medical Center an hour ago, Dean recognized that this was not the Sara he had last seen at the funeral home, not the Sara with whom he had more recently spoken on the telephone. No. This Sara, the one who bullied the staff in the cardiac unit into giving her information they preferred to deny, was in control.

As her eyes followed Ina into the elevator, Sara said: "I'm glad you came."

"I would have come sooner, but I was actually booked for a commercial yesterday," Dean said. "Sara, this is it. Stardom, at last. I'm playing a hemorrhoid sufferer. And to think we once thought my face would be my fortune."

There was no laugh, no response whatsoever, which hurt, even though Dean understood Sara's preoccupation. Still he had hoped she would understand how this one job gave him a measure of self-respect and the right to call himself an actor. It also compensated for the disappointments suffered of late when the callbacks he expected never came.

"So how are you doing?" Dean asked into a blank face.

Sara shrugged. "How does anyone do in these situations? You get through. God, but I hate hospitals!" she said, shuddering.

He understood. Outside the Medical Center he had hesitated before entering. Chris had been more in his mind than usual from the moment Sara had called from the hospital early Monday morning. Not that Chris was ever totally from his mind, but Stefan's attack, whatever its cause, and Sara's possible loss had once again brought his own sharply into focus. And yet he had been glad Sara had called. Her need for his help gave him something to do that took his mind from the one-month anniversary of Chris's death. Just a month, yet it felt like ten years and yesterday at the same time.

"It's wonderful news about the commercial," Sara said suddenly. She was smiling at him, and he could see she was truly pleased. He took her hand. She looked at their fingers entwined and asked softly: "What's it like to be alone?"

Dean considered the circumstances upon which the question was based and replied: "Worse than the loneliness you felt when you didn't know what it was like to be with someone."

Sara nodded. She remembered those years.

"The days are endless, much worse actually than the nights, which pass because eventually you sleep. Worst of all is this feeling of being displaced even though you're in a very specific place."

"Well, you've certainly helped me get my mind off things," Sara said, looking up and down the hallway for signs of stirring that might pertain to Stefan.

"You asked, and I decided you deserved an honest answer," Dean replied. "Particularly since you weren't just asking an idle question."

"You're right, of course," said Sara as she stood and stretched. "I don't think I have ever felt as alone as I have this past month. Now I wonder if I really know what alone is," she added.

"Sara, from what you've told me, you may have to find out," Dean said warily.

Sara sighed, stretched another time, and then once again seated herself next to Dean. After a very long pause she said: "I wonder how these women who pick themselves up and leave their marriages do it. Aren't they afraid? Where do they get their strength, and please, don't tell me from within or I may vomit Ina's tuna salad all over this lounge."

She was silent again, and Dean intuitively knew not to intrude on her thoughts. "There is a part of me that thinks," she began again, "I should take a walk, go out and start over again. But that part collides with the other that sees I'm forty, not a particularly well-preserved or attractive forty, and that I'm a woman with four children and no profession. Where do I go? What chance have I of finding a job or a man?''

''No more or less than many women in your situation,'' Dean answered. ''Or men in mine.''

''Oh, please, Dean,'' Sara snapped. ''We're hardly equal. You simply can't compare a fifteen-year marriage that has borne four children with a . . .'' she stumbled for words . . . ''a *relationship* of eight.''

''Who says, Sara? You, and other small minds like yours?'' Dean replied angrily. ''Well, guess again. Or look a little deeper. Beyond you. If that's possible.''

She stood, and for a moment Dean thought she would leave, not caring if she did.

''I'm sorry,'' she said abruptly. ''That was stupid of me. And insensitive. Well, I'm often both. But the truth is I just can't see us in the same boat. For other reasons,'' she added quickly. ''You're gorgeous. You have a profession. And you don't have the extra baggage of children.''

''Sara, people do overcome their obstacles. It often depends on just how badly they want to.''

''Please, spare me, particularly if you're going to sound like a self-help book,'' Sara said. ''I never felt they were real or that they dealt with how people really feel in real situations. They're all words.''

As Sara sat again, Dean rose. ''Sara, do you want to leave Stefan?'' he asked abruptly. ''Wasn't that what you were toying with or saying before?''

''I don't know what I'm saying,'' Sara replied wearily, ''mainly because I seem to be saying different things. I fluctuate. Yes, I want to leave because I'm hurt, because what's left of my pride says I should, because I want to show Stefan, you and Joanna that I'm not some spineless wimp. Then there's the part of me who's afraid. Where would I go? And I would have to go somewhere as I certainly wouldn't want to stay in Princeton, in a place that used to be our home. And how do you just turn your back on what you've created in fifteen years of marriage? I have children. Stefan and I molded them. They're terrific little people who love their father. That's what I really can't understand. How can Stefan risk throwing that away? I can't. I have a lifetime invested in this marriage, and I don't want to start over. Not unless I absolutely have to. And I may. Stefan could leave, particularly if he recovers. And if he doesn't, well, then, half my problem is solved, isn't it?''

Her voice cracked. ''There's another consideration,'' she said finally. ''We don't know what's wrong with Stefan. It could be minor; it could also be major. I can't walk out on him. Not when he's sick. Not after all he's done for me. Dean, you have an idea of what I was once like. Imagine living with remnants of that for fifteen years. It hasn't been easy for Stefan. Obviously,'' she added, her voice bitter. ''But he hung in, at least till now. I owe him. Come on. Let's walk. This sitting and waiting for answers is making me crazy.''

Dean wondered which of the answers Sara was waiting for was disturbing her most. He understood her not being able to sit as until recently he had been unable to be still in his own house. He had waited for something to happen: a phone to ring, a key in the latch, a voice calling from some other room in the house. But nothing happened, except he finally rented the downstairs office space to a husband-and-wife skin-and-diet team, and so another part of Chris had been removed from his life.

''I'm just lost,'' Sara was saying agitatedly. ''Confused and angry. Frightened, too. I wake up thinking . . . my God, what if I've killed him?''

''What are you talking about?'' Dean said, alarmed.

''We were fighting the day of his attack. I had been at him all evening, trying to make him talk. I saw how tired he was, how upset, and still I proceeded. But I needed some assurance, something to hang on to or let go of. I'm no longer certain which.''

''For Chrissake, Sara. You can't shoulder that responsibility,'' Dean replied. ''In their day-to-day lives people fight. And you had reason to fight, dammit.''

''Mrs. Schell?''

The voice, coming upon them from behind, belonged to an impassive face that betrayed nothing of the test results that he was about to relay. He took Sara by the arm and led her into the conference room where Dean could see the two engage in a brief and decidedly one-sided conversation. As the doctor was about to leave, Dean saw Sara hold him by the sleeve of his long white lab coat. The doctor's face reflected puzzlement, and whatever answer he gave Sara gave her face the same expression.

"There is no brain tumor," she told Dean as he joined her. "No neurological impairment or imbalance that they can see. He doesn't evince gall bladder problems and his kidneys are functioning normally. His blood tests don't indicate a liver malfunction and the urine analysis is normal, ruling out pancreatic difficulties."

"So what do they think?" Dean asked.

"They want to run more tests," Sara replied vaguely.

"But what do they think?" Dean pressed.

"That it might be nerves. They want him examined by a staff psychiatrist. Isn't that ridiculous?" Sara said, her laugh almost a snort. "Stefan's never been nervous a day in his life. What has he to be nervous about? They don't know Stefan if . . ."

Her sentence ended as her eyes focused on a woman walking past them down the corridor toward the intensive-care unit. "Just where do you think you're going?" Sara shouted. When her question was ignored, she shocked Dean by running toward the woman and demanding in a voice shrill and threatening: "What do you think you're doing, dammit?"

"I need to see him," the woman replied, her expression hostile and her manner indicating she was not intimidated by Sara's outburst.

"Well, you can't. I won't permit it," said Sara. "I'm his wife," she added as if the woman already didn't know the fact.

"But he wants to see me," the woman reported, her eyes beseeching.

"You don't know that," Sara sneered.

"He had a nurse call, a Mrs. Mandis," the woman replied. "Ask her if you don't believe me."

But Sara wasn't about to ask anyone. Nor was she about to let the woman pass.

"Please, Mrs. Schell, I need to see him. He wants to see me."

Sara remained unyielding. The woman's composure collapsed. "At least tell me how he is?" she pleaded.

There was a moment's hesitation, a second in which Sara looked as if she might strike the woman, before she said: "He's not in any immediate danger, but they're still running tests."

The woman closed her eyes as if in silent prayer. "I thought he was dying . . . thought he was dying," she repeated as she stumbled away. Dean didn't have to ask who the woman was. He knew. When she was a distant figure down the corridor he placed his hand on Sara's shoulder. They stood silently until Sara said: "I really didn't need that."

"And just maybe you did," Dean said as he led Sara back to the lounge.

His hands were warm, and her skin warmed to his touch. Brown upon tan, body upon body. Sun-drenched and now sun-kissed. Joanna floated, drifting in and out of her body as his lips traced the tan line of her bikini bottom, his tongue flicking into her navel and down her pelvis and around her hips. For a moment her eyes opened, seeing what she did not wish to see in the mirrored ceiling over the circular bed. She closed her eyes and her mind, preferring to drift with the sensations that drifted through her.

His hands slid up her body, strong hands, rough hands. His fingers lightly touched her nipples, lightly squeezed, and then touched again. Shivers trickled down her spine as his hands slipped under her back, supporting as his mouth traveled from her hips to her thighs and inward.

Her eyes flickered and opened again. Behind the filmy draperies the sun was descending. In a matter of hours the neon of Las Vegas would light the dark. She hated Las Vegas, but her husband loved it for the gambling, for the tennis tournaments and the never-ending rounds of golf one could play. She never played. Except now.

Joanna moaned from the feel of his tongue, now his lips, as they explored her inwardly. He turned her around, over and then over again, rocking her as his mouth continued to move deeply in its exploration. She cried out. Pleasure. Pure penetrating pleasure. She heard him groan with it. She pulled him by the hair and raised him to her. He kissed her deeply, and she could taste herself on his lips and tongue.

She would be working tonight, relieving Lilith as the second batch of press attended their client's opening in Circus Maximus, the main room at Caesar's Palace. Which is why they had come. Reynolds liked press junkets, even her own. He liked the attention, the mingling with names and faces known to millions but personally known to only a few. Of which he was one. It was a gala event, covered by the major media: How often does your number-one female film star return to the concert stage?

He arched his body, bridgelike over her, and his erectness teased as it touched her thigh, her stomach, her breasts. She heard him say how beautiful as he kissed her neck. He meant her. All of her. He lay on his side, facing her, his eyes taking in her entirety, loving her as his hand traced the curve of her hip.

His beard was scratchy and she pulled her face away from his embrace, fearful of a burn that might show or require more makeup than she wanted to wear. She began to cry, so quietly that he was unaware. Even now she was alone. Even in the one room of a Las Vegas hotel they had separate lives. She had come to hate tennis and golf and all those other distractions people called fun. They never talked. She had thought they would here, but talk was the one thing they had not done since their late Thursday evening arrival.

His mouth was on her breast, encircling her nipple, drawing it into his wet warmth. Again she closed her eyes and drifted into the feeling of being totally loved. To think that just three days ago she had worried about her brain, but the neurologist had pronounced her fit, as had her own doctor, who had ever so casually suggested that her pendulumlike moods might best be treated by a psychiatrist. She would have laughed except what was funny was also terribly sad.

His hands were firmly gripping her thigh. They traveled its length until they arrived at her calf, fingers probing, massaging, until they kneaded their way to her ankle, her foot and finally her toes. Each one now in his fingers, touched, caressed and . . .

His mouth, first on one toe, then two, and now all in his mouth; his tongue circling the topmost part of her sole. She whimpered, tossed, trying to escape from sensations she had never before known and which were far too pleasurable to endure.

She thought of Stacey, her beautiful Stacey, left at home so that she and Reynolds could be alone to talk of all the things that caused her pain. Now it pained her that she was here and Stacey there, and that Stacey didn't seem to mind that at all.

And now the other foot. Slowly his tongue flicked from her heel to the top of her sole, under her toes and over. And as each toe disappeared into his mouth Joanna felt herself disappearing, lost in a turbulent sea of sensations that took her further and further away.

She was always surprised at how little he asked for himself. His concern was only to make her happy. He was moving slowly within her now, his hips snaking their way in a rhythm that was slow and sensuous. His hands were everywhere, now kneading her buttocks as his mouth traveled from nipple to armpit, to neck, to ear and to nipple again. She was being consumed by him in a combination of tenderness and passion. She started to cry. Huge sobs that increased his rhythm. He was loving rather than using her . . . touching her . . . holding her. He whispered in her ear, the words unintelligible, unimportant, the feeling not. She was responding to the pressure building within her. His and hers. She could feel him growing larger, poised on the brink of explosion and yet waiting until he could sense she was there, poised with him.

His cries matched hers, but soon his stopped whereas hers continued, intensifying as he held her while she trembled and sobbed. She opened her eyes and stared at the familiar face smiling at her. His eyes questioned, but she could not answer. If only his hair had been blond instead of brown, his eyes blue instead of black, she could have told herself she had chosen another Reynolds since her own was not available, not while there was another tournament to play or a chip to gamble. But Barney Reardon was not Reynolds. He was just Barney Reardon, a member of a press junket, meeting her in yet another hotel room, this time in another city.

She could not leave the shower any more than she could stop her crying. The self-recriminations would not be washed away with the sweat. Her body ached, but not as much as that place of her she called a soul. She wanted to blame Reynolds. There had been reasons for the unexpected and unplanned afternoon encounter, but those reasons had to be confronted, not ignored. She sat on the floor of the tub, the water raining down on her, as she cried. She was holding her knees to her chest, rocking herself to and fro, when Reynolds entered.

He emerged from the bathroom wrapped in a huge white bath towel, his hair still damp and his skin shiny from both the sun of the day and the steam of the shower. He poured two glasses of chilled wine and brought one to where she lay on the bed, staring at nothing. She waited for him to sit or lie next to her. Instead, he opened the draperies and looked at the evening sky.

"Reyn, come talk to me," she said, patting the space next to her on the bed.

He looked at his watch. "You better get dressed, Jo. Your client opens in an hour."

"She'll open whether or not I'm late," she said, again making space for him by her.

"Not good for business," he said as he tickled her toes in passing, dropping the towel as he stepped into Jockey shorts.

She fell back onto the pillows, defeated, hoping only that the tears wouldn't start again. She was aware he was now watching her, an almost scowl on his face. "You're not happy, are you?" he asked. She shook her head, signifying she wasn't. "Nothing makes you happy anymore," he said bitterly.

"You could," she replied.

"I don't know how."

His voice was sad. She looked at the back facing her

and replied: "Maybe you try in the wrong ways." He turned toward her, either surprised or angered—she couldn't tell which—by her statement. "I don't need new cars or beach houses. I don't need these incessant weekends running for fun. Reyn, I just want you to be with me, for us to be together," she said, her voice imploring.

"You used to love people," he replied as he dressed, grimacing at the stiffness of his formal shirt.

"I still do, more than ever," she answered as she watched him button the antique gold cuff links she had bought for him in New York. "But they have a time, a place, in my life, and so do you."

"Joanna, don't talk in riddles or epigrams, for Chrissake. I have enough trouble understanding you these days without that," Reynolds said angrily. "The truth is, I no longer know what you want from me. Whatever it is it feels like too much or at least more than I can give."

"But Reyn, you're not listening. I want so little," she protested as she left the bed to stand behind him in order to adjust his black tie. "Only that we be together, really together." She looked at Reynolds in the mirror and had the sudden realization that what she thought was so little was exactly what he thought was too much.

"Make sense, Joanna. What are we now if not together? This is you and me in a hotel room about to have a smashing evening. This is me with you."

"Reyn, listen to me. Please. Don't get upset or excited, but just listen," Joanna began as she turned Reynolds around to face her. "We really aren't together and you're not really with me. Even when we make love you're not there—not you—and I'm certainly not."

She felt him stiffen.

"I'm not, Reyn. Not me, the person. Just the body. That's all you seem to require. But I need more. I want to be made love to. Me, Joanna, your wife. I want to love you while you're loving me."

She could see that he didn't understand. She could also see he was angry. "I just knew you would ruin things," he said as he affixed his cummerbund. "It was almost too good to be true. Three days without your bullshit."

"Reyn, I'm only asking that we talk to one another," she cried.

"You always have to dump on everything, make shit of things. I bought you a beach house, a car. Now, if I'm understanding you correctly, they don't matter. Then what does, Jo? Christ, but you would think given what you've been through you'd be thrilled to be living life, grateful we can afford the best life has to offer. Well, if you can't enjoy yourself I can. And I intend to. After all, how many shots at life do you think we get, Joanna?"

He faced her, his face purple under its tan. "Don't you understand? You weren't the only one who nearly died. It could just as easily have been my head lying in the road. But it wasn't. I'm here and I've learned, Joanna, even if you haven't, to live each day as if it were my last."

She started to respond, but he interrupted, his weeks of frustration and rage emerging in a volley of words. "Don't tell me, Joanna, because you already have more times than I care to remember. I know what you saw or think you saw. You believe in your experience. Fine. Let me believe in mine. I'm almost forty-five, Jo. For whatever time I have left, I want to live. The good times are right here, right now. I just wish you could see that."

"I do, Reyn. I guess we just have different ideas of what good times are. I'm just trying to find a place where we can meet, where we can both have what we want. Is that so bad?"

Reynolds sighed. The face he turned toward Joanna was filled with confusion. "Jo, I wish I understood, wish I could be whoever it is you think you want. But I'm just me. I know who and what I am. I've faced that and come to terms with it. But you . . . I don't know who you are anymore, but I do know you're not the woman I married. I'd like her back."

"She's gone, Reynolds," Joanna replied. "She died in a car crash over a month ago in New York City."

He threw on his jacket and was at the door when he turned to say: "It's just that kind of crazy talk that's pushing me further and further away. Dammit, Joanna, no matter what you think you didn't die. You're still here, and we all have to live with that as best we can. And I'm trying. I just wish you would, too.''

He would have crowned Joanna with the Yorkshire pudding had she been there. ''Get out of the house!'' she had argued. ''Make peace and amends,'' she had prodded. He should have listened instead to his instincts, which warned that he not accept Tony's invitation for a Thanksgiving Eve dinner. Damn Joanna and damn Tony, too! thought Dean as he continued to smile pleasantly at the person talking at him. Only he really couldn't damn Tony because it was funny. It *had* to be funny. Otherwise it was so damn sad he could cry.

As he picked at the roast beef for which Downing Square was noted, Dean admitted to the Inquiring Mind who wanted to know that it was indeed true that he was an actor. Yes, an actor despite the fact that his only current acting experience was in thirty- and sixty-second commercials.

How wonderful! It must be such a glamorous life, his dinner companion enthused. Dean looked at the bright and shiny face staring at him with unabashed interest and agreed it was indeed a glamorous life. His brother was pleased, his sister-in-law thrilled. At last he was someone about whom they could talk, even boast: the man in the TV ads who suffered with hemorrhoids and constipation.

As the waiter took their dessert orders Dean briefly contemplated asking for the house hemlock. He was still smarting from the shock and subsequent outrage. When he had first entered the restaurant his mind had automatically refused to accept the possibility that the table set for four was meant for any but three. Even when the tall, redheaded woman was standing nervously by the table, her hand extended as introductions were made, Dean preferred to think this was by chance, an accident, and certainly not a date, not a fix-up. Not for him. Not even if she had been a he was such a thing yet a possibility.

When he had risen he found himself staring into bright blue eyes that seemed incongruously sad, set as they were in a face made merry by myriad freckles. She was a woman of his age, more striking than pretty and a shade plumper than the designer of her sheath dress had intended its wearer to be. He had wondered about her presence at a family function but gradually had come to understand. He was the single male, available, at least in his brother's mind.

Her name was Edith Whyse and she was well read, amusing and nice. Recently divorced, her nervousness spoke of just how recent. For her sake Dean chewed on his anger as though it were one of the celery stalks served as an hors d'oeuvre.

The evening seemed endless. His past had been skirted as if the last years of his life hadn't happened. When she asked about anything that might have opened his private door, Tony drew the conversation to himself or to some other area he deemed safe. Often she seemed confused. She was trying, and it pained Dean that she was trying in vain. His sister-in-law, her friend, should have protected her. She was too vulnerable to be hurt.

He looked at his watch and explained the obvious gesture by speaking of his early-morning callback, his third, for a shaving-cream commercial. Like Edith, he could not understand why the advertising agency was making such a fuss about selecting one man whose face would be covered with foam.

"You seem distracted."

When he realized her words were directed at him Dean replied: "I was thinking about answering machines and how they're now the life-support systems of the day for many of us. I hate mine, particularly when it brings me no news or bad news, which in my profession is usually one and the same."

He was again thinking of Maurie Freissan's message left earlier that day. He had played it twice, as Freissan's words had hardly seemed possible. Not after the reaction he had received that day at the studio. But the message was clear. *At the Rainbow's End* had selected another actor. No further explanation. Not that there ever was.

"At least yours leaves messages."

"I beg your pardon," he replied.

He could see she was sorry she had spoken.

"What I mean . . . well, my kids live at home, with me and my mother. There's not much chance . . ."

She didn't finish her sentence. She didn't have to. He knew how it would end. Again he felt his rage rising toward Tony. This woman didn't need any further rejection, and he was about to reject her. For a moment Dean thought to take her home and explain en route why he wouldn't ask for her phone number, wouldn't be the one to leave a message on her machine. She shouldn't have to deal with a disappointment for which she was in no way responsible. She should know that his lack of interest had nothing to do with who she was.

In the street, as she was about to enter a taxi, she turned to the Di Nardos and thanked them for a lovely evening. He couldn't help noting the look on her face when he said nothing more than good-bye. As soon as the cab turned toward the bridge that would take her to Jackson Heights where she lived, Dean turned to Tony and asked: "What was going through your mind?" Tony looked stunned. "Don't ever do that to me again, Tony," Dean continued. "Not if you ever wish to see my face again. And for Chrissake, don't ever do it again to some nice woman who needs something I can't supply."

"What did I do? A small dinner . . . a foursome. What's the big deal?" Tony asked, his face red, his manner defensive.

"Tony, either deal with who I am or stay out of my life. Don't ever use me again to satisfy your misgivings. Just because you're uneasy with my sexuality doesn't mean you can wave a wand and change it."

"Dean, we just thought . . ."

"What? What did you think, Janice?" Dean demanded, turning on his sister-in-law with a vehemence that resembled vengeance.

"Just that if you met a nice woman you might like her."

He turned from them, walking briskly up the street as the wind that swept across Lexington Avenue was filled with the promise of winter, verified by the Christmas displays in the shop windows. The streets flew by as did in his mind the many times his family had denied who he was. He thought again of Joanna, the problems she herself was having with her own family, and yet she had suggested he see his. He thought of Sara and her waiting game to see if she even had a family, and he shuddered.

When he was finally at home, more exhausted by his anger than the fifty-block walk, he instantly checked his answering machine. The first was predictable: a nervous Maurie Freissan reminding him not to shave for tomorrow's interview as the advertiser wanted to see his face with a shadow. The second message startled him. Barbara Clarkson Langdon was in town and wanted to know if she could see him. No, she could not, he instantly decided. He was not interested in any postmortems. He was not prepared when the speaker of the last message announced:

Dean? This is Ralph Kayne. Sorry it didn't work out. Maybe we can put something together in the future. How about dinner one night? Give me a call. My home number is . . .

A call at home, not at the office. Dinner and not lunch. It could have only one meaning, Dean decided.

"And what if it does?" Joanna asked the following evening when she called and he relayed Kayne's message. "Call him anyway. He's a contact."

"But isn't my calling him some kind of tacit agreement to his unexpressed terms?" Dean asked.

"Oh, please, Dean. If that were the case few women would ever go out on a date," Joanna replied. "And stop confusing issues. Just because last night was a bummer doesn't mean all nights will be bad."

"Listen, Joanna Bennett. Last night wasn't just bad, it was the pits. It was so damn emasculating. You can't know—no heterosexual can—what it's like to sit at some dinner pretending to be who you're not so that no one will point some accusing finger or hide behind some contemptuous smile. It's killing. Only another gay man who's been there can understand. The feelings of inadequacy. The feelings of self-hatred because you're denying yourself, because your old feelings that yourself isn't good enough surface. And all this because you don't . . . can't do the expected—take the woman home to bed."

"You're right," said Joanna thoughtfully, "I can't understand, not fully, what you're talking about. But Dean, you don't know that that woman wanted you to take her home to bed."

"She was there, wasn't she? She came to meet a man."

"And she met one," Joanna replied. "Maybe not the right one for her, but Dean, that woman will go through dozens of such dinners before she meets a man she likes. But she'll go because she's learned it's a damn sight better than staying home alone and feeling sorry for herself."

"Dammit, Joanna, I'm not feeling sorry for myself."

"The hell you're not. Listen, Dean, you've been cooped up in that house for weeks . . . months. It's time to get out. If Chris were alive he'd say the same thing. He would want you eventually to meet somebody."

"What makes you so certain?" asked Dean. "Are you now receiving messages from the beyond?"

"Don't be a *putz.* Just answer me this. If it had been you who had died wouldn't you want Chris to get out . . . date?"

"Are you kidding? Hell, no. I'd want him to build me a fucking shrine and wear black the rest of his life."

"So much for you and unselfish love. Now what about Chris?" Joanna asked.

"Chris was a goddamn saint. I'm not. If I were the one who was dead I'd want him to suffer," Dean replied.

"Wonderful! Very giving of you. But I suppose, sick as what you just espoused is, I suppose it's a helluva lot better than being faithful to someone's memory out of some feeling of guilt," Joanna countered.

"God. Where do you get this crap? Faithful to someone's memory out of some feeling of guilt. It's got to be the air in Los Angeles. It makes everyone talk funny."

"Well, are you going to call Ralph Kayne or not?" Joanna demanded.

"How about I just place an ad in *Screw* magazine instead?"

"Dean, dinner with a producer can be nothing more

than that, you know. Out here it's part of the game. Acting roles are often won over the gazpacho."

"Say good-bye, Joanna, because I'm hanging up," said Dean. "Sometimes I wonder why I bother. Why should I expect anything reasonable from someone who makes heaven seem like Oz and God like the wizard?"

"Dean, do you intend to stay chaste the rest of your life?" Joanna asked. "I'm not suggesting that you tumble into bed with anyone before you're ready, but I am saying you should be open to meeting people."

"Thank you and good-bye, Ann Landers," said Dean as he hung up the telephone. The phone rang immediately. It was Maurie Freissan, announcing it was down to three possibilities of which he was one. They were talking a two-year exclusive contract if he were selected. Two years of playing a drill instructor teaching his recruits about a new shaving cream called About Face. Dean had his doubts. Would his face, if it were that closely identified with a product, be unacceptable to legitimate producers of stage and film seeking new actors? Since he didn't know, Dean realized only a producer would and decided to call one.

At least Dean had been honest, thought Sara. When invited to Thanksgiving dinner he had declined, stating that his presence would only verify how little they each had to celebrate. She had hoped he would change his mind so that neither she nor he would be alone, which was how she felt in the midst of her family. As she watched her children fight over drumsticks and wings, Sara thought how motherhood is the loneliest profession. A mother tends to her brood, but when does the brood tend to its mother? Her children knew nothing of their parents' difficulties. They preferred it that way. They wouldn't acknowledge anything that might jeopardize their sense of well-being. That they were egocentric little beings, selfish and insensitive, angered and annoyed Sara. Unlike what she had always thought, they weren't there for her.

As she forced a forkful of salad into her mouth Sara gazed at Stefan across the table. His eyes were blank, devoid of life; a dead person sharing the head of the table with her. From his weight loss his cheeks were sunken, and the effect was to make him look very old and terribly young at the same time.

It was the Valium, Sara decided. It calmed his anxiety, but it increased his depression. She would speak to the doctor. Perhaps the medication could be altered. Now that they knew definitely there was nothing wrong with Stefan's heart or any of his vital organs, they could experiment with medications to alleviate the stress they felt he was under.

They had prescribed nothing for her stress. They had ignored it. And added to it with their whispered warnings. He must have rest. He must avoid stress. He must have quiet around him. Her husband, they maintained, was suffering from depression and anxiety. What of her own? she had wanted to scream. They would not have cared. They were like her children: oblivious. As Stefan was oblivious, locked as he was within his own pain. He was a stranger, growing stranger each day.

The food in her stomach was suddenly threatened by eviction. Sara rushed from the table into the kitchen. As she sat on a kitchen chair, her head between her knees to quell the queasiness, she wondered what kind of a Thanksgiving Denise Wolfe was having. Sara suspected it was as empty as her own and was surprised that the thought gave her no pleasure.

Stefan never spoke of Denise Wolfe, but then Stefan seldom spoke, at least not in words. Only in the whimpers that punctuated his sleep. They were far worse than any words he might have spoken. During the day he sat about the den, trying to focus on journals and periodicals that seemed to exhaust him. His presence indicted her. She was guilty, although she didn't know exactly of what.

"Sara, what is it?"

The hand resting on her shoulder was Ina's. She patted it reassuringly and was about to rise from her chair when the dizziness again attacked. "Sara, speak to me," Ina demanded. "Is it Stefan? Have you told me everything? Is it something more serious than his nerves?"

"Yes, dammit, it's my nerves!" Sara exploded. "Me, your sister. You do remember her, don't you? She's the one whose marriage is coming apart."

"Don't say that!" Ina gasped as she grabbed the sink for support. "Don't even think it. Whatever is wrong can be repaired. You're just tired. It's to be expected. The strain . . . illness does terrible things to a marriage.''

''Ina, Stefan has another woman,'' Sara all but shouted.

''I don't want to hear it. You don't either,'' Ina said, turning her back on Sara. ''It never happened. He's here, you're here, I'm here, the children are here. I don't see anybody else so there can't be anyone else.''

''Ina, there is. I've met her. She exists,'' Sara pleaded.

''Sara, lots of other women exist in husbands' lives. Wives ignore them. They go on with their marriages and pretend. Who's perfect? You? Me? Don't go crazy on me, Sara. You don't know what it's like to be alone. You don't know,'' Ina repeated.

''I don't?'' Sara replied with a half-laugh. ''Then what have the last two months been about?''

''Nothing. That's what they've been about . . . nothing. Sara, don't make problems for yourself,'' Ina warned. ''Listen to me. I know.''

''He cries in his sleep, Ina. He's so unhappy. You only have to look at him to see that. Maybe if he left he would feel better.''

''Sara, it'll pass,'' Ina pleaded.

''Will it? I wonder. I wonder all the time. It's like living with an ax over your head . . . waiting for the other shoe to drop. I don't think I can take it anymore, Ina.''

''You're going to do something you'll regret the rest of your life,'' Ina warned through clenched teeth when she could finally speak. ''Don't be a fool, Sara. Forgive. Forget.''

But she couldn't forget, and later that evening, after Ina and her children had departed and her own were watching television, Sara dried the last of the dishes and then began a slow walk to the den. She had organized her thoughts and knew exactly what she was about to do.

She knocked at his door and waited. When there was no response she entered to find Stefan asleep, the light by the sofa bed softly illuminating the shadowed room. As she stood looking down at him Stefan awoke with a start, clutching the covers to him as he stared at her apprehensively. His gesture, the sheet pulled to his chest as if he were defending himself against her unnatural needs, made her feel ugly. Stefan's eyes searched and found the clock.

It was not, his expression said, an unreasonable hour, after all. He could not wage that argument.

"I'm sorry," Sara began, not knowing where to seat herself or even if she should. "But I have an idea and I want to discuss it with you. Stefan, how would you feel about our going into couple counseling?"

She thought she saw terror in his eyes. "I really think it's not a bad idea if we saw someone professionally," she continued, trying to speak above the noise of her heart pounding. "It just might clarify things. I mean . . . you haven't left, so that must mean you're here in the house for some reason. But whatever that reason is, it doesn't seem to make you happy. And it's so hard living with someone who's always depressed."

"Yes, I know," he said as he looked straight at her. "I've been there. For years."

"Well, since you know the difficulty, then help me," Sara said. "Let's try to make some sense of this. We need help. You need someone to talk to who is not me or . . . someone like me," Sara added, her voice failing.

"Sara, I'm a private person. This isn't something I want to do."

"You must, Stefan. Otherwise . . ."

"Otherwise what, Sara?" he interrupted, his voice tired.

"Otherwise it might be best if you moved out . . . for a while," she added, terrified by what she had just said. She stood alone in the room thinking that any moment her life would end, that either Stefan would walk out the door or her heart would walk through her chest. Or both. Neither happened. Nothing happened at all. Her words hung there as if waiting for someone to retrieve or claim them. Sara continued in a less assured manner: "Stefan, it's time to find out what you want so we can all get on with our lives."

Stefan lay back in his bed, drawing the covers to his neck as he turned on his side away from her. As she opened the door to the hallway the only sound beside her own heart beating was that of a man crying as he lay bundled in a ball in his bed.

NINE

As Joanna lay on the cool leather of the chaise she saw through closed eyes the beginnings—just the traces—of the Light. She tried to draw it near as she spoke to him of It, of Its love, the love she couldn't duplicate in her life, although she tried. One love, *Its* love, made her joyous: the other, unspeakably sad, she explained. He did not respond, but then he had not responded from the moment she began speaking what seemed like hours ago.

She had not cried. She had not come to him for that. But then she had not come to discuss the Light but the darkness, as she referred to her life at home and at the office. Nor was it the headaches and the nausea, for which medical specialists could find no cause but which she suspected were symptoms of some undetected brain damage, that concerned her. No, she had come to discuss her family, as it was her disintegrating relationships with her husband and daughter that troubled her.

Perhaps disintegrating was the wrong word, she admitted, as it denoted the existence of something that was now rotting away. She was no longer certain if she had ever had a relationship with Stacey. She paused, trying to collect her feelings about her child/woman daughter. She smiled, remembering how beautiful Stacey had looked the day of the fashion show, but the smile vanished when she spoke of the lunch, canceled today, as Stacey pleaded last-minute Christmas shopping to complete. Another hand she had extended had been slapped when all she had wanted was a touch. Stacey disallowed that, and often she now felt as if she were paying for some unknown crime she had committed against her own daughter.

The crime of neglect perhaps, she suggested, although it hadn't been intended, even recognized until recently. Now she missed not the years but the child within those years who had become a woman. Stacey had been there; she had not. Now, despite her search, she couldn't find what she had once lost because Stacey made it clear she didn't wish to be found.

Emotion made further words impossible. She was losing her husband, too, she said as soon as she could begin again. They were talking without hearing, making love without loving. Their distance was new, evident only since the accident, since her encounter with dying and the Light, which she could almost see when she squeezed shut her eyes and concentrated on that space between them.

Her eyes flickered open. She felt exhausted, and instead of relieved she was tense. She wondered what the doctor was gleaning from the notes he was now reading that he hadn't received when she was speaking.

His brow was furrowed as he began. "I feel what we have here is an early interrupted relationship with your mother."

She laughed.

He looked at her curiously.

"I didn't come here to discuss my mother," she explained. "She is not the problem."

"I wonder that you can be so sure," the doctor said calmly. "You describe a light, a light that is . . . how did you put it?" the doctor asked as he flipped through the pages of his notebook to quote Joanna directly. "Yes . . . 'a warm, wonderful loving light in which I felt total peace and a self filled with love and acceptance.'

"Mrs. Bennett," the doctor continued, his voice assured, "this is how an infant feels at its mother's breast, basking in the *light* of her love. Ask yourself: Can there be any brighter light or any greater sense of safety and love for a child?"

"I am not a child, doctor," Joanna replied, her voice reflecting her annoyance.

"Not chronologically, but emotionally we may have another story. Mrs. Bennett, what you describe is an adult seeking to be a child basking in her mother's love again.

Don't look so distressed. Many search all their lives to recapture the infantile feelings you describe. In lovers, mates, even employers. This search is of course an unconscious one. In your case the accident, its accompanying trauma, brought your fantasy to consciousness. Perhaps you find your current world unsafe. Perhaps you suffered an untimely emotional separation from your mother as an infant. There are many reasons we can explore for your having brought this fantasy to consciousness at this time in your life. How old did you say you were?''

Joanna sighed. ''Dr. Kossak, I came here for help with my primary relationships. Instead, I find we are talking or, more precisely, *you* are talking—if I may be so bold—bullshit about my mother. This is ridiculous.''

''Perhaps not as ridiculous as you think, Mrs. Bennett,'' the doctor countered, ''as from your hostile tone I would say we have touched some sensitive chord. I understand. Think how rageful you as an infant must have felt when your mother told you, not in words of course but in emotional signals more traumatic than words, that you must leave the light. And before you were strong enough to make one of your own. This is a terrible trauma for a child to suffer.''

''I doubt if it was nearly as terrible as the trauma I'm now suffering listening to this,'' Joanna said as she collected herself.

The psychiatrist shrugged. ''I offer interpretations that you are free to accept or reject. It may be, Mrs. Bennett, that analysis is not the approach you seek for the solution to your problems. Unfortunately your time is up. If you wish we can schedule another appointment to discuss whether or not you feel you are a candidate for the analytic approach.''

''I think not,'' said Joanna as she wrote her check for the doctor's $120-per-session fee. His face remained impassive as he took the check, only his slight nod signifying that their relationship was now concluded. At the door Joanna said neither thank you nor good-bye as she left. She felt cheated and for a moment thought to stop payment on the check, even though the money was meaningless to her. In the street, as she walked toward her car, her knees felt weak. Nausea again attacked.

She looked at her watch. It was shortly before noon, the time she had been scheduled to lunch with Stacey. Her head throbbed and she had to hold on to the car door for support as she opened it.

Beverly Hills was crowded with holiday shoppers, all of whom Joanna felt to be an irritation. She drove slowly, not certain where to go. The house would be empty, emptier than it now normally was even when Reynolds and Stacey were home. She couldn't face that. Nor could she face the office, once a sanctuary, now a prison. She felt a moment's panic when she realized she had no place to go, no place to be.

At the first gas station she called Lilith on her private line. She was there, miraculously free for a lunch Joanna knew she would not eat. Lilith suggested Colette's, which Joanna declined, knowing there were certain to be people from the industry there, people she most definitely did not want to see. She also rejected Bis Tango, as it was too near the office. Then she remembered the Saratoga, an intimate neighborhood restaurant on Sunset just east of Fairfax. Nobody she knew or who knew her dined there. They agreed to meet in fifteen minutes.

Lilith was waiting when she entered, her hands nervously playing with the half-empty Perrier bottle on the table before her. Her face scrutinized Joanna's openly. Joanna's shrug admitted she had known better days. Lilith signaled the waiter and ordered Joanna's customary lunchtime sherry. She then drew the curtains about the booth, giving them the feel of total privacy.

Joanna began to shake. Lilith took her hands in her own, trying to infuse warmth into the chilled fingers. "I'm going to cry," Joanna said, aghast, terrified of making a scene in a public place. The waiter arrived with the sherry, which Lilith took as she dismissed him with a flick of her wrist. She put the drink to Joanna's lips. Joanna sipped and then gagged. "I'm all messed up, Lilith," she said as tears trickled down her face. "I can't seem to make sense of things."

Lilith waited, knowing her hands holding Joanna's were

the only words necessary. "I don't know where to begin," Joanna said, knowing an explanation was necessary. "It's just so hard to repeat all of this."

But she did, slowly and painstakingly, with her eyes never leaving Lilith's face, needing to see that Lilith was not only hearing but not judging. She began with the accident, moving quickly to her death, lingering only to explain her feelings in the Light. Her tears renewed themselves when she spoke of both Reynolds and Stacey, their reactions and her inability to make contact with them. She did not exclude Barney Reardon or her difficulties at work.

When Joanna finished Lilith was staring into space. "Yours isn't the first time I've heard this story. My mother," she quickly explained when she saw Joanna's startled expression. "After her heart attack six years ago. She, too, talked of having 'crossed over,' as she puts it."

"Did she see the Light?" Joanna asked.

"Yes, and her past. Saw it all, she claims, in less than a second. 'Lilith, my life passed before my eyes, and it didn't seem like it was enough so I came back.' I remember her saying that as if it were yesterday. Of course I thought she was bonkers, and she is. My mother was always a nut case. The only thing her nearly dying changed was her lifestyle. Now, instead of running off to play the slots in Reno and Tahoe, she's visiting every psychic and trance medium she can find. She's really the one you should talk to about this. She'll be down from Fresno for the holidays. You'll like her. She's a terrific ole gal, although now that I think of it, I didn't always think so. Particularly after her near-death experience. She drove me crazy with her affection and her well-meant but nonetheless annoying desire to live my life. My mother was intent on saving me. Her actions made me very resentful."

"But why?"

Lilith was silent, considering a question she obviously had not asked herself. "I think I felt left out. Suddenly my mother was in some other place . . . gone. And she went without asking. She was no longer dependent, no longer the person I knew. She had upset the apple cart, the normal balance of things between us."

"Do you think Reynolds or Stacey has similar feelings?" Joanna asked.

"Well, it is possible," Lilith replied. "I mean . . . Joanna, you've had one helluvan experience, one precious few will ever or can ever share. Look at me. I hear you, but I can't really identify with one word you're saying. But I'm living with and through your changes, and I'm not going to pretend I don't resent them or that I'm not threatened. Sometimes I feel as if you're rejecting me. And I'm just your partner and friend. If I'm reacting in such a manner think of how Reynolds and Stacey might feel. They've not only been left out of your experience but left behind. You're suddenly someplace else and they can't be there, although you'd like them to be. It's like an invisible wall has been erected."

"I'm trying to break through that wall, but no one will let me," Joanna cried, exasperated, "particularly Stacey."

"Having two teenage daughters of my own, I don't know what to say. Sometimes I think between the ages of twelve and twenty aliens take over our children's bodies. Certainly they don't speak the same language. Their values are different. They're really nothing more than strangers who live in your refrigerator and on your telephone, acting as if you're the one who's weird and that they're some higher form of intelligence.

"Stacey is an odd one. Always was," Lilith continued. "She's too young to be so old and too old to be so young. She's a problem, more so now because you've done it again."

"Done what again?" Joanna asked, confused.

"Ten years ago you left her to develop a life of your own. Which you did, making it very clear that she was not the sun around which your life revolved. If she's anything like my kids, she resented that. Now, by dying and finding yet another life, you've left her again."

"But I haven't," Joanna protested. "I'm here for her. And she needs me. The child is floundering, but anything I suggest she rejects."

"Typical teenage behavior," Lilith suggested.

"Sometimes I think she hates me," Joanna continued

as she pointed the waiter toward her empty glass, signifying that another sherry was desired whereas lunch was not. "But why? She was never neglected. She had the best schools, the best clothes, even her own car. She's not wanted for anything."

"Joanna, are you listening to yourself?" Lilith asked. "Minutes ago you were talking about your relationship with Reynolds and how unsatisfying it is because he gives you *things* instead of himself. The similarity is so striking."

"Except I'm not a child who can't ask for what she wants," Joanna countered. "I've asked. I've said it's not cars and houses that I want but a feeling."

"Joanna, have you ever thought that maybe this is how Reynolds gives, that it may be the only way he knows how to give? Just as the schools and the clothes and the car were the only ways you once could give to Stacey. Have you ever considered the pleasure and the peace of mind it might give Reynolds to do these things for you when he instinctively knows he can't give you what you've received from some wacko experience with which he can in no way compete? And Jesus, Joanna, what of his own wacko experience? This man has gone through his own life-and-death experience and where were you? He's had to go it alone, and from what you tell me I think he's still reacting to the accident. He's grabbing at life. He's faced a fact we all deny: that he's going to die one day. Doctor or no doctor, that little bit of news has to scare him shitless. After all, he hasn't lived through his own death. He hasn't seen the light. And to some extent neither have you. If you had, you would know who Reynolds is. Joanna, you married the man, so only you can know if you're now asking for more than the man is or ever was."

Her mind drifted as Lilith turned to the menu and the task of ordering her lunch. She could only remember a golden god who commanded attention wherever he was, wherever they were together. She was noticed. Even her mother had thought she had done something wonderful when she had first brought him home. Finally an accomplishment of which her parents were proud. It seemed then people were always smiling at her, at them. In movies, at the theatre. She remembered her excitement. Which dress to wear, what shoes. The subsequent necking that would result in limited petting. His clothes were always impeccable, the restaurants they frequented first-class. He was fun, attentive and generous. He was all the things any girl of the 1960s could want. All the *things*.

They had never talked. They had married instead. Once they moved to glorious Southern California, it and the life she had found herself suddenly living had consumed and blinded her. Like kids in Disneyland they had played, enjoying the "rides" until Stacey was born. And suddenly Stacey had his attention. Suddenly Stacey commanded the smiles, and she was no longer standing in his glow. Which was why she had taken work with Lilith: to compete with the women in his life, be it Stacey or someone older who was interesting and exciting.

She was chilled and not just the least bit frightened. "Lilith, I'm going home now," she announced, surprising both Lilith and herself with the suddenness of her decision.

"Are you all right?" Lilith asked as she looked up from the salad that had just been placed before her.

"No," Joanna said slowly. "But you were just wonderful. Thanks for being there for me. And I'm sorry about leaving, but I can't face the office. Not today. And Lil, I think we should find that Prince Charles fellow we were discussing and hire him."

"Joanna," Lilith said as Joanna rose, "don't forget my mother."

But Joanna was gone, rushing toward her car, her head throbbing with questions about herself, who she had once been and why that person seemed even more remote to her than the boy she had married. As she swiftly drove the Sunset Strip toward Beverly Hills her mother came to mind. She was considering Dr. Kossak's words and rejected them as she inwardly felt their falsity. Her mother was not the light. Her mother had never been nurturing or accepting. It was not her nature. And she had never felt close to her mother, only separate. Her mother's very being was about accomplishment. She competed with her husband. And she had lived in her parents' shadows, in emotional darkness, not knowing there was a light in which she could glow until she met Reynolds. No wonder she had married him. No wonder she had finally felt happy and fulfilled.

Had she done to Stacey what her mother had done to her? Joanna wondered as she entered the house on North Canon Drive through its rear entrance. To an extent Lilith had been right. She had given Stacey every*thing* but the one thing her daughter had needed the most: herself. She had denied Stacey her convictions, mainly because she hadn't had any.

Joanna started to shake as she remembered when communication between the two had truly ceased. At the time when Stacey had become sexually active. They had talked then but not communicated. Instead, she, Stacey's mother, had spoken of precautions, of methods to control conception, of all the wrong things and never of the issue of a fifteen-year-old child, *her* child, having sexual relations. But of course she couldn't speak to Stacey about sex, Joanna now realized. How could she when her own feelings on the subject were so confused? She had finally accepted the truth about Reynolds and his occasional affairs and had just begun her own. If she looked at Stacey's behavior, then she had to look at Reynolds's, and worst of all at her own. She had been dishonest, as much with herself as with Stacey.

Tired, Joanna slowly climbed the stairs thinking of a warm bath and a nap. The evening was hers, as Reynolds was doing his filial duty that night by having a pre-Christmas dinner with his father, a chore from which she was spared. The door to Stacey's room was open, and it was the shaft of light streaming in from the bedroom window and falling at her feet on the hallway carpet that made Joanna nostalgic. So many years ago it was exactly at this hour that Joanna would watch Stacey waking from her afternoon nap. She would be humming as she played with her fingers or toes, waiting patiently for Joanna to come to her. And when she did, Joanna recalled, how often she would snuggle next to Stacey, feeling her after-sleep warmth and that smell that if bottled could only be called *Childlike.* But now Stacey hardly ever slept, let alone napped, particularly at this hour. Which is what made it seem so strange seeing her now in bed, a sheet barely covering her nakedness and not at all covering that of the man next to her.

Joanna stifled a cry. She stood in the doorway, trying to catch her breath and the thoughts that were leaping about unchecked. Don't panic, she cautioned herself. Don't overreact. Of course Stacey slept with men. But in *my* house? she asked. On an afternoon when she had begged off from lunch because of Christmas shopping? Was this a usual rather than an unusual occurrence while she was at work and Stacey was supposedly at school?

She positioned herself at the foot of the bed, trying not to look at the proprietary way in which the man—and now that she was closer she could see he was man rather than boy—was holding her daughter.

"Stacey!"

A moan, eyes fluttering open. Shock.

"I want him out of here. Now!" Joanna commanded.

The man looked from Joanna to Stacey to make a connection.

"You heard me," Joanna said to him. "Out. Now."

He stepped out of bed and into his jeans, at no time turning his back to Joanna.

"Get out of my room," Stacey demanded. "You have no right to barge in here."

"The fact that this is my house and I am your mother gives me every right," Joanna replied angrily.

"Then I'll leave," Stacey said as she leaped from the bed.

"He goes; you stay," Joanna said, her voice controlled and icy.

"No way," Stacey replied as she grabbed a handful of clothes from the floor by the side of the bed and began to dress. Joanna yanked the blouse from her and pushed Stacey back onto the bed. She then turned to the man who was dispassionately watching the scene playing itself before him, waiting to see if his cue was to go or stay. Joanna answered his dilemma. "If you're not out of here in ten seconds I'll call the police. She's not yet eighteen, in case you didn't know."

"I know," the man said, and moved as Stacey did; he for the door, she for the hand that was holding the telephone. Both were stunned when Joanna dropped the phone and slapped Stacey's face. The man was down the hallway steps and out the door at the same time Stacey locked herself in her bathroom. Joanna pounded on the door, insisting to be heard. "You and I have some talking to do, Stacey, and if you're wise, you'll do some heavy thinking before dinner."

"I won't be there," was the response.

"I suggest you reconsider unless you're prepared to live somewhere else real soon," Joanna said calmly. "Six o'clock, Stacey. And don't be late. You and I have enough lost time to make up for."

Of course she arrived late, as if by doing so she was regaining some kind of control. She sat at the table, her eyes swollen and her face pale. Whenever possible, she avoided Joanna's gaze. "OK, Mother, it's your scene, play it," she said finally.

"You lied to me, and I want you to know that hurts," Joanna began.

"I didn't lie. I was Christmas shopping," Stacey replied. "I came back here to drop off the gifts, and one thing led to another."

"So I observed," Joanna said dryly. "And just how often has one thing led to another in this house?"

"Oh, Christ, Mother. What difference? Ask me something important. Or tell me what the hell you want from me."

"First that you change your tone when you talk to me," Joanna replied, trying to remain calm. "Like it or not, Stacey, I'm your mother, and I insist on being treated with respect whether or not you think I deserve it. Second: Get that martyred look off your face. This isn't the Inquisition. It's a talk. I'm trying to reach you, Stacey, to understand, even to be there for you."

"A little late, don't you think?" Stacey asked sarcastically.

"Well, they say better late than never," Joanna replied. "Look, you won't like this, but I have to make some changes around here. From now on I want to know where you are and where you are going, and with whom, at all times. I expect you home by ten on weeknights and by two on weekends. And no drugs and no sex are to take place in this house."

"I'm not sure Dad is going to like that, Mother," Stacey said, looking amused.

"Also," Joanna continued, undeterred by Stacey's manner, "from now on I want to meet your dates."

"Why? So you can judge them as you have passed judgment on everything else in my life? Forget it, Mother. It's a waste of both our time. My dates wouldn't measure up to your expectations. How could they, when I don't?"

"It's just that I want so much for you," Joanna tried to explain.

"Oh, no, Mother. Not for me. But for you. You want me to be another one of your awards, something that also says Tiffany's. But I can't be that. I'm just me. So let *me* live my life. Don't try to run or ruin it."

"Stacey, why do you dislike me so?" Joanna asked, deciding dinner, no matter how dry it got sitting in the oven, could wait. "It's all right, Stacey. You can tell me," Joanna said when she saw Stacey looking at her warily. "I won't say I will have heard worse in my life because I probably haven't. Particularly since it's coming from my own daughter."

Stacey shrugged and then closed her eyes. For a moment Joanna thought she might even put her hands to her ears.

"All right, then why don't I begin by telling what it is about you that I don't like?"

Stacey's eyes opened.

"You're dishonest, but then we've already covered that. And you manipulate people who are weaker than you. Like your father, and yes, when it comes to dealing with you, he is the weaker. You're sarcastic, insensitive and hostile. You have brains you refuse to use and looks you use to use others. Only guess what? They use you. Should I go on?"

"There's more?" Stacey asked, looking suddenly as if she had been punched in the stomach.

"I hate the way you treat me. I deserve better," Joanna continued.

"But you don't," Stacey spat out. "You're plastic. Your values are strictly Rodeo Drive. You care more about being the goddamn Tiffany of public relations than you do about being my mother. You're never home, and when you are, it's like you're doing us some great big favor."

"What else?" Joanna asked, almost relieved to be hearing what she had long suspected to be Stacey's true feelings.

"You're self-centered. Everything revolves around you. It's obvious why you only had one child. You just hate to be inconvenienced. God forbid you should muss your hair or smear your makeup. It must kill you that I'm so much younger and prettier. But then you never liked me."

"But I always loved you, and that's even better," Joanna countered.

"How can you love someone you don't like?" Stacey asked, her bruised feelings showing.

"I never said I didn't like you," Joanna explained. "I mentioned those things about you that I find dislikable. There's a difference." And then noting the expression that continued to hover over Stacey's face, Joanna asked: "Should I now tell you what I do like about you?"

Stacey shrugged as if to say it would make no difference, when Joanna could see that it would.

"I like the way you laugh from deep within you when you're amused or happy. And I love the energy and the joy you bring to dancing. It says something about who you are, and how you are. I like the spirit with which you compete at tennis, the way you like to win. I even like the fact that you'll fight with me. Yes, I do," Joanna added when she saw the surprised expression on Stacey's face. "It's just your methods of fighting I find reprehensible. I wish you would fight more for yourself than against me."

"And what's that supposed to mean?" Stacey asked defensively as she crumpled a seeded roll and began to pick at its pieces.

"That there is a difference between going for what you want and going against another's wishes," Joanna explained.

"Bullshit. Why can't you be honest and just admit you hate the fact I'm growing up and that you can't control me any longer?"

"I doubt if I ever controlled you," Joanna replied, "and I think now I should have because you certainly haven't learned how to control yourself. Stacey, I wouldn't have a problem with your growing up if I felt you truly were. But your actions say otherwise."

Joanna stopped, not wanting her words to become a tirade. Softly she asked: "Stacey, do you ever give a thought to your life and what you're doing with it?"

"By that, of course, you mean do I think about finishing school and then going on to college."

"Yes, I suppose so. And why not? Want something from life," Joanna encouraged. "You're entitled. Prize yourself, Stacey. Don't sell yourself so cheaply."

"Which is your indirect way of saying that's what I'm doing when I sleep with a man," Stacey said accusingly.

"I'm not against sex, Stace. I'm just saying you don't have to, or *shouldn't have* to, sleep with a man just so he will pay attention to you. Or to enhance your feelings of self-worth."

"How about of being loved?" Stacey challenged.

"But you are loved, Stacey. God, how you are loved! And not just by me but by . . ."

"Don't say it," Stacey commanded, interrupting. "You embarrass me when you come on like one of those ridiculous TV evangelists."

"I was about to say . . . not just by me but by your father, but since you brought it up, yes, by God, too," Joanna replied testily.

Stacey groaned.

"I understand you find it difficult to accept what happened to me," Joanna began. "Perhaps you even feel excluded or rejected by it."

"How about getting to the truth of it? I think you're nuts," Stacey interrupted.

"Stacey, I really would like you to understand that my experience was real, at least it was real to me. But if you can't that's OK. I won't jam it down your throat anymore. But don't put a gag in mine. Let me be who I am, and as much as it is possible for me, *your mother,* I'll do the same for you."

"Don't you think giving me a curfew and putting tabs on my whereabouts is stuffing a gag in my mouth? Sometimes, Mother, you are so full of shit."

"Stacey!"

"Please. All this talk of my selling out cheaply, of sleeping with a man so he'll pay attention to me. Did you ever think to ask whether I might be in love?" Stacey asked angrily.

"You're only seventeen," Joanna said in both defense and protest.

"So? Have you now established some kind of age requirement?" Stacey challenged.

Joanna took a deep breath and asked: "Are you in love with this man?"

"Yes . . . I think so."

"So he was the father," Joanna mused.

Stacey looked confused.

"Of the child you aborted," Joanna explained.

"You just put one and one together and got two, but it may be the wrong answer," Stacey replied.

"He wasn't the father?" Joanna asked, trying to comprehend.

"I don't know. I'm not certain," Stacey replied.

"For God's sake, Stacey, then how can you say you love him?" Joanna yelled despite her determination to remain calm and nonjudgmental. "That was only a few months ago. You can't be sleeping around with Lord knows how many and then turn around and claim to be in love with only one."

"Really?" Stacey said sarcastically. "Then you better quick talk to Dad about that, Mother, or is it possible you haven't heard the stories?"

Joanna looked at the cruelty, heard it, but did not know how to respond.

"Not that I blame him," Stacey continued, not bothered by the expression on Joanna's face. "You know, Mother, you really should clean up your own life before you interfere in mine. Maybe then I could take you a lot more seriously."

* * *

Weekends were always the worst. Although there was the occasional but rare audition, normally Saturdays dragged into Sundays with nothing to do but creatively fill time. Which was particularly difficult in December, the season to be jolly.

Perhaps now is the time to visit Joanna, Dean thought as he dressed for a dinner engagement he did not want to keep. In Los Angeles he would not only be out of the house but out of a life he now had to put behind him. His ribs had healed, but he hadn't. But Joanna had not offered as she talked of a first Christmas in Malibu, and so he was faced with spending the holiday alone. Unless he went to Sara. Also not likely as Sara still had Stefan at home, babylike in his demands and moods. He really didn't wish to be subjected to that, Dean thought as the telephone rang.

It was nearing eight, late for Ralph Kayne to be canceling dinner, but a possibility considering how twice before Kayne had postponed at the last minute due to problems at the studio. He would not mind if that were the case. In fact, he would be relieved. His questions could wait, particularly since he had not heard a word about the shaving-cream commercial in ten days. About Face, it seemed, had done exactly that in their interest in him.

It was not Kayne but his brother Tony, inviting him to Christmas dinner. With the family. It was a kind gesture, yet Dean felt reluctant to accept since he had not heard from his father since his one visit to the hospital. He also knew the invitation would not have been offered if Chris were still alive. Experience had taught him that. And so he declined, saying he had already accepted another engagement.

Suddenly what he would or would not wear to dinner seemed totally unimportant. He wasn't out to impress or attract, thought Dean as he reached for an old but serviceable blazer to wear over the blue button-down oxford shirt he had chosen. He had been shocked when Kayne suggested they meet at the Ginger Man. It was the one restaurant he and Chris had frequented, as it was near Lincoln Center where so many of the activities they enjoyed took place. He had suggested the Slate instead, knowing it would be without memories that would make an already difficult evening worse.

Kayne was seated at a banquette table, his back to the exposed brick wall, when Dean arrived. His face was buried in a massive script, read through glasses that were perched precariously on the edge of his nose. It surprised Dean to see the beginnings of a bald spot on the back of Kayne's full head of hair. As Dean approached the table Kayne, as if with a sixth sense, put down the script and removed his glasses, rising to greet Dean with an outstretched hand. He was smiling warmly, a gesture that made him look exceedingly young. He is still an attractive man, made more so by an assurance that wasn't there when they were younger, thought Dean as he seated himself opposite Kayne at the table.

They chatted over drinks, and predictably Kayne spoke of New London, waxing nostalgic over their seasons of stock as if they had been glorious days, which Dean imagined they were when viewed from Kayne's current professional position. But to him they were but a painful reminder and an embarrassment.

Away from the studio Dean noticed Kayne was less the cheerleader and more low-keyed, which Kayne explained through yawns of exhaustion rather than boredom. "When you're doing two hundred and sixty hour-long shows per year, twelve hours a day, often six days a week, it takes a lot of psyching to maintain the level of enthusiasm necessary to keep a long-running show fresh."

"Ralph, why didn't I get the role?" Dean asked, surprising himself as much as Kayne with his bluntness.

"I'm glad you asked. The question has been hanging there from the moment you sat down," Kayne replied, not looking the least discomforted by Dean's invasion. "It was a joint decision, and that's not a copout. I am the producer, but I have a casting director and a head writer with whom these decisions are made."

"I thought I was good," Dean said.

"You were," Kayne replied as he pushed his half-eaten entrée to the side where the waiter could take it. "But good wasn't good enough when someone else proved to be better.''

''Swell. Now neither one of us feels like eating,'' said Dean as he placed his utensils on his plate. ''You could have lied. I'd be a helluva lot happier hearing you cast younger or older, or even a different color. But better? Shit. I don't need that.''

''If it helps any,'' said Kayne as he ordered coffee but declined dessert, ''I wanted you for that role. Your résumé made it clear things haven't exactly been easy for you. Frankly, I was surprised. You showed a lot of promise in New London. But my hands were tied. This isn't stock, and roles don't go to friends past or present, not if I want to maintain a certain level of excellence in my work. The guy we hired is your age but brand-new to the business. He's going to explode. Hollywood will grab him from us in two years because he's got the magic.''

''And I don't,'' said Dean, his voice filled with resentment.

Kayne replied softly: ''You were good, Dean, and I'd test you again in a minute if something else came up.''

''But the truth remains, I wasn't magic,'' Dean pressed.

''For Chrissake, Dean, face up,'' Kayne said impatiently. ''Don't you think if there was magic you'd have made it by now?''

''I laid off for eight years,'' Dean replied defensively.

''And what about the eight before that?'' Kayne persisted, matching Dean's stare. ''Dean, I'm not trying to crush you, but c'mon. Be real. Most careers have happened by your age. That doesn't mean you're not good. It doesn't even mean that you won't still make it. But it will be by hard work and a few breaks rather than any magic. It's no big deal. And listen, you want to start working more? You're hitting that age where you should be thinking about character work. Making that transition will broaden your possibilities.''

''I really hate this conversation,'' said Dean as he played with the spoon in his coffee.

''Sorry,'' said Kayne as he shrugged his shoulders.

''Don't be. Even though I'm acting like a shit, I'm grateful for your honesty. You're right in what you say. I just hate your being so right,'' Dean said, sighing. ''But what the hell. You did say I was good.''

''And that I'd test you again if something suitable came up,'' said Kayne. ''You know, you've aged well,'' he added as he studied Dean's face. ''Actually, you haven't aged at all. You just look older, not as pretty but better-looking. Do you still work out?''

Dean felt uncomfortable rumblings, warning signals that the conversation was turning into an area he wished to avoid. He did not want to look attractive to Ralph Kayne, except on a professional level. ''I want your advice on something,'' he said hurriedly. ''I'm up for a commercial. It's a pretty big deal. I'd be the face and voice of a new product.''

''Hey, that's great!'' Kayne enthused.

''That's what I wanted to ask you. Is it? If this job comes through it'll mean print and television. Mass saturation. Can that kind of exposure hurt my stature as an actor?''

''What stature?'' Kayne asked bluntly as he looked Dean directly in the eye.

''No magic, no stature. Great. Tell me, Ralph, what else haven't I got?'' Dean said, his sarcasm apparent.

''A sense of reality. Dean, c'mon, this commercial will give you stature, not to mention recognizability. Look at Selleck. He was the Chaz man before he was Magnum.''

''And it wouldn't hurt my credibility as an actor?'' Dean asked. He noted the expression on Kayne's face and gave himself his own answer. ''Right! I don't have any.''

''If it's offered, Dean, grab it,'' Kayne said of the job.

''You've convinced me. Now maybe you can convince them to offer it to me. And I wish they would already,'' Dean said, his words surprising him. He had not been aware of how much he wanted the job until Kayne told him it was all right to want it. ''This business really sucks,'' he said. ''It's about nothing if it's not about risk, disappointment and anguish.''

''Just like life,'' Kayne replied, the bitterness of his words surprising Dean, as they were not in keeping with Kayne's character. He waited for further words that might explain, but there were none. Until he said almost angrily:

"Do you want a nightcap? I live just up the street at the Dorchester."

It was stated, out there now in front, where it could not be denied. The inevitable: the after-dinner pass. Hike! "Sorry, I'm just not up for that kind of thing, Ralph, but thanks," Dean said.

"Up for what kind of thing?" Kayne asked, confused. "Oh, shit!" he said as comprehension dawned on his face. "You flatter yourself, Dean. As I just said, you're good, but you're not magic. And me, this dirty ole man producer hasn't gotten laid in more months than he can remember. I've neither the strength nor the courage."

Dean was embarrassed. "Listen, Ralph, I'm usually not such an asshole. It's just that this was a difficult evening for me. I haven't been out solo in a long time, and I didn't know where you were coming from. I was uptight. My lover was killed in an accident three months ago."

"I'm sorry," Kayne replied. "Christ. Now I really feel bad that you didn't get the role. You needed it, didn't you?"

"Yeah, but not as badly as I thought," Dean replied as Kayne paid the check before he could. "I mean . . . with everything that's just happened, I'm still here even if, as you just witnessed, I don't always know how to be. Not as a single person anyway. That's tough after eight years."

"Tell me about it," said Kayne bitterly. "I'm recently single myself," he explained, his face and voice anguished. He turned his head away from Dean and whoever else might be watching. Dean ordered two brandies and waited. When Kayne was composed, he said, "I miss my kids. They're down in Houston, and I just can't get used to it."

It had never occurred to Dean that Kayne might have married. Kayne read his mind. "I never stopped being a switch-hitter, not in my head anyway. I stopped playing it out several years ago when I first read about this AIDS mess. It might have been different if I had only been playing Russian roulette with my own life, but there was my wife's to consider. So I cut out the after-work excursions to the baths. I wanted to live for the life I had created. She took it from me last spring, announcing she had fallen in love with a recent widower and was moving to Houston. She took the kids and I took an apartment. So what was that you were saying before about risk, disappointment and anguish?"

"Ralph, I'm sorry," Dean said, feeling helpless.

"Yeah, well, which of us doesn't have some sad story to tell? Everyone has one," said Kayne. "That's why people love the soaps. Misery loves company, and we give our viewers plenty of both."

They were standing on Columbus Avenue, each about to find his way home, when Kayne said: "If I wish you Happy New Year, don't think I'm being snide or sarcastic. I mean it. You'll recover, Dean. We'll both recover. That's the great lesson soaps teach you: People get knocked down or fall down, but they get up."

Although in recent years she had not been a beach person, Joanna could not resist the sun when she saw it shimmering upon the sands and the ocean from the terrace of the house. Taking a new towel from the linen closet, she walked down the steps leading to the beach and sprawled near enough to the ocean where she could hear and feel its vibrations as it pounded the shore. Despite existing problems, Joanna felt peaceful. She stretched, luxuriating in the warmth of the afternoon winter sun.

At breakfast that morning Stacey had made it clear she was not about to give up control easily. She was argumentative and demanding, threatening to move out if Joanna insisted on imposing curfews and other regulations that Stacey felt demeaned her.

Joanna insisted.

She would take her own apartment, Stacey reiterated.

If you so decide, Joanna replied calmly, and then advised Stacey she would receive no financial support from her family if she took such action.

I'll get a job, Stacey countered.

I'm sure you will, Joanna responded and then spoke of the difficulties of finding work when one has no job skills.

She would waitress if necessary, Stacey maintained.

Yes, she would, as it would be necessary, Joanna replied. But had Stacey checked apartment rentals lately?

She doubted if the tips Stacey would receive would cover the security, let alone that first and last month's rent so many landlords required. Then there were beds and chairs to be bought and electric and gas bills to be paid.

She had money from her grandfather, Stacey said angrily.

That would last about three months, Joanna replied.

There are rooming houses, Stacey said hostilely.

And some don't have bugs and do have toilets and baths in your own room. But none have swimming pools, saunas or garages in which to park a car, Joanna countered.

And so it had both proceeded and ended with Stacey finally storming out for her ophthalmologist appointment without a good-bye. Joanna had been distressed. Of course she would have to speak with Reynolds about what had transpired between her and Stacey, but she would do so in such a manner so as to minimize Stacey's transgression and hopefully therefore Reynolds's distress. Of course she would say nothing about Stacey's seeming knowledge of his affairs.

As the sun drenched her body in comforting warmth, Joanna thought of the warmth missing from her bed last evening. Reynolds had called from his father's, where he had elected to remain for the night due to the amount of wine he and his father had consumed. She had thought that wise but nonetheless felt rejected. She slept late, enjoying the fact that the office was closed for the holiday weekend, and came to the Malibu beach house shortly after noon, marketing en route for specialties that would make the long weekend seem much too short. She arrived at the house just as the local florist was delivering the near floor-to-ceiling Christmas tree that now reigned over their newly furnished Mexican-style living room. The bedrooms, too, she had completed, her own featuring a hammock for two that hung across the picture-frame window that looked out on the ocean.

When she heard the sound of feet on the steps leading from the house to the beach, Joanna thought it was Stacey. Rolling onto her stomach, Joanna was surprised to see Reynolds kicking off his shoes and strolling slowly across the sands toward her. As the sun bathed his face in an almost mystical light, he looked as he had the night they first met. Once again her reaction was physical. She could feel the longings stir within her. He was standing over her, casting a shadow, his eyes on the ocean, when he said: "This would be a great place to entertain clients."

"Why would I want to?" Joanna asked, her intonation indicating such an idea was furthest from her mind.

"For tax purposes. A party or two a year would give us enormous tax write-offs," Reynolds said, still gazing at the water rather than looking at her.

"I'd rather pay the taxes and keep this place private, just for us," Joanna replied as she sat up. "I'll not only sleep but feel a whole lot better that way."

"You're being impractical," Reynolds said, waging a dispirited argument. "The money is better in our pocket than the government's."

"Happily we've money enough for both," said Joanna, as she stood next to Reynolds, her arm hooked through his. "I'm glad you bought this house," she said as she snuggled next to him, her eyes fixed on the distant shoreline. "It is so beautiful out here, about as close to heaven as you can get in this life."

He stiffened at her use of the word *heaven,* and although he continued to look out on the ocean Joanna had the distinct feeling Reynolds was looking without seeing. "Are you hungry?" she asked. "I have a picnic basket in the fridge. We can either eat on the terrace or in bed."

He acted as if she had not made a blatant attempt at seduction. Saying nothing, he turned toward the house. As they walked on the cool sand Reynolds's body felt rigid to Joanna's touch. Perhaps some wine would relax him, she thought. Perhaps the weekend spent as children in the sun could restore the play to their lovemaking, or just the lovemaking itself, considering how absent it had been ever since Las Vegas.

Once in the house, he ignored the tree and the delicacies so artfully ordered and carefully arranged in the picnic basket and took only the offered chilled wine from Joanna. "Stacey was by to see me today," he said after he had taken a sip. "She called me at the office insisting on seeing me. Frankly, Joanna, I don't like what I heard."

"As well you shouldn't," Joanna replied calmly, thinking Reynolds was referring to the scene upon which she had stumbled but a day ago.

"Why did you threaten her?"

His question was more an attack than an inquiry. "I think you better explain," she said, her body tensing.

"Did you say we wouldn't support Stacey if she elected not to attend college, that in essence we would put her out on the street if she didn't do as you say?"

"Not quite, but get to your point," Joanna replied.

"Listen, Joanna. I want to make something very clear. I meant it when I said I didn't like what I heard this morning. Don't speak for me anymore when dealing with Stacey. I don't want my kid being frightened half out of her mind."

"The only one out of his mind is you, Reynolds," said Joanna angrily. "You've been had. Stacey is using you, again manipulating you against me. And it's incredible that her device is working. You don't like what *you* heard? Let me tell you, Reynolds, I'm not thrilled with what I'm hearing right now. Your child, *our* child, is consistently driving a wedge between us to get what she wants, and you can't or won't see it."

"Joanna, the one driving wedges between people is you, and it's been you ever since the accident. Suddenly you know what's right and what's wrong. You're writing the book on everything, including a chapter on what's good or bad in bed. Frankly, Joanna, I don't need your help in that department. Nor do I need a tour director or a drill sergeant in bed, giving me orders. I do just fine on my own, thank you. I have lots of experience and few complaints. Except for yours."

Joanna was reeling from what was tantamount to a confession of his infidelities.

"And Stacey doesn't need your ordering about either," continued Reynolds. "I want it stopped. I've said it before, Joanna. Let up on Stacey. Otherwise you're going to lose her for us. She's going to turn her back and walk out."

"Only if you permit it," Joanna said.

"And if and when she does," Reynolds continued, "I'll hold you responsible."

"And what of your own responsibilities? Stacey knows

you, knows you haven't the balls to be a father. No! You listen now," Joanna shouted. "I refuse to be the heavy in all this. Tell me. Did Stacey just happen to tell you about yesterday, about how I came home early from work and found her in bed with a man?"

"No, she didn't. But what difference does that make? Where should she go? To some dirt-bag motel? Grow up, Joanna. If you hadn't come home early you'd never have known, and none of this would be taking place."

This wasn't happening. This could not be Reynolds. Certainly he had more moral fiber than that.

"And where my balls are concerned," Reynolds continued, "they're just fine. The only problem is that they're not as big as yours at the moment."

"I don't understand you," Joanna replied. "This is your daughter we're discussing, a daughter who seems to think she can solve her problems in sex and that she can do whatever she pleases when she pleases. Reynolds, Stacey won't make it in life living as she does now. And if that doesn't frighten you it sure as hell does me. She needs rules, regulations, needs someone to say no."

"Oh, lay off, Joanna. Can't you see what a pain in the ass you've become? Stacey is eighteen; I'm forty-five. We're both old enough to know what's right for us. Unless you now think you're the only one with wisdom and insight, who has seen the *light* . . . so to speak.

"Joanna, listen to me good," Reynolds continued, his voice low and therefore twice as threatening. "If Stacey moves out I'll never forgive you. And if she does go I'll give her everything she needs to make her life safe and comfortable."

"No, you won't, Reynolds. You can't. You don't know how," sighed Joanna. "You haven't even a clue as to what I'm talking about."

"I haven't for months, Joanna," replied Reynolds as he walked out to the terrace, down the steps and once again onto the beach. Again Joanna saw the sun bathe his face in the same mystical light, but it looked different. Reynolds looked different. Joanna suspected from this day on he always would.

* * *

She felt so foolish. Once again people had conspired behind her back and she knew nothing. Until now. She looked at his face, blank, not remorseful, and couldn't speak what she was feeling. Her anger slipped into resignation.

"I just don't understand," she said finally as she paced the den. "There's to be no discussion, just a decision? *Your* decision?"

"There's nothing to discuss, Sara, as it *is* my decision," Stefan said as he sat in the Wallaway chair.

"But where does that leave us?" Sara asked, her heart pounding.

"It's not about us right now but about me," Stefan said wearily.

"But we went for couple counseling," Sara persisted.

"No. You went for couple counseling. I followed because you gave me no choice. Now the doctor has given me one, and I'm going to be seeing him privately."

It was hard to comprehend. He, who had been so opposed to any counseling whatsoever, was now seeking counseling for himself. "And that leaves me exactly where? Or doesn't anyone care?" Sara asked.

Stefan shrugged. He didn't have that answer, nor would he look for it, Sara could see as Stefan yawned, an indication that his medication was demanding another nap. She left him in front of the television watching *Donahue*.

The phone was answered on its second ring.

"Dr. Reich? This is Sara Schell. My husband has just returned from what appears to have been a session with you. He tells me you will no longer be seeing us together as a couple. Don't you think this should have been discussed with me?"

She listened, not believing what she was hearing.

"Of course I'm interested in my husband's full recovery, but what has this to do with our marriage?"

His answer in the form of a question stunned her. What had the ten sessions they had already experienced since Thanksgiving done for their marriage?

Precious little, she had to admit. The counseling had not been visibly successful. Most of the time they sat for the near fifty minutes without communicating. Mainly she spoke and Stefan listened, or Dr. Reich spoke and they both listened.

They had not moved an inch closer toward recognizing or solving Stefan's problems. He was still accusing her of using him, of making him be what he was not, a tower of strength, a port in the storm and other clichés that said the same thing. And he complained that he had never been young and that neither had she; that they didn't know how to have fun. And he wanted to have fun and be young.

Often it seemed hopeless. Some days she thought to steal his Elavil, a change from the Valium, to ease *her* depression.

"I think this is very unprofessional, Doctor. This should have been discussed with me before a decision was reached," Sara said, surprising herself. "After all, you are my therapist, too."

Again she listened and again she was stunned. He was no longer her therapist. He couldn't be, he explained, as it would not be in Stefan's best interests. He was referring her case to a colleague in New York, a very competent psychotherapist, highly experienced in cases such as hers. He hoped she would call.

And what kind of case was that? she wanted to ask. Instead, she inquired about Stefan. "What progress do you feel my husband is making?"

He is making *his* progress, was the doctor's response; he then urged she not ask as he could no longer answer such questions. It violated patient confidentiality.

She hung up the phone and returned to the den, where Stefan was watching without seeing the images on the television screen. "I'm taking the kids into Manhattan, to the Music Hall," she decided spontaneously. "It *is* their Christmas break and we haven't done a thing together as a family. Do you want to go?"

"No," he replied.

"Then I'll go without you," she said.

"Can you manage?"

His question infuriated her. Planting herself in front of the screen, she said: "I can sure as hell try."

She stared at the phone and then walked away. The office was still, being as it was the end of the workday. She dialed before she could think. Lilith answered. They chatted. Lilith sounded more exhausted from her week away from the office than she did when she was in it. Pleasantries were exchanged and maintained as conversation until Lilith said: "You want to talk to my mother, don't you?" and Joanna replied: "Yes, I do."

He hung up the phone and immediately heard a yell, more a whoop and a holler than a scream, reverberating through what had been for so long a quiet apartment. He would not look for Chris, would not feel his absence. He would phone Joanna or Sara. Both.

There was no answer on Joanna's private line at the office; at Sara's, Stefan announced that Sara had taken the kids to the movies. Dean almost told Stefan, so great was his need to share his excitement. He hung up, his mood beginning to turn from his sense of isolation.

He dialed. The secretary at the studio said Mr. Kayne was on the studio floor but she would have him call. As he sat idly, Dean wondered for the first time in more than eight years how and why he had allowed his life to become so singular, so involved with one person who didn't have the courtesy to be here when he now most wanted him.

The phone rang. He leaped toward it. Ralph Kayne was returning his call.

"Ralph, I got it!" Dean shouted. "I got it, Ralph, got the commercial!" No sooner had he said it than Dean felt foolish. Why should Kayne give a damn about someone he hardly knew and about something as paltry as a television commercial?

Kayne's enthusiasm crackled over the telephone lines, his voice as pitched in excitement as Dean's. Yes, Kayne could buy him a drink to celebrate, said Dean. Better still, he would buy Kayne a drink, several drinks. Dinner, too.

He hung up the phone and danced around the apartment. The day after New Year's he would be on a sound stage. Within the week a commercial would be filmed. Within the month it would be aired, the product and he launched simultaneously. Life was about to do an About Face.

The office smelled as offices do after an in-house party—bad. A stale smell of cigarettes clung to the heavy air, as did the odor of Scotch and Champagne rising from half-filled plastic cups as often as not serving double duty as ashtrays. The partially consumed tray of hors d'oeuvres added to the offense, the three hours they were exposed to the air helping neither their color nor their scent. Joanna looked about the remains of the office party and wondered why she and Lilith had bothered. Their employees' goal hadn't been to have a good time but to leave early in preparation for the real good time that evening.

Joanna was not looking forward to her own evening, an annual New Year's Eve event at her father-in-law's, where "names" from medicine, music and art intermingled. Reynolds, however, loved the black-tie affair at which the guests dressed much like extras from an old MGM extravaganza—*Grand Hotel,* if past New Year's Eves were any barometer. In the past Joanna had enjoyed the hoopla. Now it seemed a chore, which made her wonder if Reynolds was right. Perhaps she was becoming a bore, uninterested in the everyday things most normal people enjoyed.

But she had enjoyed their weekend in Malibu. Miraculously all parties in what had been warfare accepted a truce. There had been no arguments or scenes. Just light, meaningless chatter. She had particularly loved the mornings, the strolls on cold, wet sands, the sounds of gulls demanding whatever it was gulls demanded from one another and their world. That she was alone on these sunrise walks did not truly disturb her, as she never felt alone. Not on a beach, beneath a rising sun that brought warmth into her life.

Her phone ringing startled Joanna. It was Barney Reardon, calling to wish her a Happy New Year. They chatted, he inquiring about her work and the house in Malibu (had she told him or had he heard about the house from some other source?) and she waiting for him to state what was really on his mind. But he didn't, and Joanna felt uncomfortable. She should see him, she realized, the sooner the better; doing so would eliminate much of the tension she was feeling.

The persistent knocking on the door to the office announced Elaine Winters. Making her apologies, Joanna promised to return Barney's call and then quickly turned her mind to the reasons she had asked for this meeting. Instantly her headache returned and, with it, her first rush of nausea.

Elaine Winters stood in the doorway, a smile splashed

across her face, looking like an older version of her daughter. A mound of streaked blond hair perched like a bird's nest atop a tiny head that sat upon a body that surpassed Lilith's in size.

"I'm living proof that all good things do not come in small packages," Elaine said as she breezed into the office, removing a pink scarf thrown very Mick Jaggerish about her neck. She was wearing a white polyester pants suit and could have been, Joanna decided, an off-duty nurse.

"From the way you're staring, I would guess I'm either a sight for sore eyes or a sight to make eyes sore," Elaine said as she sniffed about the room. "Smells like I missed a good party."

"Would you like a drink?" Joanna asked, remembering her manners.

Elaine demurred. "Good heavens, no. I never drink. I just eat," she said as she reached for a wedge of salmon on black bread from one of the trays. "A rather superfluous admission, I would guess," Elaine said as she patted her considerable girth. "Ah well, it is one of life's pleasures." She seated herself abruptly and totally, collapsing into the one leather sofa in Lilith's private office, where they had somehow wandered.

"You're very pretty," Elaine said as she looked deeply into Joanna's face. "I was expecting Grace Kelly, but you're not her at all. You're much more . . . *there,* available." Her face screwed up as if she were wrestling with some thought or feeling she could not yet accept or understand. "But things are difficult for you, aren't they? You don't have to answer, you know, but I do see that in your eyes. And I do understand."

Joanna could see that Elaine did indeed understand. "My life has been . . . *different* since my near-death experience. Different and difficult," she said slowly.

Elaine put up a hand to stop Joanna from speaking further. She reached into her handbag and removed a newspaper clipping. "My dear, you are not alone. It says here, according to the Gallup poll, about eight million people in this country have had your experience. And Joanna, I'd be willing to bet if you and I were talking to those eight million right now, we'd hear that they too have found their lives different and difficult. I know I did. Nothing quite feels the same, does it?''

Joanna thought. ''Hardly. Some days I have difficulty recognizing myself. I can't seem to focus on the very things I used to find important. Like my work. Like television. And I can't bear to watch the news as violence appalls me.''

''Well, of course, Joanna. It has to appall you once you've seen the meaning, the preciousness of life. When you've felt such enormous love, you've seen the light, so to speak, and you just can't understand how the rest of the world can persist in demeaning life and living in darkness.''

''But it's so confusing,'' Joanna said. ''Sometimes I feel like a snake that's just shed its skin. I feel fresh, new. Other times I'm frightened.''

''By?'' Elaine asked proddingly.

''Anger, resentment,'' Joanna replied.

''Toward your family, of course,'' Elaine concluded.

''How did you know that?'' Joanna asked, somewhat uncomfortable that someone could look into her mind.

''Joanna, talk to those eight million. We're either all in or have been in the same boat,'' Elaine said. ''And besides, who but our families is closer to us? And they haven't seen the light and often they refuse to consider it.''

''You know what a psychiatrist told me?'' Joanna asked. ''That the light was nothing more than my unconscious wish to be joined again to my mother.''

''What the hell do psychiatrists know? They're the same as scientists. Nothing!'' Elaine replied vehemently. ''If they can't see it, can't touch it, it therefore doesn't exist. A-holes. Actually, there are many scientists who now say what you and I and the other eight million people call an NDE is actually a self-contained experience; that as death approaches chemicals called endorphins are released in the brain, and that these chemicals account for the feelings of peace and euphoria. Which is a possibility, I suppose. But,'' Elaine added as she waved her finger at an imaginary adversary, ''this theory cannot explain why many people can recount events that occurred during or after their accidents, or events that happened in their hospital rooms while they were ostensibly unconscious.''

''Like me, seeing me dead in the roadway from a height

of at least thirty feet,'' Joanna added. ''And later again on the operating table.''

''Exactly! These so-called experts make me so mad. Ye of such little faith is what I say to them. They have no explanation for the tunnel that most of us have been swept through, or for the light that most of us have seen. Cynics call it hallucination, but that's bull. Hallucinations don't have profound transformational effects on people.''

Elaine sighed. ''You'd think if thousands—forget about millions—of people tell the same story, it would have credibility. Particularly if those thousands aren't Holy Rollers, which I sure wasn't. My religious upbringing took place in parochial school at the hands of Attila the Nun. I didn't believe in much of anything until my NDE.''

''So I'm not some nut,'' Joanna said with relief.

''Hell, no. You're just a normal, everyday, garden-variety neurotic. Like the rest of us,'' Elaine replied. ''And you won't even be that if you get your act together. The secret, Joanna, is to accept your experience and to live your life as you now see fit and not as others would prescribe. And I know that isn't always easy. People start getting nervous, particularly husbands and children, when we don't fit any longer into the little circles or squares in which they have pigeonholed us.''

''I just wish I didn't feel so out of sync,'' Joanna said.

''How else could you feel?'' Elaine asked with a shrug. ''You're not you as you used to be. You're not you as others would have you be. And you're not yet the you you should be, the *you* you are.''

''I feel as if I'm losing everything important to me,'' Joanna said, her voice a whisper.

''I know, and I can only say in support that sometimes you have to lose to gain,'' Elaine replied. ''Think of all you've already gained. Joanna, have you any doubt any longer about who you are—I mean who you *really* are—or about your intrinsic worth?''

''None,'' Joanna replied instantly, not needing to think about the question. ''But Elaine, if I told my husband . . . 'Listen, dear, I'm a child of God and He and I are one . . . you and I are one . . . He, It lives within us and we live within Him,' Reynolds would groan, call up the Funny Farm Hilton and reserve the first available room."

"Yes, husbands are difficult," Elaine said wistfully. "Children, too. After my NDE my marriage was like the Battle of the Bulge, which may be a bad analogy considering our respective girths. But you get the point. Constant battle, warfare, with him trying to change me and me trying to change him. It finally became either a Mexican standoff or a Mexican divorce. We settled for the standoff and returned to our own corners, and we've never come out again. At least not to do battle. We live compatibly enough. We let each other be. And I always know where he is: in the same place he's been for the fifty-four years of our marriage. But Joanna, he is happy there. I became happy when he stopped restricting me from living my life. What the hell, I was on the road to higher consciousness and he was on the road to Mandalay. The twain never meet. Only they do. In simple ways and in familiar places, and that is nice."

Elaine grew quiet, absorbed in thoughts Joanna wished she hadn't shared when she finally spoke. "My marriage was in trouble before my NDE, only I didn't know it. We never had much communication. Frankly, neither of us felt the need. We lived together simply, in harmony most times, and if not *in* love, then with love. And you know what, Joanna? That love survived only when I stopped asking him to be what he wasn't—to do what he couldn't, which was change—and he stopped asking me to do what I couldn't do—not change. Was I often lonely in this kind of arrangement? Sure. But deep down I had always been lonely. I just never knew it. It took the Light to make me see it."

Joanna felt the emotion rising first in her stomach and then settling in her throat. Of whom was Elaine speaking? Of which marriage? She began to cry. "Sometimes I think I don't like my husband very much. And sometimes I feel a love for him that overwhelms me. The same is true for my daughter. She isn't always very nice. Sometimes it seems as if they've changed overnight, but now in listening to you I realize they haven't changed but I have. And it's making me very unhappy. I feel like an outsider, the weird one who interferes with their lives. I don't know how to reach them, and I must. After all, I left a place I didn't want to leave, a love I had never before known, a tranquility, for them. For Reynolds. For Stacey. But the more I reach out, the more they pull away."

Elaine took Joanna's hand. She held it for several seconds before speaking. "Joanna, after my NDE, I found, hard as I tried, I couldn't live Lilith's life for her. And believe me, I tried. I thought it my duty to make Lilith see the light. But Joanna, people see what they can see. None of us can be another's eyes. And Lilith, as you know, is doing fine without me or my sight. She's a very happy barbarian and I'm very proud of her. And she knows essentially what love is. She lets a body be even when she thinks, as she did in my case, that that body should be in a straitjacket."

Again there was silence as Joanna digested Elaine's words. When she finally spoke, this time it was Elaine who was taken aback.

"Elaine, if you had been younger would you have divorced your husband?"

"Joanna, this is not the time to be thinking about divorce. It's too soon. You still don't know what's happening to you. Find yourself. Who knows? In doing so, you just might find your husband."

"Where do I look?" Joanna asked.

"There are tons of places," Elaine replied. "The library, for starters. You'd be amazed at the number of articles on people like us. And have you read Shirley MacLaine's books? They'll help, as will Dr. Kenneth Ring's *Heading Toward Omega,* which is a compilation of scores of near-death experiences. And you should contact IANDS."

The name was familiar. Joanna searched her memory.

"It's the International Association for Near Death Studies. They're in Connecticut," Elaine explained when she saw the quizzical look on Joanna's face. "They helped me; they can help you."

Joanna connected. The nurse at the hospital. These were the very same people she had suggested she call.

"I have to go," Elaine said suddenly as she looked at her watch. She edged toward the end of the sofa and then, gripping its arm, she hoisted herself to an upright position. "Do you mind if I take these leftover cookies with me? I'd tell you they're for my grandchildren, but I don't think you'd buy that. You wouldn't, would you?'' Elaine asked with mock hope. When Joanna was silent Elaine shrugged. ''What the hell, it's bad for their teeth. Mine come out so it doesn't make a helluva lot of difference.''

At the door Elaine turned and again stared into Joanna's face, this time touching it with her hand. ''You're a lovely woman.'' She flung her arms about her and said: ''Don't hesitate to call if you need to talk more. But better still, call IANDS.''

Joanna promised she would. But first, she thought, as she closed the door behind Elaine, she would call Barney Reardon. Just as she had promised she would.

There was little time for a rendezvous, what with her father-in-law's party and Reynolds and Stacey to consider, but Joanna decided it was just as important right now to consider herself. And Barney Reardon was paramount in her mind.

He was surprised by her choice of hotel and even more surprised that she met him in the lobby, where they could be observed. He didn't protest but followed as she led him not to the elevators but to the Polo Lounge, which was crowded with peers and acquaintances despite the early New Year's Eve hour. He looked at her wonderingly as they were seated, aware he was about to learn her reasons for selecting this place for their meeting.

When the waiter arrived Barney fumbled, becoming embarrassed and even apologetic when he realized that after all this time he didn't know what she drank. She patted his hand and told the waiter a dry sherry on the rocks. He ordered a Scotch and soda and then smiled, still obviously unsettled.

''We don't know much about one another, do we?'' Joanna began.

''I know enough.''

His reply was said neither smugly nor salaciously. When the drinks were served she came directly to the point. She would not be seeing him anymore . . . couldn't. The reasons, although important, were not important to this discussion, she maintained. They were personal and had nothing to do with him.

He did not argue. His response was a simple: ''I'll miss

you." His words again lacked a leer or any hint of what he would be missing.

"It's not me you'll be missing, Barney," she said. "You don't even know me."

"If you need to think that, do," he said quietly. "But it's not true."

She laughed. "Of course it's true, Barney. We *know* each other on one level only. It's called *biblical* in proper circles."

"And you think that level can be divorced from the others?"

She stared at him, confused. This Barney Reardon was unknown to her. What was he saying? Who was he being?

"Joanna, you can't make love with someone for two years and not know them. Whether you call it fucking or making love, there's a lot of communication that takes place even if no one says a word. Also, you can't watch someone at business, see how they dress, how they act, how they hide their nervousness, see the way they preen when they triumph, sag a little when they fail, and not know them. As I said, Joanna: I'll miss you."

"I'm married, Barney."

It sounded stupid, and yet it was exactly what she wanted to say. Whereas before it hadn't mattered that she was married, now it did.

"I'm sorry you're married, Joanna. I always have been. But I've put up with it."

He was confusing her, upsetting her, too. She rose. Out of habit she signaled to sign for the check. His hand stopped her.

"Thank you," she said as he reached into his wallet for some bills.

"Thank *you*, Joanna. For everything," he added as an afterthought. "I guess this means I shouldn't call on your private line anymore. And just when I had it memorized. By heart."

TEN

THE rocking motion of the train brought back memories of her childhood, of sitting next to her mother in a subway car, her legs not yet long enough to reach the floor, rocking back and forth as she hummed some tuneless song in rhythm to the rhythm of the train. Now Sara sat and watched life as it sped by her shatterproof, spattered windows, a lady on a train dressed for her visit to New York. She felt glamorous, as if there were more to this visit than usual. And there was. Today was her luncheon at Sardi's. Her mother would have died!

She remembered their noontime luncheons at Sardi's spent in the kitchen of their home on Thirty-fifth Street. With Arlene Francis on WOR radio. Arlene and a celebrity would dine daily with her and her mother. Such wonderful small talk. Her mother had always said the one place she wanted to visit before dying was Sardi's. But she never had. Now her daughter was, lunching with Dean before journeying farther uptown to the Central Park West offices of her therapist.

Sara saw his face reflected in the window. He was looking either at her or the countryside, a striking-looking man with a full head of white hair, worn long about his somewhat boyish face. She had noticed him on other Tuesdays and Fridays when she took her usual later train from Princeton to New York. He was there when she boarded, involved in his newspapers, oblivious to everything. Except once he had looked up and their eyes had met. She had gotten flustered and had taken a seat as far behind him as space would permit. Today she was seated across the aisle, wondering what she would do if this man in a business suit and tie spoke to her.

Her eyes closed, but she couldn't close out his image and other images his face produced. Her heart began its race against her commands to stop this insanity, the fantasies her therapist suggested were defenses she used to put distance between herself and her anger. Therapists. All they ever wanted to discuss was anger. Not theirs, but yours, thought Sara as she continued to press shut her eyes. If anger hadn't been invented there would be no therapists. It had been four weeks with the good doctor, four weeks of being told she was avoiding her feelings. What of it? Her life was hardly one she enjoyed facing, particularly these mornings when she awoke alone in her bed, aware her husband was in the den thinking God only knew what, as he never shared his thoughts with her. At least he had returned to work after the New Year. What happened at the university, and with whom, she refused to contemplate. She preferred avoidance. It was much like living on air, floating about untrammeled, distanced . . . safe.

The stops flew by. Sara had them memorized and loved the fact that their order never varied. Each time she traveled, the same stops were made in the same towns. There was something so very comforting in the well-known fact that some things never change.

The smallness of the office pushed in, making him gasp for air. For a moment his inability to breathe made Stefan think to call Dr. Reich. The medication wasn't working. They had reduced it so he would be more clear of mind when lecturing. But when he wasn't teaching or working in the lab, the anxiety threatened to detonate, exploding pieces of him all over his cubicle.

Stefan checked the time. He had the hour before lunch free, time enough for the drive home, time enough to find the safety lacking in his life. With Sara and the children away, there would be no faces to cause further anxiety and guilt.

The knock on his office door startled him. He wouldn't answer but pretend he wasn't there. He watched as he saw the doorknob turn and the door open. She stood there, staring at him, her eyes expressing their normal concern. He clung to her, burying his head in her bosom, wondering why she had insisted they spend their hour here and not in her home. She stroked his hair, murmured to him as his hands undid the buttons of her blouse. She let him nuzzle like a child, until she sharply withdrew. She straightened her clothes, and with tears streaming down her face she spoke to him.

He listened. He had to make a decision, she insisted. She would not . . . could not continue this way. With hope. Without hope. If he couldn't act, she could. She would leave the university.

She was sobbing, clutching her arms to and about her bosom. Worse than her fear of losing him was her fear of not having him, she cried. Not in the way she must have him for her life to make sense. As her husband. She did not wish to hurt Sara or his children, but she could no longer continue to hurt herself. He must make a decision or she would.

He reached for her but could not leave his chair. She came to him, dropping to her knees by his chair, looking up into his face. She loved him. She needed him. He loved her. She knew this. He knew this. What then? she asked. What?

When Stefan didn't answer, she rose quickly and quietly left the office.

Their bodies brushed as each was pushed in the crowded aisle. He nodded and stepped back, signaling for her to debark before him. She walked on, feeling his footsteps behind her. On the platform she hesitated, wondering which way to the exit nearest Eighth Avenue. He pushed by her, the Burberry he carried lightly touching her arm. He did not look back.

It was near noon. Both the train and she were on time. With the day cold but clear Sara was tempted to walk, to test herself in a densely populated part of town. A taxi, however, would be quicker. Finding one was not. The uptown bus deposited her but a block from the restaurant. As she stood under its canopy she twirled slowly, enjoying the moment despite the curious concern of the doorman who almost reluctantly opened the door when she decided to enter. Seconds later, the maître d' showed her to the table where Dean was waiting, a bottle of Perrier standing next to his half-filled glass.

"My God, Sara, I hardly recognized you. It's great!" said Dean as he took her in.

Sara's hand flew to her hair as she seated herself. "It's called Dark Warm Brown, courtesy of Loving Care by Clairol. The style is Pietro of Pietro of Princeton. The hair, however, short as it now is, is all mine."

"Well, it's terrific," Dean enthused.

"Mr. Pietro will be so pleased. I'll tell him the next time he lands," Sara said.

Dean laughed. "I never thought the day would come when Sara Rosen Schell would make hairdresser jokes. Particularly with me. Also, your body looks different. But your face isn't thinner so it can't be your weight."

"It's the aerobics classes. I hate every goddamn minute of them. So why do I do it? According to my big-mouth therapist, it's just another of my ways to put distance between me and my anger. She's a very sick woman."

"I didn't know your therapist was a woman," said Dean, surprised.

"Neither did I when I first went to her," Sara explained. "The shrink in Princeton just told me to call a Dr. Sydney Schauzer, and I did. Imagine my surprise when I entered her office. However, although she's a woman, Sydney Schauzer ain't no lady. All she ever wants to talk about is anger or sex. Which she says in my case may have been one and the same thing. I only hope my seeing her helps. Her, I mean."

"I couldn't spill my guts to a stranger," said Dean thoughtfully. "I did that enough as a kid in confession, and I hated it."

"I'm not too thrilled with it myself," said Sara, "but I have a problem that needs solving. God knows I had more than enough couch work in Brooklyn, but Dr. Sydney thinks not. She doesn't use a couch, by the way, at least not with me. And just because I tend to crawl right on it, curl up in a ball, suck my thumb and go nighty-night.

Somehow she does not think this is what good therapy is about. Besides, she's not interested in deep, long-range analysis with me. I sit in a chair facing her and we talk of the present, although it often seems my present is covered with the slime of my past. Or so the good doctor thinks."

"And what do you think?" Dean asked as the waiter brought Sara the Perrier she had ordered and then handed them each a menu.

"I don't. With the money she's earning per session—and thank God for Stefan's medical insurance—let her do the thinking. She's paid enough to think for two. For two? For twelve is more like it. By the way," Sara said, changing the subject as she reached into her handbag, "I have a little something for you. No!" she cautioned as Dean began to untie the ribbon that surrounded the simply wrapped package. "Don't open it now. It might not be the time or place."

But he had, and the expression on Dean's face proved that Sara had been right and yet wrong.

"You're not going to be upset," said Sara as she watched Dean's face while he examined the framed picture of him and Chris taken the afternoon of the bar mitzvah. "It's such a lovely candid, I just thought you would like to have it," she said almost apologetically.

"It's a great gift, Sara," Dean said softly, touched by Sara's gesture. "Oh, c'mon. Now don't *you* be upset. I'll be fine in a minute. I'm really pleased you thought of me."

Sara absorbed herself in the menu, giving Dean time with his feelings and his picture. Then her eyes took in the details of the room and the people in it. She wondered at which table Arlene Francis and her famous guests had gathered. And then she wondered why her mother hadn't come to Sardi's, treated herself to something she had so much wanted. At the waiter's behest, she ordered the filet of sole, broiled plain without butter, and a salad without dressing. To Dean she explained her actions with an almost embarrassed admission that she was watching her weight.

"But you look wonderful," Dean protested.

"Me? You should see you," Sara replied after the waiter

had departed. "Mr. Gorgeous. And you're going to be rich and famous," she enthused, rubbing her hands together at the prospect. "Maybe now is the time for me to leave my husband and run away with you."

Her words hung there between them, each aware and yet each reluctant to further explore their meaning. Finally Sara broke the awkward silence by saying: "My therapist will just love that. *If* I tell her. She says many a true word is said in jest. Very original. I just bet she'd love to get her hands on Don Rickles." She laughed nervously, feeling awkward, and then with a rush of words asked, "So what's it like being the star of a production? It must be exciting beyond belief."

"It's a little weird," said Dean. "I mean I'm still not into it, although now that we're filming I believe it more than I don't. Also, I'm not as nervous. In the beginning just the sight of the limo waiting each morning to take me downtown . . ."

"A limo?" Sara shrieked. "They send a limo for you?"

"Not as big as the one Joanna sometimes makes her home in, but yes, a car with a driver who takes me downtown to some studio on the Lower East Side with the unlikely name of Mother's. And for the next eight to ten hours people carry on around me, fixing my hair, whitening my teeth, removing lines and circles from around my eyes and blemishes from my face. They couldn't fuss more around Warren Beatty."

"You don't sound thrilled," Sara commented.

Dean shrugged. "I keep it in perspective. After all, I'm just some guy whose face and body were right for a particular product. Although I'm pleased as hell, I don't kid myself that it took a particular talent to win the job."

"Well, I'm thrilled for you. Just think. Soon your face and body will be seen on television and on billboards all over the country. And if it's on the Princeton train station, I can draw in a mustache and a beard."

"I tried both in the sixties. It wasn't me," said Dean. "However, I suppose a mustache is preferable to some of the other *things* that will be scrawled on my face.

"You know," Dean said as he looked beyond Sara at something no one in the room but he could see, "Chris would have loved all this. He was such a hick, a real rube, totally lacking in the kind of sophistication we New Yorkers think we have. Chris would have been out photographing every billboard in town and probably telling anyone who would listen, 'Hey, that guy's my lover.' "

His face clouded. The hand that reached for his surprised him. It was as odd to see as Sara's new hairstyle. So out of character. "He really would have enjoyed this more than I am."

Sara squeezed Dean's hand, trying to understand and yet still unable to imagine two men loving each other with such intensity. It just didn't feel real or possible to her. Seeking to restore the good humor of the luncheon she said: "Well, I know I'm being repetitive, but I'm thrilled and I can promise you yours will be the only shaving cream I will allow Robert and Evan to use."

"What about Stefan?"

"I don't want to talk about Stefan," Sara snapped, "and I wish you wouldn't push me. You do that, Dean, and I don't like it."

"I only meant, wouldn't he be using the product?" Dean said softly.

"Who knows what Stefan will or will not do," Sara said impatiently. "When he's not making any decisions, he is making others that are staggering. But that's between him and his Maker, which currently seems to be his therapist."

"Sara, goddammit, I'm your friend, and like it or not I have to ask what the hell you're doing with your life. You can't just sit around waiting."

"Now you look, Dean," Sara said as her hand pointed to her hair. "Does it look as if I'm sitting around waiting? Give me points for what I'm doing. I travel the train twice weekly. With no problem, I might add, I drive . . . a lot and for great distances. Probably just another means of putting space between me and my anger. And I'm thinking about possibilities in work. But why am I justifying myself? I know you and Joanna both think I should leave Stefan, but when you're walking in my shoes that's when I'll listen."

"Sara, it's not what I think that matters—although just

so it's clear between us let me say that yes, I do think you should leave Stefan. And you're right, I'm not in your shoes so it's easy for me to say that. But what bothers me is you. What do *you* think? Or is that between you and your Maker?''

''Yes, dammit, it is,'' Sara said. ''Look at the time. Dean, please, get the check. If I'm late for my hour, ole Sydney gets nuts. She actually believes my lateness is yet another way—are you ready for this?—of my not dealing with my anger. That woman is a bore. A total bore. I honestly don't know why I bother. Only I do, Dean,'' said Sara as she once again reached for Dean's hand. ''I really do.''

The snowstorm had been a legitimate reason for missing her last session, Sara argued.

An inch snowfall does not constitute a storm, Sydney Schauzer maintained.

Traveling conditions were difficult, Sara insisted.

But not that difficult, was Schauzer's response.

Sara grew silent, her thoughts asking why she didn't leave rather than subject herself to such harassment. She decided to act on her feeling and was at the door with her coat in hand when Schauzer with her usual calm said: ''Perhaps now you can see what you do with your anger. You run from it. Or you leave. Or pretend it doesn't exist. Certainly you can leave, Sara. I won't stop you. But be aware, your anger leaves with you. It goes where you go, causing anxiety, palpitations and tremors.''

Sara sat in the armchair facing Schauzer, who remained seated behind her desk, again commenting on the difficulty in talking Sara had experienced since her luncheon with Dean. And that day, Schauzer pointed out, Sara had arrived late, dallying by her own admission in the building lobby.

''It had been a lovely day and I just didn't want to disturb it with disturbing thoughts,'' said Sara.

''But I wonder just how lovely it was and if you weren't already disturbed before you ever came to your session,'' Schauzer pressed.

And Sara had barely spoken, certainly not about the

lunch or her words said in jest that day. Nor had she mentioned Dean's words, meant in their honesty to be helpful and not hurting. But at this session, a week later, Schauzer was trying to retrace Sara's resistance.

"So you were angry with your friend Dean," Schauzer ventured.

"Well, he did ignore my changes and made it seem as if I had been doing nothing for myself," Sara said reluctantly. "And I have made changes . . . my hair, my clothes, even my body to some extent."

"And he didn't notice." Schauzer's statement was a question.

"He noticed my hair right away, said he liked it a lot. He also mentioned that I looked different . . . good," Sara replied.

"So he didn't ignore your changes then."

"But I felt as if he did," Sara said, agitated. "He was pushing me, and I even told him to stop."

"And how was he pushing you?"

"He wants me to come to some sort of action with Stefan. What the hell does he think I'm trying to do? And Stefan, God knows, doesn't make it any easier. Suddenly he's much worse. Much more nervous and agitated. He jumps at me for everything. So critical and complaining. And then he's apologetic. Or sullen and withdrawn. Sometimes I feel he's pushing me to my limits, but I don't know why. Maybe he wants me to tell him to leave or for me to just say it's enough . . . I'm leaving."

"Sara, these changes you've made, who are they for?" Schauzer asked.

"I don't understand you sometimes," Sara exploded. "I'm talking about Stefan, and you suddenly mix apples with oranges by asking who my changes are for. Obviously if it's my hair, my face, my body, then it's for me."

Schauzer remained silent, a device that continually infuriated Sara when Schauzer applied it. Sara remained just as silent, although internally she was seething. "Dammit! So they were for Stefan, all right? Satisfied? And they were for Joanna and Dean. Even for you. So that Stefan would find me more attractive, more viable—and isn't that a lovely word for a wife to want to be for her husband—

and you all wouldn't think I was such a nerd and that what has happened wasn't all my fault."

"You think it was your fault?" Schauzer asked matter-of-factly.

"Well, there has to be some reason for a man up and leaving."

"He hasn't left yet," Schauzer reminded her.

"It feels as if he has. Only just the other day," Sara mused, "I remember thinking that Stefan really left some time ago, when we stopped sleeping together. We were never very successful in bed, you know."

"And that didn't bother you?"

"To the extent that I felt I was failing him by not giving him something he needed, it did."

"Sara, in listening to you it appears that your reasons for cutting and coloring your hair, for your aerobics classes, are all about Stefan, pleasing him. Even your attitudes about sex are more geared toward pleasing the man than yourself. What about you, Sara? Why do you do these things for men but not for yourself?"

The room began to spin along with her head. Suddenly she was worried about the winter weather and the train ride home. She was afraid. She should leave. Thank God the hour was nearing three and her fifty minutes were up. She couldn't breathe. Schauzer gave her no help.

"I think, Sara, it would be productive if you thought about these things we just mentioned between now and our next session. You might explore how you feel about yourself and what those feelings have to do with the significant male figures in your life."

Sara fled, thanking the therapist, promising she would act on her suggestion and knowing, hoping, she would not.

The ball slammed off the wall and onto Dean's racquet, where it was instantly struck with ferocity back to and off the wall, then charged by Ralph Kayne, who struck the ball with all the force a forty-two-year-old man standing just under six feet and weighing one hundred sixty-two pounds could muster. Kayne was sweating, his chest heaving, from what was meant to be relaxing exercise. But for both Kayne and Dean, the game had become something else, just as it had on the other occasions they had played. As Dean returned service the ball became the unseen but felt enemy, the driver of the car that had spun out of control and destroyed more than just the car in which he had been driving.

The game ended with Kayne smashing the ball out of Dean's reach, the point and game won. Kayne seemed to take no pleasure in his win, yet he didn't look like the loser who had appeared on the court thirty minutes ago.

It was nearing ten, closing time at the Health and Racquet Club where Kayne and now Dean had memberships. The men met here Tuesdays and Thursdays after Kayne "wrapped" at the studio. Now that his work on the commercials had been completed it gave Dean something to do with a portion of his day. The agency estimated it would be two to three weeks before the first in the series of TV ads aired. There was nothing for Dean to do now but wait.

Kayne did not speak in the locker room, his face remaining set in a singular expression that Dean now recognized. He suspected, looking at Kayne, that dinner would not be a lot of laughs. As Kayne stripped down Dean donned his swim suit. His twenty-five laps in the pool would do for him what the steam room did for Kayne—deflate and defray the anger even further.

As he waited for a lane to open in the deep end of the pool Dean debated whether to fly to Los Angeles for a few days. He thought it the perfect time, as he had nothing but time until he would be seen in the commercials. Joanna thought otherwise, maintaining that introductions would be easier for her to make once he had product that producers and agents could see. She was right, of course, yet the idea of waiting around New York in February, the city's bleakest month, was depressing.

His body felt heavy in the water, more mentally than physically. He wondered just how much longer he would feel angry. And the anger had shifted—from the driver of the car to Chris's family, to his own and finally to Chris himself for not having fastened his seat belt. And all because he, the doctor who saved lives, did not believe in death. Still, the anger was better than the grief and the deadening depression. It not only enlivened but kept him warm on these winter nights.

The mechanized voice on the intercom announced the club's closing time. As Dean climbed out of the pool he was mindful that his body was attracting stares despite the fact he was among the older men in the club, particularly at this hour when singles dominated. Of late he had found himself curious about the stares, tracing their source and then becoming guilty because he was feeling an interest in someone other than Chris. His sense of self had changed with his work. For the first time since Chris's death he had been feeling sexual. There was something about the work itself, his accomplishment, the challenge, that ignited him. He felt differently, and it was apparent from the reaction he was receiving that others felt that difference. But his sexual reawakening increased his feelings of loneliness. Casual sex not only didn't interest him but was dangerous, the rate of increase in the number of AIDS cases staggering, which was why he was grateful for Kayne's company. Since their pre-Christmas dinner he had someone to be with and something to do twice a week. Often on weekends, when the days seemed endless, he thought to call Kayne to catch a movie or a show, but he didn't, embarrassed that Kayne might think he had no one else to call.

There was no pressure in their relationship. Kayne was interested in but two things: his work and his children. One he had, the other he didn't. Not since the week between Christmas and New Year's had he seen his children; his wife was not generous in allowing the teenagers to fly from Houston, and he, busy at the studio, often could not get away. But this Sunday Kayne was taking the first flight to the Texas city, spending the day with his children and flying back that night, a total of almost seven hours in the air and nine hours of travel altogether for a few precious hours.

Kayne was towel-drying when Dean entered the shower room. The question he was about to ask was answered when Kayne suddenly looked up and said: "Pick someplace simple for dinner. I think I'm drinking rather than eating it tonight." Minutes later they were seated in the Richoux café, Kayne nursing a Miller Lite while Dean attacked his salad with a gusto produced by exercise. From his funk Kayne said matter-of-factly: "I think I'm going to have something for you, something to keep you busy until you flood the airwaves with your face."

Dean looked at Kayne inquiringly. Kayne shrugged. "I'm going to need an actor, someone who can play tough. The role is that of a doctor on a witness stand, crucial to the prosecution and deadly to the defense. It'll keep you off the streets for a few days."

Kayne's offhandedness moved Dean as much as the offer. He had told Kayne only recently of his difficulty still in filling time. "Listen, Di Nardo," Kayne pursued. "Don't get your hopes up. This isn't going to win you an Emmy. It's just a role, and it wouldn't hurt you or the role if you two got together."

Dean thought. The terms of his About Face contract permitted him to do stage and film as long as the roles he selected did not compromise his image as spokesman for the product. This would not. As he played with the rim of his own beer glass Dean thought of ways to thank Kayne.

"Listen, you want me to meet you at the airport Sunday night when you get back?" he asked. "It's no big deal, you know."

"Why the hell would I want that?" Kayne replied, sounding annoyed, which Dean knew he was not.

"Cut the crap, Ralph. I've seen how difficult these trips are for you. You're a basket case afterward."

"You sure as hell have given me a lot to look forward to," said Kayne as he chugalugged his beer and then ordered another. "You know, sometimes I think I married just to have kids," Kayne mused. "Then I remember how much I liked Donna. I mean *liked.* We were friends. It was better than being in love. It was more reliable. It was steady. I needed that. I thought she did, too. Shit. You don't want to hear this crap, and neither do I."

"Ralph, it's OK. I understand," said Dean softly. "I've got my own boring story and you listen. I know you're struggling and you know I am. It's not easy learning how to be a single person again."

"Even tougher when you don't want to be. I mean . . . what's the point? What's so damn great about being single? Example," said Kayne, settling into the discussion, "the show has gone up another point in the ratings. You know what that means? The network is shitting gold and silver bricks because they can now charge more money for each commercial minute because we're reaching more people. I'm a big success, a big fucking success. But who cares? Who have I got to share the triumph with? When you're young you do it for yourself because anytime you score something big, you feel as if it increases the size of your dick by two or three inches. Success is a sexual stimulant. No doubt about that. But when you're older and you've had a chance to see what success really is, an extra rating point doesn't mean a helluva lot in comparison to those things that really make a man feel successful. Like your family, your marriage that's going on seventeen years."

"Yet you played around," said Dean, voicing what he was thinking.

Kayne shrugged. "I had to. It was a part of me I couldn't deny. I mean, I never kidded myself. My drive was always toward men. I was a real bed bouncer. In fact . . . this is awkward as hell but . . . I'm curious. Did we ever . . ." Kayne's question remained unfinished as his courage faltered.

Dean spat pieces of lettuce all over the table as he choked on his laughter. And then suddenly Kayne's question wasn't funny.

"What do you mean, did we ever? Well, thanks a lot. First you insult me by saying I have no magic. Then you insist I have no stature. Next you claim I lack credibility. And now, shit, Ralph, you'd think you'd remember if we screwed or not!"

"The hell I would! It was the goddamn sixties, man. Everybody was jumping on everyone's bones in those days. If it moved and didn't say no, you jumped it," Kayne protested.

Dean laughed, causing Kayne to feel even more uncomfortable.

"What's so funny, dammit?" Kayne asked, annoyed there was seemingly some joke that he wasn't getting.

"Us. I can't remember either if we did or we didn't.

But I suppose if it had been any good we'd remember. What the hell do you think that says about both of us?''

''That there was just too much candy in the candy store. Not like now. Shit. What are you doing about sex these days?'' Kayne asked.

''The same as you . . . talking about it. Except for those times when I take matters into my own hands,'' Dean replied.

''Sometimes I wonder if anyone ever died of horniness,'' said Kayne.

''Of loneliness, maybe, but horniness . . . I doubt it.''

''Well, I'll be the first,'' said Kayne as his eyes searched for a waiter and the check.

They were on Sixth Avenue, walking toward Central Park, where they would separate—Kayne went west and Dean east—when Kayne said: ''About Sunday night, if the offer still stands, meet me at the Brasserie. I should be back in town by eleven. It will give me something at least to come back to, even if it is only you. Life is so unfair,'' Kayne sighed. ''Why couldn't you be some twenty-five-year-old blue-eyed surfer?''

''For the same reason you're not Mikhail Baryshnikov,'' Dean replied as he pushed Kayne aside to take the taxi that had stopped at Kayne's signal.

No one ever thinks of New York as quiet or empty, thought Dean as the taxi drove through the deserted East Side streets. The hour was just past midnight, not late for a Friday evening, and yet, other than for the occasional dog walker and straggler, people were scarce, hiding from the elements and other dangers of the New York winter night. Dean smiled, recalling his parting shot to Kayne. It was one of the few times he had beaten Kayne with a witticism. He was sure he would hear about it Sunday night. Which was fine. Now he, too, had something to which he could look forward.

He was comfortable with Kayne, Dean realized. As if they had been friends of long standing. At New London Dean could only recall that Kayne had been highly efficient and insistent on managing *his* stage. If they had hit the sack, thought Dean, it was because Kayne had been attractive and available—but then, who wasn't?—and not because there had been any romance involved. And now they had loss in common. They could empathize with one another and with no strings or overtones that would make a friendship awkward.

Dean saw the man standing in the doorway, looking down from the brownstone to the taxi even before the cab pulled to a stop in front of the house. Standing in the shadows atop the stoop, he seemed an unnatural accoutrement to the building's quiet. A sense of warning told Dean to ask the driver to wait. The man understood and stepped out of the cab with Dean. The man in the door extinguished his cigarette, stared directly at Dean and then called from the distance: "Di Nardo? Dean Di Nardo?"

"Yes," Dean acknowledged, still not moving from the side of the taxi.

The man came down the stairs swiftly, his hand extended. "This is for you," he said as he slapped an envelope into Dean's hand and then quickly turned and walked away.

It was too sudden to comprehend and too dark to see. Only seconds later, when he was standing in his own apartment behind the safety of his locked door, would Dean examine the *thing* he was holding in hand and see that it was a summons. An incredible summons that caused him to drop the paper on the floor and to dial the phone, demanding to speak to the person who had so summoned him. But the sleepy voice on the end of the line said that Barbara Clarkson Langdon wasn't home and that she didn't know where she could be reached or when she was expected.

It was a conversation she had not been meant to hear, and as Joanna listened to the unguarded voices—they thought she had not yet returned from an early-evening screening—she wondered if she were really hearing it, hoping she was not. She had not meant to eavesdrop, and yet how could she not when she heard Reynolds say as she was about to enter their bedroom: "I think it best if we don't tell your mother."

For a moment she had considered breezing into the room

and with false gaiety asking: "Don't tell Mother what?" But she feared that what she might hear and what she might say would cause a scene, and they had all been so careful these past weeks to avoid that. And so she clung to the wall and listened as Father said Mother must not be told that he had given daughter permission to weekend with her boyfriend, that Mother should not be upset any more than she already was, that Stacey should be sensitive to Mother's mental condition.

Joanna leaned against the wall. Instead of her usual anger, there was only a deep, pervading sadness and a sense of loss. She rested, breathing deeply, wishing she were already on the plane that would take her east in the morning, away for a weekend that her daughter would use to spend with some man.

Her daughter was staring at her now, horrified when she realized her mother had heard all. Her rather loud "Oh shit!" brought her father to the bedroom door. His face blanched when he saw his wife leaning against the wall. She could see in his eyes that he was worried, wondering how much of his conversation with their daughter she had heard.

She turned and entered their bedroom. He followed, signaling Stacey to go to her own. Joanna sat heavily on the bed, all thoughts of packing for her early-morning flight gone. "It just makes me so sad," she said finally. "All of it. All of us. You really don't understand what you're doing, do you?"

He did not sit but stood, facing her. "I'm holding on to my daughter by letting her go, trying not to impose my will and values on her."

"Can't you see I'm only trying to do what's best for Stacey in the long run?" Joanna replied quietly. "There is no order to the girl's life, no sense of design or purpose. That worries me."

"She wants to be an actress," Reynolds replied.

"Reyn, she hasn't been in a school production since the second grade. She hasn't even been in a theater for years. And the movies she sees are teenage exploitation and are more about tits than talent. And she has not made one move toward an acting career, probably because she expects me or you to open that door for her just as you opened the door for her weekend with her boyfriend."

"It's just a weekend, Joanna. For God's sake, wake up! This is the nineteen-eighties."

"Do you realize you are contributing to the delinquency of a minor? No, I'm not referring to the fact that she will be sleeping with some man she has undoubtedly already slept with," Joanna said quickly when she noted the look on Reynolds's face, "but to the fact that you waited until I was away, *will* be away, and then gave her license to look for shortcuts, to go behind my back to get what she wants. Really, Reynolds, that's such a shabby thing for you to teach and for her to learn."

"Christ, but I'm sick of your moralizing. Have you any idea how difficult it is to live with a saint?" Reynolds asked disgustedly.

"Can't you hear what I'm saying? I'm not attacking you. We have a problem—a daughter who thinks she can go far, instead of just *so far,* in a wet T-shirt and sawed-off jeans—and I wish you'd help instead of hinder. Do you even know the man Stacey is weekending with?"

"Yes. He's a rock-video producer . . . bright, sharp. You met him actually," Reynolds said as he lit a cigarette. "He's the man you threw out of the house a few months ago. He's twenty-six, divorced, and he's been dating Stacey for about eight months. Which, by the way, says something about her adult ability to make a commitment."

"Reynolds, adults rarely get pregnant because they find the pill an interference with sexual spontaneity," Joanna replied.

"Joanna, it was no big deal. Abortion isn't the crime it was with people of our generation."

"Abortions leave scars, Reynolds. No woman just walks away scot-free from one, no matter what her reason. It's something she lives with, if not at the time, then later. And with some sense of dread and guilt."

"You're doing it again, Jo. You're moralizing. Leave Stacey be, Jo. Please. I already lost the woman I married; don't make me lose my daughter, too."

"But I'm here, dammit, I'm not lost. Just look. What

are you so afraid of? Everything I say, everything I am, it's only about love and caring and hope. Or in another word . . . God."

"And it's exactly talk like that I can't handle," Reynolds said angrily, interrupting Joanna's plea. "If only you could hear yourself. You're not real. *It's* not real."

"Then none of what the research doctors and scientists have done is real either," Joanna replied. "We are all bogus, both those of us who have lived through our deaths and those who have researched and recorded them. Reyn, you're an intelligent man, a doctor; why not read the literature before you damn it? Why not give me and us that chance?"

"Because it's not scientific. It's all your basic mumbo-jumbo. None of it can be proven," he replied.

"And just maybe it can," Joanna said. "Reyn, my trip to New York isn't just about finding a vice-president for our office. I'm actually flying into Hartford first to visit the International Association for Near Death Studies at the University of Connecticut."

"Jesus, Joanna. When is enough enough with all of this?" he groaned.

She sighed. "I don't know, Reyn. Maybe when I find what I'm looking for."

"Which is what?" he asked, his annoyance obvious from his tone.

"More of me, more of who I really am and what my purpose is in this life," she said simply.

"Years ago you would have laughed at that kind of jargon and the people who spoke it," Reynolds said bitterly.

"Yes, I suppose that's true," Joanna replied. "But that was years ago. Or, to be more exact: a lifetime ago."

She rose from the bed and walked to the closet where her suitcase was stored. With her back to Reynolds she said: "At least get a phone number where she can be reached. That would make me feel so much better. Would you do that, Reyn, please?"

The alarm rang at six, the phone shortly thereafter. It was Lilith announcing that she had canceled Joanna's limousine and that, despite the ungodly hour, she, the "morning mess,'' would drive Joanna to the airport. Lilith didn't explain why and Joanna didn't protest, glad as she was for the company, particularly this day. The morning was cold and wet, not unusual early February weather but a shock to Joanna, who still expected endless clear and bright skies in Los Angeles, particularly on those days when she felt cloudy and murky.

She showered, hoping the running water would wake Reynolds. It didn't. She dressed, thinking the opening and closing of closet and bureau drawers might rouse him. It didn't. He remained asleep, as he had from the moment she had slipped into bed the previous evening, hoping for but never finding a release from her sudden anxiety. She thought to wake him, to kiss him good-bye, but somehow knew he didn't want to be disturbed. In the hallway she listened at Stacey's door but heard nothing to dispel her feeling that she was alone in the house.

The single quick sound of a horn announced that Lilith had arrived and was waiting in the driveway. Joanna opened Stacey's door, looked at her daughter asleep, and then carried her single suitcase down the stairs and out the back door. The rain drenched her beaver-lined trenchcoat, and her hair quickly frizzed from the moisture her plastic rain hat collected. She removed it as soon as she was in the car.

"I hate those things," Lilith said as her good-morning. "They make me feel like a walking terrarium."

Joanna laughed. Her hands were cold, and as she was about to rub them together Lilith produced a container of steaming coffee from a paper bag in the backseat of the car. Joanna clutched it eagerly.

"I feel like your local Saint Bernard," said Lilith, "and probably look it, too," she added as she gave herself a cursory once-over in the rearview mirror. "This is not my best time of day, you know. Actually, I look best at night. Between the hours of midnight and three A.M. I'm gorgeous."

"And to what do I owe the honor of your company this morning?" Joanna asked.

"I always see my children off on their first day at school," Lilith replied.

"I am not going to school. The IANDS office is located at the university, that's all," Joanna said.

"And I'm suffering with the same anxiety," Lilith continued. "How well I remember the first time each one of my little monsters toddled off to school. 'Bye, Mama.'

"Bye, Mama, shit! I knew the kid I was sending out of my house, but I hadn't the vaguest idea what kid I would be getting back. Like I know the woman I'm putting on a plane, but I have no idea if I'll know that same woman when she returns."

"You'll know me, Lilith, because you know me now," Joanna said softly. "You're the one person in my life here who hasn't been and isn't afraid to know me."

"So I've learned from past mistakes. I lost a lot of years with my mother because I was afraid to know the person she had become," Lilith replied as she turned onto the Santa Monica Freeway.

"But you've become closer," Joanna said.

"We've become closer," Lilith echoed, "but it's different. As it will be with you. As it already is with you. And that frightens me. I like having you in my life, Joanna.

"But this is not what I intended to say at all," said Lilith as she attempted to change the mood with a change of tone in her voice. "I just wanted you to know I'm here . . . that I want you to be anything you want to be, that nothing will be too crazy as long as it makes you happy. OK? Enough said."

"Lilith, will you hug me?"

Lilith pulled off the road onto the shoulder. She opened her arms and Joanna leaned across the bucket seat into Lilith's all-embracing warmth. She was trembling, fighting off the pervading anxiety and the mounting memories of the previous evening. As if reading her mind, Lilith said as she stroked Joanna's hair: "They'll come around, Jo. They need time."

"And if they don't, Lilith?" Joanna asked.

Lilith had no answer. Joanna didn't suspect she would. But she hoped those on the other end of this cross-country trek would.

* * *

She sat huddled and hidden in her coat, cold despite the comfortable room temperature. As beads of sweat materialized on her forehead, she fought her mounting nausea and a racing mind. Her entire body was now wet beneath her clothing, and her throat was closed as her heart raced.

Sydney Schauzer observed Sara's struggle, her own being not to speak and interfere but to wait for the breakthrough she felt was imminent. Sara began to cry. "I'm just so afraid," she said, sounding to Schauzer like a frightened child. "I'm afraid," she reiterated before her sobs made further speech impossible.

"Of what, Sara?" Schauzer pressed gently.

Sara shook her head to signify that she didn't know. She lowered her head between her knees to fight the feeling of faintness. The nausea, usually a morning occurrence, heightened and then subsided as Schauzer again suggested these were the signs of anxiety, signs that increased in their intensity as Sara neared the heart of her problem.

"Did anything in particular happen today to make you more anxious than usual?" Schauzer asked.

The reply came from a far-off place. "He was not on the train."

"Who wasn't, Sara?" said Schauzer, leaning forward as though her physical nearness might give Sara some additional emotional support.

"The well-dressed man, the one who usually rides the same train with me into the city. He wasn't there today," Sara said, sounding strained. "And Dean wasn't at home when I called just before leaving the house. I don't know where he is, or where he's gone."

"He's probably working," Schauzer offered, her eyes closely watching Sara for physical responses.

"No, he's just gone," Sara replied, burrowing deeper into her coat.

"You understand there's a difference between someone being 'gone' and being away for a weekend?" Schauzer asked. When Sara nodded, she continued. "Why should Dean's absence disturb you?"

"I just expected he would be here."

"Like a safety net or a familiar landmark that helps you get your bearings," Schauzer suggested.

"Yes," Sara said, sounding interested in Schauzer's analogies.

"Like the man on the train . . . familiar . . . comforting," Schauzer pursued.

"Yes," Sara agreed.

Again there was a silence. Again Schauzer observed the physical signs of anxiety as they appeared on Sara's person. "What is it, Sara?" she asked.

Sara was breathing heavily, having difficulty drawing in air. Still she responded: "I'm afraid to leave the house, and once I do I'm afraid to go home. I'm afraid if I leave Stefan will leave. I'm afraid when I return he won't be there. And he is going to leave, I just know it. I can feel it . . . see it. I just wish he would do it already," Sara cried.

"Sara, listen to yourself. Did you hear what you just said?" Schauzer asked, trying to keep her excitement out of her voice. "You gave reasons for your fear of leaving the house. Do you understand them?"

Sara's eyes widened. She was looking without seeing. Her eyes focused on the gray felt walls of the office and traveled to the fuchsia floor-length spreads that covered the round end tables on either side of the sofa. She could sense Schauzer's presence, but she could not speak.

"Sara, tell me your fantasy," Schauzer pressed. "What do you see will happen once you leave here to go home?"

"I open the front door and it's quiet," Sara began slowly. "I look in the den, but he's not there. I try the kitchen, the bedroom, but again he's not there. I think maybe he's with the kids, in their rooms, the garage, the backyard. But he's not. He's nowhere, and I'm alone in the house and frightened."

"Sara, how old were you when your father disappeared?"

Her head jerked back as if her face had been slapped. She began to sniffle. "Seven or eight," she replied.

"And how did you discover he was gone?" Schauzer asked.

Sara drifted away from the question and toward the night. To sleep. She had trouble sleeping these nights, her mind turning ideas over and over for examination. She had decided to prepare for the national teachers' exam. She would become licensed in New Jersey to teach. She would become active and involved, perhaps even taking additional courses at the university in special education with a goal toward working with "special children." Like her. She had to do something before he left. And Stefan would leave. Each day he grew more agitated and less communicative. Not that he abused her, although his silence often felt like abuse. She would have preferred arguing, yelling, screaming, sounds of life rather than the silence of death.

Her mother should have done something. Each day he had become more agitated and less communicative. She remembered their suppers as a child, her mother sitting silent at one end of the table, her father deadly quiet at the other. It had frightened her. He never spoke to her, never asked about her work in school. Sometimes she would have preferred a spanking to his silence.

"I woke up one morning, came down to breakfast and he wasn't there," Sara finally replied to Schauzer's question. "I looked upstairs, thinking maybe he was late and still shaving or dressing. But he wasn't. I asked my mother if he had left early, and she mumbled yes, he had left . . . early. I went to school thinking he would be there later, at dinner. But he wasn't. And he wasn't there when I went to sleep or when I woke up the following day. I asked and was told to be quiet. I didn't understand. Nobody talked. I thought they all were angry at me."

"Did you think your father was angry at you and that's why he went away?" Schauzer pressed.

Sara thought. "Yes," she replied.

"What else?"

"That he didn't like me, that his leaving was my fault, that I had embarrassed or failed him in some way. My mother never talked about the reasons for his leaving. She just said it had nothing to do with me, but I didn't believe her."

"Did you ask Ina?" Schauzer continued.

Again Sara's face contorted in thought. "Ina didn't want to talk about it either," she finally said. "Ina was upset because her friends were talking, the teachers were talking, the neighbors were talking. Everyone other than Ina and my mother were talking.

"My father never wrote to me," she said softly. "Not a word. As if I had never existed."

"And you continued to think you were the cause of his leaving?" Schauzer asked, noting the time and that the hour was drawing near a close.

Sara thought, and the thoughts continued to build upon other thoughts cascading into her consciousness. She replied, and Schauzer responded with a question that pushed Sara still deeper into her thinking. About other men, other leave-takings—the many men with whom she had slept and all of whom had left, leaving her thinking it was her fault.

Sara's mind rebelled, shut down and closed off. Sex as a symptom had been suggested by her first analyst, but without his suggesting what that symptom suggested. Now she was hearing Schauzer maintain that sex was often a tool for some, even a weapon, the one device a grown woman had that a little girl didn't to hold on to a man. A device that also gave her the affection and approval and affirmation from a man. But it was false affection, Schauzer maintained, false approval and false affirmation. Sara had looked for each man to be her father, to give her what he hadn't. None of them could. Except for the rejection. The man on the train was fantasy, Schauzer continued, a transference of feeling from her father to a stranger. The man had not abandoned her any more than Dean had. And her sexual fantasies with this man were merely means to control, to hold on to something she didn't have to begin with.

Stefan's words flashed into Sara's mind. She could hear his recriminations—how she had bound the children to her. She now understood his words and realized their veracity. She held on to those she loved too tightly, fearful that if she didn't they, too, would leave. Just as he, Stefan, would leave.

"But there's a difference, Sara," Schauzer maintained. "Stefan has told you he might leave. There will be no shock or unexplained surprises, and you will survive because regardless of how you feel, you are not *that* little girl anymore. Or his either."

ELEVEN

THE summons had been his initial shock. Chris's lawyer, refusing the case without benefit of explanation, was yet another. With Barbara Clarkson Langdon still refusing to take or return his calls, Dean's anxiety mounted daily. Not knowing what else to do, he conceived of a plan that both Joanna and Ralph thought foolhardy, each concurring independently that the case was best left in the hands of the lawyers. Only he didn't have one, and time was running out. According to law, he had but another ten days to reply to the summons. Traveling to Kansas City to see Barbara was, Dean felt, the best reply he could make.

Normally Dean was not a white-knuckled flier who gritted his teeth and gripped the armrest from takeoff to landing. But this was no pleasure trip, and Dean expected that the turbulence that threw the United jet around the not-so-friendly skies would be nothing in comparison to the turbulence awaiting him on the ground. He was the uninvited and sure-to-be-unwelcome guest. Still, he was counting on the surprise element to work in his favor.

He was not seeking a confrontation but a meeting, a chance to show Barbara the evidence, the notarized documents that stated clearly his Joint Tenancy With Right of Survivorship. He would convince her of her misguided and possibly even ill-advised action, and leave. There would be no threats and no recriminations.

As the plane began its descent Dean decided that at best, and at worst, Barbara's was just a nuisance case, her intention being to force him into acting on Chris's behalf and bestow some token financial settlement upon her. If he must he would, but she deserved nothing and hopefully that was what she would get.

But what if . . .

In the worst of his fantasies Dean envisioned the headlines on the tabloids that passed themselves off as newspapers. WIFE AND GAY MALE MODEL BATTLE OVER HUSBAND'S ESTATE. Only there was no estate, and therein lay the problem. Barbara's legal complaint made that all too clear. With no estate from which she could collect her pound of flesh, she wanted the brownstone. *His* brownstone. But there was no way that could happen, Dean assured himself as the plane touched down noiselessly. It was a ruse, one he hoped his visit would rout.

It was well after the workday before she answered her phone. He recognized her voice immediately and identified himself as a phone company representative checking on reported trouble on the line. Minutes later, a taxi dropped him at the ivy-covered apartment house on East Concorde. Entry to the five-story building was simpler than he had hoped. The door was open, its lock jammed. He climbed the two flights to her third-floor apartment and knocked on the door, nervously wondering what he would reply when she asked who her caller was. But she didn't ask, opening the door quickly, obviously expecting someone else. Her expression was equal parts surprise and disappointment.

"Yes?" she asked.

He suddenly realized that although he knew her from pictures, she had never seen him. He looked at her puzzled face, the owlish gray eyes set into the top half of an oval, the thin-lipped mouth partly open in question, and said: "I'm Dean Di Nardo."

She could not move, not her or the door, which remained as open as her mouth. She stared at him speechlessly, trying to find answers in her examination of his face and body that had continued to elude her. "I've nothing to say to you," she said finally. "You should be talking to my lawyers, not me."

He remained calm, resisting his impulse to shout that she had plenty to say to him and that an apology followed by an explanation would do for openers. "I think we should talk,'' he replied, ''and not here in the hallway where your neighbors can hear your business.''

Aware of her choices, she stood aside, permitting him to pass through a long, dark hallway that entered into a small living room, blue in color and mood. Its furnishings were comfortable, although hardly luxurious.

''I don't know why you're here or what you hope to accomplish,'' she began as she continued to stare at him. ''This is between Chris and me and has nothing to do with you.''

''But I'm the one you've summoned, the one you're threatening with legal action. It's my life you're playing with. Chris's ended months ago,'' Dean replied, fighting to maintain his control.

''Look, I really think this is pointless and that you should go,'' she said as she continued to stand facing him. ''I have a lawyer just so I can avoid this kind of thing. What you're doing simply isn't done. It isn't fair.''

''And do you think you're acting fairly?'' Dean replied. ''Barbara, have you any real idea of what you're doing?''

''Only what's right,'' she answered angrily, shaking her blond hair off her face. ''Now look. I have a friend due here momentarily. You've come a long way. Suppose you tell me exactly why.''

He reached into his coat pocket and extracted the documents. ''These definitively prove I own the building legally. Those are forms drawn up by a lawyer, Barbara, and notarized.''

''I don't give a damn about your so-called legal documents,'' she exploded. ''Are you so certain that they're worth the paper they're written on? Look, Dean, it's not you I'm trying to get or hurt. Frankly, I don't give a damn about you one way or another. I'm not even out to get Chris, so get that out of your mind. I'm only trying to get what's mine.''

''How the hell do you figure anything to do with that building is yours?'' Dean asked, his temper rising.

''Dammit, I'll tell you how I figure,'' she exploded again. ''There was no divorce settlement. Chris was killed before we could agree upon one. And one would have been agreed upon eventually since we had both decided divorce was best. But the point is, he would have settled something on me had he lived. But he died and I got screwed. Right! Screwed I got; laid I didn't. An old story. So tell me. What other recourse have I?"

"You're not entitled to one," Dean said angrily. "Not after all the money we sent you each month for the past God knows how many years."

"What's this 'we' shit? It was Chris, not you, who sent that money. How dare you mention that! You have your nerve coming in here like this," she added, shaking from anger. "Whatever your *friend,* my husband, sent me was hardly enough. It'll never be enough.

"Look, I don't want to go on with this, OK?" she said suddenly. "You're reopening an old wound, and frankly I don't like it. I don't want to hurt anymore."

"Oh, Jesus, but I am sorry," said Dean with mock sincerity. "You're feeling hurt. Imagine. And after almost ten years. Who the hell are you kidding?"

"How do you know what I went through? Where do you get off with your holier-than-thou attitude? An attitude that's pretty damn funny considering this is Middle America you're standing on and we don't find anything holy about types like you or your attitudes. Let me make it as clear as possible. What I went through with Chris is none of your business," Barbara said as she walked toward the door, hoping Dean would follow. He stood his ground.

"It's my business when you threaten to take away my home," he replied, no longer trying to contain his anger. "I gave four years of my life to that building, built it brick by brick. Not for you to take but for Chris and me to live in. I gave up my work, my career, a part of me to build it, and I'm not giving up one single thing more because you in your warped thinking believe you are owed."

"Boy, but does this sound familiar," said Barbara as she poured herself a shot of Scotch, not offering to do likewise for Dean. "What *you* gave up. And for whom? For Chris. Since you've come such a long way, let me tell you all that I gave up."

"I've already heard, and it's not a story that bears repeating," Dean replied.

"I left college after my sophomore year," Barbara began.

"He said he never asked you to," Dean interrupted.

"He never said I shouldn't either," Barbara countered. "I took some shit job so that he could attend med school. We lived in a crummy apartment. I wore crummy clothes, ate crummy food and felt crummy each time I entered a crummy office to do an even crummier job. But it was all worth it because it was for *us*. One day we'd have a home with a two-car garage. I'd have nice clothes and a baby. Two babies. Maybe even three. I'd be the wife of a doctor. More important: I'd be the wife of a man I loved, *had* loved from the moment I had met him as a freshman."

"OK, it sucks, but it wasn't intentional. Chris didn't marry you under false pretenses," Dean interrupted. "He didn't know who he was until later."

"Let me tell you about *later,*" Barbara said, "the months of wondering about me, the years of doubting my womanliness, even my sexuality. I became afraid of men. I don't suppose you know that. I couldn't have an orgasm. I became phobic where sex was concerned. Chris wasn't the only man I felt I had disappointed. There were others afterward.

"Then came the nagging, niggling thoughts. I would lie awake nights wondering who had he really been fucking when he was supposedly making love to me? Was it someone like you he was thinking of and not me? And what disgusting acts was he imagining to get himself hot so he could make love to me? Those thoughts made me sick then. They make me sick now," she said, shuddering. "I had a near breakdown. Oh, nothing serious because as the doctor maintained I kept functioning. I worked. I kept house. I kept alive. But I was dead, to myself and to others. And you tell me I'm not *entitled,* that my thinking is warped, that I deserve nothing? I think you better think again because I'm telling you now I'm going to fight for what's right, and I've got support. My parents and Chris's are right behind me."

"But taking my home is not going to make anything right for you!" Dean cried. "It's an act of revenge!"

"Damn you!" Barbara cried. "Can't you see there is a

difference between revenge and restitution, and it's the latter I'm seeking? No matter how you feel, you have nothing to do with this.''

The downstairs buzzer rang, startling them both. Barbara stared at Dean, tears streaming down her face. ''I've nothing more to say. You've heard it all and you'll hear it all again in court, I'm sure.''

''You'll never win,'' Dean warned.

''Neither will you,'' she replied as she showed him to the door.

It was nearing six when the hour-late United jet touched down at Bradley International. Joanna, as she raced toward the baggage-claim area, looked for a phone to call the IANDS office, fearful it had already closed for the weekend. Nancy Evans Bush answered and said she would wait the forty-five minutes it would take Joanna to drive from the airport to Storrs, where IANDS was housed on the University of Connecticut campus.

A car rental had been arranged from Los Angeles, and as soon as she had collected her one piece of luggage Joanna was sitting behind the wheel of the Nissan. The directions she had received from Bush were clear, but still travel was slow, what with the roads being covered with a thin sheet of ice. The wind, too, was a factor, as was the visibility. An already darkened winter sky promised snow.

Nervous, Joanna again questioned why she was making this trip and what she would ask Bush. The executive director had already answered many of her unasked questions and had assuaged many of her fears by sending a packet of material that established IANDS's credentials. The names and titles of the board of directors—doctors, senators, military men and sociologists—had been reassuring. And the material didn't proselytize or promote a party line. There was a simple statement of purpose stressing that the organization's function was to further understanding of near-death and other transformative experiences, and to help people integrate these experiences into their lives and culture. Furthermore, they were a research-oriented organization that actually encouraged perspectives on near-death different from their own. That,

Joanna felt, would satisfy even Reynolds and allay whatever doubts he might have about IANDS's authenticity.

Joanna felt a chill as she drove onto the campus, located in a typical New England rural setting. Little ponds dotted the landscape, and numerous trees, laden with ice and the first layer of falling snow, gave the mile-and-a-half-square area the feeling of a belated Christmas card. The campus was an architectural smorgasbord of modern to Gothic buildings, with IANDS located in a three-story, red-brick-and-cement affair whose insides were as Bush had stated . . . a maze. With some difficulty Joanna found the IANDS office on the second floor and, with it, the woman she assumed to be Nancy Evans Bush sitting behind a neatly cluttered desk in the windowless, boxlike room. The furnishings were best described as renaissance—from the local used-furniture store or office-supply room of the university.

''Joanna?'' Bush asked as Joanna entered.

From the sound of her calm and reassuring voice on the telephone, Joanna had expected Nancy Evans Bush to be blond and petite, a Dr. Ruth of death. What she found standing before her was a more than ample woman of five feet seven whose face was a combination of interesting features. High cheekbones, a firm jaw and a fixed no-nonsense expression gave Bush a look of strength. The wide-set blue-gray eyes added vulnerability, and a full mouth sensuality. The large nose, Joanna decided, was . . . a large nose.

Bush was chatting, making the initial encounter easy by commenting on the weather, the difficulty with airline schedules, airline food and accommodations. Speaking of which, she had made a reservation for Joanna to spend the night at the nearby Altnaveigh Inn, where Bush thought they might also have dinner. ''I'm sure we'll be more comfortable there than here,'' she explained.

And they were. The Altnaveigh was an old white colonial situated atop a stony walkway. Its twin dining rooms, separated by a staircase to the upstairs bedrooms, were flower-laden and candlelit. Pink napery mixed and matched with floral pink wallpaper and matching curtains and draperies. It would have been a lovely inn for an evening with a lover, so similar to many of those in which she and Reynolds had dined in Westchester during their courtship, Joanna thought as she remembered.

He was very much with her this evening, which surprised and unsettled her. She wished he were present, as interested in learning about her experience—*their* experience—as she was.

"How can I help you?" she heard Nancy ask shortly after the waiter had taken her customary dry-sherry-on-the-rocks drink order.

"You already have," Joanna replied as she munched on a celery stick, hungry for the first time that day. "Having seen the office, its decor . . ."

"Its *decor?"* Nancy hooted. "Oh, but you *are* nice. That office has been referred to in many ways by many people, but never has anybody in their most generous of descriptions ever referred to what we have there as decor. And you haven't even had a drink yet!"

Joanna laughed. "But it's the very lack of a 'look' that gives the office its clout. It looks and feels authentic, as if real work is done there by real people and not by a bunch of loonies."

"Now there's a word I recognize. It's one we've often heard used to describe us," Nancy replied.

"Weird is the one I hear most often. It's my daughter's favorite adjective to describe her mother," Joanna replied as she examined the menu handed to her by the waiter.

"And your husband?" Nancy asked casually as she, too, perused the bill of fare.

"And so we come to one of the many reasons I am here," Joanna replied, "and the beginning of my response to your earlier question of how you can help."

"I'm listening," Nancy said after she had ordered and handed the waiter her menu.

She proved to be a very good listener, never interrupting as Joanna related the before, during and after of her near-death experience and the problems she now faced. She was surprised when she had concluded by how upset she felt. She was even more surprised but grateful when Nancy reached across the table to touch her hand.

"It's just that . . . I feel isolated," Joanna explained.

"It's almost like being a ghost, seeing and hearing people clearly without their being able to see or hear you. If you know what I mean."

Nancy nodded, signifying that she did indeed know.

Joanna paused, trying to choose her words carefully before speaking. "My life is not in a shambles, yet it feels that way. I wake up mornings next to a stranger who happens to be my husband of almost twenty years. This makes my marriage feel like an upset stomach looking for some remedy to settle it. The same is true for my work. There's a sign on the door to my office that tells me who I am and what I'm about, but I can't relate to it. My life is upside down and I don't know how to make it right side up. I'm just so confused, and alone in that confusion," Joanna added, fighting back tears.

"But you're not alone, and that's the first thing I can say that might help," said Nancy. "Joanna, I've heard your story many times before, from both men and women who have found themselves standing at your very same crossroads. There are solutions. There are also resolutions. What you're going through is not only understandable but predictable. After all, you've had a very powerful experience. I wish I could say I have powerful answers, but I don't. There aren't any. Frankly, I've yet to meet anyone who has had a near-death experience who has had an easy time of it.

"So how can we be of help, you want to know," Nancy continued. "By sharing ourselves. By sharing our collective experience. This often helps to dissipate a person's sense of aloneness. What I would like is to put you in touch with people in California much like your Elaine Winters friend. She sounds like a wise old owl. I agree when she says you should do nothing rash."

"You're referring to my marriage," Joanna said in question.

"I'm not here to give advice, particularly on marital problems," Nancy replied. "But I can tell you that yours are not unique. Actually, they're predictable as well as understandable. Joanna, you're the one in your marriage who has had the NDE. You don't have a choice as to whether or not you can reject its authenticity because you lived it. Your husband didn't, and therefore he has that choice."

"The choice he has made," Joanna said, feeling and looking grim.

"I'm not going to shield you from the facts," Nancy said. "Many marriages do not survive when one member has had an NDE. But there are others that have not only survived but been strengthened. That can occur when both partners are willing to work."

Were they? Joanna wondered. Was Reynolds? Was she?

"What would you suggest?" Joanna asked, turning away from the questions she had just asked of herself.

"Continue to read, to explore. Attend the seminars. You are coming tomorrow?" Nancy asked. When Joanna nodded, she said: "Good. Kenneth Ring is speaking. He's one of our board members and teaches psychology at the university. In *Heading Toward Omega* he put together the most comprehensive collection of persons'-near-death experiences to date. Also, you'll hear Elisabeth Kübler-Ross, perhaps the world's most renowned expert on death and dying. She even wrote a book by that name. And you'll meet some of the IANDS members, women if not quite like you then similar enough to offer a unique support system. Barbara Harris will die over you . . . if you'll pardon the expression. She tries to shoulder much of our public relations, and could use your help to take the fear out of the very word *death*. It's not very glamorous and it certainly lacks charisma. Barbara finds it difficult out there selling our experience, even though we know it's undoubtedly the best trip one can ever take in a lifetime. Only we can't prove it as none of us took pictures of the other side or brought back souvenirs. Death has a lousy image. If you're interested, you could help Barbara get across the message that we're not selling death but life, the one here on earth and the one that awaits later.

"And you'll like Barbara. You and she have much in common," Nancy continued. "Which makes me think you might find one of our Friends of IANDS groups helpful. They're scattered throughout the country, but there's one in the San Francisco area that I think you'd find particularly worthwhile. In addition to its members being other experiencers like yourself, there are doctors, nurses, social workers and other lay people who work with the ill. This kind of group support and contact could help you."

Joanna thought before she spoke. "I don't think so. I'm just not the group type. I would have trouble speaking openly before strangers. That's for my clients, but not me. I could never be public with my emotions and problems."

"Don't be surprised if that changes," Nancy said. "You just might want to one day. When you're ready."

Sara's eyes fluttered open and then closed again. It was there, nothing concrete that she could see but something intangible that she could feel. In the pit of her stomach. It frightened her much as it did every morning. Knowing better than to make any sudden move, she slowly eased her legs off the side of the bed, sitting up carefully, for any quick motion would cause the room—or was it her head?—to spin.

She had known for weeks now but had refused to acknowledge what she knew. Today would be no different. There were other matters more pressing. Stefan, for one. Their marriage, for another. She listened for sound and heard the voices above the music that carried from the kitchen below. Saturday . . . the children were up and about, preparing breakfast for themselves and their parents. A weekend ritual.

She didn't feel good about rituals. Not this morning, when she just didn't feel good. About anything. She would not be able to look at food. Tea and perhaps toast, at best. She would not think about it, either "it." She would think instead about Joanna's happy phone call last evening just before ten. Joanna, in the East and in New York late this evening. Luncheon at the Conservatory Monday. She, Joanna and Dean, who, Joanna informed her, had been in Kansas City.

The kids were calling for her. She begged for a minute, trying to erase the doomsday feeling with which she had again awakened. She struggled to the bathroom. The mirror revealed a puffy face and a body looking as full as the breasts that heaved against her white cotton nightgown. She stepped into the shower, hoping a dose of hot followed by a dash of cold water would wash the apprehension down the drain. She slipped into a housecoat, ran a brush through soft and silky hair, and looked longingly at the bed and its pile of covers under which she yearned to hide. But she couldn't. She had tried that twice this week but found each time she couldn't escape the feeling of dread or the knowledge that followed her throughout the day. Who was it who had said: Too much knowledge is a bad thing? They were wise, whoever they were.

She had not spoken of it to anyone. She couldn't. They would laugh, and rightfully so. It was, after all, a joke. A big joke. Even the gods must be laughing. She should be too. It was so ridiculous and impossible.

Go to breakfast, Sara, she urged. Organize the day, the boys' with their father; her own with the girls. Tomorrow, if Stefan—and wasn't that a big if?—was about, around, they would all do something together as a family. She couldn't think what, although she thought prayer might do for a start.

The smells in the kitchen had their usual effect upon her. She rushed for her tea and sat at the table, pretending enthusiasm and appetite as the girls piled banana pancakes on her plate. She gagged. Banana pancakes? Yes, the girls enthused. They had blended the batter with two bananas and some honey. She tasted it as they watched, eager for her praise. She smiled as she swallowed, a big, wide smile, and hoped it would be enough to turn their attention away before another bite could send her over the edge . . . of the kitchen sink or the bathroom bowl. She waited for some relief from Stefan. Normally he arrived in the kitchen before she did on Saturdays, shaved and dressed, ready to plan the day with the boys. She looked for his coffee cup on the kitchen counter, thinking he might have risen early, made some instant and left with it for his room. But the cup was there, alone on the kitchen counter, the word FATHER printed in script on it.

Again she knew, only this time she really knew. She turned to Robert and asked: "Have you seen your father?" The boy shook his head. Evan offered to fetch him, but Sara quickly interceded, saying she would go. She walked slowly toward the den, knocked once on its door and entered. She was not surprised to see the sofa bed in its upright position, as though it had not been used in the night. Nor was she surprised to see that his clothes had been removed from the closet, his toiletries gone from the downstairs bathroom. She breathed deeply and returned to the kitchen. "Your father's gone out," she said, keeping her voice even. Robert looked at her quizzically as Evan groaned. She did not offer more information and they didn't ask. But they would, and Sara knew eventually she must have something to say and a face with which to say it. Perhaps he would return by lunch . . . or dinner . . . the following morning. She could stall till then.

Her mother came to mind and the morning—or was it the mornings?—in their kitchen when she had waited for something to be explained, *anything* that would help her understand where her father had gone. Her mother, too, had stalled. Life was repeating itself. Déjà vu. Only she would not lie to her children. She might not tell them the truth, but she would not lie. She would never allow them to think that they were the possible cause of their father's abandonment. She would protect them from that. As she should have been protected. But her mother, she now understood, had been more the child and she the parent, even at that age. And even if she had been able to parent, how do you tell your children that their father had found something lacking in his life and it was you? Her father had only left for another country. That was bad, but it wasn't ignominious. As leaving for another woman was.

Sara began to tremble. With a great show of smiles and approval, she excused herself from the table, causing cries of disappointment over her lack of appetite. She made one last show of stuffing her mouth with yet a few more bites of the pancakes and then silently asked God that He let her retain them until she was up the stairs and in the privacy of her bathroom.

It was nearing dinnertime. The kids were occupied and hadn't asked about Stefan all day, assuming that one of the possibilities she had suggested to explain his absence—that he was working at the university or attending a nearby out-of-town conference—was correct. They seemed almost unconcerned, and as much as that pleased her, it also angered her; their insensitivity often did now. She was still in her housecoat, not having bothered to dress for the day. After all, where was she going, where could she go, while she waited? She went to sleep wearing the same housecoat, pulling a blanket over her as the reassuring flickering light from the television accompanied her night.

Invisible hands were pulling her to safety from the turbulent river into which she had fallen. Waking suddenly, she was surprised to find herself in a bed and not a boat. She looked at what had awakened her, dragged her from the deep waters of a dream. A telephone, ringing mercilessly. She stared at it, knowing who it would be at this early hour of the day and what he would say. It was almost unnecessary to answer.

She had considered all the possibilities, particularly nurturing the one in which she told them the total truth. His lies. His deception and cunning. They collected at the breakfast table with her still not knowing what she would say until she began saying it.

"You know, your father has not been himself for a very long time," she began. They stared at her.

"Is he ill again?" Naomi asked timorously.

"No. At least not in the way you mean," Sara explained. "Your father has problems he needs to work out. He called me early this morning to say he can't work them out here, that he needs to be alone . . . needs space. You know how that is. When you have homework, a task from one of your teachers, you know the total quiet you must have. So your father has gone away for a while to think things out, to have some quiet, so that he can make right his life again."

She was not imagining it. Those were tears in Evan's eyes.

"When is he coming back?" Dana asked.

"I don't know," Sara replied, grateful her daughter hadn't asked, *Is* he coming back. "But fairly soon, I suppose. And he'll talk to you much sooner than that," Sara added, suddenly deciding that contrary to what she had just told Stefan he could indeed talk to the children. "Your father needs you now to understand. Try. He always tried to understand you. You all know that. Whenever you had a problem, it was him you went to because he would listen. Because he loves you. And that, too, you know." She never mentioned her sense of loss or her anger or her hurt. Those she kept to herself until she could no longer breathe or function. Then she dialed the phone. She reached the service. It was Sunday, she was informed, as if she didn't already know.

"Tell Dr. Schauzer it's an emergency," she said before disconnecting.

The callback came within minutes from the therapist, who, when apprised of the situation, cleared time to see Sara the following afternoon. She encouraged Sara to talk in the meantime, but Sara had nothing to say, having already said it all. Except for the undocumented and unacknowledged fact that she was pregnant. Four months and counting. So much, dear doctor, for anxiety and stress being the cause of her nausea and discomfort.

Ralph Kayne held up his hand, signaling for Dean to stop, much the way a traffic cop would. He wanted to hear no more, had heard enough, too much, he declared, in the less than forty-eight hours that Dean had been back from Kansas City. "You should be talking to a lawyer, not me," Kayne protested. "There's a long mile between what you and I agree to be right and what the law might say in such cases. My own experience in the courts proves that. Donna got a bundle even though she was leaving me to marry another man. And she received almost exclusive rights to the children, even though my abilities as a father were never questioned. So don't count on our legal system for justice. Get a lawyer, one who can talk as fast as he thinks. Get the best."

From a drawer in his desk, Kayne removed a script and handed it to Dean. He then returned to his revisions in the text for the afternoon's taping, the hand he was waving directing Dean to sit somewhere but not too near him while he worked. As he stood feeling stupid and somewhat angry at Kayne s dismissal, Dean thought about the one lawyer he knew. He would see him that afternoon, first for an opinion and then, if necessary, for a referral. Despite Ralph's pessimism, Dean knew his was an open-and-shut case. Still, he would relax only when it was settled, another closed chapter, the least pleasant, in what had been his life with Chris.

Dean looked at Kayne, now the picture of a man totally absorbed and focused on his work, and not on the actor before him who belonged to next week's tapings and problems therein and therefore not of concern now. Dean smiled, enjoying Kayne's preoccupation with his work and his ability to shut off and down any outside distractions. It was the mark of a professional. Chris had been like that—able to remove himself from any setting or situation to concentrate on a patient's medical problem.

He seated himself and opened the script that would open yet another door in his professional life. The character he was to play was named Clark. Dr. Clark Kensington. He liked him already. His name was one of strength. Very macho and yet elegant. He assumed what he believed to be the physical characteristics of the man as he began reading. Forty minutes later he closed the script and stared at Kayne, who was still involved—now with the scenic designer—and still oblivious to his presence.

It was a gift, thought Dean as he slipped out of the office, the script clutched in his hand. A role in which even a bad actor would look good and a good one look great. As if he had magic. It was a role he would have killed for last fall when he was about to meet with Joanna and Sara after so many years of estrangement. Now, as he walked the few blocks from the *Rainbow's End* studio to the Mayflower Hotel and his luncheon, Dean was thinking not only of the role but of the man who had made it possible. He was a friend. His first really among men. And the role of a friend suddenly felt even better than that of Dr. Clark Kensington. It made him smile when he realized he didn't have to assume any characteristics to play it.

She was fine. Absolutely fine, Sara insisted, trying to halt the debate within herself. No need to panic. So the rabbit had died. Which was exactly what she had expected. She would not turn around and go home, although every part of her yearned to. She couldn't, although she could call and cancel her lunch. But she couldn't cancel Schauzer. She could, but the doctor would find that indefensible. And so would she.

The train seemed particularly crowded. She never expected crowds on a Monday, somehow thinking people reacted to the day as she did. An awful day, fearsome. She hated it, had since childhood. Then it meant leaving home for school. Later, it had meant leaving home for work. Now it meant leaving home.

She felt the panic rise. As she breathed through it, Sara elected to free-associate, a Schauzer suggestion to implement her therapy. Stefan was not home. Nor would he be home when she returned. Who else would be missing? Would the house still be standing, her mother still there? Her heart stopped for an instant. Her mother was dead. But somehow mother-and-house were interchangeable, entwined. Safe places both, no matter how messy, with draperies drawn or open. Her mother had always been there. Just like the house. There no matter what. Havens. Safe arms into which she could fall.

Her mother was dead, Sara said angrily as the train lurched from station to station. Her mother had been dead for years. Quite possibly she had died long before her father had deserted but had not bothered to be buried by others. Only by herself.

The image of a tree trunk came to mind. Her father. Little leaves—her mother, herself—clung to the tree, dependent on it for nurturance, support. She watched the leaves fall, unable to fend for themselves with the first winds of winter.

Stefan was a tree trunk. Or so she had thought. She had married her father. A predictable cliché. Trees might sway in the breeze, even bend as they should, but they didn't break. Hers did, and she hated it for doing so. She had thought him as "solid as an oak." She had wanted to think of him as that. But he had been a sapling and she a sap for thinking otherwise. She began to shake as the train pulled into Penn Station. Long after the last passenger had exited she remained seated, thinking: "There is no one to take care of me. Except me."

But she couldn't do it. She *wouldn't* do it. It wasn't fair that she or anyone else should ask that she do. She should have what she never had: someone to take care of her. She laughed. The sound was bitter and yet free. She had always had people taking care of her. From her mother and Stefan to her children. They had never proven either sufficient or efficient. She had never really felt safe, so perhaps it really was time to try something else even if she hated the idea.

But as she stood on the corner of Thirty-third Street and Eighth Avenue Sara realized she didn't really hate the idea at all. If everyone had failed to take care of her, maybe she could do better on her own. Certainly, she decided as she pushed her way past another who thought *her* name was written on the windshield of the approaching taxi, she could do no worse.

"I don't understand. How did it happen?" Joanna asked, her face reflecting the amazement she felt.

"Oh, in the usual fashion," Sara said coyly. "Well . . . to a point anyway. You've heard of coitus interruptus? Well, I got caught in the coitus part, even though there was interruptus. It seems one of those little sperm fellows got loose despite there not being an ejaculation."

"But I thought you and Stefan were sleeping in separate bedrooms," Joanna sputtered. "When?"

"The morning of the bar mitzvah," Sara answered. "I was feeling all warm and gushy. Like a mound of fresh chopped liver looking for an onion and a seeded roll to make life complete." She stopped, suddenly aware that she was speaking about sex, *her* active participation in it, something she seldom did even with her therapist. They were sitting in the Conservatory restaurant, their table facing traffic on Central Park West. Sara had been the last to arrive, catching the end of a conversation in which Dean was reveling in a role he was about to play, courtesy of someone named Ralph. The name was spoken by Joanna now as she suggested Dean might speak to this Ralph not only about Sara but all their recent lives. "Surely there are six years of story lines in just the past four months."

"Who is this Ralph person exactly?" Sara asked impatiently.

"He's a producer . . . a friend," Dean replied.

"Oh, really? Well, ever since we sat down, or I sat down, it's been Ralph this and Ralph that. Is something going on between you two?"

Joanna burst out laughing, surprised by Sara's directness and pleased; it was a question only Joanna's own tact and taste had prevented her from asking.

"Sara, I've already told you," Dean replied. "He's just a friend. Besides, he's not my type."

"Why not? He's a man, isn't he?" Sara countered.

"It doesn't work that way, Sara," Dean answered. "Being homosexual doesn't mean you're attracted to every man you meet."

"What's not to be attracted to in this case?" Sara asked. "Is he an ugly? No? Well, then, I don't understand. He's single, attractive, and a producer. That's not too difficult to take. If that's not your type it could be mine. By the way, which way is he inclined? And does he like children? I seem to have a bunch."

Joanna was laughing, trying to decide as she stared at Sara if she was drunk from her one wine spritzer or just being a Sara she dimly remembered from what seemed like a hundred years back.

"He happens to have two kids of his own he's crazy about. He's divorced," Dean explained.

"It gets better and better," Sara said, rubbing her hands together. "Do you know how he feels about New Jersey?"

"The way most people feel about toxic waste," Dean replied. "Now just stop. Ralph is not for you. To use your delicate phraseology, he's not so inclined. And how the hell did we get to Ralph Kayne when I still haven't quite yet come to grips with the fact that you're pregnant?"

"Welcome to the club," Sara said as she extended her hand in greeting to Dean.

"It's a lousy break, Sara," Joanna said, "such a bad time for this to happen. How is Stefan handling it?"

Sara shrugged.

"Haven't you told him?" Joanna asked, alarmed.

Sara stared at her menu as she replied: "I haven't seen Stefan to tell him. He left. Sometime between Friday and Saturday."

Joanna's right hand flew to her mouth as the other reached to take Sara's. Sara withdrew her hand angrily. "Don't look so upset, Joanna. This isn't a tragedy, so don't make it into one. I'm all right."

"You don't have to have this baby, Sara. Not now," Joanna said.

"Of course I don't," Sara snapped. "But I want to."

"Sara, be reasonable," Joanna persisted. "You may be endangering your life. After all, you are past forty."

"It's not my first child, Joanna, and I'm healthy as a horse," Sara replied.

"Well, you are going to take the amniocentesis test, aren't you?" Joanna asked.

"No, I refused," Sara said. "It's irrelevant. And dangerous. Did you know that one slip of the needle can kill or damage the baby? Also, God willing, this child is perfect. If it isn't, it's still mine. I would not abort it. Loving a child is not conditional."

"Sara, be realistic," Joanna argued. "Being a single parent at this stage in your life will be terribly difficult."

"Stop undermining me," Sara cried. "I'll manage. I'll have my teaching license soon enough, and once the baby is a few months old I'll do some substitute teaching to supplement my income. And there will be help. Robert will be almost sixteen by the time the baby is born. The girls, too, will be older. I can't keep them children forever and I wouldn't want to. Not anymore. It's time we all grew up."

The words were spoken with such bitterness that Joanna again reached for Sara's hand. "You should tell Stefan. He's entitled to know. It is his child."

"It really isn't," Sara replied. "His is an accident of fatherhood. He was hardly there, would not have been had I not coaxed him into it. Imagine having to coax your husband into making love. No. This baby is mine, dammit. More so than any of my other children. It's what I get as *my* settlement. Barbara wants a house and I want my baby. And I'll have it!"

"Let me know how I can help," Joanna said softly, moved by this Sara whose struggle for emergence in some strange way felt similar to her own.

"You just have," Sara replied as she stared at Joanna without flinching, despite the tears in her eyes.

Dean looked uncomfortable, his unconscious shaking of his head making his negative feelings apparent. "Sara, are you sure you've thought this through?" he asked.

"Don't be ridiculous. I'm reacting emotionally," Sara replied. "But I don't want to outthink myself. Dean, I'm no fool. I'm scared, but dammit, I've been scared all my life and have acted or not acted because of my fear. Not this time. I want this baby. The truth is: I'd want any baby. That's *my* role," she said, the tears again welling up in her eyes. "It's what I do . . . who I am."

Dean nodded, his mood lightening with his understanding. "I'd make a fairly decent uncle, I think," he said.

"Not decent. Not you, ever," Sara replied jokingly. "But good? Without question. You got the job."

They watched as she dashed by their window, too hurried and harried to see them observing from their table. Her footing was uncertain on the melting snow, and when Sara slipped Dean started up from his chair. He sat again when she righted herself and disappeared up Central Park West in the direction of her analyst's office. They sat silently, each thinking of Sara, but differently.

"I envy her," Joanna said wistfully. "Sara knows exactly what she'll be doing the next five months of her life. And even after that. No matter what her other difficulties, and obviously there will be many, she'll be a mother mothering. Me? I have no idea what the next five minutes, let alone the next five months, hold. Which, I must admit, is of some concern."

She looked out the window, unaware that Dean was studying her face, thinking she had never looked or seemed so vulnerable. Not even when she was just a girl.

"You know, until this past weekend, the seminars, there was still some part of me that thought maybe I was a little bent, a little loony,'' Joanna continued. ''But Dean, I'm not. I'm just a woman who has had an unusual experience which is causing me to have even more unusual experiences. But I'm no crazier than the doctors, scientists and researchers who took part in the conference. And they weren't crazy at all.

''Dean,'' Joanna began after a slight pause, ''help me. Maybe by understanding you, I can understand others. You've been terrific and all about my NDE, but still, I know you're somewhat skeptical. Why is that? What stops you from accepting that what happened to me did indeed happen?''

He thought, trying to crystalize his feelings. Of course she was right. Although he had never totally discounted Joanna's experience, he had never quite credited it either. ''I guess it's because it's too much to hope for,'' he said finally. ''Maybe it's something we need to believe in so badly that it becomes impossible to accept. Then, too, it throws open all kinds of questions about God and the meaning of both His and our existence. Simple things like that, Jo,'' Dean added, smiling.

They sat quietly, watching the sun disappear behind onrushing clouds that were dark and heavy. ''And to think we once sat in a restaurant not very far from here and didn't, or couldn't, talk,'' she said, pretending a lightness both knew she wasn't feeling. Dean's hand touched hers. She smiled. ''I hate to leave, but I must go hire my vice-president and then make my plane back to Los Angeles.''

''What's the rush?'' Dean asked softly.

''None,'' Joanna replied. ''And that's the reason I had better hurry. Somebody must need me back there. Somebody or something, or I've got big troubles.''

Dean felt dwarfed by the immensity of the office building. It towered over the city, casting a giant shadow upon its brethren on Sixth Avenue. Much like the giant shadow the office's occupant had cast upon him much of his life. Still he felt it. His successful brother, a self-made man, doing his business from the thirty-eighth floor in a high-rent district . . . He should have sought his legal advice elsewhere, Dean thought as he entered the glass monolith.

The receptionist buzzed him through the glass-plated doors that separated the steel-and-leather waiting room from the offices that overlooked Central Park. Tony was waiting in the end office down the hallway, a handsome man in a three-piece suit, his hair carefully styled and cut. He looked as well appointed as his office. He also looked only somewhat more comfortable than Dean, which was not very comfortable at all.

His sister-in-law, Janice, smiled from a silver frame on Tony's desk. She looked, as she so often did, willing to please, the *picture* of the dutiful wife. The framed photo next to hers, that of the boys, proved she had dispensed her duty well. From the pictures and the office they adorned, it was obvious to the most casual visitor that the office's occupant had done well. Any parent would be proud.

They chatted, small talk, with Tony asking about his fractured rib. Long healed, thank you, Dean replied. Their last meeting at Thanksgiving hung in the air, not mentioned. And when there were no more pleasantries to make, Dean knew that an explanation of his presence was due. It would not be enough to say he had legal difficulties. He must also explain, if not to Tony then to himself, why he had come here to a man who only made him feel awkward.

He handed Tony the summons, watching his brother's face for any reaction as he read. The wait seemed interminable. What he had purposely withheld from Tony throughout his adult life, Tony was now holding in his hand. His life. His very private life.

"I know this isn't serious, that it is just a nuisance suit," Dean began when Tony put down the summons, "but I need someone who will not only deal with the summons but with this crazy woman. I need someone to find out what she really wants."

"What she really wants may be exactly what she says she wants—your house," Tony replied.

"But I have Joint Tenancy With Right of Survivorship," said Dean as he produced the papers that would bear out his statement.

Tony read them carefully and then asked: "What happened to your lawyer, the one who drew up these papers?"

"He was Chris's lawyer, not mine, and he says he doesn't handle this kind of case," Dean answered.

"Sure. I just bet," said Tony disdainfully. "Wise up, Dean. A lawyer who draws up a Joint Tenancy agreement handles this kind of lawsuit. Unless he's afraid his slip will show. He wouldn't be alone. Lots of lawyers would turn down this case. It could attract a lot of unwelcome notoriety."

"How can a simple nuisance case attract notoriety?" Dean asked angrily. "I met with the woman. She's angry. She feels dumped on. She and Chris were about to reach some sort of financial agreement and be divorced when he was killed."

"What did the will stipulate?" Tony asked.

"There wasn't any," Dean answered. When he saw the look of surprise and then disgust on his brother's face, he added: "He was only thirty-five. He wasn't expecting to die."

"No one expects to die. Not even the dying. But wills are made anyway. Usually to protect loved ones," Tony said as he stared at Dean. He shook his head. "Two grown men and not a mature mind between them."

"You didn't know Chris, so keep your fucking judgments to yourself," said Dean as he grabbed the summons from Tony's desk. "Sorry for wasting your time, but I think I made a mistake. I better find someone else."

"This stuff costs, Dean," Tony replied.

"So what? I'm not a charity case. I can pay."

"With what? A good lawyer runs a couple hundred an hour. That's steep for an actor," Tony said matter-of-factly.

It was a moment Dean would relish, a time when he would finally triumph. He hesitated, trying to find the right words, the exact words, that would humble his brother. They wouldn't organize in his head. Instead, he heard a flat voice say simply: "I'm working. I'm the face and voice for a new shaving cream, the spokesman. I've already filmed four commercials—the pay puts me in the six-figures-per-year bracket."

His brother did not look humbled, only pleased, with

a silly grin that looked so incongruous with an oh-so-serious face. "Well, hot damn. That's just great," Tony said.

The reaction left him undefended, something he tried not to be with Tony.

"It could be a problem," Tony finally said.

"What are you talking about?" Dean demanded. "What could be a problem?"

"This bit of news you just laid on me. Does this Barbara Langdon person know?" Tony asked, his expression no longer that of someone who was pleased about anything.

"No. Why should she?"

"I suggest you keep this quiet," Tony advised.

"Oh, sure. The ads break in a matter of weeks, maybe even days, and you want me to keep a national campaign quiet. Why, for God's sake?" Dean asked, exasperated.

"Her lawyer will now know you won't be too hot to go to court. Your success is his success. It gives him ammunition. It's not just that you have bucks now, Dean," Tony explained when he saw the confusion on the face opposite his, "but visibility . . . status. Maybe even fame."

"I don't get it," said Dean.

"Dean, if this goes to court, how do you think your advertiser will react to his star being labeled a pansy, and according to one woman the reason she lost her husband and her home?"

"But that's a crock of shit," Dean said angrily.

"Can you convince your advertiser or a jury?" Tony asked calmly.

"What are you telling me, Tony, that I'm in trouble?"

Tony stood and came from behind his desk to seat himself in the chair next to Dean. "I'm not telling you anything. Not until I review the law anyway. I need to make certain—or whoever represents you needs to make certain—that there is no legal precedent upon which Barbara Langdon could wage her case and win."

"But she can't win," Dean shouted. "I have notarized legal papers here. They should hold up before any judge or jury in this country."

"Forget the *shoulds*. There are no *shoulds* in law.

There's only the law, with all its loopholes and legalese that often can be interpreted to mean what a judge wants it to mean."

"You're talking as if this will come to court when it's clear it can be settled out," Dean said, anger and alarm mixing in his voice.

"You could be right," Tony conceded. "But lawyers are paid to give clients the downside. That doesn't mean I'm trying to alarm you. I can tell from your face you already have all the alarm you can handle."

"Well, for Chrissake, it is my home. I built it for four fucking years of my life. Now I'm hearing from a lawyer that I could lose it. That's enough to shake anyone up."

"I know," said Tony softly, "and I'm sorry. Now what do you want to do? As you know, you have to move quickly. The summons has to be answered. Then you can stall for time."

"How? And why would I want to stall? I want to get this fucking mess out of my life," Dean replied.

"You stall for time by answering the complaint and asking for a Bill of Particulars, which are questions your lawyer asks of her. It's a fact-gathering device. And it gives you time, which you will need to prepare your case *if*—and I said *if*—it should go to trial. Which it may not. You may be right. She may just want a settlement. And a quick one, as this has to be costing her a bundle. Since she's suing you in New York, she has to hire a New York attorney. She and her witnesses have to travel here—at her expense—to give their depositions. Does she have the bucks for this?"

"No. But Chris's parents do. She said they're supporting her claims," Dean replied.

"They're really out to screw you, aren't they?" Tony asked as he rose. "Everybody wants his revenge."

Dean looked at his brother, surprised that Tony was ascribing motivations to his persecutors identical to his own conjecture.

"Don't look so damned surprised, Dean. It doesn't take any great legal mind to know gays aren't the most popular people in the world," Tony said. "And AIDS hasn't exactly helped their popularity, just their visibility."

They sat quietly, each considering the options. "So what's your decision?" Tony asked. "Do you want a referral or do you want me to handle the case?"

"What do you want?" Dean asked.

"For Chrissake, Dean. What I want is not what's important. This is your life here we're talking about. A lawyer is like a doctor. You must trust him, believe he's working his ass off to save yours. Since we don't have what people call a warm, loving relationship, maybe for your peace of mind you should go elsewhere. But since you've asked I'll tell you. I'd like to handle your case. For two reasons. The first because right is on your side. The Langdon woman is out of line. It's clear that Chris's reason for obtaining Joint Tenancy was to make the building yours in the event of his death. And it strikes me as being morally and legally wrong for anyone to contest that. So I'll take the case if you want, even though our father will have a shit fit."

"What's he got to do with this?" Dean asked.

"When you're page three of the *Daily News*—should this come to court and the shit fly—how do you think it will go down with his buddies in Queens? He's going to feel humiliated. The world will really be on his ass."

"And what about your ass, your buddies?" Dean asked.

"Fuck 'em. They either owe me too much money or too many favors to open their mouths."

"And your kids?" Dean asked.

"You mean your nephews, the ones you never ask about or bother to see? Let me tell you about those two guys. I'll be a hero in their eyes if I take the case. They don't seem to give a shit about who's gay or black or Jewish. They operate from a whole other bag. Too bad you never had the time to know them."

"I never felt welcome in your home," Dean replied.

"That's right. You never *felt*, but I never said you weren't."

"Bullshit! You didn't want me around any more than Dad did. I made you just as uncomfortable," Dean said angrily.

"Damn straight you did. And not because you're gay. Shit. I never knew what the hell you were. How could I? You never told me. I was like some fucking stranger. You were always so damned secretive, pushing me away. Dean, I'm your older brother. I would have listened, but you didn't trust me enough. So I got angry. No one likes to be rejected, Dean, and you rejected me. I understood why only later, when you were nineteen or twenty and I figured out you were swinging in the other direction. But even then I wasn't certain. And when I tried to open the conversation you closed it."

"How the hell do you hold a conversation with some macho geek who's always making cracks about faggots?" Dean asked.

"Dammit, Dean, all guys talk about gays that way, particularly when they're growing up. And why not? Shit. I never knew a gay guy personally. Then suddenly I'm confronted with the fact that my brother is one of those guys, and it fucks with my head. Because I hate the idea. When I think about *it*, what you guys do to one another in bed, it makes me nuts. I get sick to my stomach. I hate the idea of anyone screwing you, whether it's this Langdon bitch in her way or some guy you've got something going with in his."

"You said you'd represent me for two reasons," Dean said. "I've heard one. Now what's the other?"

Tony drew in a breath before he answered. "Because you're my brother and that matters. I don't want to see you hurt. Dean, you're family even if you pretend you're not. I love you, OK? And you don't make that easy. You're so fucking angry all the time. You want something from me I just can't give . . . approval. Dean, I hate your being gay, but I've come to accept it."

"How much?" Dean asked. "Your fee," he explained when he saw the look of confusion on Tony's face.

"Two twenty-five an hour. You can get a lawyer for less, but he won't be as good," said Tony as he watched Dean for a reaction. "I'll also do it for nothing and with the same attention and dedication. You decide."

Dean understood the gesture and the feeling behind it. Although touched, he quickly said: "I'll pay." He then abruptly stood, wondering how he could exit the office without tripping or crying. Or both. As he fumbled for exit lines, the reason he had come to this office this day became clear. Where else should he have gone? Tony was his brother, his big brother, the one he had always looked up to even when he thought Tony was looking down on him.

They were sitting in matching leather club chairs, facing one another, the hum of the dishwasher in the kitchen the only sound in the apartment. Dean was struggling with his feelings and his words. "He's my brother. I loved him as a kid. I had forgotten how much. It was real hero-worship stuff, the little kid with the big crush on his big brother."

"I like him," Ralph Kayne said as he put his feet up on the teakwood coffee table separating the two chairs and thus the two men. "He put himself on the line. That took guts. You need someone you can trust right now. It's just too bad you didn't feel you could have before. You might have grown up with a much-needed friend."

"He sure threw the responsibility for our nonrelationship right back at me. Maybe he's right," Dean said. "Maybe I did fuck up. But he was a prick. One of those typical macho men trying to prove their balls are bigger than the next guy's. I never felt I could compete with Tony, that I could prove anything to him. Not about my masculinity anyway. And I couldn't tell him what I was feeling, although God knows I needed then to tell somebody. But I was afraid of what he would say, afraid of being put down and humiliated."

"Dean, if you're like most gays I've known, Tony couldn't have put you down any more than you, at that time in your life, were already doing," Kayne said as he downed the remainder of his brandy. "All kids who know at an early age that they're gay go through the same shit. No sense of self. Just a feeling that we're less than other men. Or not quite men. We're bummed out because of what we hear from others about homosexuals. It's a bitch. But, there must come a time in our lives when we come to grips with who and what we really are versus what people think or say we are. When we do we see we're just as good, or bad, as anyone else. I've learned from my somewhat checkered and often sordid past that homosexuality, *any* sexuality, is what you make it. Or maybe," added Kayne as he considered a new thought, "it's what you make of yourself."

Dean's eyes were closing, both from exhaustion and relaxation. It was his first visit to Ralph's, and he had expected the apartment to be a place where one hung his hat but did not call home. He had been wrong. The apartment was large, airy and very much a residence rather than a crash pad. The living and dining areas were furnished in dark woods with largely leather and hide upholsteries and many brass accessories. It was spare but not austere. And it was spotless, as if Kayne had nothing better to do with his days than clean. The second bedroom, the sunniest in the apartment, had windows facing south and east. Fully carpeted, it contained twin beds and a wall-to-wall unit that housed a collapsible desk, a typewriter, a television, a tape deck and a VCR. The closet was filled with clothes, some still with their labels and price tags attached. They were high and casual fashion for teens. The rack in the bathroom was stacked with freshly laundered towels, and the medicine chest had an ample supply of toothpaste, dental floss, deodorant and other necessary sundries. It saddened Dean when he realized that the entire apartment, from the freezer, with its overload of ice cream that Dean knew Kayne never ate, to the record shelves stocked with rock/pop releases Dean knew Kayne would never play, was in constant readiness for the arrival of children . . . Kayne's.

"You know," Ralph mused as his eyes struggled to remain open, "Tony nailed it. We isolate ourselves. We pull away from people we like, maybe even love, and all because we don't trust them to like us for who we are. We reject them. But by our actions we are really rejecting ourselves."

"Ralph. Don't oversimplify," Dean argued. "What about those who do trust and then get that trust abused? What about those kids who come to their parents and then get disowned? And those guys who die of AIDS, alone because their parents abandoned them?"

"What about the parents who didn't?" Ralph responded. "Let's hear about them. Let's hear it *for* them. Sure, some get bruised, even battered when they put their trust in the wrong people—and that's the key here: the *wrong* people—but it's better to have your feelings hurt than to deny your feelings. Better to be who you are and have that rejected than to deny who you are and reject yourself.

"I should have trusted my wife. Before we married, I should have said here's who I am, can you accept it? Yes, that would have been risky. Yes, I might have lost her, lost out on having a family, but at least I would have liked myself better. And there wouldn't have been a wall between us, one that grew bigger from guilt every year with every lie I told. No wonder my wife left me. I'm sure she felt deprived, cut off from me in so many different ways."

"Ralph, if your kids ask one day, if they want to know why you didn't marry again or why they never see you with a woman, what will you tell them?"

Again only the hum of the dishwasher could be heard as the men sat quietly considering the question Dean had asked.

"Well, I suppose I could say I haven't found the right person, with the accent on person. That wouldn't be a lie," Kayne began. "Or I could tell them the truth," he added as his eyes closed. His face looked pained and, for the first time, like that of a man in his forties when he said quietly: "It would be awful to be rejected by my kids. Probably the worst thing that can ever happen to a man. I'm glad you asked the question. It gives me something to think about, something I really *don't* want to think about. But I will. Because I owe you an answer, I'll owe them an answer, but mainly I owe me an answer. One I can live with."

TWELVE

SARA stood in the middle of her kitchen wondering what to do with her immediate life. Robert was sitting at the table, staring at her, something, she was sure, on his mind, and Ina was due momentarily for a luncheon she had all but demanded in her near-hysterical phone call that morning. Where once she used to love the weekends because everyone was home, now Sara hated them for precisely that reason. During the week she was alone, no other face but her own with which to contend. Now she saw the look on Robert's face. It was similar to one she had seen earlier that day and the day before that . . . and before that, on her other children's faces. But Robert wore something else about his eyes. It made her uncomfortable.

Lunch had to be made. Food always stalled Ina in midthought. She would finally have to tell Ina something—something other than she was gaining weight. Unless Ina didn't ask, which was unlikely. Ina was always asking these days. And her answer was always a lie, which she suspected Ina knew but denied. Things, despite her words, were not fine.

Chicken salad. With lots of cut-up vegetables. Sara checked the cold-storage bin. Tomatoes, green peppers, romaine lettuce. The red onion, where was it? Behind the carrots. She would grate those too into the salad. Ina would love that. She would deny the presence of the mayonnaise and dub it a low-calorie lunch. Her figure would remain intact. Which was nothing wonderful, as Ina was built like a small but solid wall whose few indentations spoke of an altercation or two with an onrushing truck. No matter. Ina prided herself not so much on her shapeliness but the fact that her weight hadn't changed since the day she was married. Which in her mind meant *hope,* hope that another man existed in this world attracted to small walls.

Sara was ignoring Robert as she chopped vegetables. She should send him on an errand, ask him to sit elsewhere.

"Is something wrong, Rob?" she heard this crazy other woman ask, the one who seemed to have a mind of her own even if that mind was shared with her.

"I saw Dad today, Mom," Rob began.

She stiffened. She had not known until earlier in the week that Stefan was still in Princeton, fantasizing that he, like other escapees from reality, had fled to California or Hawaii. She hadn't bothered to ask when he first called that Sunday. It was only when he called Thursday and asked if he could arrange to have some things he had left in his den removed that she realized they were sharing the same town—he undoubtedly with Denise Wolfe. Then Friday he had sent her her money, exactly two thirds of his salary, with a note saying he would like to see the kids. She felt as if she were being bribed.

"I didn't know Dad asked to see you when he called," she replied, thinking Stefan perhaps had gone behind her back.

"He didn't. I saw him at the mall. With a woman. I've seen her before. . . ."

Her hands clutched the knife as Robert spoke. As she chopped, pieces of Stefan fell onto the cutting board in tiny chunks of green.

". . . at Evan's bar mitzvah. Do you know the way Dad used to hold you under the arm when you'd be out walking? Well, that's the way she was holding him. They went into the market together. I waited until they came out. They did shopping together."

She waited out his silence, knowing he was about to ask a question she didn't want to answer.

"Mom, is Dad living with this woman?"

She would tell him everything, she decided. She would enlist him as an ally. He would know of his father's duplicity, of the months, years in which he had been cheating. And hadn't they lectured Robert on the concept of cheating, of how wrong it was? She would tell him how abused and humiliated she felt, how selfish Stefan was, how his own needs came before anyone else's.

"Yes, he is," she said softly as she turned from her salad making to face Robert.

"How long have you known?" he asked, suddenly no longer looking like a child. Don't go, not yet, she wanted to plead.

"For a while," she replied as she wiped her hands on her apron and sat down next to what till moments ago had been a boy.

"That sucks. That really sucks. Why?" he asked.

She shrugged, searching for the words she had been intent on speaking. The other mind, *her* other mind, was again operating. Independently. "That's something you'll have to ask your father. It was his decision. But it had nothing to do with you."

"Bullshit!"

She was startled. Robert was never profane around her. She wouldn't permit it.

"When my father walks out you can't say it has nothing to do with me. It's not just you he's leaving, after all. He made a choice."

"I made him make one," Sara said. "I couldn't let him have it both ways. So maybe you should be angry at me, too."

"So he chose her," Robert said angrily. "What's the story, Mom? Doesn't he love you anymore?"

"You'll have to ask your father, Robert. Only he knows what he feels."

"Don't cop out on me. What about you? What do you feel? Don't you love Dad anymore?"

She thought back to that other kitchen, the one on East Thirty-fifth Street, and the questions, so similar to the ones she was now hearing, that she had wanted to ask. It seemed so inconceivable then that her parents could stop loving one another. She imagined it seemed that way to all children. Robert's question was similar to the one Dr. Schauzer had asked just yesterday. Did she love Stefan and if she did, why? Why had she ever loved Stefan?

"I loved your father very much," she replied.

"Don't you still?" Robert asked, his eyes, like his question, a dentist's drill in her head.

She considered the question. Was waiting, without being aware that's what you were doing, for a key to turn in the lock, for a car to pull into the driveway, to feel the bed drop on the other side when someone slips into it, loving someone still? She hardly knew. She had no time to know. Not when she had more immediate concerns. Like the baby and its defense. Like the position she had taken for herself on having the baby and its defense. Which made her again think of Ina. She shivered. Don't tell her, she advised. Wait until it becomes too obvious to hide. Like the moment your water breaks and you enter labor.

"Mom, I asked you something," Robert said.

"Rob, your father and I aren't exactly sure what we feel for one another, although when we had you we loved each other very much."

Did they? she wondered. Well, you felt loved, so therefore you were loved, she told herself.

"And only recently has something changed between us. How, when and why are questions you really must ask your father."

"You make it seem as if you have no say in all this, as if it all happened without your being there."

He wasn't far from the truth, but she didn't know if she should tell him that. She also wasn't sure if that was totally true. Perhaps if she had been less like her mother Stefan might not have left, either emotionally or physically. But then had she been less like her mother would he have been attracted to her initially? She wondered again why her parents had married. Had it been arranged, which often happened in the old days in Europe, or had they been attracted to one another? But what could that attraction have been? Of late, when she thought about both, she found neither attractive in any sense.

"Rob, I wish I could help you more with this, but I'm not sure I can. The only thing I want to reiterate is that your father loves you. He always has. What has happened is between your father and me, and unfortunately you're caught in the middle. I wish it were otherwise. I guess you're now having your first adult lesson. This is an imperfect world. I didn't make it. I'm only part of the imperfection. You'll have to live with that. I'm learning."

She wanted neither to talk nor to listen but to continue drifting pleasantly. She was thinking of her body, growing fuller each day, ripening, like a bud about to flower. Such a lovely image. She stretched languorously, enjoying her middle months of pregnancy, the time when she looked her best. Her hand rested lightly on her stomach, occasionally making soothing circular motions. Behind her closed eyes she saw a tiny pink baby with a bow mouth, from which little gas bubbles dribbled. She smiled.

"Sara, there's more to having a healthy baby than good nutrition," Schauzer said, interrupting Sara's current flight from reality. "You've heard the expression sound of mind, sound of body?" Schauzer pressed. "Well, your mind needs work. For your health, which therefore affects your baby's."

Sara's eyes fluttered open. Suddenly she was there, involved. This baby was to be perfect, just because nothing else in her life was.

"I gather from what you started to say but didn't that Ina wasn't very supportive," Schauzer said, beginning cautiously.

Sara shrugged. "Just because she fell on the floor and lay there kicking and screaming is no reason for you to jump to such a conclusion. Actually, she made it seem as if I were Little Eva crossing the ice, or as my kids would say: Ina freaked. She wanted me to abort on the spot. She blamed it all on my underwear. Too sensible. I should have worn frilly black lingerie. Then Stefan would still be at home."

"I'm glad you're amused," Schauzer said as Sara sat opposite her, laughing. "Other women in your position might be somewhat anxious."

"You know I'm anxious," Sara replied. "And you also know I want this baby. We discussed this."

"Not really," Schauzer corrected. "*You* discussed it; *we* didn't. It wasn't open for discussion at your last session. You didn't want your decision questioned, which to an analyst means there is some doubt in your mind."

"There is no doubt," Sara said harshly. "None. I want this baby desperately."

"Why *desperately,* Sara?" asked Schauzer, pouncing on what she saw as an opening.

"Oh, for God's sake, it was just a figure of speech," Sara protested, annoyed that she was being pressed to discuss a subject she felt was closed.

"Are you desperate to have a baby, Sara, or is it just possible you are desperate to replace one object with another?"

"Stop it. A baby is not an object," Sara yelled.

"It is if it's being used as one," Schauzer replied.

"Dammit, why are you trying to undermine my confidence?" Sara asked.

"I'm trying to establish your motivation. Sara, this is a major life decision. Your reasons for having this baby should be clear in your mind, even if they're neurotic reasons. Understanding that they are can almost neutralize their power. Just be honest with yourself."

Sara heard. She also reacted. From deep within she began to feel her answer. It brought a warmth to her body. "I feel best when I'm mothering. I love the fact that something is growing inside me. I love the idea, the feeling, that I, this rather ordinary person, am doing this rather remarkable, even incredible thing—making a baby. It doesn't matter about the millions who have done it before and who will do it again. That's about them; this is about me. Me, Sara Rosen Schell, giving life to life. And when I hold that baby against my breast, it will give life to me. Nothing else matters. Nothing."

She was remembering how each of her children had felt in its infancy. The early years with one's child are like living within a golden glow, she explained. There was no warmth like the warmth one felt with a baby's fingers tucked in your own. She would nurse this child, as she had her others, treasuring those minutes that were unlike any other in a woman's day . . . life, that time when she understood the meaning of her existence.

"Sara," said Schauzer softly, "have you considered whether it is fair to the child to raise it alone? Have you thought of your own difficulties as a single parent?"

Sara turned toward the analyst. "Why must you do this? Why are you trying to dissuade me . . . make me feel guilty of some wrongdoing?"

"Sara, if you hear an accusation in my question, then it is the one you're hearing in your own head," Schauzer replied. "Mine was only a question to prevent you from later feeling guilt for some real or imagined wrongdoing."

"Money will not be a problem. Besides what Stefan will contribute, I'll eventually work. The kids are old enough to help, so I won't be alone. And many children these days are brought up without a father. I was."

"And look at the result," Schauzer said. "Your entire adult life has been a search to find with some man that safety you felt with your father as a child. Do you think that was fair to Stefan? Do you think asking him to be all the things your father was and *wasn't* is appropriate?"

"In any marriage people parent one another," Sara said. "You yourself said there's nothing wrong with that."

"That's part of a healthy relationship," Schauzer verified. "But Sara, did you want Stefan to be anyone other than the man you created in your mind, a strong, fatherlike figure who would and could cope with the world for you?"

"It wasn't just me but Stefan," Sara cried angrily.

"We're concerned with you here. This is your session, *your* life."

She felt harassed, pushed into corners she did not wish to explore. She had hated Stefan's breakdown, his ridiculous explosions of anger, his equally annoying depressions that often resulted in those embarrassing displays of tears. He was not supposed to do that. No man was. If they did, where did that leave her? Vulnerable . . . unprotected.

"You didn't want a man, Sara. You wanted a father. And not even a human father but a fantasy figure a child creates in her mind," Schauzer said. "Sara, men have feelings. They have weaknesses. Most just don't show them. And they suffer for that. And just as they suffer for not allowing themselves to *be,* to *be,* Sara, you suffer because you don't allow them to be. Your relationship with Stefan wasn't real. Can you honestly say you know this man who was . . . is still your husband?"

She thought, hating both the question and the answers

it produced. "Six months ago I would have said yes. But six months ago I would also have said we were happy, I was happy. Now I don't know." She grew silent, remembering pictures of her past. She *had* been happy. It was more than his physical presence, she explained to Schauzer. That was more comforting than it was happiness-making. He was kind to her. He listened. He advised. He was helpful. With her problems and with the children. He was not one of those husbands and fathers who took no interest in his family. Not Stefan. He was there, providing more than just income but input. And he took care of her. As she took care of him. As couples take care of one another in a marriage.

And they had fun, she said, her voice arguing with an unknown adversary who questioned her memory. In quiet ways that were pleasing to both. An occasional movie. A concert at the university with dinner, perhaps, beforehand. She had not required greater stimulation. Nor had he. Or so she had thought, obviously incorrectly. She liked their house and their evenings spent either with both reading—he his reference material, and she whatever her selection from her book club—or watching public television. So she wasn't one of those movers and shakers she read about. It was enough that Stefan one day might be if his research produced some extravagant result. The tempo of their relationship had always been thus. It hadn't changed from the time he had first called.

She had never understood why he called that day so many years ago, or why he called again after their first date. Had she asked? Why, no, she replied, surprised by Schauzer's naïveté. It simply wasn't the kind of question one asked. Except of oneself. They had just . . . *assumed* one another. One date into the next, with her too grateful to be questioning or demanding. He took her to Lincoln Center, to hear people she had heard or read about but never seen. Although she wanted to, much the way her mother wanted to see Sardi's and Arlene Francis. He never asked that she meet him at their destination but instead called for her at home, a gentlemanly gesture that pleased her mother. And no car door was ever slammed behind her as taxi fare was thrust in her hand. He took her home, which pleased her even more than it pleased her mother. He was steady, dependable and there. He was always there. Which was why his not being there now was so hard to understand.

She started to cry. "I wish I could be angry. It would be so much easier. But after the anger I'm left with feelings that hurt so much more. We had so much. How could he just give it all up, leave? I think of her and I feel so small."

"Sara, you mentioned everything but talk," Schauzer said. "Did you ever? Did you ever ask how Stefan felt, what he was thinking? Not about things or children but his life, himself, about his dreams and fears? Did you ever ask him why he was largely uninterested in you sexually?"

"It never seemed important to talk," Sara replied. "His actions spoke so much louder than words."

"Did they?" Schauzer asked, her voice soft and sympathetic.

"He was what I wanted him to be," Sara said, "and I didn't ask, I suppose, because I was afraid of what I might hear. That he wasn't what I thought, *we* weren't what I felt. I didn't want the peace disturbed. I was happy. As you've heard, ignorance is bliss."

She rose somewhat unsteadily to her feet. "We still have more time," Schauzer said as she glanced at her watch.

"No, we don't. *I* don't," Sara said. "I'm having a baby in a matter of months. Also, if I'm lucky, I'm having an adult . . . me. There's nothing more to say here today. Any further talk is now between Stefan and me."

His body was atop hers, yet its weight, as she lay face-down on the bed, a pillow beneath her pelvic area, was not oppressive. He moved slowly, steadily, his chest pressed to her back, the side of his face to hers. As his arms encircled and encapsulated her, his hands meeting and locking at her breasts, she could feel him strain to draw her yet nearer. Physically. He required closeness, extreme closeness, and had ever since her return from New York, the day her father-in-law had suffered the first of his two strokes.

Let me give that closeness to you. Truly, let me give it,

she ached to scream until he heard her. Let me be close in ways other than this.

His cheek was wet against hers, and Joanna didn't know if it was tears or sweat that oozed between them. But then she knew so little because he said so little about what he was feeling. It was always like this. Only she had never noticed. She hadn't then the need.

She had never understood his deep concern and love for his father, but then she had not known such a relationship with either of her parents. From the beginning of their marriage it was understood that Reynolds would spend an evening a week with his father. She had never interfered. Now they spent seven nights a week, or a portion of the same, together, with Reynolds sitting and watching his father die, hoping he wouldn't, and certainly not while he was sitting there.

Their communication had died while they were both sitting there. And lying there, in their bed, in their comfortable lives in which they never truly met, not one let alone seven nights of the week. That he had just been there had seemingly been enough for her . . . then. They had asked so little of one another. And that was what they had received.

As his mouth and tongue moved along her neck, down to her shoulder, Joanna yearned to give some other kind of comfort to Reynolds, one that was more substantial, that proved she loved in other ways. She wanted so much to share something more than the bed and the physical sensation of sexual contact.

His was not an act of love. He never said he loved her. He never spoke at all as he clung to her. But the fact that he clung to her, he would have argued, was all the proof she should need of his love. She felt otherwise. He needed her presence and was grateful for her willingness to be there for him. Only she wasn't really willing, just compliant and desirous of doing something to alleviate his terrible pain.

But she felt negated, not there. She felt used and yet not used enough. He wanted the woman, not the person. Although that angered her, she nonetheless ached for the little boy in the man who could neither talk about nor accept his father's death. Even after the second stroke, a massive attack that left Selwyn Bennett unable to move anything other than his eyes and lips, Reynolds refused any kind of relief other than the sexual. He preferred to renew his sense of life, of omnipotence, than discuss the inevitable. Joanna felt frustrated, needing to discuss death with Reynolds, knowing that if he would just listen he might hear, and she could therefore help him through this crisis.

He was lying in her arms now, trembling, needing to be coddled like a baby. She knew from his closed eyes and his heavy breathing that he was again elsewhere, undoubtedly with the man who lay inert in a nearby hospital.

"I read the books you left for me," she heard him say shortly after he had lit a cigarette. She was stunned and overwhelmingly gratified. She was present and accounted for, after all.

"They're well written and moving, and I can certainly understand why you're drawn to them."

The "but" was coming. She could feel it.

"But Jo, they do lack scientific data, and I find everything but their sincere intent difficult to accept. To me it's all fantasy, God knows an appealing one—they solve so many human concerns about dying. Jo, has it occurred to you that your NDE may simply be the dying brain's way of playing out long-repressed mental images, its ultimate and final defense against annihilation?"

"After all I've told you, is this what you believe?" she asked, hoping he would admit to at least some doubt.

"Unfortunately," Reynolds replied softly. He turned on his side to look at her. "Jo, I know it's real to you, although I think in time it will become less so. I wish I could share in your belief. It would make present matters so much easier to deal with. But as a doctor I know there is life and there is death, and all that passes in between. After that, although I, too, lack proof, I believe there is nothing. And what difference between our beliefs? The dead are gone, lost forever, no matter what you or other reincarnationists believe. All that's left behind are memories and worldly possessions. As if they could erase the sense of loss."

"Let him go, Reynolds," Joanna whispered as she lay by his side. "He's in pain and he's suffering. He wants to go. Help him to."

"What are you talking about?" he asked angrily.

"Reynolds, you're holding him here with your loving."

"We don't have that power," he replied as he turned his back to her to show his annoyance and disdain.

"But we do. And it's selfish, Reynolds. Let go. Let *him* go," she repeated.

His response was to stiffen, roll off his side of the bed and head into the bathroom, once again away from her.

The day seemed interminable with calls from clients and press that required time and effort. Now, as it neared four, Joanna was straightening her desk, preparing for an early departure so that she might spend an hour alone with her father-in-law at the hospital. His stroke saddened her. No longer was Selwyn Bennett the imposing man, the not-so-gentle gentleman who had survived his wife's death a decade ago without pause in either his work or his life. And he had loved his wife, honored her with his fidelity. Of that Joanna was as certain as she was of the clear fact that Selwyn had not loved the late Myrna Bennett as much as he loved his son, his image and shadow.

He had approved of her from the first, liking her credentials for his son. The daughter of professional people, a high school principal and his teaching wife. He enjoyed Joanna's good looks and thought them the perfect complement to his son's. At first skeptical when she had entered business, later he referred clients to her agency and boasted of her expertise. She had made him proud by enhancing the Bennett name. But he had never loved her. Love was reserved for sons and grandchildren. It was not his or her fault. Selwyn Bennett was a product of a generation that believed women, and daughters-in-law in particular, were meant to be mainly of service and serviceable.

She had always respected her father-in-law, appreciating his wit and a style that, although gruff, was honest. Others respected Selwyn Bennett too. In hushed tones at parties throughout the circuit people talked of the excellence of his work, the breakthroughs he had achieved in reconstructive surgery. And many the person at those parties who turned up his or her nose at the Hollywood lifestyle did so with a nose created by Selwyn Bennett.

Her private line rang, and Joanna stared at it, wondering if this was the call that would announce his passing over. She used to think that such a strange and almost funny euphemism for death, but now she felt that passing over was exactly what one did—pass over from one plane of existence to another.

She was surprised to hear Donald's voice and was even more surprised to hear his reason for calling. She was past due at his office for her collagen injections. She should not delay any further, he cautioned. As Donald talked, Joanna wondered about her face, particularly how it looked; she had not been aware of it in a very long time. Not even on those days when she wore stage makeup to play her role of press agent at various functions. She thanked Donald for his concern but felt it and further injections were unnecessary. He was stunned to the point of disconcertedness. He did not accept the aging process and did not expect any of his clients to. He urged her not to do anything foolish that she might later regret. His words made her smile.

The intercom buzzed. The receptionist announced that Damita Miles of D.M. Productions was on the line. Joanna stared at the blinking button on the telephone, loathing the caller's intrusion. Another stood in the doorway to her office: Lilith, now asking if she intended to pick up the telephone or was she using a telepathic communications network these days. Joanna understood Lilith's anxiety. Miles was a major account and a woman not used to waiting for anything or anybody. Least of all her press agent, to whom her production company paid a four-figure fee per week.

She greeted Damita briskly, knowing that effusiveness did not play with this kind of no-nonsense type of woman. She listened, pretending to knowledge she didn't have as Damita explained why she couldn't use Stacey in her next film. She was actually contrite, sorry that a girl who photographed so beautifully tested so poorly. She thanked Joanna for sending Stacey to her and asked if she would convey her best and yet, at the same time, the worst of all possible news. Joanna said she would not, momentarily stopping the woman who was not used to taking no for an answer in this, the fiscal year when her tease-and-tickle films for the teenage market had grossed as much as some recent Spielberg productions.

She had only thought to have the blow cushioned, Damita explained.

But who had cushioned the blow for her, Joanna wondered, upset by the fact that Stacey had used and misused her contact without her knowledge, that Stacey was once again taking shortcuts, being dishonest with herself and others.

"I'll tell her, Damita," Joanna said, changing her mind. "And thank you," she added, not wanting the client to think she was not grateful.

She was keenly aware of Lilith leaning against the wall, studying her as she took small bites from an apple meant to dispel the blood-sugar sag from which she suffered at this hour of the day. Joanna was experiencing her own sag, a drop in energy as the depression she had been fighting against since early morning won the battle. She bolted up from her chair as Lilith seated herself on the sofa.

"Not this time, Lilith," Joanna said as she began to stuff her attaché case with work she would read later at home. "There's nothing to talk about, nothing to say. At least nothing you haven't already heard. I mean . . . what's new about a husband who doesn't share your outlook on life. Or on death. Or a daughter who manipulates and lies."

Lilith continued to sit quietly, munching her apple. "That call from Damita informed me that Stacey has been using my name, our contacts, to push for film work," Joanna explained. "I felt like such a fool. Oh, to hell with what Damita thinks. What a shock. What a slap in the face. Why couldn't Stacey ask me? What's wrong with me that I can't get through to these people? I just seem to alienate them."

"Maybe it's not you, Joanna," Lilith said softly.

But Joanna wasn't listening, not to anything but her own thoughts. "I would help her if she asked. I would only insist that she finish school, take some acting lessons. Why won't she talk to me?"

"I'm sure thousands of mothers have asked the same question about their daughters," Lilith said. "Not me, of course. I'm always delighted when any of my children spare me from anything that's on their childish minds. That's what they have a father for. I'm a rotten mother. I accept that. Some not-so-rotten mothers have rotten children, and they have to accept that."

"I'll talk to her," Joanna said, not hearing Lilith's words. "I can't have her using our clients that way," she added as she struggled into a light coat that would do nothing to protect her from the unusually cold late-winter day.

"More important, Jo, you can't have her using *you* that way," Lilith cautioned. "You deserve better."

He was awake when she entered, staring somewhere in the direction of sound emanating from a suspended television set, its flickering images the only real sense of life in the room. She was momentarily startled when she realized she could feel his dying, sensed something in the room that made her rush to the bed to stare at what remained of the once overwhelming presence of her father-in-law. He did not see her until she sat at his side and took the hand hanging limply, dead to him and to the people he had once surgically served. She wondered if he could feel her touch, since she could feel his fear and exhaustion.

She talked to him. Little words about little things. Like the day, of the coming arrival of spring, of Stacey. Tears formed in the corners of his eyes and seemed, like the man, too weak to do anything but lie there. They hurt her. She stroked his forehead and bent over his shrunken frame to kiss his cheek. His breath was foul, but still she held her face to his, crooning words of reassurance. His lips moved, but there was no sound. Still she heard him. He was afraid, as so many others in his condition had been and would be. As she would have been had she not died.

She hesitated, debated, decided and then debated again. Ultimately there was only one decision she could make.

Because it was for him. "Sel, I know you're tired, but I want you to listen closely. Don't fall asleep. Not yet. Later you can sleep as long as you wish, for as long as you wish. Selwyn, death is nothing to fear. I know because I died twice."

She didn't have to ask if he was listening. She could feel it in the quickened pulse in his wrist and in the eyes that focused with an intensity that belied his sickness.

It was as if she, too, had fallen asleep, lost track of time and place. She had re-entered a world she had once thought was lost to her but now knew was not. The colors had been blinding, the aromas overwhelmingly pungent. And the music had been . . . heavenly. She wept, thinking again of the Light, becoming slowly aware first of the hand in hers and the tubes in his arm that sustained life, and then of the man standing in the room's twilight shadows.

"What have you done?" he demanded, his voice accusing even in its whisper.

"I told him about death and life," she explained.

"You're letting him die," he accused, moving from the shadows to where she could see his stricken face. "You're taking away his fight."

"Who's he fighting for, Reyn, himself or you?" she asked. "He's so tired, in such terrible pain . . . so sick."

"You're the one who's sick, Joanna. Now get out and leave me alone with my father."

"I only meant to help, Reyn," she said, shocked and hurt by his reaction.

He did not answer but pulled a chair to the side of the bed where he could sit and watch. Or was it guard, Joanna thought as she gathered her things. Her husband, a watch guard against death, now and, it seemed, forever.

As he sat in Tony's office Dean was wondering why he had subjected himself to the harassment. And Barbara Clarkson Langdon's Bill of Particulars was harassing, if not particularly enlightening. She said nothing she hadn't already said that day in her apartment, but the manner in which it translated onto paper was another matter. It was very matter-of-fact and austere. It was black or white but never gray. The information could have been given on the telephone, and Dean wondered why Tony had been almost insistent that he drop by the office at the noon hour. He should have refused. He had another commitment cross-town in a matter of minutes, and he couldn't be late. Not this day. Not for what awaited.

He forced himself to attend to Tony's words. Depositions must be taken. Which would require Dean speaking with Barbara's lawyers. A standard operating procedure. Although in this case, the questions the lawyer would ask would not be standard, Tony advised, his eyes focused on Dean. Some might be awkward for Dean to answer.

"Like what?" Dean asked, feeling the apprehensiveness begin again to throttle his stomach.

"Like the nature of your relationship with Chris. The physical and the financial," Tony replied, continuously watching Dean for reaction.

He thought about his private life made public to a stranger. But only one stranger, he said to comfort his misgivings. Better that than to risk having it told in court where it could be fodder for the press and public. His mind raced ahead, to the deposition and what he would explain. The truth. Surely then the lawyers would find a compromise that would allow him to get on with his life. Which was actually proceeding very nicely, except for this, thought Dean as he stole a glance at his watch.

"We're early, aren't we?" Tony asked as he looked up from his notes.

He didn't understand Tony's question or the statement he was making beneath it. Rather than challenge it he said: "I have a lunch date at one."

Tony's reaction was surprising. His voice matched his expression when he said: "I thought we'd have lunch here." His brother was disappointed. But why? "Didn't Blanche ask you for lunch when she called?" Tony said.

Perhaps she had, Dean replied, but obviously he had misunderstood the secretary when she asked that he come in at the noon hour. "Sorry," Dean said. "Next time."

Tony nodded but didn't respond, and Dean was confused; he had the impression that Tony's feelings were hurt. He was trying to understand when Tony proceeded as if the entire interchange that had just passed between them had not taken place. "I think we can stall this case indefinitely. If I work all the angles we can tire her out. It might take as much as two years before a judge hears the evidence.

"No. No long, drawn-out affair," Dean said. "I want this settled. Out of my life. *It* and her. I don't understand why she just doesn't name a figure instead of putting us all through this bullshit."

"To her and her in-laws it may not be bullshit," Tony replied as he chewed on the tip of a fake cigarette, a prop in his continuing campaign to quit smoking.

"I don't see how you can call Chris's parents Barbara's in-laws when Chris and Barbara have been separated for more than a decade," Dean said as he again looked at his watch, now anxious to be at his next appointment, the little ripples of anticipation throughout his body telling him just how anxious he was.

"In the eyes of the law, whether they've been separated ten minutes or ten years, if they have not divorced they are still married, and the Langdons are still the plaintiff's in-laws," Tony responded. "Your relationship isn't defined by law. Except as a joint tenant. There are no provisos for lovers."

"You've made my day. Thanks," Dean said as he rose from his chair. "I've got to move . . . got a lunch date with my producer." He paused and looked as though he might laugh. "That used to sound so phony when others said it . . . a lunch date with my producer. I never thought the day would come when those words would fall out of this mouth."

"I can sweeten the pot by asking which one," Tony replied. "Your soap or your shave cream?"

"Good God, you're right! How about that? The soap. My segments begin airing next week," Dean said.

"I know. We're taping it. In fact, I've asked Dad to join us Friday evening. We'll run a Dean Di Nardo film festival," Tony said as he stood smiling at the man across from him.

Touched, although not certain why, Dean pointed to his watch and said: "I really have to move."

Tony walked him down the hall toward the reception area. By the coat closet, as Dean was buttoning up his Burberry, Tony asked: "When do you want to give your deposition?"

"Next week. Tomorrow. I don't care. Just soon," Dean replied as he rang for the elevator. "Tony, please. Press for a settlement."

He was standing alone when the elevator doors opened and Blanche, Tony's secretary, emerged, carrying an elaborate tray of sandwiches wrapped in yellow cellophane, a bottle of Champagne trapped precariously under her arm.

"Where's the party?" Dean asked. He heard the response just as the doors closed.

"In Mr. Di Nardo's office. Someone he knows has a television commercial airing at one."

It lasted less than a minute. His face, his body flashing across the screen, a strange-sounding voice coming from a mouth he knew was his. He had looked without seeing, hating what he did see when he saw it. Finally the screen turned to black and then to the usual sports programming on the ESPN cable station. He sat stunned, waiting for someone to tell him how he should feel.

He heard the pop of the cork and felt the drizzle of Champagne as it slopped onto his hair and down his face. There was a loud whoop from an exuberant voice and Dean looked up to see Ralph Kayne, his face glowing with pleasure. Suddenly he was swooped from his chair, danced about and hugged. A bear hug that took his breath away.

"You were fucking terrific," Kayne was exclaiming. "I believed every second of the goddamn thing. And you looked hot. People all over town will want to jump on your bones."

Dean looked at Kayne as though he were a man who had gone mad in his own office in the middle of a workday. "It's going to blow it open for you. You really turned it on. Christ, you turned *us* on!" Kayne said, shaking his head.

Dean looked about the room, wondering who the "us" was, and suddenly remembered Sara sitting there being very pregnant and looking very much the proud mother.

She lifted herself out of the once well-stuffed but now sagging couch and wrapped her arms around Dean. He was pleased Ralph had thought to invite Sara, surprised by his gesture and hers. He knew that it took considerable effort for Sara to travel. She did so, he knew, to share his Minute, his first among many that would begin airing this week. She was murmuring how proud she was, how pleased, her cheek pressed to his. He thought of Tony and again felt bad, sorry that he had once more missed a connection Tony had tried to establish.

He began to relax, watching and listening as Sara and Ralph replayed the commercial for one another, each verbalizing or acting out a particular part they had especially enjoyed. He laughed at the silliness of it all, a big-time producer carrying on as though the minute he had just viewed would win them both an Emmy. It was just one lousy little commercial, Dean reminded himself. But if it was only that, why then was he thinking alternately of his father and Chris, wishing both were here, as if their presence would give some further credence to the moment? It suddenly seemed as if he had waited for just such a moment and his father all his life. The pain intensified before it was dispelled, gone with the understanding that neither his father nor Chris could be here, both absent for different reasons, but absent nonetheless. He returned to the room, to the festivities, to Sara and Ralph. He turned to his friends and asked in an almost childlike fashion: "Was I really OK?"

Sara watched as Ralph Kayne's hand touched and rested on Dean's face as he said: "Even without a cape, without a rabbit to pull from a hat, you had the magic." She saw the expression on Dean's face and she wanted to laugh—for him—and cry for herself. It made her that lonely. And she heard an embarrassed Ralph Kayne quickly pull his hand away and say: "Let's eat."

But it was Dean who moved her the most, Dean who asked to use the office telephone, who said: "I want to call my brother first." In that moment Sara knew exactly what her course of action must be.

It was late afternoon when she arrived on campus, uncertain whether Stefan would still be in his office. She was trembling, both from the winter cold and her anxiety. Even if he were in his office he might refuse to admit her, just as he had refused to see her ever since she had asked for a meeting. She walked slowly, careful not to slip on the ice, her balance no longer what it once was now that she was carrying a football, which if true to her past performances would be a rather large-sized watermelon by her seventh month. Still, Stefan didn't know. Not that she had wanted him to know. Not that he had allowed the possibility of his knowing. She wondered how exactly to tell him without confusing the real issue, which was them, independent of her pregnancy. Independent of all her pregnancies.

He need not know. Not if she didn't remove her coat. She could hide the fact and the baby. She shivered, chilled by her thoughts. What would he do if he knew she was pregnant? Suppose even that changed nothing? The thought made her feel as bleak and gray as the late-winter sky. Outside his office, she surprised herself by pulling a brush through her hair and freshening her lipstick. For what reason? Because she wanted to look wonderful, she decided, as wonderful as she imagined he would look now that he was settled in his new and *passionate* life.

The voice responding to her knock was his. Panicked, she thought to run but clutched her coat to her and entered. He did not look up, absorbed as he so often was in paperwork. She stood in his doorway staring at a stranger, her hand to her mouth, preventing either a laugh or a scream, she was not sure which. The Stefan she imagined was not there. No tall, tan and happy man sat at his desk. The Stefan who suddenly turned his face toward her was old, gray, without life, without passion. It frightened her. He frightened her.

She sat in the chair nearest his desk although he had not asked that she enter or sit. She wanted to touch his face, his arm, his hand. Had they been at home, she would have put him to bed and fixed a hearty cup of tea. He was telling her she looked well. He asked how she was.

"I took the national teachers' exam this week," she said, hating herself for seeking to impress him.

"Did you?" he asked, his voice somewhere other than in the room.

"Yes. I could be teaching by the spring semester," she added, unable to stop the selling of this Sara she wanted him to view as aggressive and in control.

His phone rang and he stared at it stupidly as if not knowing what to do. He finally picked it up and mumbled his greeting. A brief pause and then his: "I can't talk now." Sara didn't have to ask. She knew who the caller was. His hands, trembling as he returned the receiver to its cradle, were verification. The unseen enemy . . . Denise Wolfe. The victor. To the victor goes the spoils, and Stefan certainly was the spoils, Sara thought as she sought for something to say that would ease his discomfort and her own.

"You shouldn't have come," he said quietly. "I asked you not to. This isn't fair."

She almost laughed. Who was he to talk of *fair?* He had left children at home. Without a word. He had left her at home. With too many and yet not enough words for her to make sense of their lives.

"The kids miss you," she said finally. His face crumpled. For a moment she thought he would cry. "They don't understand," she said, speaking hurriedly. "Why haven't you called recently? You said you wanted to see them."

She avoided his eyes. She avoided his face. She couldn't stand the pain she saw there.

"I don't know what to say to them," he said finally. "I'm afraid, afraid of what they might say, what they will ask. I'm afraid they will hate me if they don't already."

"No one hates you, Stefan," she replied, suddenly realizing her words were true. "Stefan, these are your children. You're their father. They love you and you . . ." She couldn't finish. "You always were there for them before you were there for . . . anything else," she concluded.

"I left them," he said.

She waited for more, for some further explanation, but soon realized that his one sentence contained all his anguish and guilt.

"I told them you left me, not them," she said.

For the first time hope flickered in his eyes. It left abruptly as he broke down, dropped his head into his hands on the desk and wept. "It's so painful," he said. "So painful," he repeated as if she might not have heard. He raised his head and displayed a tear-stained face that looked as if it would break if she said or did one more thing to upset him. "I miss them. I miss being their father. I walk around the house looking for them. It seems so empty. *I* feel so empty. It's not a life without them. I'm half of who I am without them. And I worry I may have done them terrible harm."

She was resentful. He was speaking more eloquently than she could ever remember, and about whom? The children, not her. She would not be moved by his words or his condition. She would remain dispassionate, uninvolved. She had come to this office for her, not him, to make her world right. Still her hand moved to his arm, where it rested as he stared at it, unable to speak.

And what of the harm you've done me? she wanted to ask but didn't. Instead, she adjusted her coat about her, clutching it at its top, and said: "What were we together, Stefan?" And when he looked at her oddly, she explained. "Our marriage. What did it mean to you? What did I mean to you? Why did you marry me?"

They seemed like reasonable, simple questions to her. She could not understand his discomfort or why he withdrew his arm from under her hand. He did not immediately respond, and for a moment Sara feared he wouldn't. And why should he? His answers were only important for her life, not his.

"Is this necessary?" he asked.

It was not the answer she hoped for. It wasn't even one of the possibilities. Still, she replied: "Yes. I need to know or I wouldn't be here. Don't ask me why because I'm not certain. And it isn't easy to ask or to be here, but I need answers; some you can provide and some you can't."

"You were a very nice girl," he said wearily, "the kind a family like mine expected their son to marry. You were educated. You were Jewish. You were intelligent. You wanted a home and a family. You were all the right things."

"I was also cracked, in the middle of a paralyzing breakdown, in case you've forgotten," she responded.

"That, too, was attractive. It stressed your vulnerability, which seemed very appealing to me then. It also made you seem more sensitive than most, and sensitivity can be a very seductive trait to someone who has little of his own and has seen even less of it in his life. It was obvious you would make a good wife and mother. You loved me. And I loved you. You were pretty, you know. No, you didn't know, and that somehow, too, made you all the prettier."

Say it again, she wanted to scream. Tape it for me so that I can replay it later for myself. Dissect it for every meaning, both hidden and not. This is my legacy and my passport; say it again, Stefan, or for God's sake say more about fifteen years of marriage. Lie, but say something about passion.

"And you were weak and that made me feel strong," she heard him add almost wistfully.

"I wasn't all that weak, Stefan," she replied as she gathered herself. "I only thought I was."

Hers would have been the perfect exit line, but he topped her as she stood at the door, clutching her coat as if it were her pride. "And I wasn't that strong. You only thought I was."

She had always viewed fear as weakness, and now Schauzer was insisting the two were not necessarily one and the same.

"The man cringing before the poisonous snake at his feet is not weak, just afraid and rightfully so," the doctor emphasized as Sara sat before her, examining her weaknesses and Stefan's strengths.

Most of her life her fear had immobilized her, made her a coward, Sara said harshly.

Not so, Schauzer maintained.

"I always lacked courage," Sara argued.

"I would say, considering how fearful you always were, that you had enormous courage. To act when one is afraid is what courage is all about," Schauzer stated firmly.

"Were you afraid yesterday?" Sara nodded. "Still you went to see Stefan. *That* took courage."

Sara rested in her chair, momentarily forgetting yesterday and remembering so many other days when she had been afraid. Like the first day of every new term in the school year. Of people she didn't know with whom she would spend the next six months of her life. Of gym classes where she was certain she would look foolish. Of locker rooms and showers after gym classes where other girls would see how small her breasts really were. Still, she had attended school, and although she had never mastered her fear, it also had never mastered her. She had been a top student, a member of the honor society, liked but not popular because her fear had kept her separate.

She recalled her graduation day from college and then the morning after when she was consumed by fear. Within a day she had lost a world and her standing as a child. Now, a degree made her in the eyes of others a "grown-up," responsible for herself and her own life. She had never felt quite so terrified. Except, perhaps, the day she realized her father would never be coming back. But she had somehow gotten herself out of her house and into the very things that frightened her. Like a job in the city, subways, relationships with men, sex. All those "little things" most people took for granted but which for her had never been easy or "little things."

That was courage as defined by Dr. Sydney Schauzer.

Then she was courageous, she agreed sarcastically. In fact, considering how afraid she had been to marry, to have children, to own a house, she must be one of the world's most courageous people, she said with a wry laugh.

Schauzer thought that indeed not only possible but probable. "Sara, after your breakdown it took something other than Dean's hand and your mother's arm to get you out of the house. What do you think it was?"

She resisted the answer and Schauzer pressed, wanting to know why, wanting to know "the emotional investment in thinking yourself as weak, without courage.

"He's never coming home again, Sara. Your father is gone. The terror you felt as a little girl was justified, but it isn't now. Give up that little girl, Sara. Be the woman you already are. All it takes is what you have plenty of: courage."

She was slicing the cherry pie into five equal pieces when she said: "There is something I must tell you, something I should have told you sooner but didn't because I was afraid." She watched their faces for reaction and was not surprised when she saw none. It seemed her children had become expert in not revealing their feelings ever since Stefan had left.

"I'm going to have a baby," she said as she handed the first piece to Dana. "And I'm very happy about it," she added, confronting each of them with her eyes.

There was the expected silence, which lasted longer than she would have liked.

"Is it Daddy's?"

Robert's question stunned her. She was also offended, and by her own child. "Yes, and for you to think otherwise flatters but annoys me," she replied.

He shrugged. "Anything's possible these days," he said, his bitterness obvious even to the younger ones at the table.

"Will Dad be coming home then, Mom?" Dana asked.

It was a logical question and an even more logical assumption for a not-quite-child, yet hardly-an-adult to make. She hesitated. "He doesn't know yet about the baby. I haven't told him. And please, don't any of you tell either when he calls."

"*If* he calls," Robert shot back.

"He will call, Rob. Believe me. And I want you all to promise you will let me be the one to tell your father when the time is right."

"Why isn't it the right time now?" Naomi asked, looking frightened. "Don't you think he'll want the baby?"

Sara was trying to read beneath the question. Was Naomi asking whether or not her father wanted her? She handed her a slice of pie and said softly, trying to keep any sense of condemnation out of her voice: "I don't know what your father wants right now. I'm not sure he does either,'' she added, thinking of the face that had continued to haunt her since their meeting.

''Mom, how will you manage?'' Evan asked.

''The same way I always have,'' she replied.

''I think you should get rid of it.''

The boldness and severity of the statement frightened her. She looked at her eldest child and didn't know whether to slap or to hug him and whether his hurt was worse than her own. The other children were watching, each undoubtedly with a point of view he or she wasn't as quick as Robert to express.

''I think you should get rid of it just as he's gotten rid of you and us,'' he continued.

She put down the knife with which she was cutting, contained her anger and replied: ''He has not gotten rid of you. Or me either, for that matter. Nor does he wish to get rid of you, despite appearances. I saw your father the other day. He misses you. He loves you. He just isn't able to call right now. I know that's hard to understand . . . even for me, but it's the way things are.''

''Are you getting a divorce?'' Robert asked confrontationally.

It was a question she avoided, particularly when she asked it of herself.

''I don't understand why you would want to stay married to someone who doesn't want to be married to you,'' he persisted. ''And look how he's acted. Look at what he's done.''

She struggled for patience, struggled for the understanding she knew Robert and all her children needed. Still, she was angry. ''Robert, you're asking me questions to which I have no answers yet. Except one. No abortion. No getting rid of this baby. It was conceived in love. My love. For your father. And that's enough reason for its life and mine. Now eat your pie.''

And they did, digesting it along with her words.

THIRTEEN

It was chaos bordering on hysteria. She wanted to disconnect the phones, but Lilith refused, just as she refused police assistance to bar the press from their office. Which was now overrun with reporters and cameramen, each trying to capture on film something that would excite or incite the six o'clock news viewers. Their concern was not for the subject of their story but for the story itself, which would pour out over the wires and airwaves for days into weeks.

Joanna retreated into her office, where she was followed by Lilith and Anders Byrne, their new vice-president. Her private line was ringing and Lilith was staring at her accusingly, wanting to know why she wasn't answering the call. Because she had no answers, not for the caller or for the newspersons who had taken up their vigil both at Stone and Bennett Public Relations and at Cedars Sinai Hospital, where Lileen Lavery was a patient listed in serious condition. For months rumors had rebounded between the coasts that Lileen was again drug-addicted. Her weight had plummeted, along with her energy level. Rumors reached their crescendo when Lileen had collapsed at the Denver airport, following a concert during which she had also fainted. At Cedars preliminary tests suggested a liver malfunction. For a day leukemia was suspected. Last night the final diagnosis was made, ostensibly only to the singer and her people. Lileen had AIDS. And since she was not a male homosexual or a Haitian, it was assumed that she had contracted the disease through intravenous drug taking. Unless the record producer with whom she was cohabiting was a bisexual, a possible deduction that had that record producer, along with Lileen's manager, each yelling at the other, each wanting the agency to immediately release a statement that would protect everyone's reputation, each demanding to know how the diagnosis had leaked.

Joanna withdrew, feeling alienated and ashamed for those involved in the situation. She looked around the room, listening to the various strategies being proposed, aware that none took into account the very real fact that the person they were discussing was dying. Only once had Joanna interjected, suggesting the truth be told immediately.

The manager's answer had left her stunned. "What would such an admission do to her career?" he had wanted to know. An insane question considering her career, like her life, could be over in weeks to months. He denied that possibility, speaking of experimental medications, of hope and even of miracles.

The record producer/boyfriend championed honesty and then threatened to tell the truth himself of Lileen's drug abuse if they didn't follow his suggested course of action.

Lilith could smell his fear, his self-concern. She had remained silent until now. Her voice mesmerized the room as she decreed, not spoke. Lileen would go public, doing what she did best: repent. She would throw herself on the mercy of God and the mercy and goodness of the public. She would praise the Lord as she damned the devil, who was the greatest drug pusher in the world. She would share the responsibility for her fall with the force of all evil. And she would ask all those who had ever strayed to pray for her.

It was calculated and manipulative, and Joanna couldn't help looking at Lilith with disgust. Not the others. They liked what Lilith had proposed. One even said it had "a ring to it." They were pleased, *their* problems solved.

Joanna looked out her window. Her car, with its telling "Joanna" license plate, was surrounded by reporters, intent on capturing her or at least her statement about Lileen. As the others conferred, she dialed a car service, gave her account number and asked that someone meet her at the building's back entrance in ten minutes. Only

Lilith overheard. Her reaction was instantaneous. She motioned Joanna out of the office and into the conference room, where she berated her for jumping ship at a time when she was desperately needed. Joanna held firm. She wanted out.

But she is a client and you are a partner in this company, Lilith said angrily. Joanna walked away. She had no heart for the matter, no heart to watch the press bury Lileen before she was dead or Lileen's public relations counsel issue statements that might serve everything but the truth. Death was just too private and personal a matter to be the center ring of a circus.

"This really isn't a public relations matter, Lilith," Joanna said as she took her coat from the hall closet. "How Lileen Lavery chooses to die or how she admits to her illness is something between Lileen and her own conscience and not between Lileen and the press or the public."

"For Chrissake, Joanna, grow up! This is Hollywood. This is life," Lilith pleaded.

"Wrong. Hollywood is not life. They're antonyms, not synonyms."

Joanna pushed by the press collected at the doorway, rushed down the stairs, avoiding the elevators, and exited from the rear of the building. The car was waiting and she entered it quickly, not beginning to breathe easily until the car was speeding toward Beverly Hills. She felt terrible, empty, as if she had suffered a twenty-four-hour virus. Perhaps it had been wrong for her to leave. For *her,* no, she decided.

For a public relations person, yes. She sighed deeply, thinking of the rift she had created. It seemed unimportant when she thought of Lileen, a crazy, wild, uncontrollable girl. But a girl. Not yet thirty. How does one deal with a death sentence at that age? She would visit her. Perhaps for the first time in their association, she, her paid counsel, could finally be of service to Lileen without reservations or resentment.

She was shaking when the car pulled into the driveway at North Canon Drive. She entered the house from the rear, surprised to hear at this relatively early hour Reynolds's voice almost chirping from the direction of the living room. It was a change from the depression into which he had settled since Selwyn's merciful death a few days after her visit. The funeral, arranged by Reynolds, had been a "beautifully orchestrated affair"—so said the *Times*—with hundreds of well-known mourners. It resembled your typical Hollywood premiere.

Joanna came upon the couple with Reynolds as they drifted from the living into the dining room, extolling the virtues and flaws of both. Joanna struggled to understand what strangers were doing in her home, looking into her closets, examining her drains and disposal units. As they wandered the house, she trailed, feeling as if she were in some dream, unable to call out or make her presence known. In some ways it was not unlike the scene she had just left at the office. It, too, was totally unreal.

As soon as the couple left, she was at him, demanding to know why he was showing her house to strangers. He looked at her as might a little boy with a wonderful secret. The will had been probated, he explained. She looked at him dumbly. Selwyn's will. The Truesdale estate had indeed been left to him, he said, his eyes alight with excitement, expecting that she would share it.

Her reaction was instantaneous. She hated the house that wasn't a home but a museumlike mansion with more rooms than she or anyone else had use for. It had an indoor and an outdoor swimming pool, a miniature golf course and tennis courts. It had all the taste and style of a Mercedes with a license plate that bore the owner's name. Not again. She wouldn't be party to this.

"And you showed our house without asking me?" she said.

"The buyers fell into my lap. Dad's lawyers are affiliated with these people. They're moving out from Philadelphia and were in town only until the morning, so I brought them by. And Jo, I think they'll make an offer."

"This house . . . my house is not for sale," she said. "It suits my needs."

"Well, it doesn't suit mine," he replied angrily.

Sensing the challenge in Reynolds's voice and words, Joanna realized that further fighting would be destructive.

He was not about to be defied or denied. She turned away, toward the kitchen to prepare dinner, when his hand stopped her. Feeling his fingers tighten on her arm, she turned to face him and stared into the face of a small boy, a very disappointed small boy.

"Don't do this," he said. "Don't turn this into shit, too."

"But Reyn, we don't need it. Such a huge house. It will require live-in help, caretakers, a staff. I would hate that," she said softly.

"Jo, the house is free and clear. We have nothing but upkeep and taxes to pay on it. Think of the profit we could make selling this one," he argued, his voice cajoling, almost seductive.

"We don't need the profit," she replied. "We're more than just comfortable."

"So why not enjoy it?" he asked. "Jo, the house is a showplace."

"I don't want a showplace. I want a home," she replied.

"But I do want it, Jo. I've earned it. I can afford it. This is what work, even life, is about. Moving on up. Enjoying your money, reaping the harvest of your labors. You've heard of that before, haven't you, Jo? What is it you now want, to live like some goddamn ascetic?"

"I would hardly call North Canon Drive in Beverly Hills living like an ascetic," she said, wondering how both could win this conversation or at least finish it with neither feeling like the loser.

He turned from her and went back into the living room. "Any other woman given this opportunity would be thrilled. But then you're not any other woman. You're not even close. For God's sake, Jo, that house makes a statement. About its owners. And there's nothing wrong in making that statement. My father worked hard for it. So have I. Why can't you share my successes?"

She actually felt pangs of remorse stirring. To remind him that they seldom used his other "sign of success," the house in Malibu, would be cruel. It also wouldn't matter. That they *had* the house, could *say* that they had the house, was important. To him houses and cars were the affirmations of a life lived successfully, of the pursuit of happiness and the capture of same.

He was right. Probably any other woman would be thrilled to move into the Truesdale estate. She looked around the living room, furnished over the years with great care, each piece a major decision. It was not a perfect room by any means. But nor was the house perfect. The family room was awkwardly placed too near the living sections, but it was sunny and it faced the garden. She had planted that plot shortly before Stacey was conceived. Not on her hands and knees but by the side of a Japanese gardener who followed the specific design she had sketched. There were now cherry and apple trees that yielded beautiful blossoms. She wondered if Reynolds ever noticed.

"Can we each think about it?" she asked, conciliating.

He nodded, but she could see that his thinking was finished. He was counting on her changing her mind, coming around to his way of thinking. She thought of the house in Truesdale. She would never feel comfortable in it. It lacked intimacy. Persons could not be a family there. She hated the thought; it raised an unpleasant question. How often in this house, her home, did she feel intimate, or did they, as "persons," feel like a family?

There was no time to consider her answer. The front door crashed open and Stacey came stomping in, complaining in a loud voice: "You won't believe what she did now."

Joanna realized Stacey was talking to Reynolds even before she saw him and that the *she* Stacey was referring to was her.

"And what did I do now?" Joanna asked as Stacey entered the room.

Stacey's face registered shock. "Your car isn't in the driveway or the garage," she offered by way of explanation.

"And just what did I do now?" Joanna asked again.

"Why didn't you tell me you had spoken to Damita Miles?" Stacey began accusingly. "I felt like such a goddamn fool. 'Didn't your mother tell you?' she asked. No, my mother didn't tell me, although I don't know why. She just let me go on hoping for some dumb-ass role in a movie. I don't understand how you could do that. Haven't you any regard for my feelings?"

"Your feelings?" Joanna hooted. "What about mine? If you felt like a 'goddamn fool,' then imagine how I felt when *my* client calls and tells me my daughter has used my name to gain herself an audition."

"Why didn't you tell me?" Stacey screamed. "This is my life you're playing with!"

Joanna took a deep breath before she responded. "Frankly, it wasn't topmost on my mind. In case you didn't notice, I was busy with your grandfather, your father and little things like a funeral. I'm sure these are all relatively unimportant in your life, but they're not in mine."

Stacey turned to leave when Joanna stopped her. "I want to know why you used my name with one of my clients without asking."

Stacey spun around as she replied: "Because Dad said it would be all right. We talked about it the weekend you went east. So what's the big deal?"

"The *big deal* is that Damita Miles is a client of Stone and Bennett, and no one has the right to use Lilith Stone's or Joanna Bennett's name without asking first. Is that clear?" Joanna asked as she stared angrily from Stacey to Reynolds.

"Jo, I called Damita because Stacey needed an intro," Reynolds explained. "I couldn't see any harm in it. We're not strangers. We've been guests in her home; she's been a guest in ours. So I traded on your name. I just can't see it as a big thing. Jo, don't make this into an issue," Reynolds commanded. "Helping one's daughter really isn't a crime in anyone's book. And it certainly shouldn't be in yours."

He left her sitting there, taking Stacey, who shrugged as she left, deciding this had nothing to do with her. Joanna sat in her favorite wing chair, facing the fireplace, humming as she stared at the sconces it had taken weeks to find so many years ago. Her eyes flitted from the Fabergé egg to the Steuben glass owl that shared her mantel. Her "things" in her home. But just "things." She burrowed into the chair, relishing the feel of the damask and remembering exactly where she had found the material and the smell of the fabric showroom that day. She kicked off her shoes and rubbed her feet against the plush carpet, recalling how she had taken the sample to her cheek to see how it would feel against her body when, not if, she and Reynolds lay on it before the fireplace.

Her memories made her lonely. The day's events made her sad. She felt confused, hurt, and thought to call someone, but there was no one. Lilith was now very far away, and Dean and Sara had troubles of their own. There was only one person she could think of who would understand and perhaps share her grief: Nancy Evans Bush. But she couldn't call her. Nancy wasn't the answer, but, Joanna remembered, she had offered one.

Sara was drifting from thought to thought, choice to choice. Stefanie, for a girl; Stanley, for a boy. Stefanie and/or Stanley Schell. Pretty, she decided. She stretched and then allowed her body to sink still further into the upholstered seat, out of which she would soon have difficulty rising. It was warm in the train. Cozy. Almost as warm and as cozy as the office she had just left. Not that she had wanted to. Bliss, she decided, would be spending her day, each day of the remainder of her pregnancy, in that office next to the other women in their various stages of pregnancy. No other place in her life felt quite so safe and protected. Certainly not Schauzer's office, which lay ahead, menacing in her mind. She thought about her obstetrician's words: Mother and baby are doing fine. And they were.

Except for those moments when she thought of Stefan as the father of the baby. Perhaps she should tell him. Not exactly yet, but soon. If he decided to do the gallant thing she would deal with it. And if he didn't do the gallant thing she would deal with that too. Later, however. Everything right now was later. She really was feeling good, due in part to the Do Not Disturb sign she had hung over her feelings since her meeting with Stefan.

The train lurched, and Sara's eyes opened to find a man in the aisle staring at her. His eyes were friendly and exploring. He wasn't *the* man, but a man who suddenly sat next to her, although he could have had one of many seats to himself in the half-empty train. He rose and Sara thought he was thinking better of his choice, but once he removed his coat and folded it he sat again, this time his knee finding her own. She crossed her legs, grateful that that physical act was still possible at this stage of her pregnancy. She could feel him looking at her. Not furtive little glances but stares that frightened even as they excited her.

"You take this train often, don't you?" he asked.

She didn't know what to answer. What constituted *often?*

"I come into the city twice a week," she said, trying not to do anything more than answer his question. Her eyes remained focused everywhere and anywhere but on his face.

"I've noticed you," he replied. "You're always deep in thought."

He noticed her. Why? She wasn't the kind of girl or woman a man usually took note of. Although Stefan had said she was pretty. Was she? More so now, perhaps. Pregnancy always enhances a woman's face. So they say.

She had never noticed him. He wasn't the kind of man she would have noticed. He was nondescript. Certainly not ugly, but no Stefan. Nothing about this man—except perhaps his chin and maybe his full mouth—was particularly commanding. But he smiled a lot and his eyes took in more of her than she was used to having assessed.

He was making conversation, trying to elicit responses that would make for a dialogue rather than a one-man show. She wasn't good at dialogues. She had certainly mangled the one she had intended to have with Stefan. Why hadn't she pressed him for a decision, to act on his plans for the rest of his and thus their lives? Probably because she didn't know what she wanted to do with her own. But he had said she was pretty.

Did she work in town or was she a shopper?

She wondered what kind of women he knew who took a train twice a week into the city to shop. I'm neither, she wanted to say. In fact, I'm nothing more than some crazy lady who comes to the city twice a week to see her shrink.

Instead, she said she was a buyer for an important children's concern. Not exactly a lie. But then she never exactly did lie to men. She just never really told the complete truth. Which was why Stefan had undoubtedly thought her intelligent and a proper choice.

He was a patent lawyer with a pharmaceutical company, he revealed. Not an uninteresting profession, she thought. He reacted as if she had said she would join him in bed that evening. He turned his body toward her and asked about the magazine in her lap. She made some comment, wondering how she could make *Good Housekeeping* seem more interesting than it was. Or if she should.

His hands were in her lap, taking the magazine. She found his action terribly intimate. He thumbed through the pages with one eye fixed on her face, asking if she intended to try all the recipes. She doubted it. I believe in trying everything, he said as he carefully returned the magazine to her lap. Particularly exotic foods. I love to eat, he revealed, with something in his tone making the simple declaration sound obscene. He invited her to lunch. She declined. He suggested dinner. She almost giggled. Feeling giddy, she thought to open her coat and flash him, give him a peek of Stefanie or Stanley in her or his formative days. Then she thought she should thank him, not just for the invitation but for making her day, maybe even her entire adult life. This time she did giggle. She, a Sara Schell, a Mrs. Sara Schell, married lady from Princeton, giggling like a schoolgirl. Only she had never giggled as a schoolgirl. But then no one in recent years had ever tried to pick her up on a train—or anywhere else for that matter.

She decided she liked his chin even if it lacked the cleft that would have made him romantic. And she liked his hair. He had a full head of it. Which was important to a woman having her first pass made at her in more than a decade and a half. Again she giggled. This time he laughed with her as his knee again "accidentally" touched hers. He fished a business card from his wallet and handed it to her, stating that his lunch or dinner invitation was an open one. He did not offer his home number, and his wedding band made it obvious why. She tried to appear casual as she took his card, scanning his eyes briefly to see if they were as blue as she imagined. They were. And with long lashes, which she found strangely erotic in a man.

He offered her a cigarette. She declined. And still there was another quarter hour's time before they arrived in the city. He had closed his eyes, slumping in his seat, his legs open, a knee still bumping against hers in rhythm to the movement of the train. He had dropped off into what sounded like a deep sleep, if his occasional snore was any indication. She had the distinct feeling suddenly that she was sharing an intimacy with him, that they were lying in a moving bed, preparing to move with it. Her eyes were slits, pretending to be closed as they took in his calves, his thighs and, finally, his crotch.

She began to cough, unable to draw air into her lungs. She bolted from her seat but suddenly was quite all right, able to breathe but sweating. He was staring at her and then asked if she did Jane Fonda's workout or some other. Such an odd question. Her breathing stopped again. Some other, she replied. To which he suggested in a voice heavy with innuendo that she must look great in a leotard.

She thought she would faint. When the train finally pulled into Pennsylvania Station, she let him lead her from it and toward the subway, which she decided to take uptown to Schauzer's office. It wasn't until the doors of the car had closed behind her and she saw the graffiti-stained walls that Sara realized she was in a subway for the first time since her breakdown. She was wet with a nervous underarm and between-the-breasts sweat, which was common and not unknown to her. But the other wetness, the one between her legs soaking her pantyhose, was not common. And just as it was frightening, it was also exciting. She opened her purse, looked at his business card, thought of its owner's face as he had handed it to her and then tore it up in tiny pieces.

Centered by the familiarity of the surroundings and the face across from hers, Sara was finally calm. "He was either terribly nearsighted or very desperate," she said of Aaron Adelman, patent attorney for Kruger & Kreig Pharmaceuticals.

"Perhaps not. Perhaps he found you attractive," Schauzer suggested, her voice adroitly casual.

"Yes, men burn with desire when they meet me. I tell you, it's a curse," said Sara, trying to dismiss the situation.

Schauzer wasn't about to let her. "Stefan, too, said you were pretty."

"But I didn't exactly make him mad with desire," Sara responded.

"Perhaps that had less to do with you and more with him," Schauzer said. "Remember, this is a man you now understand has difficulty showing emotion. Sara, don't you consider passion, sexuality and sensuality to be part of one's emotions?"

She thought of Stefan and how he had looked these past years. Despite his words about his relationship with Denise Wolfe, there was no sign of passion about the man or his being. There was nothing. At his office he had looked so poorly and had seemed so lost.

"I feel this enormous hurt for Stefan when I should feel hurt by him," Sara said.

"Why not feel both?" Schauzer asked.

"He's not the man I married."

"No, he's not," Schauzer agreed.

"He's so much less than what I thought he was, and yet . . ." Sara struggled. "He's so much more. There's something comfortable about him now even in his discomfort. If only he hadn't posed. If only I had known who he was from the beginning. It would have made . . . *being* so much easier. I could have liked me more and him just a little less if I hadn't felt so inferior to him."

She thought about her words and the memories they elicited. "Of course I wanted to feel inferior. The superior ones take charge, make it all right for their charges . . . we inferior ones. They need us just as we need them. And what's then viewed as love is often hate. It all becomes so damn confusing."

"Until you make sense of it, which you're in the process of doing," Schauzer reminded.

"It's really all about one thing, isn't it? Growing up. Maturing in mind as well as in body. The aging process takes care of the latter automatically, but to mature in mind, not just to say but to know I'm an adult, an adult woman, independent, in charge of my needs, that takes doing."

"But you're doing it," Schauzer said. "You did it on the train. You gave yourself an option, which is a very adult act."

"What are you talking about?" Sara asked, confused and beginning to feel annoyed, although she did not know why.

"Sara, when a man talks of seeing you in a leotard, unless he is your physical-fitness instructor, he is already in the act of making love. There is more to foreplay, you know, than touch. You permitted it. Furthermore, you encouraged it."

"Don't be ridiculous," Sara exploded. "The man sat next to *me!*"

"And you could have moved at any time. You could have also cut him off *at the pass,* so to speak, with a word or with silence. But you didn't. You engaged in a flirtation. You were giving yourself an option. Even if that option was to say no, which you did. In other words, you were engaged in adult behavior, consciously or not.

"Oh, stop looking so horrified, Sara. It no longer becomes you. So you've had a raunchy fantasy. You even looked at a man's crotch. Welcome to the women's club. What you choose to do about your fantasy is what you choose to do about it. Your adult decision, in other words. But don't deny it, Sara. Don't deny that part of you that is as valid as any other," Schauzer urged.

Sara remembered her words to Stefan spoken months back. *Passion at my age is the least of things in a marriage. A home, a family, a marriage are more important than passion.*

And his response suddenly had a different meaning. *And that's enough for the rest of your life?* he had asked.

Obviously it wasn't, although then she had thought it was.

"Sara, once you accept who you are—*all* you are—you can then decide what kind of marriage you want. Whether it is to Stefan or to some other man, providing you want marriage at all. And contrary to any example Ina may set, women your age, with and without children, do meet men.

You do have options, Sara. You do not have to settle. And fond as you are of saying nobody gets it all, some do. *If* they work for it and *if* they are lucky. But the point is: In knowing who you are and what your needs are, you can begin to make choices that aren't made from conflict but which are real choices."

She looked at Schauzer, aware that she was being given something she had never received from her mother or sister: permission to be a woman. But Schauzer was granting that permission only after she, Sara Schell, had made it clear she wanted to grant it to herself.

"Life is strange," Sara mused. "There I was, sane, sensible Sara Schell, sitting on a train minding my own business, when this pervert, and not just any pervert, but this Jewish pervert . . . a Jewish lawyer pervert, sits next to me and plays kneesies. Next thing I know, sane and sensible Sara Schell is a hot-to-trot preggie in search of a vibrator. I don't know, Schauzer. Given that, how can anyone still doubt the beneficial effects of psychotherapy?"

One more lap and he would have run five miles in thirty-five minutes on an indoor track. He was struggling, breathing heavily, gasping for air: unable to think, which was good; unable to feel, which was even better. He had come directly to the gym from the lawyer's office, where he felt not only had his deposition been taken but some part of him. He was angry and humiliated. Barbara's lawyer had pried as he probed, insinuated as he questioned, his voice, like his face, filled with judgment and disdain. He examined the *exact* nature of his relationship with Chris. How they had met, where they had met and when. He asked about finances and whether Dean had received an "allowance" during their eight years together. He had succeeded in making a marriage, a partnership, seem like a play-for-pay liaison.

Tony had been all but helpless. Although he frequently interceded, he could not shout "objection" as he would have had it been a court of law and Dean on the witness stand. And so Dean had shouted his objections, which made Barbara's lawyer, Allister Casey, smile and his questions even more invasive. He had fled the inquisition as soon as it was over, not waiting to analyze the proceedings with Tony, who looked saddened by the experience.

Dean finished his run with wind sprints and then moved to the Nautilus equipment, loading the press with more weight than he normally used. He pushed, straining against the one hundred eighty pounds of steel, the veins in his neck popping as his pectoral muscles expanded. He sucked in oxygen and then exhaled, trying to release the sick feeling in the pit of his stomach. It clung to his intestinal walls, determined not to leave its home. He pressed again, pushing not just the steel weights but the experience from him. Another came into focus; the day he had climbed the four flights to his crummy dump on the Lower East Side to find it ransacked, clothes and drawers from dressers thrown about as if they were Frisbees. He had been physically ill then when viewing the violation, and that sick feeling had stayed with him for weeks. And then it was only his *things* that were manhandled. Today it was he himself.

Sweat glistened on his brow and his military T-shirt clung to his damp chest as he again heaved himself into the press, pushing away the lawyer, Barbara and a process that allowed a person to be so humiliated. And if giving a deposition had been so painful, what would it be like to give testimony in a court of law, should it come to that? Which it mustn't. Barbara must settle. Perhaps next week, when she and Chris's parents and her psychiatrist came to New York to give their depositions, her attitude would change. Let Tony do to her what her lawyer had done to him.

He glanced at the clock on the wall. An hour remained until closing time. He would swim, exhaust himself to the point where going home would no longer be difficult. He would sleep despite his anxiety. And there was nothing to be anxious about. His fears were groundless. He did have Joint Tenancy. With Right of Survivorship. A legal piece of paper said he did.

Do you hear that, Barbara?

But why did he feel that Tony didn't share his confidence in that legal piece of paper? He should call Tony. He should ask. Unless Tony was sparing him from some hidden and potentially dangerous legal fact. Nonsense. His mind was being overactive. He was frightened and angry. They were trying to steal his home just as they had stolen Chris's body.

Damn Ralph for being away. Of all possible weeks for him to be on location shooting, this was the worst. Ten days in the Bahamas, the last four to be spent with his children during their spring break from school. Which was nice for Ralph but rotten for him. Although he could call, but might not the children think that strange? Even though he was just a friend. He needed advice. Not that Ralph would give it. He had this infuriating habit of turning the responsibility over to him. Sometimes he just didn't want it, even if it was for his own life. An ongoing role in a new cop show was being considered, as was his co-starring in a not-very-good made-for-television movie. Was either a smart career move? And now Joanna thought this might be a good time for him to make the rounds in Los Angeles. Only he couldn't leave New York. He was too afraid someone might move into his home and move him out while he was gone.

He pulled at the pool waters, trying to hoist himself farther afield and apart from the few remaining late-night swimmers. He cramped, a sudden but sharp blast of pain in his gut. He gasped, catching a chlorinated miniwave in his mouth, and choked. A hand steadied him, a man who grabbed him by the arm and held him upright until he could signal he was all right.

He went from the steam room to a cold shower and back to the steam room again, where his overused muscles began to unwind. Twenty minutes later he was standing outside the club, watching the steady drizzle of early-spring rain, not knowing where to go except home, where nothing waited but the day's memories.

"Do you need a lift? My car is parked just up on Sixth Avenue."

Dean turned and recognized the face of the swimmer who had steadied him in the pool. From the smile and the intensity in the eyes, Dean knew it was more than a car ride that was being offered. He quickly studied the man. Tall, slender, but well built. He felt the adrenaline suddenly flood his system as warmth rushed to his groin. Suddenly the sick feeling in his gut disappeared. There were other matters now to occupy his mind.

The car was parked in front of Lamston's, and as the man bent to unlock it Dean's eyes fondled the shape of his buttocks, the look of his leg in the Levi's jeans. He was becoming aroused for the first time in six months. His mind stopped working as he concentrated on only one thing.

As they drove uptown, silently agreeing that the driver would choose the location of their assignation, Dean fantasized the various sexual acts to be performed. He was only half aware of the conversation being made. About workouts and the Eat to Win diet, as opposed to the one that promised to strengthen the immune system. Of interest to everyone in this day of acquired immune deficiency syndrome. And then silence. It was only as they neared Columbia Heights, where the man lived, that Dean realized the man in his sexual fantasies was faceless and not the man in the car. He looked again at the driver and, despite a face that was strong and handsome, even with the thick glasses he wore for driving, he held no interest for him. It was just another face, different and yet not different from hundreds—or was it thousands?—he had known and touched before Chris.

Before Chris. After Chris. It was the in-between that now stood in the way, that slowed the rush of adrenaline and cooled what had just been a firestorm in his crotch. This man could not give him what he needed, other than a release from six months of pent-up sexual frustration and someone, anyone, to get him through the night.

They stopped at a drugstore; the man, somewhat embarrassedly, said he needed something and for Dean to wait in the car. But Dean elected not to wait, leastways not in the car, as his legs were now cramping. He stretched and flexed in the street, and then peered through the window into the store, where he saw the druggist pointing toward a display of condoms.

Dean began walking, slowly at first and then quickly, knowing he should stay and explain that it wasn't his fear of AIDS that was making him reconsider but his fear of another kind of death, the one brought on by too many meaningless one-night encounters where the body was valued but the person wasn't. He couldn't go back to that.

But he turned back; he could not just leave without some explanation. He owed both himself and the man that. It was a responsibility. "I'm sorry," he said as the man eyed him oddly, the panic dissolving from his face as Dean returned. "This has nothing to do with you. Nothing at all. Which is the problem." He didn't know if the man understood. But it didn't matter. He did.

They fought over the house often, and Joanna would leave their arguments with her head hurting, somewhat dizzy and more than just a little sick to her stomach. To please him, she examined the Truesdale estate and found rooms of little function other than to opulently fill up space. She noted, however, as they walked gardens and tennis courts just beyond the pool and its surrounding cabanas, how like a child Reynolds was with his potential new toy. She saw then that although she didn't need the house, he did, and that she would acquiesce; she couldn't deprive him. It mattered more to him than their home, whose true foundation, even elegance, was its memories. Nearly two decades of their lives had been lived there. That meant much to her but seemingly little to Reynolds, who was only impressed that their initial investment in the Cape Codder had now quadrupled in value.

Joanna's head ached. Her watch said she had the twenty minutes that would serve better than an aspirin or any other headache remedy. She closed the curtains in her bedroom, took a light blanket from the closet and covered herself as she lay on the thick-carpeted bedroom floor. Behind closed eyes she drew inward, going deeper into meditation with every inhalation.

It appeared slowly. Just a pinpoint of light at first, and then it grew larger, spreading like oozing oil as it flooded her system. The light was brilliant but not blinding. She could see into it and feel its warmth as it moved slowly from the top of her head down through the neck, to her shoulders, rib cage and into her stomach. Relaxing, as one would in a warm bath, she could feel the light wash in and through her, from without to within. The headache vanished, taking with it the nausea and dizziness.

It was a process Joanna had accidentally discovered during Lileen's first stay in the hospital, when she and Lilith had fought bitterly about the agency's role as liaison between their client and the public. Battered at home by Reynolds and the issue of the house, and badgered at the office by Lilith on the issue of professionalism, she had retreated one particularly difficult afternoon behind her closed office door. As she lay on her couch, her head pounding, depressed and disturbed, she closed her eyes and, by deep breathing, slipped back to that recent time when she had felt the most calm, the most peace and the most love. The experience was still available to her. Hot in all its sense and smell or brilliance, but enough to make it feel as if it were once again happening.

Thirty minutes later she had been startled by the knock on her offfice door, thinking she had closed her eyes and mind for but a minute. Lilith had been strained when she entered, but Joanna's calm had calmed her. And so her meditation had begun, and it proved to be healing each time. Not only did her headaches disappear, but so did the anger and depression that always accompanied them. It became her haven, her place to go in times of stress. It became her most important home and it could not be valued. Best of all, it was mobile.

Joanna rose from the floor feeling light-headed but not dizzy. She walked slowly down the stairs, knowing the exact number of steps to each landing. In the hallway, on the table where she always placed the day's mail, she left her note, reminding Reynolds she would not be home till very late that night. He believed it was business. She let him think that. He never questioned her, and she wondered if that was because he was having an affair. She suspected he was. She thought that should bother her but was more bothered that it didn't.

Just as she had pulled out of the driveway and into the street the stretch limousine stopped at curbside. Stacey exited, schoolbooks in hand. As Joanna watched, Stacey leaned into the car, obviously kissing its backseat occupant. Her video-producing friend, Joanna deduced. After all, from what she knew, Stacey saw no one else. Not even her.

* * *

The woman in bed staring out the window, her bony hand resting on the Bible that lay open on the top sheet, seemed smaller to Joanna than the last time she had seen her. Yet the sickness seemed so much larger. Even from the doorway, Joanna could see it hanging like a cloud over the room, its thickness making breathing difficult. As she approached the bed, still not understanding why she frequently visited this woman she had never liked, Joanna could see the effects of Lileen's recent bout with pneumonia. Oozing blisters clustered on her lips, testimony to the 105-degree fevers that had accompanied the bronchial infection. Whatever dislike Joanna had once felt for the woman had now turned to concern and a need to say or do something for the child who was in such obvious need of more than just medical attention. Joanna took Lileen's hand, an act that meant much to the singer, who till recently had had thousands shrieking for a touch, but who now had twice that many seeking to avoid any physical contact with her.

Neither woman had been comfortable with the other when Joanna had first visited, with Lileen particularly confused by Joanna's attention. She associated Joanna with aloofness and attitude, two things she experienced often when with certain kinds of white ladies. Initially Lileen had just watched from her bed as Joanna came and went, saying little but being there in ways that Lileen could not define but that she could feel. Days ago, when Lileen was rushed to the hospital for the second time, it was Joanna she had called, although neither knew exactly why.

As Joanna continued to massage her hand, Lileen looked from the Bible to Joanna and said: "There's nothing in here that helps." Lileen was not one to cry, but Joanna could see that the girl was on the edge of her emotions when she said: "It only makes matters worse." Joanna didn't know what to respond so she said nothing, letting her hand, as it held Lileen's, do her talking. "This Good Book says I'm going straight to hell and that I do not pass Go or collect my two hundred dollars. This is God's judgment, Joanna. This is His punishment."

"I don't think so," she heard herself saying, although she had not intended to speak. "God doesn't punish, Lileen. Only we do that. To ourselves and one another.

Somewhere deep within us all there is a judge and jury for our every action, and when we find ourselves guilty, we sentence ourselves.''

''And my sentence was AIDS,'' Lileen said derisively. ''Honey, a simple cold would have done the trick nicely. One hundred Hail Marys would also have been fine. But this hell is heavy-duty stuff, and it's damn hard for me to believe I put it on myself. No, this is God's judgment. And I understand it.

''Joanna,'' Lileen whispered after a brief silence, ''I may not have gotten AIDS from a needle. Years ago, I used to party a lot, particularly after the shows when the only way not to go way down from a performance was to stay up. And sex is an up. It stops you from crashing, from feeling that there's nothing until you step onstage again, getting all that love from people you don't even know. So I got all that love offstage from a whole lot of men I didn't know. And it was better than drugs because it didn't leave no tracks, no needle marks in the arm or leg. And I didn't have to deal with the scuzballs who always knew when to be there with the stuff at the right and wrong time. So I got laid and now I'm fucked for it.''

The laugh was a wry one and it unnerved Joanna. She looked about the room, bare of visitors and flowers whereas weeks ago it had overflowed with both. There were telegrams and cards, but not in the number Lileen had first received when she initially entered the hospital. Joanna hesitated, debated and then realized she had no choice other than to speak. ''Lileen, God doesn't judge,'' she said almost as a pronouncement.

''Girl, dost the Lawd speak on you directly these days or is this the gospel according to Pat and Shirley Boone?'' Lileen asked, her eyebrows raised in mock sarcasm.

''He doesn't judge, Lileen. Not ever. I know that. For a fact,'' Joanna added softly.

She had the girl's attention. She could tell by the pressure suddenly applied to her hand, the eyes that widened and the lips that parted, preparing to speak. ''Lileen, last September, in that auto accident you may remember, I died.'' She watched Lileen's face, felt the spasmodic jerk that went through her body. ''I know. It sounds weird, but

I died and went to that space we call heaven. And Lileen, I heard God, although He never spoke, not in audible words anyway. More important: I felt Him. Lileen, you know how loved you felt on that stage? It's nothing in comparison to how loved you feel standing before God. And it's not frightening, Lileen. It's just beautiful because it's all about love. Nothing but love."

"You saw God?" Lileen asked, struggling to sit upright in bed.

"I *felt* God," Joanna corrected. "In a glowing light that infused my entire being. Lileen, it still infuses it. And as the Bible says, He is the father; but Lileen, He is the father of love and of infinite patience and acceptance."

"And He's not saddened by our sins . . . He doesn't judge?" Lileen asked in the voice of a child.

"Lileen, recently I remembered something I had forgotten about my experience. In that Light, before God, I was asked to assess my life and in particular what I had to show for my forty years on this earth. My life passed in review as if flashed on a wide, circular screen. And God watched with me, helping me to see how I had lived, where I had succeeded and how I had left much to be desired . . . and learned. All without judgment. It was odd. The things I thought would matter—like my work, my awards—meant nothing. It was the simple gestures I had made without thinking, gestures toward others, kindnesses, the things we simply don't pay attention to . . . these are the things that mattered. I came up short. In my mind."

"I don't think I've exactly got a stockpile of simple gestures of my own," said Lileen. "And it doesn't look like I'm getting a second chance to amass them."

"It's not too late," Joanna said. "Lileen, your illness gives you a chance to examine your life. Maybe it even sets an example to others. You have time to learn from this. Go for it. Live each day as if it were your last, but know that it isn't. And let go of the past. With all your mistakes. It's a new day, Lileen. Commute your sentence."

She had no idea where her words were coming from, and she was so surprised by her spontaneity that she had no time to judge or censor them. For a brief moment she felt embarrassed. Lileen was staring at her, not knowing what to believe but wanting to believe it all. She was thinking, trying to sort through Joanna's words and experience and apply both to her own life. Her words, when she spoke, came with a rush. "That home I started for teenage unwed mothers. It was a pile of shit. Something to get the heat off my back. But I think it's a good thing. No . . . I *know* it's a good thing. But I don't know what's happening with it. My lawyers and accountants know. 'Cause to them it's a tax shelter. Joanna, can you find me somebody who will teach me my own business? Somebody has got to make sure nobody has his hands in the cookie jar or on the cookies either."

"I can do that, Lileen. Not to worry," Joanna said as she fluffed up Lileen's pillow and arranged it comfortably beneath her head. Lileen leaned back, her body limp, her face drawn. As she closed her eyes she said, a smile playing about her lips: "You are really something, white-bread lady. You take one hell of a trip and you don't use ludes, smack or acid as your private jet. Come back soon. We have some heavy-duty stuff to rap about."

She had it timed. From the moment the plane touched down in Oakland and she picked up her rental car, it was twenty minutes to the John F. Kennedy campus in Orinda, an Oakland/San Francisco suburb. Enough time to become anxious. And to think about what had transpired with Lileen in her hospital room. The people she would soon see would have been surprised at her verbal abilities, considering how silent she had been the one time they met her a month ago. But then, despite her need, she had been hesitant to speak. From the moment she entered the classroom and saw the chairs arranged in a circle, her every warning signal screamed, "Group!" And she was not a group person, not the type to "share"—the current buzz word—her "gut reaction," a buzz word from her past that still had unpleasant memories.

Still, she had returned. She needed the environment and the people in it, people concerned simultaneously with death *and* the quality of life. If she couldn't speak she could listen, and in that way "share" something perhaps pertinent to her own life. The meeting last month had been informative and with none of the outpouring of emotions she had so feared. There had been a topic: *Are You Really Not Afraid of Dying?* and it made her think about the differences. Death did not hold fear for her, but dying still did. Only because she was not yet ready to leave this life, and when she was she wanted to do it quickly, without pain, and with a written guarantee of same.

Room *303* in the flat-roofed, ranch-style building that housed a series of classrooms was filled by the time she arrived. She blanched again at the seats arranged in a circle but focused instead on the faces of those in attendance, trying to intuit which were experiencers like herself and which were "concerned others." Like doctors, nurses and social workers, the peripheral members of the group. She returned the smile of the group leader, a pert woman with wash-and-wear permed hair and hazel eyes that sparkled even through the heavy prescription lenses that covered them, and took a seat, smiling at both her immediate neighbors to her left and right. The group began. She listened.

She was unaware of the exact moment she stopped listening but began participating, not with words but with her emotions. The topic had been discarded as one member, a round and unassuming-looking man, spoke of his inability to do his job since his NDE. He had been a policeman and now found it impossible to carry a gun. His wife didn't understand. His friends on the force didn't understand. And he didn't know how to make them understand. She thought about her own job, and in particular about Lilith. The relationship was dying. And that was worse, more painful than the death itself. She was already mourning the loss of Lilith, just as this man was mourning the loss of his partner, the man with whom he had driven for twelve years in a squad car.

A woman started to cry—it wasn't her, thank God, she thought—speaking of the distance that she felt existed between her and her family ever since she had "passed over," as she referred to her near death. And she couldn't bridge the distance. She felt as if she were on a ledge, trying to get back to safety, her hand extended, but with no one to take it.

Joanna thought about all the times she had reached out for Reynolds and all the times he hadn't been there. Yet he felt she hadn't been there for him. Which is what Stacey felt. They were all feeling the same thing. But whose hand was extended?

She didn't want to feel, let alone listen, as one distraught young man—he could not have been thirty, thought Joanna—spoke of his divorce, of a wife who belittled him now to former friends and family because he couldn't provide as he once had—as a boxer. He couldn't be violent anymore, couldn't misuse his body or abuse another's. The former policeman nodded, understanding mutely.

Although her eyes had been open, she started to see. None of the nonexperiencers were smirking or laughing or looking snide. All seemed most concerned. She felt safe and suddenly glad she was seated in a circle, where if she wished she could see everyone's face.

The problem, she realized, was endemic to those who had experienced near death. Their families removed themselves as they felt removed from lives they had been leading prior to their demise. Loneliness, even despair and depression, were usual. The function of the group, the leader interjected, was to help with those problems, to help integrate the near-death experience into a life and into the job and a family. Joanna doubted if that were possible, doubted if she would ever again feel Reynolds or Stacey close to her. She felt a hand on her arm, and was surprised and then confused by its touch. Why was the group looking at her? Because she was crying, she suddenly realized, showing her emotions despite her intent to remain aloof. And the tears wouldn't stop. Through them, she saw the concern on the faces of those about her. She also felt it and thus knew she was no longer alone in her own experience, that finally there were others willing and wanting to share it. And so she continued to cry. For all she had lost and for all she had just gained.

FOURTEEN

SARA looked again at the official notification. An ordinary piece of paper, a form letter actually, with nothing personal about it. Except her name. Her glorious full name: Sara Rosen Schell. Who now was, according to this nondescript yet official piece of stationery, licensed to teach in the state of New Jersey. She would have danced, but dancing was difficult. She would have laughed, but she was crying. She reached for the phone in her excitement and dialed without thinking. An old number and a familiar one. There was no answer.

Thank God, she thought as she disconnected, wondering how, even for a moment, she could have forgotten that there was no longer a Stefan to share this event or any other in her life. She would not suffer it, she decided. She would find someone else with whom she could celebrate. But not Dean; he was too troubled with the endless depositions that were being taken in his life. Sara looked at the kitchen clock. Early to call California, but not that early where Joanna would be terribly disturbed. She reached for the phone just as it rang. The voice that asked to speak with Sara Schell was not familiar. It had a controlled edge to it, particularly when the caller said it was Denise Wolfe phoning.

She listened as Denise Wolfe hurriedly apologized, for what, Sara wasn't certain. Just as hurriedly, as if she were embarrassed, Denise Wolfe said that Stefan had been hospitalized again, taken by ambulance late last evening, seemingly suffering from a heart attack, which so far proved again to be nothing more than hyperventilation caused by extreme anxiety. Still, the woman rushed on,

Stefan had not been well, suffering with insomnia, recurring nightmares when he did sleep, a loss of appetite resulting in a loss of weight. She felt that Sara and the children should know.

Sara heard herself asking intelligent questions, unemotional and detached, inquiring about his blood pressure, pulse and cardiogram. She listened to the responses as if she were not on the phone with the woman her husband had left her for. She was civilized. Denise Wolfe was guarded but cordial.

The question stunned her momentarily. Would she visit? Sara didn't know, so she didn't respond immediately. There were still too many questions in her mind left unanswered. But she couldn't ask why she was being called and if Stefan had asked to see her. Instead she listened as Denise Wolfe apologized for being the one to bring such bad news.

Sara almost laughed. It was funny. In a way. Here the woman who *was* the bad news, and who had been the bad news since last fall, was apologizing for being the bearer of sad tidings. Indeed. She finally did laugh and didn't give a damn what the woman on the other end of the line thought.

She took Stefan's telephone and room number and hung up, thinking how ridiculous that she had said, Thank you for calling. She sat heavily into the sofa in the living room where she had wandered, forgetting the difficulty she would have later when getting up. The small football had become the expected watermelon. A kicking watermelon that often doubled her with pain. Imagine bringing that into Stefan's hospital room. If he hadn't suffered a heart attack before, he surely would when confronting her and "it."

The tone in Denise Wolfe's voice. She could identify it now. She was tired of him, tired of the mess and of the cleaning up after it. And why not? Sara asked. It wasn't Denise Wolfe who had promised to love Stefan Schell in sickness and in health. She was trying to dump the responsibility. Well, that wasn't possible, Sara decided. She tried to think clearly. About what *she* wanted. If she didn't go to the hospital she was making a statement. Yet if she went she was also making a statement, albeit a very different one. And if she didn't tell the children she was making lots of statements, some that she might regret greatly if Stefan's condition was or grew to be more serious.

She would call Schauzer. She would gain her input. The idea made her angry. She didn't need her analyst to make a decision. She hoisted herself up and off the sofa, the letter with the New Jersey State imprint falling from her lap to the floor. It could stay there, she decided. Whether it be on the floor or in her hand, the fact of it didn't change. She was licensed to teach. She had an avenue and a mode of transportation. Both made her feel freer than she could ever recall feeling.

She decided not to tell the children until she could ascertain the severity of Stefan's illness. The children needed no further shocks, having made several adjustments within a few months' time. After his prolonged silence, Stefan, but two weeks ago, had begun to phone frequently, spending awkward minutes with each child via a cordless phone. It was a beginning and she had been pleased. If he were seriously ill the children would need to be told something—they would wonder why he wasn't calling again. She suddenly realized that she, too, needed to be told something. She reached for the phone and dialed a number she knew by heart even though she had never dialed it. Denise Wolfe answered on the second ring and was taken aback by Sara's questions. She only assumed Stefan would be pleased to see her. She only guessed that he would be more upset by her absence than by her sudden appearance, she answered.

Again Sara had the feeling she was being pushed, a replacement for the tired troops, a relief pitcher brought in to mop up at the end of the game. Sara thought how the situation had reversed itself. Months ago it had been Denise Wolfe pleading to see Stefan. And she had refused, not wanting this woman, particularly this woman, to have any communication with her husband. So wasn't it strange that Denise Wolfe felt no such proprietary feelings? Wasn't there some kind of unspoken statement, and truth, in that?

Dinner was almost ready. She could slip out of the house now and the children need never know. The visit to the hospital could, however, wait.

Stefan would be all right. And if he wasn't, her life wouldn't change. His illness had nothing to do with her, only with him. But perhaps it would be best to go now. For her own peace of mind. The doorbell startled her. Instinctively she reached for the phone, thinking that possible while an unexpected visitor was not. She peered through the living room window but could not see the face of the figure in her doorway. Yet there was something about the man's stance, the way his hands were stuffed in his pants' pockets, that made him seem familiar.

They hugged, and as they stood in the doorway, neither anxious to separate from the other, she wondered which of them had just heaved such a heavy sigh. She studied his face and saw it could just as easily have been Dean.

"I don't suppose you'd believe that I just happened to be in the neighborhood so I dropped in," he said, feeling that some explanation was necessary. She didn't respond but led him to the kitchen, where the table was already set for five. He didn't protest as she added another setting, except to say he must leave shortly after dinner if he were to meet Ralph's eight-fifteen plane at Newark Airport.

She handed him the letter that had arrived that morning as she stirred and fried. He read it, and his first smile of the evening appeared on his face. "Hot damn, S.R. A baby and a license to teach all in the same year. Now that's what I call cooking," he said as he hugged her from behind while she labored at the stove.

She fixed him a Scotch and soda and steered him toward the living room, where they sat facing one another, each still unable to speak his mind. The ice broke with his glass, which fell from his hands, smashing against the leg of the coffee table. She hurried for the paper towels while he took to hands and knees to pick up jagged glass, cursing his clumsiness as he did.

"What is it, Dean?" Sara asked softly as they worked together to mend his mess. They were sitting on the floor, which was no easy task for Sara, when Dean replied: "I met with Tony this afternoon and asked him some questions I should have asked weeks ago.'' He paused. She waited. ''Sara, I could lose my home.''

Sara leaned against the back of the sofa for support, her hands folded across her stomach. She was shocked and horrified, knowing how she would feel if some court of law during a divorce action awarded her home to Stefan. She shivered involuntarily. ''But how?'' she asked, knowing of Dean's legal right to the brownstone. ''How can a document drawn by lawyers be worthless?''

It was what he had asked Tony, and he could still see his brother's face, ashen and pained as he responded. He had listened, trying to understand the law that Tony admitted was often open to a judge's interpretation and prejudices. But what he heard he could neither fathom nor assimilate. His mind rebelled, and so Tony had had his secretary make a copy of his notes and of a judgment recently passed in a similar case. Dean took it from his breast pocket now.

''You know, Chris died intestate. Which means he died without a will,'' Dean began. ''Well, it says here in article four on Descent and Distribution of an Intestate Estate, the property of a decedent, not disposed of by will, after payment of administration and funeral expenses, debts and taxes, shall be distributed as follows: A spouse and both parents—that's Barbara and the Langdons—with no issue—that means there were no children—twenty-five thousand dollars and one half of the residue to the spouse and the balance to the parents.''

Sara gasped. It was unthinkable. It surely couldn't happen. Which was exactly what Dean had said to Tony, who assured him it could.

''From what I learned this afternoon,'' Dean said wearily, ''no matter what proof I furnish, Barbara, because she was still legally Chris's wife when he died, will receive at least half the worth of the brownstone. Not the worth when we bought it but the worth now, after I've busted my chops restoring it. Of course, she might not get half. She might get it all. Or she might share some part of it with Chris's parents. I might even get lucky and some kindly judge might decree she must even share the worth of my own home with me.''

''Can't Tony do anything?'' Sara asked, feeling helpless.

''Oh, yes. He can stall the case indefinitely, keep it out of the courts for years—which at least gives me a place to call my own until some judge says I can't. He can also go to court and prove that my work as an architect and builder has given the house its current estimated value. And the judge, Tony thinks or hopes, will then order a partition. Which means I would win . . . something. I would have to sell my home, and once the loans and mortgages were wiped clean my value to the house would be ascertained, and I would be given that while Barbara would receive the rest.''

''Is there no chance you could win all?'' Sara asked.

''There's always a chance,'' Dean said, repeating Tony's words to the very same question he had asked but hours ago. ''Tony feels we can fight. He also feels we can win. He adds that we could lose, that the final decision rests with the judge. A decision, he is quick to add, that just might hinge on the judge's reaction to my being a homosexual, to the fact that Chris and I—as Barbara's deposition reads—were 'engaged in a homosexual relationship.' ''

Sara reacted, and Dean noticed. ''Yes, there's something ugly about those words. . . . Dirty-sounding . . . as if Chris and I were doing disgusting things to one another. Funny, but if you and Stefan went to court, your lawyer couldn't do much with the fact that Stefan is 'engaged in a heterosexual relationship.' What a difference a word makes.''

She was shaking her head, trying to make sense of the senseless. Although she still felt Barbara was entitled to something, something wasn't all. She searched for words to express her outrage but could find none that he hadn't already expressed.

The kids trooped in from their outdoor play, dragging baseball bats and gloves. Their faces were flushed from the unusually warm early-spring evening. She told them to wash—dinner would be ready in a matter of minutes. They said their hellos and vanished. Except for Naomi, who remained to eye Dean suspiciously.

"You remember Mr. Di Nardo from Evan's bar mitzvah?" Sara asked. "He's an old friend."

"Friend or boyfriend?" Naomi asked bluntly.

Sara laughed, not the least flustered. "Friend, missy. *Friend,*" she repeated. "But I like your thinking. He is gorgeous, isn't he?"

Naomi giggled and scampered upstairs, where she was greeted by Dana with fervid whispers that resulted in still more giggles.

"She's such a hoot, that one," Sara said, smiling in the direction in which Naomi had fled. "Of all my children she's the most outrageous. I'm glad she's the youngest and not the oldest. What an example she would have set! God help me." Again she laughed. "If this new one is anything like her, it will be a laugh riot around here."

"When is it due?" Dean asked, staring at the prodigious mound that was Sara's belly.

"In about eight weeks. Time does fly when you're having fun, doesn't it?" she asked, her humor somewhere between black and gray.

"Have you heard from Stefan?"

"Only about him. Just today actually," Sara replied, trying to sound casual. "His 'heterosexual relationship' called to tell me he's in the hospital. He's complaining of chest pains, but I gather it's just his nerves." She laughed. "Just his nerves. As though that were nothing at all." And suddenly she was in tears. "It's just that I'm frightened," she explained. "For Stefan. I just don't want anything to happen to him. I'm trying to decide what to do—to see him or not, trying to decide what's best. For me as well as for him. I don't want to be hurt any more, Dean."

He held her hand, playing with her fingers, an intimate gesture that at one time would have threatened them both but now didn't. They sat silently until Sara said: "Dean, you are going to fight, aren't you?"

He shrugged. "If I did I just might win the battle but lose the war."

She looked at him questioningly.

He explained. "There's a moral clause in my About

Face contract. Also, I'm about to film a pilot for a cop show. If I fight, Barbara's lawyer will lash back with every means possible. The case is certain to hit the newspapers, and that's when the shit could hit the fan—the tabloids thrive on this kind of thing. And there could go the About Face contract. They could claim I am in violation. Let's face it: The company would have trouble selling my macho image once the rags got through with me. And what producer would want me to play a cop? Wouldn't the NYPD just love it if I did?

"Funny," Dean continued, "if I were still a nobody this wouldn't attract more than a small paragraph dumped somewhere in the middle of the papers, if that. But the commercials have given me visibility and so I'm news. If this goes to trial, if I fight I could lose more than my home. I could lose everything."

She knew about losing everything, knew now that it was purely attitudinal.

"Which is why Tony is urging me to stall, to delay the case, keep it out of court as long as possible. Wear them down. Maybe when Barbara's hurting financially, she'll settle and I'll escape with my ass intact. But it's a helluva way to live. Like waiting for the other shoe to drop. But I'm considering it. What the hell is a little anxiety in return for keeping one's home and livelihood?

"God, but I'm glad Ralph is getting home tonight!" he said suddenly. "He knows how to sort through this kind of thing and settle me down at the same time. He's had to be careful for so long himself—had so much that he could lose—that he knows how I feel."

When I can only imagine, Sara thought as she watched fear change Dean's facial expression once again.

"But I'm sort of worried about Ralph," Dean continued. "He didn't sound right when he called. And it's odd that he wouldn't just hop in a cab from the airport. He's never asked that I take his car and meet him before. Maybe he broke his leg or arm in the Bahamas or Houston, where the kids live, and needs some help. But why wouldn't he say just that? Why the mystery?"

They sat again without speaking, each considering private dilemmas. When the timer on the oven emitted its loud buzzing noise, Sara tried to get up from the floor but couldn't. "Give me a hand, Dean," she said. "On second thought, give me both hands . . . and a foot and maybe even a tow with your car."

He laughed as he somehow helped her to her feet. As he escorted her to the kitchen she said: "I'm really glad you're here, glad I can give you something even if it's no more than dinner."

"No advice?" Dean asked.

"Me?" she said, laughing. "Hardly. I'm too busy giving, taking and rejecting my own. What I will give you, however, is chicken soup. It might not help, but . . . it couldn't hurt."

Ralph came through the gate, his face frozen, his manner distant, as if the plane had landed but he were still airborne or in Houston. His greeting was perfunctory and his silence punishing. But despite the feelings that Ralph's attitude and condition aroused within him, Dean kept the distance Ralph so obviously wanted to maintain.

The twenty-minute drive into Manhattan seemed twice and three times that, the only sound between them that of the radio. At Ralph's apartment house, after he had garaged the car and helped with the luggage, Dean made to leave. Ralph's hand on his sleeve stopped him, but not so much as his words. "Stay the night." There was no upset or pain evident in either his tone or his face. It was a flat request made in a flat voice, but it moved Dean. Without further question he told the doorman to cancel his request for a taxi.

His senses were awake before he was, nose and ears responding to the coffee maker as it gurgled and belched in the kitchen. His eyes blinked several times before they reluctantly remained open, staring at a wall and a picture that were familiar and yet not. It was not his bedroom. It wasn't a bedroom at all but a living room, where he was uncomfortably sprawled on the leather-cushioned sofa. He remembered, fighting his headache to do so. He had thought about using the kids' room the night before but hadn't wanted to enter and disturb that part of Ralph's life.

And so he had crashed on the sofa, and his body felt as if it had done just that.

They had watched television, Friday night music videos, which were as confused as those aspects of his life he wanted to discuss with the man intent on discussing nothing. And so they both consumed copious amounts of alcohol until the images on the TV screen faded from view and Ralph had staggered into and collapsed in his bedroom, seemingly peaceful at last.

Dean stretched. Despite his aching head, the mood of the morning felt better. A blanket he didn't remember taking covered his stripped-to-his-shorts body. He heard the whir of the blender; his stomach turned as he realized Ralph was making his usual morning drink of soy milk, a raw egg and two tablespoons of vegetable protein powder. He rose, feeling somewhat unsteady, and was greeted by a naked Ralph Kayne emerging from the kitchen to hand him a cup of steaming black coffee. His nudity discomforted Dean, although he had never had a conscious reaction to it at the gym. But there it had seemed natural among the other partially clad or unclothed bodies. Here, in the early morning, before his teeth were brushed and his bladder emptied, it seemed uncomfortably intimate.

He took the coffee into the bathroom and placed it on the vanity as he stepped into the stall shower. As he soaped he was hoping Ralph would be dressed by the time he emerged, would be communicative rather than morose. He did not want to spend a silent Saturday but would, he suddenly decided, if that was what Ralph needed. He had never seen Ralph act in such a fashion, and his concern was therefore greater than it would have been for Chris, who often, when work went badly, when a patient failed, withdrew to escape the world and its discomforts.

Ralph was wearing jeans and a sweatshirt, thumbing through *The New York Times,* looking at the theater and film listings, when Dean re-entered the living room. "How about we work out at the gym and then catch a matinee?" he asked as Dean seated himself, a fresh cup of coffee in hand.

"Fine with me," Dean replied. "What do you want to see?"

Ralph examined the paper again and then disgustedly crumpled and flung it across the room. "Not a goddamn thing. And I don't want to work out either."

"I think we better talk," Dean said as he settled into the leather chair that faced the sofa.

"There's nothing to talk about. It would only come out as excuses. The truth is: For all my goddamn talk I fucked up, and I don't like myself much for doing so."

It was hard for him to think Ralph capable of fucking up. Not the producer who took charge and care of a cast and crew of nearly a hundred. Not the man who took charge and care of his own life, health and body. No, not Ralph. Yet there was a plea in Ralph's eyes that told Dean he best set aside his own ideas of who this man was and listen.

Ralph was on his feet, pacing, lighting cigarettes he never smoked, pouring a second cup of coffee he never drank and which he continually chastised Dean for doing. He watered the few plants in the apartment, and then he sat again on the sofa and launched into a travelogue on the beauty of the Bahamas, the near-perfect weather and how idyllic it had seemed once his children, Kevin and Cassie, had joined him. Despite the location shootings and the tight schedules and even tighter budgets, he had felt relaxed, happy. The kids had mingled comfortably with the cast. Too comfortably, it resulted; the actors had let their guard down and played like children in a sandbox. But in ways foreign to Cassie and particularly to Kevin, who had been furious when he realized two of the actors preferred to play with one another rather than with the actresses to whom they made love on camera. He was even angrier when his father had defended his position when asked why he employed "fags" instead of "real men." Didn't his father know of the disease of mind and body these *kinds of people* bred?

Dean flinched at the words and at what he now understood had been a no-win situation.

"And I fudged," Ralph said in a tired, defeated voice. "I ran a perfect line of reason and bullshit by him. I dodged the real issue and said I hired actors, and that their sexual orientation and preference was none of my business. My only concern was what any employer's should be: Could they do the job? And then I attacked him, attacked my own son. I asked why these men's sexuality threatened him. I psyched him. I scared the shit out of my *own* kid by asking whether he was afraid of his own homosexual feelings.

"He left the next day. Took off for Houston while I was out doing some underwater filming. He called his mother, got her to arrange the transportation and left, taking Cassie with him. I followed a day later, but he wouldn't talk to me. And Donna wouldn't discuss it, except to say she thought I should think twice about the environment into which I was taking the children. I stood there wanting to hit her. That might have been better than doing nothing, saying nothing. But it really wasn't Donna I wanted to hit. It was me. For copping out . . . being dishonest . . . being full of shit."

They sat silently, Dean not knowing what to say and Ralph stewing on what he should have said. He sighed. "Funny how only weeks ago you wondered what I would tell my kids if they ever asked why I wasn't remarried. Well, this is damn close to that issue, isn't it? And I lied."

"You didn't lie, Ralph," Dean interjected.

"No. I just didn't tell the truth."

"And not many men in your position could or would have," Dean said. "Goddamn, Ralph. Give yourself a break. It was a tough situation. We both know how difficult it is for a son to come out to his father, but that's got to be diddly-shit in comparison to a father coming out to a son."

Ralph nodded but didn't speak. He lit another cigarette, coughing and choking as he inhaled. "I feel like shit," he said hoarsely. "I can't remember when I felt so bad. There's my son and his feelings. Then there's my daughter and my wife. And finally there's me. How do I make it come out right for everybody?"

"Maybe you just can't, Ralph. Maybe you just have to make it come out right for you," Dean said. "Do what you can live with, even if it's not the ideal or *your* ideal solution."

Ralph thought. As he walked toward the bathroom and

a shower, his hand rumpled Dean's hair. "You're right. I've got to do what's best for me, which may also be the best I can do for my family. Or anyone."

"Stefan?"

His eyes remained closed, and Sara stood at the foot of his bed looking at the face that had once been such a constant in her life. She began to hurt, a deep inside-to-out ache that threatened the buttered toast she had hurriedly eaten before leaving the house for the hospital that morning. The words of Stefan's doctor, cornered moments ago as he finished rounds, echoed as she watched Stefan breathe, occasionally crying through his shallow inhalations. "His blood pressure is low, not high, and his heartbeat is only somewhat irregular . . . although his heart is sound. A simple case of severe strain."

She was struck by the "simple" and "severe," seemingly so contradictory in their meanings, and as she continued to look at Stefan's face Sara saw just how contradictory they were. He looked like an old child as he slept, framed by the white linen of his bedclothes. Although his features hadn't truly changed, his face seemed as if it had. He looked vulnerable, like any one of her children she had watched during one of their many illnesses.

She had not rehearsed her feelings or her reactions before leaving the house. Awakening late, she dressed for her visit without thinking, not paying particular attention to wardrobe or hair. The children did not ask, and she did not volunteer, where she was going. She was acting independently, and they had come to both expect and accept that.

It wasn't until she cornered Stefan's doctor that the enormity of what she was doing struck her. She was becoming involved, acting like a family member . . . a wife. But then, she realized, she had been involved from the moment her call with Denise Wolfe had been concluded. As she had parked the car in the hospital's lot, she briefly wondered if they would meet. Should she have phoned first? But the idea of phoning to see *her* husband in the hospital stopped her. If a meeting occurred, she would deal with Denise Wolfe, and Denise Wolfe would have to deal with her.

"Stefan?"

This time his eyes opened and he looked at her as if trying to connect the dots. He looked as he often had when she had awakened him from sleep: confused, even frightened. She remained silent, waiting for him to focus, to become aware of his surroundings and who she was. It happened slowly, and as recognition passed over his face fear accompanied it.

"Am I dying?" he asked, thinking that could be the only reason for her being there. "Am I?" he again asked, this time somewhat urgently.

"No," she assured him. "The doctors say you could be—" (She almost said *home* but thought better of it; that might upset him. Or her.) "—out of here in a few days. It's not your heart, Stefan. It's your nerves."

But how do you separate the two? she wondered. When her nerves had gone so many years ago, wasn't it because her heart had hurt, been ailing, pounding away at her for reasons she was still discovering?

"I didn't change the insurance policies," he said. "You're still the beneficiary."

Did he think she had come to see to her interests?

"How are the kids?" he asked, his eyes somewhere other than on her face. She followed his eyes and understood what he was looking for. "The kids are fine. They're at home. I thought it best not to tell them you are here. They've had enough worry these past months."

He nodded, understanding, which was more than she now did. They were his children. They should have been told.

"How are you feeling?" It was a dumb question, and she hated the irrevocable fact that she had asked it. Other than a delivered mother or one who is about to be, how does anyone who is in a hospital feel?

"I'm in pain," he replied, touching his chest with a finger. "I have trouble breathing sometimes."

"You're working too hard," she said quickly, again hating herself for having stated the obvious. Hers was the answer so many used to diminish or verify an illness. "You always worked too hard,'' she continued, unable to stop herself.

He smiled, and then, as if remembering something very important, he tapped his forehead and struggled to reach the nightstand near his bed. His hand searched its top and found a letter. He handed it to her, saying: ''Princeton is giving me an award.''

He watched as she read the letter on Princeton University stationery, waiting for a reaction. Like a child, she thought, wanting his mother to see the gold star the teacher had awarded his efforts. ''That's wonderful,'' she said, again feeling the ache and pain she had experienced earlier. And it was wonderful. But it was also terrible. A year ago she would have rejoiced. But a year ago she would have felt part of his accomplishment. Now she felt cheated because the award was only partly hers, but he wasn't.

''There's going to be a ceremony,'' he said, ''a black-tie dinner at the Prospect Association.''

Was he asking her to attend or was he taunting her?

She knew the place, the home of Woodrow Wilson when he had been the university's president. Its dining room looked out on private gardens. She quickly read that the award was being bestowed for distinguished service in chemistry . . . for ''commitment beyond the usual.'' She almost laughed. Commitment beyond the usual. To a *what* rather than a *who.* She was angry, furious actually, that he had taken this moment, when she was basically his captive, to share his news.

''I've been licensed to teach,'' she said suddenly and then was again hounded by the stupidity of her remark. As though she were in competition. He was silent, totally nonreactive, which made her anger even greater. ''You made your point,'' he finally said, a smile beginning to change the downward curve of his mouth. He turned to look at her, the smile widening with his eyes that suddenly saw her as if for the first time that day. The smile froze, as did the focus of his eyes.

''Are you pregnant?'' he asked, squinting as though his eyes were either failing or deceiving him.

She stood helpless under his gaze, looking back at the confusion and disbelief in his face. All of her reasons for not telling him surfaced as excuses to be made now, once he asked.

"Whose is it? No, you don't have to tell me," he added hurriedly. "It's your business."

She almost laughed. Like Robert, Stefan was flattering her. Whose baby could it have been if it wasn't his?

Aaron Adelman's of Kruger & Kreig Pharmaceuticals, she thought and suddenly felt much better.

"It's yours, Stefan. Do you remember the morning of Evan's bar mitzvah?"

She watched as he turned his head away, retreating, not just from the memory but from her. Just as he had that morning, as he had for years.

"I remember," he said, just loudly enough to be heard. His hand again fingered his chest and she heard his breathing become labored.

"It turns out we were more successful at our lovemaking than either of us thought," she said. "In fact, you're a regular ball of fire. Or *balls* of fire might be more appropriate."

She was amazed at her bitterness. He said nothing, nodding, trying to take in this new development in his life.

"I want nothing," she announced, speaking to what she was certain were his fears. "Mother and child are doing fine," she added vehemently.

"Don't hate me, Sara," he said, turning toward her.

He seemed so pitiful that she couldn't resist touching his face with her hand. "I don't hate you, Stefan. And although I did hurt, I hurt less now. I also know you didn't mean to hurt me. You just did."

He took her hand. "I'm sorry."

"Me, too," she said as she took her hand away. "Stefan, I'm sorry you're not well. That's why I'm here. I wanted you to know that. If you need me to do anything I will. And if you want me to bring the children to see you I will."

She prepared to leave, putting on and buttoning the light coat she had removed when she entered the medical center. She debated and then decided, stooping to kiss him on the cheek no matter what he thought or what she might think later. She was at the door when he said weakly: "Sara, do you need money?"

She suddenly knew it was the best he could offer, that there was nothing else he was able to give, and that didn't anger but sadden her. "No, Stefan. We're fine. We really are fine." And in saying the words, Sara realized they were true, and that made her both happy and yet terribly sad.

She glided through the crowded room, a stunning woman in a flowing chiffon gown, greeting guests in the style for which she was famous and to which they had become accustomed. She chose her moment to touch a friend's arm or air-kiss an offered cheek, her laugh radiating above and through the crowd, adding still to the already festive atmosphere of the flowers and balloons a crew of ten had affixed to the ceiling and walls that afternoon. Despite what she was feeling, she was giving a near-perfect imitation of Joanna Bennett.

Waiters with trays of Champagne and platters of hors d'oeuvres negotiated through the crowd, trying not to ogle the famous faces who had come by invitation to the party. Servers stood like sentries at the buffet table in the dining room, ready to appease an appetite at a signal. And the band, a small combo locked into the small confines of the patio, played on, soon to be relieved by the tapes prepared by Stacey's "friend," as Joanna called the rock-video producer whose name, no matter how many times it was mentioned, she could not remember.

Joanna stood in the midst of the packed room, trying to make comfortable people she barely knew, although she herself was not. She had wanted a small party, a private family dinner to mark the last occasion they as a family would celebrate in this that had been their home. But Stacey had preferred what Reynolds had suggested—that her eighteenth birthday be very special, which is what they felt a "bash" would be but a family dinner would not. And so two hundred mix-and-match personalities had been invited to a home that now resembled Noah's Ark with its two of everything parading and preening.

Stacey was making yet another entrance, this time gliding down the stairs with what's-his-name by her side. The sequins and beads on her micro-minidress barely covered her essentials, and the black wig with the skunk stripe running from front to back gave her a hard if current look. Her daughter was bright-eyed and . . . too bright-eyed, Joanna realized, reacting as Stacey's laughter joined that of others in the room. She pushed toward the stairs and then stopped. There was nothing she could say—not now—to a daughter who was stoned and with people who perhaps expected no less.

Joanna turned away, watching the dancing that was not supposed to take place in her living room. Champagne sloshed from glasses onto a carpet she had once chosen so carefully for its erotic softness. Cigarette ashes were being stomped into its pile. Her eye followed a dollop of caviar as it fell from cracker to damask-covered chair, soon followed by a cocktail sauce that blended poorly with the fabric on her sofa. What matter? Reynolds would say, when so many of the furnishings, *her* furnishings, were either being stored or sold once they made the "big move."

From the patio Joanna watched the people dancing, their arms flailing above or about their heads, which bobbed as their bodies jerked. Stacey, too, was spasmodically twitching, her eyes closed as each of her legs moved in syncopated rhythm even though they seemed to be moving in opposite directions. From the expression on her daughter's face Joanna could see she was no longer there in the room as she danced. Whether it was the music or drugs or both, she didn't know.

The Champagne flowed and, with it, people's tongues. Guests were having fun, but she wasn't. She searched the faces in the crowd, looking for some clue to her mood and her behavior. She saw people dreamy-eyed, lost in the beat of the music, transported, dancing and acting with abandon. She saw her answer.

She didn't want to lose or abandon herself, didn't want the excesses of liquor or pot or music played much too loudly to take her away from or out of herself. She simply didn't want to abandon Joanna Bennett. Not again. Not ever. Not for any reason. Too many others were already abandoning her for her to do that. And then she thought of those who hadn't, the people at IANDS who had held her as she cried, wept about the fact that she had been set adrift as on an ice floe, left to her own devices and by the very people she most loved.

As she watched the dancers, Joanna thought that when she danced again she would move from the inside out, as an expression of who she was and what she felt. And it would be a joyous expression. Once again she heard the sounds of glasses tinkling, corks popping . . . laughter, and with her first genuine smile of the evening she turned from the room toward the garden. A voice called out: "Lovely party, Joanna." And she answered without turning or stopping: "Yes, it is, isn't it?"

Within the noise she had found her quiet moment, making peace with the fact that soon this house, her home, would be another's. She was sitting on a swing, rocking gently to music, not the tapes now playing but a song she heard in her head. She was remembering the playground on Flatlands Avenue near East Thirty-fifth Street and those rare afternoons when her mother would take her to the swings and push as she kicked her little feet and laughed as the ground below and the sky above merged and moved. She had built this swing for Stacey, and many had been the afternoon when she had hummed the same song as she pushed her daughter higher and higher.

She suddenly felt herself pushed, gently, a slow movement upward, a gentle swing down. She looked up and the stars flew across the sky as the swing accelerated. She came to an abrupt halt and she felt herself pushed to one side as a large body crammed onto the swing next to her. And pushed. Just off the ground at first and then higher. Two grown women on a swing acting like little girls.

She squealed, so much like a child, as the world and her head began to spin. And she laughed. She kicked off her shoes as they each exerted force to take them higher and higher. And then they relaxed, allowing the laws of physics to do their work. When they were just swaying gently, side by side on the swing, their hands touching, Joanna said: "I'm sorry if I've hurt you."

Lilith shrugged: "It wasn't me you were hurting but the

business. There's a difference. One's personal, the other isn't."

"Are you still angry?" Joanna asked.

Lilith thought before she spoke. "No. It's what you have to do, and I know now you don't mean it to be at my expense."

"No, I don't. Not ever," Joanna said, squeezing Lilith's hand for emphasis. "Lil, my life is changing so fast that I'm frightened. I wish I could just let go, as I just did on this swing, and let it take me wherever it's meant to go."

"If it's like this swing, then it's going higher and higher," Lilith said.

They sat quietly, each listening to her own thoughts. "Do you think you'll remain with the business?" Lilith asked, expressing her main fear.

"I don't know," Joanna said thoughtfully. "Lileen has asked that I find someone to administrate her halfway house. I'm thinking it might suit me to do that, although I have this great desire to work with the terminally ill. There's a volunteer program at Cedars Sinai, and they're taking applications for a training program that starts this month. Lil, I think I can be of service there. And that matters to me a lot. I think I can help these people face their fears about death and maybe even help them to see that they're groundless."

"Sounds like laughs. A real up! I say go for it," Lilith replied. "Why, with your public relations expertise you could make death *the* thing. And just by calling it the vacation capital of the world, the international playground of everybody who's anybody. And wouldn't that be the truth!"

Joanna was laughing, but her mind was working, trying to discover why Lilith's words, although spoken in jest, seemed familiar.

"And you have more than a concept to promote," Lilith continued, warmed now to her rap. "You have an actual person and a product—of sorts. I can hear Merv now: 'And now, ladies and gentlemen, direct from his run in Las Vegas let's have a hand for . . . the Grim Reaper.' And wouldn't that also make a great name for a wrestler?

What fun! I'm telling you, you could give death a whole new image."

They were a reasonable facsimile of the words Nancy Evans Bush had spoken. Then they had made no sense. Now . . . she wondered.

"What are you people doing up there?"

Joanna looked into the bemused face of Maryn Peters.

"I've been looking for you all evening," the woman said to Joanna.

"Maryn, you're not going to hit on me in my own home, are you?" Joanna asked the woman who produced the top-rated *Los Angeles Woman* morning show.

Her face reflected hurt as Maryn replied: "Joanna, you've known me for years. Would I be so pushy as to press you for a date you've been promising me for months at a private party? And not just a private party, but your own? How about next Wednesday? We need a guest then," Maryn ended, her expression blank even as her eyes laughed.

"As if we haven't got enough pollution, you want to put her on the air?" Lilith said.

"Maryn, if I finally do your show I want your promise that there will be no questions about our clients and in particular about Lileen Lavery," Joanna said.

"Agreed!" Maryn replied instantly.

"Then what the hell are we going to talk about?" Joanna asked. "Public relations is not exactly a scintillating subject."

"We'll talk about you, Joanna. Face it, Bennett, you *are* the Los Angeles Woman, and I have the magazine and newspaper articles to prove it," Maryn said.

"And what am I?" asked Lilith huffily.

"Anaheim . . . maybe Pomona, and if we really push it . . . Redondo Beach," Maryn answered.

"I never did like you, Maryn," Lilith replied, as she began to push the swing.

"Wednesday, Joanna. What do you say?" Maryn persisted.

"If she can squeeze it in between the seesaw and the sliding pond she'll be there," Lilith responded as she took the swing higher and higher. "Now get lost before I bomb you with a spitball."

"Wednesday, Joanna," Maryn called as she returned to the party.

"Wednesday," Joanna agreed as she linked her arm through Lilith's and began once again to push for the stars.

She had somehow become separated from Reynolds just as the birthday cake was being wheeled in. As she stood next to Lilith, watching Stacey's face glow above the tiered whipped cream and roses, candles dripping their blue and yellow wax, she felt sad, almost bereft, as if in mourning. Her "baby" had reached yet another milestone. She wondered as she watched Stacey, her eyes closed, her lips moving as she silently made the ceremonial birthday wish, if other mothers saw images of their children's past birthdays dance in front of their half-closed eyes at occasions that somehow seemed momentous. She smiled as the crowd cheered the huge exhalation that blew out most of the candles. She laughed as Stacey was engulfed by her friends, who were suddenly calling for a speech.

Stacey was giggling, looking at the "friend" at her side—Sam! His name was Sam, Joanna remembered—and searching for something to say. The crowd quieted. Stacey tried to talk but giggled instead. The crowd giggled with her. Again she tried to speak and again she faltered. Then, after taking a deep breath, she came out with a triumphant shout.

"I'm getting married!"

Joanna watched as Stacey held up her hand to display the ring on her finger. Joanna's legs buckled, and but for the arm Lilith had placed under her elbow, she would have fallen. Her eyes found those of Reynolds, but he quickly looked away, the smile on his face set as if in stone. Friends were rushing Stacey, hugging as they congratulated. Friends were rushing Joanna, doing the same, and as she lost contact with Lilith, she felt as if she were drowning in a sea of congratulatory embraces and emotions.

She was alone, watching the dawn begin to light the night sky but not her mood. The last of the guests had left hours ago, but still Joanna sat in the smoked-filled living room, unable to think of sleep. As she had for many years, she was waiting up for Stacey, aware this night, or this morning as it were, Stacey might not come home. Nor might Reynolds. His whereabouts were a mystery, whereas Stacey's she could guess.

She ached for Reynolds. He also had not known. She had read that in his face as they each shook hands with well-wishers, each embarrassed that their daughter was getting married. No girl in today's world marries at eighteen unless she's pregnant or so lacking in imagination she thinks marriage is the only way to escape her parents.

Joanna heard the car in the driveway pulling toward the rear of the house. She knew it was Reynolds; Sam never had his limousine drive Stacey to the door but deposited her at curbside, where he watched from the backseat until Stacey had entered the house. It was another of Sam's traits that she disliked.

Reynolds entered through the rear of the house, acknowledging her with a look but not words. She saw both the tiredness and the pain on his face.

"I blame you," he said as he moved toward the stairs. "You made her life impossible."

She was stunned, unable to speak or defend against his attack. The cruelty of his words matched those of her own inner critic, who taunted by asking if his words were true. "Reynolds, we should talk," she said as he began to mount the stairs. He stared at her, as one would at a stranger whose face was familiar, and then continued his slow climb to the bedroom. She did not follow.

It was light when she heard the front door open. Through eyes still half shut from a twilight sleep, she watched Stacey enter the house, carrying her wig in one hand, her shoes in the other. She looked fresh, as if she had slept. Her hair was still damp from what Joanna assumed was a recent shower and her face was devoid of makeup, making her look younger and prettier than she had anytime that night. She also looked happy.

Stacey stopped when she saw Joanna curled in the chair observing her. She held her finger aloft so that the rays of the morning sun streaming in through the living room bay window could reflect off the diamond of her engagement ring. "It's pretty, isn't it?" she said, chirping almost as loudly as the birds in the trees that surrounded the house.

"You might have told me," Joanna said as Stacey plopped into the damask-covered chair still to be cleaned of its caviar stain. "I really am hurt. So is your father."

"And good morning to you, too," Stacey replied, still measuring her ring in the beams of sunlight playing about the room.

"Don't be cute, Stacey. Not now when you've already got me down," Joanna said, her voice tired yet firm.

"So this is about you for a change. And here I thought this was my evening," Stacey replied.

"Stop being such a bitch!" Joanna exploded. "You owe me an explanation."

"I owe you nothing!" Stacey replied. "But for your information, I didn't know Sam would be giving me an engagement ring tonight. It was as much a surprise to me as it was to you."

She was not lying. Joanna could read that in Stacey's expression. "Do you know what your father thinks?" When Stacey shrugged Joanna answered her own question. "That you're doing this just to get out of the house, away from me. Are you?"

Stacey shut her eyes and in a mock Valley Girl voice intoned: "This is *really* boring. *Really.*"

"Answer me!" Joanna demanded.

"It's a reason, but it's not *the* reason," Stacey said. "He's running a number on you, on himself too. Dad knows how I feel about Sam because I've told him. I guess he's no better at listening than you."

"How *do* you feel about Sam?" Joanna asked.

"He makes me feel good," Stacey replied as she picked at the polish on her fingernails.

"Could you define 'good'?" Joanna asked, thinking Stacey was about to talk in physical terms.

"He makes me feel valuable, like I'm worth something."

The response shocked Joanna. "But you know that. I've been telling you that all along."

"Actions speak louder than words. Or didn't you know that, Mother?" Stacey responded. "Obviously you didn't."

"Stacey, I did the best I could, loved you as best I could. If it wasn't enough I'm sorry. But don't do something rash, something you might live to regret. Finish school. Consider college. Don't leave one cocoon for another. At least be on your own for a while. Take two years at an out-of-town college, then if you want to marry this man . . ."

"His name is Sam, Mother. S-A-M spells Sam!"

"Then marry him later," Joanna continued as if Stacey had not interrupted. "Marriage should not be something one does to escape—to go from a situation that feels bad to one that one hopes will feel good. Believe me, I know."

"Mom, this isn't the big deal you're making it. Haven't you heard of divorce? It's a piece of paper a judge grants when you ask for it," Stacey said mockingly.

"Stacey, listen to me. Please, just listen for a minute," Joanna pleaded. "Marriage is not something you drop in and out of. Like school. And divorce isn't as simple as you make it. Even when a marriage is bad people just don't pick up and pull out. Not from a life you've shared with another person, be it for a year or twenty."

"Speaking from experience, Mother?" Stacey asked, her question calculated to draw blood. " 'Cause if you are it's a mistake. In fact, considering the way Dad plays around I think you're hardly qualified to advise me on anything to do with marriage."

"It's exactly why I am qualified," Joanna said calmly.

Stacey was looking at her oddly, a mixture of concern and upset on her face. "I'm moving in with Sam after graduation. Later, if it feels right, if I still love him—a little emotion you don't seem to think I'm capable of feeling—we'll get married. With or without your approval or attendance. You either come along for the ride or you don't. Your choice. But get off my case. I don't want to hear it from you anymore."

"Stacey, I don't know—and frankly I no longer care—what your reasons are for hating me as much as you do. But I do care if they're going to ruin your life. So let me throw back your own advice at you. Get off my case. *You'll* feel a lot better if *you* do."

"I feel good now," Stacey replied defiantly. "I'm leaving here to get married, to be an actress or a model. I'm going to live in a big house with lots of cars and lots of famous people for company. It's going to be a much better life than I'm living now. Don't look so dismayed, Mother. Everybody has a right to come and go as they please. After all, isn't that what you've been doing ever since I was a child?"

And there it was . . . again.

"Give it up, Stacey," Joanna said wearily. "Not for my sake but yours. Carting that kind of baggage with you into a new life will only weigh you down. Put it to rest, Stace. It will make your life so much easier when you do."

She didn't think but acted, something she hadn't done in a very long time. Within minutes of her confrontation with Stacey she packed a small bag of essentials—toiletries, makeup, a change of pantyhose and a blouse—and drove to Los Angeles International, where she boarded the early-morning 747 flight. She hadn't thought to leave a note for Reynolds, but then she hadn't thought but acted on something she suddenly felt she had to do. She was strangely calm, no longer angry or hurt. Ignoring food and the movie, she slept the five-hour distance between her two points, feeling refreshed when she was nudged awake by the stewardess.

There were problems in obtaining a taxi, as none of the drivers wanted to make the trip to Long Beach, certain a return fare would not be probable. Her offer of double the meter finally snared her a ride, but not before the driver received, at his demand, half the estimated round-trip fare in advance.

Within the hour she was standing in front of the brick building that would have held no particular anxiety for her if she hadn't had a particular relationship to one of its residents. She was trembling as she entered its antiseptic interior. Although she had written monthly checks to the institution, she seldom thought about the home, knowing it was there but not wanting to know more than that.

At the reception area she was directed down a long corridor that led to the nurses' station. There she was once again directed down another corridor, this one lined with bodies in wheelchairs, discards and relics, with drool and dribble running down their chins. Some called to her, thinking she was a daughter, a sister, a mother. Still others asked of her things she could not do—like remove the straps that tied them securely to their chairs.

The door to the room she sought was open, one of its occupants recently departed or deceased if the stripped bed was any indication. The other bed was occupied by a small form covered by a sheet. She approached it slowly, hesitantly, watching for any sign of life. The woman was lying on her side, her head turned toward the wall away from Joanna. The once-henna-rinsed hair was now white, the skin below the hairline a near match except for the liver spots. The room smelled of rotting. Joanna went to the other side of the bed to peer into the face lying near the guard rail.

The shock momentarily stopped her. It was not her mother but her remains, the likeness but not the woman. The open-without-seeing eyes were still deep brown, but they were lifeless. The mouth drooped and the cheeks were sunken, caused in part by the removal of her dentures. Joanna lowered the guard rail and sat on the edge of the bed, taking her mother's frail hand in hers. It was cold. She began to stroke it, hoping to bring some warmth into its marblelike touch.

The face that had once been so austere, autocratic and prepossessing was that of a child, a blind child who saw nothing. Her mother's mouth suddenly moved; Joanna put her ear to it but heard sounds rather than words. She sat back and looked at the woman in total. How could she ever have hated her? she wondered. The realization that she never truly had was like a punch to her stomach. She had only pretended to have hated because to have admitted she had loved, and had so much wanted that love returned, would have been more than she could have borne.

She looked, she stared, trying to reconcile the woman she remembered—so articulate, precise in her demands, her tastes—with the frail little person whose hand she now held. They were one and the same woman, *any* woman who had done her best, which wasn't always the best for her daughter. And it wasn't that her mother hadn't loved her, she just hadn't been able to love her in the way she had needed. But she *had* loved her. Imperfectly, perhaps. Just as she had imperfectly loved Stacey.

She continued to hold the hand she hadn't held since childhood. She stroked the face that was as soft and as wrinkled as a baby's. She prayed that somehow, in some way, her mother could feel her touch, could take some comfort and pleasure in another person's warmth. And love. She slipped into the bed, lying on her side so that she could hold her mother as one would a child. And she wished her mother could speak, could say something she would hear for the rest of her life. She lay her cheek next to her mother's and began to sing, much as she used to croon to Stacey when she was an infant.

The nurse woke her an hour later, disturbed to find a visitor in the nursing home's bed. Definitely against regulations. Joanna dismissed her with an imperious manner that she suddenly realized, with a laugh, she had inherited from her mother. She then asked an attendant to phone for a taxi, which the attendant did once Joanna offered the five-dollar bill. She then kissed her mother good-bye but found that she couldn't leave. Not until she was advised her taxi was waiting.

She stood in the doorway, looking at her childhood and, to some extent, her present, and with tears streaming down her face she whispered: "I love you, Mom. Take care." She waited the briefest of moments and then left when there still was no response.

She had told Ina, when she called, not to come and Schauzer, when she had called her, that she was not coming. She preferred to handle Stefan's illness alone, without either woman's interference or harassment. She needed her quietude, her time to mourn the loss of a man she had loved. He was gone. That had once again been made so evident at the hospital. It was no longer deniable, no matter if she still tried.

There was another man answering to his name, and she did not yet know how she felt about him. But then there seemed to be a new woman in her place, and she did not yet know how she felt about her. But he was not her strength or her very own answer man. He was more like Robert and Evan, or Dean perhaps. And he was nothing like her father.

Whom she barely remembered, she thought as she entered the kitchen, turning on ovens and timers to prepare the evening meal.

He was a stocky, blond man who seldom laughed and most certainly never cried. He spoke little, but when he did the household listened. Or was it, obeyed? She remembered his holding her, not often but often enough for her to remember the security she felt as a child in his arms. From the back of the car, where she had fallen asleep after a late night at his sister's, to her bedroom. From their blanket on the beach into the water, so that the soles of her feet wouldn't burn on the hot sand. And in the water, wrapping her arms about his thick neck, clinging to him as waves broke over and about them. He had never once allowed her to slip from his grasp.

When he left them she was certain she would drown. Even on land.

She remembered that week. It was in the kitchen with her now as she scraped carrots she would later glaze with honey. Waves of fear and nausea. She had blamed her mother then, not in words but in some unconscious fashion that even she had not realized. And suddenly she had the strangest thought, strange in that she had not thought it before and strange in that Schauzer had never suggested it.

How strong could her father have been if he had just disappeared without a word? He had been too weak to face the situation and so he had run. Run from what would have been painful. Not very brave. Not very strong. It was the action of a coward.

Too strong, she decided of her word. Her father did what people do, everyday people who don't always act in the way they should, even if they want to. It made them human.

Stefan was human. He had his strengths—the award he was soon to receive from Princeton proved that—but he was also weak in that he was like her father. He, too, had run away rather than deal with a confrontation. Her father had run to Israel, Stefan to Denise Wolfe. What difference? And she had blamed herself just as she had blamed her mother. Neither was to blame except in part.

She was crying again. The one inescapable fact and truth upset her. Despite everything she missed him, missed her life with him, missed being Mrs. Stefan Schell. There was yet another fact and truth. Despite mistaken identities she loved him. She hated what he had done, how he had acted, what he had become, but she loved him.

What she both loved and hated was all him, she reasoned, wishing the Schauzer seemingly now forever buried within her would shut up and leave her be. It was so much more comfortable living in fantasy instead of constantly facing up to reality, she thought.

But was it? the Schauzer within again intervened. If it had been all that comfortable, why had she always been so anxious?

She lived with much less anxiety now, which was strange considering how much less with which she lived. No Stefan. No assurance that she would be his or anyone else's wife. No identity other than her own. And still she no longer awoke afraid, just concerned, and she could feel the difference between the two.

She wandered through the house, what had been Stefan's den, what had been their bedroom. For the first time the idea of selling entered her mind. Perhaps it might be better to be somewhere other than behind a wall, one made of both brick and memories. Of course they would need a house; apartments were simply too small for a family as large as hers.

Hers. Not *theirs*. She had thought that.

The front door opened, and despite her repeated command it slammed instead of shut softly. Robert found her in the living room. From the expression on his face she realized he was carrying not just his schoolbooks but the world on his shoulders.

"I just left Dad," he said. "He wants to come home."

FIFTEEN

IT was funny, although he couldn't see the humor in his traveling three thousand miles to Los Angeles to make a TV pilot about three rookie cops in New York. But then, Joanna had noticed rather quickly, he didn't see the humor in anything. From the time they had met for breakfast, each needing to break away early for their respective dates before the TV cameras, he had been agitated, anxious to leave Los Angeles, regretful he had come and not the least interested in any doors she could open now that he was finally here.

She watched him as he made halfhearted stabs at the scrambled eggs he had spread about his plate in an effort to make it seem as if he had eaten something. She had not seen Dean this upset since his stay in the hospital. She listened as he spoke about the lawsuit, the possibilities involved and his concern for Ralph Kayne. She did not know what to reply, knowing that platitudes like: "It will all be all right" often weren't true.

Except perhaps in Sara's case. She had not known how to react when Sara had called, as Sara had not sounded overjoyed with the news that Stefan wanted to come home. She had attributed Sara's seemingly laconic reaction to shock, perhaps even disbelief, for the story had been relayed by a child rather than delivered by the man himself. Still, Joanna imagined they would reconcile, would do what so many others in their circumstances had done and would continue to do: pick up the pieces.

She touched his hand. He looked up from his eggs and smiled. She thought what a beautiful-looking man and how lucky he was finally to be doing the very things he had once dreamed were possible but then had thought were not. His life had changed so from that morning when they had each left the hospital, different people trying to enter the same lives they had once lived. Dean, it's just a house, she wanted to say but didn't, knowing it would only serve to denigrate what he was feeling.

He asked about Stacey, Reynolds, her work—all the things a friend would and should ask, but she could see he was only going through the motions, that his mind was elsewhere. She wanted to tell him it was all right, that she knew he cared and that he was hurting. And that the hurting prevented him from really being there. Instead, she gave half-answers, knowing that was all he really wanted to hear.

He paid the check; she thanked him. They separated on the street corner, each moving to where they had parked their respective cars, his rented at the airport. She heard him call. She turned as he came walking swiftly toward her. He hugged her, even though he just had. This time he added words. "I'm not always a drag."

It was his explanation and apology, rendered, even though she hadn't felt it necessary.

She had worn her not very new cream-colored silk suit, chosen for its simplicity rather than for any fashion statement it might make, and found herself drawn into a discussion on power dressing for women. That she stated she did not think of herself as powerful, only successful, surprised the other panelists and particularly the program's moderator, Aileen Herta, herself a power due to the strong ratings of her daily *Los Angeles Woman.*

Didn't the fact that she often manufactured and manipulated the news make her powerful? Herta asked, and then topped her question with yet another. "After all, it is you, isn't it, who is deciding what the public should or should not know about Lileen Lavery's condition?"

"I work for and with the client. Seldom do I make arbitrary decisions," Joanna replied.

"And what happens when the client—in this case Ms. Lavery—becomes too ill to participate in the decision?" Herta pressed.

"Then I act. But I personally do not consider that power," Joanna added. "Only an obligation . . . to the client and to the job."

She was asked by a panelist, a psychologist, if she feared power, thought perhaps it would make her less feminine and therefore less attractive not only to men but to members of her own sex. She was spared an answer as the psychologist answered for her, if not specifically then generally. Women, she stated unequivocably, were afraid of power for the very reason she just offered. And she had two hundred and eighty-four pages of her just-published book and her presence on this program to prove it.

Joanna was bored. Women . . . power . . . were subjects that no longer held much interest for her. She wished the program would end so that her real day could begin. She stole a look at her watch. With one more ten-minute segment, her obligation, a promise made to Maryn Peters months ago, would be fulfilled.

"That's what I'm talking about," the psychologist said as she pointed accusingly at Joanna, who wondered what the woman had been saying. "You just glanced at your watch," the psychologist explained. "Undoubtedly measuring time, racing, running from here to some other appointment where your presence is needed. This is the new executive woman. This is how woman is emulating man in the worst way. This is why the incidence of heart attack and stroke are increasing for women at an alarming rate."

The head of a Beverly Hills investment firm agreed, admitting her frenetic schedule had placed her in the hospital several months ago for treatment of a bleeding ulcer.

Hadn't she recently been in the hospital? Herta asked as she glanced through her notes.

Joanna nodded but quickly added that her hospital stay had not been stress-related.

But hadn't she nearly died? Herta pressed.

"Oh, no," Joanna answered too quickly, her mind not as fast as her words. "I did die."

There was a hush, a total quiet. Even the usually unflappable Herta found it difficult to respond. Joanna felt constrained to explain.

"Twice, actually," she began, wondering how this could

be happening. "Once, just after the other car hit the one in which I was a passenger, and then again, later, while on the operating table."

The others continued to sit silently. Herta seemed lost, as if searching but not finding in her mind the notes she had prepared recently on a similar subject when she had interviewed Shirley MacLaine. Still, she waved off the director's cue to go to commercial in thirty seconds in order to proceed with the kind of questioning that had made hers the top-rated program at nine A.M.

"Are you telling us you had a near-death experience?" Herta asked.

"I guess I am," Joanna replied, almost laughing in spite of her "what-have-I-done" feeling.

"Can you describe it?" Herta asked, using her best you-can-tell-a-friend voice.

"Not really," Joanna replied enigmatically. But she tried, and when she was finished she again felt a sense of frustration and failure at her inability to capture in words the feelings of perfect and total love, and complete understanding and acceptance she had known within the Light.

She was aware of the silence of the studio, aware of Herta leaning toward her and in an almost conspiratorial voice asking: "So you believe in an afterlife."

Joanna thought. "Having seen something else, some-*place* else, I now think sometimes what we know here on earth is the afterlife, and the real life, the very essence of life, is in that place we think of as heaven."

"Joanna, has this experience changed you?" Herta asked. "Has it changed your relationship to your life, your family, your work in any way?"

She did not want to answer, did not want to involve those in her life who saw her changes but remained blind to what they saw. She answered hesitantly: "My work means less to me than it once did. There are now other priorities."

"And by that you mean—?" the psychologist asked.

"The quality of life," Joanna replied softly. "Actually, the quality of all life, not just mine but everyone's. And the power, the intrinsic, internal power we all have, even those who think they have none."

"You're referring to the power of God?" Herta interjected, leading Joanna to a place many of her viewers would laud while others laughed.

"I mean the power each of us has as a part of God, as part of a whole that is God and the universe," Joanna responded, wishing she could be clearer, more succinct. She could sense the impatience building in the investment counselor, could feel the derision of the psychologist, could see the red light atop the studio camera glaring at her. Again, she almost laughed, thinking how she had been insistent on not discussing her clients' personal lives when she should have perhaps applied that mandate to herself. Then she might not be dealing with the question Herta now asked as she ignored her other guests to focus on her, the Los Angeles Woman, the Tiffany of public relations and now . . . curio.

It was past eight that evening when she turned the Mercedes onto North Canon Drive, her mind spinning, starting and stopping. Exhilaration had turned to exhaustion. Her second in the eight-week series of hospice training classes at Cedars-Sinai had been particularly draining, mainly because it was dull, concerned as it was with helping the dying patient to make such final arrangements as a will and an obit. Then, too, she had been cautioned, but not exactly warned, by a departmental head who had seen the *Los Angeles Woman* telecast in the morning that although the hospital program was interested in and sympathetic to the near-death experience, the directors felt until further research was done, it had no place in their treatment of the terminally ill. She understood, she lied, wondering why they felt so threatened.

In a matter of weeks, she knew, she would be working on the floor at the hospital in some general capacity. Soon thereafter she would be assigned to work with a terminally ill patient either at home or at Cedars. In either place she would be of service. That thought both sustained and comforted her. Her guilt was assuaged when it had become evident that her volunteer work wouldn't interfere with any of her duties at the office.

She began to smile, thinking of the office and of the

''coming-out'' party—Lilith's words—arranged that afternoon by her partner. Although her talk-show appearance had caused considerable comment among their clients and contacts, little seemed to be negative. Only a few ''stars'' had sniffed, not at her near-death experience but at her thinking her work could possibly mean less.

Lileen had called, from her home and from her bed. In a raspy voice that was lively although weak she said: ''Lady, you're the only person I know who can take death out of the closet. And in a Valentino cream-colored silk suit. Talk about an image change. But the name has to go. Death sucks. Call it pussy, baby, and you'll have half the population running to get it, *dying* for it—so to speak—while the other half runs after those who be doing the running.''

She smiled again, thinking of Lileen, and then her mind turned to her strangest—as well as briefest—call that afternoon.

''I think I finally understand,'' Barney Reardon had said and then hung up, leaving her hanging, both figuratively and literally. She hadn't thought about Reardon in months, Joanna realized as she pulled into her driveway, and to think of him now for some reason made her anxious.

She heard both the television blaring and the phone ringing when she entered the house. She was surprised no one was answering the persistent ring. She reached the phone just as the answering service connected with the caller. She listened briefly to Damita Miles's ''urgent'' message.

''Why didn't anyone pick up?'' she asked as she entered the den, where Reynolds and Stacey were sitting in front of a television neither seemed to be watching.

''We picked up,'' Reynolds replied. ''We stopped after the first ten or twelve calls in the first half hour we were both home.'' He was staring at her accusingly. ''You wouldn't guess how many religious fanatics there are out there who seemingly want nothing more than to touch the hem of your garment.''

''I'm sorry. I never thought . . .''

''Exactly, Joanna. You never thought,'' Reynolds interrupted as he punched the off button on the remote control. "And you should have. You really should have."

"Honestly, Mother, what a dumb thing to have done," Stacey said. "I was humiliated. The girls at school think you're some kind of joke: They call you 'Space Cadet Mother.' Of course the druggies think you're a hero. They want to know what you're taking and where they can get it. Such weirded-out shit. Where do you come off with this . . . *a part of God, a part of the whole that is God and the universe* crap? You sound like Yoda in *Star Wars*. How could you do this?"

Joanna was so unprepared for the attack that she stood there, unable to retreat or defend.

"Did you ever think of the effect your going public with your so-called experience might have on my practice?" Reynolds asked, prepared to tell her before she could respond. "My clients are already frightened when they come to me. Contrary to some public opinion, face lifts are not casual happenings for casual people. They are potentially dangerous. There is, after all, anesthesia and a knife involved, as well as the sure hands and what is hopefully the sure mind of the surgeon. My patients do not need the added worry of whether or not I'm as crazy as my wife. And you are crazy to go public with this. Do you know what you sound like to most people?" Reynolds asked. "Like *Looney Tunes*. Dammit, Jo, you have no right to involve me. I have a position to uphold, in the community and at the hospital. I can't be suspect because of my wife."

"What, for God's sake, makes me suspect?" Joanna demanded.

"You must be kidding," Reynolds snapped. "Jo, in case you haven't noticed, the average person, let alone the wife of a doctor, doesn't go on talk shows claiming she died and went to heaven to see God. Do you know that Stacey and I have had to deal with your mess all day? There were reporters at my office and even at the house when I first came home. And have you checked with your answering service? There are calls from *The National Enquirer* and *The Merv Griffin Show*. They all want you, Jo. You're a goddamn media event, the latest freak show. Get rid of them, Joanna. Don't talk to a single damn one of them. Forget the whole thing, and just maybe they and all this will go away. Make it stop, Joanna. I've had it.''

Staring at her accusers, Joanna shook herself as if that action would awaken and free her from what could only be a bad dream. ''I don't believe this,'' she began. ''I feel as if I'm standing in the middle of one of those puzzles that asks: What's wrong with this picture? This just doesn't compute.

''You,'' Joanna said as she pointed at Stacey, ''come and go around here, doing as you please, never asking, never consulting. You even decide to get married without so much as a word. And you,'' Joanna continued, turning toward Reynolds, ''you buy and sell houses, cars—*my* houses, *my* cars—also without asking or telling. You do exactly as you please. You take off to play tennis, to go sailing, to play. Sometimes you're home when you're expected; sometimes you're not. Is it any wonder your daughter acts just like you? You've set the example. Well, then, why is it I don't have the same privileges? In case you haven't noticed this is my life, and if I choose to speak about it that's my decision. We're not exactly talking ax murder or child abuse or sexual depravity here. We are talking about real life-and-death issues, which I spontaneously chose to discuss in public. It was for me. It had nothing to do with you. Unfortunately, I might add.''

She paused, nursing a growing hurt, watching their faces for some kind of softening. ''What a joke,'' she said finally. ''I put myself out there today, all but hang by my thumbs in front of a few hundred thousand people, and I get this reaction from my own family. Amazing. How about some support instead of condemnation? How about some respect for my rights, my freedom and my experience, which just might be valid in spite of anything you might think?''

''Your freedom ends at the tip of my nose,'' Reynolds countered.

''Then I suggest taking that sure mind and sure surgeon's hand of yours and shortening it, if for no other reason than to get it out of my business,'' Joanna said. ''And Stacey, I wouldn't worry about what your friends at school think of me. In your case, given your track record, I'd be much more concerned with what they think of you."

She was at the den door when she turned. "I just can't seem to reach you people, can I, and I must tell you I'm getting sick and tired of trying."

He wasn't quite awake, although he had never quite fallen asleep. In his dreamlike state he heard the alarm in the whispers of others but was too groggy to be anything more than just passively concerned. His stomach pitched along with the plane. Neither quite righted itself as different storms buffeted each. His mind continued to drift.

It should have been exciting, fun, an experience to remember—even treasure—whether or not the TV pilot ever sold to a network. Instead, the ten days had felt like a prison sentence with only the knowledge of release and a return to home sustaining him.

He had been unable to relax or to relieve his anxieties. His hotel room felt like four contracting walls of floral, flocked paper, and the telephone his only link to a familiar life.

He had called Ralph daily but stopped midweek when he felt Ralph withdraw, seemingly unwilling to deal further with his fears. Without Ralph his anxiety had worsened, which perhaps caused his greatest foolishness—or at the least the first of his foolishnesses. He had called Tony the day he learned the cast and crew would be held through the weekend for additional shooting, thus preventing his Friday night return to New York.

Dean thought about that phone call as stewardesses navigated the rolling aisles of the 747 to caution awakening passengers to remain in their seats with their seat buckles securely fastened. Just a local thunderstorm, one chirped brightly to a particularly frightened flier.

Tony had also been aloof when he called, his recalcitrant manner saying more at first than his words. Dean had pressed, and Tony finally revealed they had received a Note of Issue and Statement of Readiness from Barbara's attorneys. Tony explained that this meant the case was ready to proceed . . . to court, to conclusion. He had felt his stomach drop then just as it was dropping now when the plane plummeted from one cloud to another. Despite the fact it was what he had repeatedly told Tony he wanted—a swift end to this lingering horror—he had panicked, choking on his fantasies and the reality of what might happen once he entered the courtroom. It would indeed not be a trial by jury but a hearing before a judge. He would be at that judge's mercy or lack of same.

He had panicked, losing his resolve with his courage, and thus agreed to Tony's suggestion that he deny the motion, claiming that before they could proceed to trial, more information from the plaintiff was needed. This would borrow time, at least weeks and maybe months, and then, Tony added encouragingly, they could have anywhere from six months to three times that before the case reached the docket, given the current overload in the courts.

He had blundered through the rest of the week on the set, his concentration gone with his nerve, forgetting lines he had learned before leaving New York. Repeatedly he had to remind himself he was an actor, a professional, and that he must gain control. On Friday he had called Joanna, hoping to fill some portion of what loomed like a year's time in a weekend, but found her Saturday occupied. They agreed to meet Sunday, with her sounding no happier than he felt. He had again called Ralph, but even at the early eastern hour of seven A.M. could only reach the answering service. Two hours later he called again, reaching the service once more—Mr. Kayne had indeed phoned in for messages; they would indeed tell him that Mr. Di Nardo had called once more.

He could feel the plane turn, its wings dipping to the west as it once again began circling the New York airport. Almost an hour had passed since they had arrived in the metropolitan area, only to be repeatedly waved off by the air-traffic controllers, who were concerned with the sudden wind-shear factor.

Not knowing where Ralph was and why he wasn't returning his calls made him angry, furious actually, and he had stormed out of the floral, flocked hotel room, his gear in hand, thinking only of the tension-releasing workout he would obtain in the hotel's health club. There had not been any other thought in mind, he later repeatedly assured himself. And although that was true, it was also a lie. In health clubs all across the country there was always the possibility of meeting someone.

Which he did, almost immediately, a familiar face who spotted his familiar face and eyed it as each went about his workout. They began talking naturally, although their conversation was unnatural, given the undercurrents that remained submerged until they agreed to meet for the euphemistic "drink."

In one respect their lives were parallel, with each in Los Angeles to make a television pilot. For Dean, it was his first; for the other, his third since his last show had been canceled five years ago. They talked about careers, the one that was seemingly happening and the one that was not—unless this new pilot eventually sold.

He hadn't stopped to think. He didn't want to. He only wanted to feel. Not emotionally but physically. Within the hour they were engaged in *safe* sex. And not only was there no exchange of bodily fluids, as prescribed by the medical experts on the prevention of AIDS, but there was no exchange of anything resembling a feeling. It was ostensibly the release he had craved. For a moment his anxieties had been allayed. With someone, even a stranger, he had felt safe. In that floral wallpapered room with grass-green carpeting he had been an old self . . . distant, uninvolved, using sex the way some people use food or drink or drugs.

But as the plane began its final descent into Kennedy he realized the sex hadn't been safe at all. It had awakened feelings and stirred buried remembrances . . . of being close to someone, of loving a person as you made love to and with him. And making love was not just making someone come. It was making someone happy in more ways than the obvious one. It was an involvement that had only in part to do with parts of the body.

He had wanted to touch Joanna that Sunday on the beach at her Malibu home, needed to feel an intimate contact that was based on true intimacy. But Joanna was unavailable, unreachable; she remained buried in the privacy of her thoughts. He had worried about her, and that, too, stirred memories. He missed worrying about someone's happiness even as he resented that person for infringing on his own. He needed to feel close even as he cried out for distance.

He was standing in front of the brownstone on Ninety-second Street, his luggage at his side, searching for something he had imagined was there but wasn't. It was only a house, he saw. A not terribly attractive brick building that looked not much different from scores of others in the city. And for this he had pined. For this he had suffered anxiety.

The apartment was dark when he entered, and it smelled the way apartments often do when they've been empty for ten days with windows closed and plants unwatered, a dried soil smell that only another houseplant owner could identify.

It was the feeling of completion he had missed, that feeling of being two instead of one, that certainty of identity when seen through the eyes of another. A *real* other and not a stranger.

The clock read just past seven. He would sleep a few hours and then call Ralph at the office, perhaps join him for lunch if he was free. There was undoubtedly an explanation why his calls had not been returned. He wanted to hear it so he could feel better about things.

The jumbo jet shook and rattled, dunking in and out of huge gray-black clouds before it plummeted. He placed his head on the pillow in his lap, bending his torso to his knees, preparing for the inevitable crash. Beyond his whimpers he could hear the wail of a siren, of perhaps a fire truck or a police car.

He bolted upright, a half-scream constricted in his throat. The wail of a siren became the phone ringing beside his bed. Confused, he looked about the darkness and found the digital clock on the bedside table. His ''just a nap'' had turned into an all-day sleep.

Lifting the receiver from its hook, he heard Ralph's voice. He struggled to respond, his mind and body still in the throes of his dream and its obvious implications. His trembling stopped as he identified several objects in the room. He was home . . . safe, and at the other end of the phone a man he knew was explaining how he had been trying to reach him since yesterday. Hadn't he checked his machine for messages? He hadn't, having chosen to unpack and then fall into bed instead.

Dean wanted to interrupt and ask: Where the hell have you been? But he refrained; there was something in Ralph's tone, something vague and foreign, that made him mindful of more than just his own concerns.

Was he free for dinner? Ralph asked.

He was.

He would pick up steak and salad and be by the brownstone by eight, Ralph said.

He agreed without thinking. Only later, as he showered, did Dean wonder about the arrangements. In all their times together Ralph had never suggested he come to the brownstone, and he had never encouraged it, keeping the space private, as if an outside intrusion might erode whatever memory he was trying to preserve. He found himself cleaning, dusting even as he vacuumed. He asked if flowers were necessary and decided they were, even though Ralph was a friend and not a date. And once out, he wanted wine. Not just any wine but a good French import. As if they were celebrating. Which they were not, unless Ralph knew something he didn't. And a dessert. Not a honey-filled nutritious bit of baking from the local health food store but some sugary slab of whipped cream and chocolate from the patisserie.

Only when the table was set, the wine chilled and the flowers arranged did he remember his answering machine. With notepaper and pen in hand, he prepared to learn of the events in his life.

Maurie Freissan was the first and fourth call, each time asking anxiously about the pilot and whether *he* had heard anything. Dean knew that the next time the phone rang that evening it would undoubtedly be Freissan.

Sara's message was surprising. She had been in the city Monday. To terminate her therapy. And, it resulted, with her shrink's blessing. She wanted to celebrate. She thought Dean might want to roll her around Central Park.

Joanna's voice startled him; it sounded so near. She was apologizing for having "not really been home Sunday."

She offered no explanation, just a closing: "I love you." He was touched.

His sister-in-law, Janice, invited him to dinner the first Sunday in June. He found that odd, as the invitation had no history or historical significance. Like a birthday or anniversary. But Tony's message clarified the seemingly senseless. The family's annual visit to the Long Island cemetery where his mother was buried would be that Sunday. Would he attend?

He hadn't in recent years, refusing these family "reunions" for many reasons and preferring to remember the anniversary of his mother's death in some way other than visiting a plot of ground and a slab of stone. But the fact that Tony had asked, had again extended a hand, moved him. In some peculiar but nice way, he thought Tony's invitation was the same as Joanna saying she loved him.

And then Tony again, on a later message. He had not as yet denied Barbara's Statement of Readiness but would as soon as they talked again and if indeed that was still Dean's decision. Dean was thinking about Tony's intent when the doorbell rang. Ralph was early.

He stood awkwardly in the doorway, not knowing quite how to greet the man who stood before him buried behind a shopping bag that seemed filled with far more than steak and salad. A handshake with his arms full would be impossible; a hug . . . uncomfortable.

"I shopped; you cook," Ralph said in a tone that defied contradiction. "Where's the kitchen?"

And despite his thinking that he was prepared, suddenly there was another man in his kitchen, opening the refrigerator, moving things about. A man who suddenly said: "I've been at the studio since eight this morning. I need a shower."

And just like that someone was in his bathroom, passing through his bedroom to get there. It was odd, somewhat uncomfortable but not upsetting. As he seasoned the steaks, listening to the sound of water running up above his head, Dean realized he had never dealt with how he would feel about sharing again. His mind went to the man in the health club and then in his bed. Why had that been simple? Because he had truly shared so little of himself, it was inconsequential.

They were at the table eating, little pieces of information exchanged between big bites of food. He was surprised by Ralph's restlessness. He listened as Ralph spoke of leaving the soap, of wanting a change, a distraction perhaps, or something new and challenging. He wondered who was this man and who did he think he was talking to when he said: "Let's go to Europe this summer, cruise around the Greek Islands, hit Egypt and the pyramids. Maybe even go on to Jerusalem."

Dean did not respond, at least not to the suggestion, but did say: "I called several times over the weekend." It was his indirect way of saying: Where the hell were you and why didn't you return my calls? He watched Ralph's face for a signal, some sign of either guilt or contrition.

"I was in Houston," he heard Ralph say. "I couldn't call. Then when I could, I didn't feel like it."

The words, spoken more to a medium-rare piece of beef than to him, were surprising. Ralph had not mentioned previously any plans to visit his children, particularly since they seemed to be rather adamant about maintaining their distance ever since the Bahamas and the incident that had followed. He had many questions, which Ralph answered without him asking.

"It was something I had to do," he said as he pushed his plate away. "Something I knew I would do the morning I told you what a mess I had made of it in Houston. So I just hopped on a plane and presented myself. Boy, did I present myself," Ralph said, a wry laugh almost drowned by the slug of wine with which he washed his words down, or away.

Dean studied the face across from his. He saw the eyes and quickly turned his away. He saw too much pain.

"Hey, it's OK."

The words were Ralph's when Dean felt it should have been the other way around. He stumbled up from the table, collecting himself as he collected the coffee. All he had to do was pour it. Which he did, his hand involuntarily shaking as he poured.

"OK, tell me," Dean said as he settled himself at the table.

Ralph played with the spoon in his cup, stirring despite the fact he took neither sugar nor cream in his coffee. "I came out to my kids, Dean."

Once his shock had passed, Dean asked: "But why?"

"Because from my point of view it was something they had to know and something I had to tell them. If they were to know me, really know me, how could they if I kept secret a vital part of who I am?"

"It's not always necessary for people to know everything about you. Even the people you love," Dean defended.

"Ah, but what about the people who love you?" Ralph asked. "Dean, don't you see? How can I, can you, can anyone who is gay really feel loved by someone who's straight if he's being dishonest about his identity? Always in the back of my mind has been the thought if so-and-so knew the truth, he or she or they wouldn't love me. Well, I can't live with that anymore. You either love me or you don't, and if my sexuality makes a difference, so be it. I mean . . . Dean, if my kids are to love me, they have to love who I am, and being gay is part of who I am."

He arose from the table, and Dean watched as Ralph began to pace. When he turned his face was flushed. "When I pounced on my son, on *his* sexuality, the last time we were together, you know what I was doing? Hiding. Trying to draw the attention away from me and who I really am. That made me feel like shit, Dean. I don't want to do that, not to me or my kids."

Dean remained at the table, not knowing what to say, reacting as if what Ralph was saying, was feeling, applied to him. "So what happened?" he finally offered. He saw the shrug, watched as Ralph turned his back and heard him say with a wry laugh that spoke of pain: "It's not every day a father gets to lose his kids . . . again. You'd think once would be enough for any man to suffer that in his lifetime."

He knew he should speak, act, move from the table to his friend, but he couldn't. He felt helpless.

"My daughter said nothing. She just sat there while my

son glared. At that moment I saw he hated me. Admitting to being gay was worse than if I had admitted to murder.

"Dean, you know how I love my kids—not quite so much right now because I'm hurt and angry—but I love them. I always said, as most parents do, that I would die for them. And if there was a truck bearing down and it was a choice between them or me, I would make it me. But Dean, although I would die for them in that circumstance, I won't give up my life for them. I won't give up who I am, because if I do I'm not anything."

He heard that. And although Ralph continued to speak, he continued to hear those last words. They were like termites, eating away at him from the inside.

"They told their mother, of course," he heard Ralph saying. "She accused me of making our marriage a mockery. Which it wasn't. I loved her. I loved our life together. And then she panicked. She wondered if I might have given her AIDS. She became hysterical, threatening to go to court to change the visitation rights, to block my seeing my children. In Texas the courts just might grant her request, and if they don't the kids might. But no court can change the fact that I'm those children's father. They'll have to deal with that and with me one day."

Dean sat with his head in his hands. He was thinking about the second bedroom in Ralph's apartment, its closet stocked with the children's clothes, its shelves lined with their books, records and tapes. How would Ralph deal with this?

They were silent, Ralph standing at the window, his back to Dean, while Dean remained rooted at the table.

"I did my best, Dean. And I really think coming out to my kids was not only best for me but best for them. It makes me free, and hopefully, somewhere down the road, it will set them free from narrow-mindedness. I mean . . . I really feel terrific about what happened. Except for one thing. I am in such godawful pain."

Dean heard the pain, felt it even from across the room. His reaction was to clear the table, scrape the plates and load the dishwasher. The phone rang. He knew it was Maurie Freissan. He ran to answer it but caught sight of Ralph's face as he did. He forgot the phone, forgot his own fear and walked to where Ralph was standing looking out the window. He slung his arm around Ralph's shoulders, and although he said nothing, he continued to stare out the window with Ralph as if they were not just looking at a cross street but at the most interesting event in the world.

"What are you going to say?"

"Ina, for the tenth time would you stop asking me that? I've already told you. I don't know. I haven't even thought about it. God, but I wish Robert hadn't said anything to you or to me either about Stefan wanting to come home," Sara fumed. "It may not even be true. Certainly Stefan hasn't given me the slightest reason to think it's true."

"He's called, hasn't he? He's coming here in a matter of minutes, isn't he?" Ina said.

"But that doesn't mean a thing," Sara persisted. "Ina, you know how children are. Robert may have only thought he heard Stefan make some sort of remark about coming home. It may be all in Robert's mind."

"Well, then why are you taking so much time with your hair?" Ina asked, as she watched Sara fuss with a hairbrush and comb.

"For God's sake, Ina. There's not much else I can fuss with. An elephant is an elephant no matter what you drape over it. And in my case, I'd need the proscenium curtain from Radio City Music Hall."

Ina stared at Sara's reflection in the full-length mirror. "I have never understood how anyone who initially carries so small can become so big," she mused.

"Just lucky, I guess," Sara replied. "Now go, Ina. It was truly nice of you to come, uninvited though you were."

Ina stood firm. "You're nervous and you need my support. The moment the doorbell rings I promise I'll disappear. But not a minute sooner."

Sara steeled herself. "Ina, if I'm nervous it's because you're making me crazy. This is my life, Ina, not yours. My reconciliation, not yours."

"See?" said Ina triumphantly. "You just said it. Reconciliation. You are planning to say yes."

"Ina, get the hell out of here now. And fast. 'Cause if I haul off and hit with nine months of baby, you won't need a car to get home. An ambulance will drive you there."

Ina gathered her things, pouting and protesting, urging Sara to call as soon as Stefan left. In fact, she could remain in Princeton, sightsee and shop, and then come right over. So Sara wouldn't be alone.

"So you can get the scoop before it's on *World News Tonight*, you mean," Sara responded. "I'll call, Ina. But don't hang by your thumbs waiting." She looked at her sister's downcast face. "All right," she relented. "I'll call tonight. *After* the kids are in bed."

She wandered throughout the house, straightening pictures and plumping sofa cushions. She once again arranged the flowers in the cut-glass crystal vase on the piano and finger-dusted the tops of the little frames that held the many family portraits. She thought about the upstairs bedroom and how a Dresden blue might be nice; something different from the pink that was so one-sided—hers. The cost to refurbish would be almost that of a week's trip to London and Paris. Ina could stay with the kids. It was a possibility. Except for one thing. She was having a baby.

She stared at the telephone, wondering if she should call Schauzer to discuss the mind that was running away with her. Schauzer would call her fantasies "revealing." They made it clear she was hopeful of a reconciliation, a new beginning for two people who had changed and would continue to change.

Schauzer had always said that fantasies weren't harmful as long as they were kept in perspective.

The baby kicked, and perhaps even punched, so great was the pain. Not now, little one, Sara cautioned. You've waited this long, wait a little bit longer. She entered the kitchen and, after checking the wall clock, set the Mr. Coffee in motion. As it began to bubble she began to wonder if he still drank coffee or whether the doctors had convinced him to cut down on his caffeine. She wondered what other changes might have happened in his life. She wondered about her own.

She began to cry, not gently but violently. The months of estrangement, of humiliation, anger, fear and loneliness were no longer at a distance but before her, not to be ignored or denied. Once again she was amazed by the turn her life had taken. She had married forever. It was what she was about. Marriage, being Mrs. Stefan Schell, was as integral to her being as her left or right arm. Yet she had functioned without Stefan. She had achieved and had made real changes that had made her feel good, confident. But she had never felt fulfilled. Each day she had awakened with the distinct feeling that something was missing, misplaced, and if she just looked she would find it.

She knew she would work, teach and perhaps study for an even more advanced degree that might lead her into counseling. She understood that within that process she would meet some—perhaps even many—like her on the teaching staff who were divorced. There would be companionship, perhaps male as well as female. But she couldn't imagine starting over again, learning how to be comfortable with another person, so comfortable that you could admit without fear of ridicule or censure that sometimes you just felt frightened even if there was no particular reason. So comfortable that you didn't have to look your best or be at your best because that person knew who you were anyway. The likelihood of finding another relationship, a man with whom she could build a history, seemed improbable, mainly because she doubted whether she could ever risk that much of herself again.

But she didn't feel desperate or even particularly frightened. She could and would survive and make some kind of life in the process. But that life would be so much nicer in a Dresden blue bedroom with white lace curtains and furniture, stripped and painted antique white with a Dresden blue trim.

The doorbell rang. She moved toward it, wondering why he didn't use his key, if he still had it, and whether he was entitled to both have and use it. After all, what rights did he have? she wondered. What rights do you want him to have? was her response.

She opened the door, and he stood on the threshold, looking considerably better than when she had seen him last. His face was fuller, and it had color beneath and above his closely trimmed beard. Only his eyes hadn't changed. Life still hadn't returned to them.

He refused the coffee, asking for decaffeinated tea instead. She was surprised when he accepted her offer of a sandwich, never thinking he could eat at a time like this. Just looking at the egg salad—he had always loved her egg salad—made her queasy. But then she had things other than food on her mind. She couldn't believe he was making small talk and that they were exchanging pleasantries. Yes, the spring had been lovely. It had been a tonic for him. His work, too, was going well, and he was particularly pleased about the awards dinner that would close the school year at the end of the month. Would she attend?

Would she? She didn't know. It depended, she realized without putting voice to her thoughts, on whether *she* would be there. And suddenly she wondered where *she* was, Denise Wolfe, at this moment and what she would think, how she would feel, if she knew Stefan was here.

She thanked him for the invitation and said she would let him know. He nodded, seemingly understanding her need to be noncommittal.

He sipped his tea, never looking about the kitchen, at its new curtains or the total lack of clutter on the counter, where everything that didn't have a natural place of its own used to be thrown. He asked about the children, and they chatted about each of their offspring's school year. He casually mentioned choices of colleges for Robert. She refused to listen, let alone consider what he was saying. Robert was only to be a junior. He rose abruptly, and she had the distinct feeling that now that he had eaten, spoken of the children, he would leave. She followed into the living room, where he sat not in his usual chair but on the sofa, crunching the very same pillows she had just fluffed and plumped. He was trying to get comfortable, working from without to within, which she knew from her own experience was an impossible task.

"Stefan, you're obviously here for a reason. Shouldn't you get to it?"

She couldn't believe her temerity. Only it wasn't her but

that crazy lady mouthing off again, rushing in where no one wise would tread.

"I'd like to come home," he said simply.

She could not tell whether it was the baby or her heart that pounded and kicked. Although she had heard from Robert that Stefan would say this, hearing it directly from Stefan was quite another thing.

His eyes were lowered as he spoke, as was his voice. "Sara, I'm not happy separated. It's not what I want. I miss my life as it was, miss my home, my family. It was good. It was comfortable. I didn't think I was happy, and to some extent I wasn't. But I was content, more content than I realized. Sara, I regret what I've done. It's been a mistake. A big mistake," he added as if she hadn't heard.

He said nothing more, although she waited. There had to be something more. Please God, there had to be.

Finally he spoke again. "I've told Denise. She's being very good about it, allowing me to remain in her house until this is all settled." He looked sad. "This isn't easy for her."

His eyes sought hers. She neither blinked nor flinched. "I know what you think, Sara, but you're wrong. Denise is not a bad person. She's really very good, very kind and understanding."

"No!" Sara said suddenly, her voice flat but vehement.

"No?" Stefan echoed. "Sara, that's not fair. You don't know Denise."

"No, you cannot move back," Sara said, knowing this was no crazy lady speaking this time. "You're not ready. At least not for me. I don't want you as you are."

He looked shocked, as though her words had no connection to any reality.

"For God's sake, Stefan, you speak of this woman, but you have never once spoken of me. You spoke of the house, the family, and if we had a dog you'd probably speak about him too. But you never mentioned me, never said a word about missing me. I *am* the house, Stefan. I *am* the family. You're supposed to be coming home because of me, because you miss what we had, what we were together, what I am in your life, because you love me, if I might be so bold or so stupid—I'm not sure which. I'm not interested in your other reasons. I'm only interested in what's good for me."

He looked confused, lost, his expression so unlike any she could remember seeing on his face throughout their years together.

"Don't you want to be married, Sara?" he asked.

Her laugh was bitter. "Oh, yes, Stefan, I want to be married. I need to be married. It's what I'm really about and I no longer make apologies for that. But I need to be married to a man who needs not only to be married but to be married to me. Me, Stefan. Sara Rosen Schell. And Stefan, I want more than just a husband. I want a friend and a lover, and given what you have said, I don't know if you can be either."

He stared at her, his eyes solemn and dry. "Nor do I," he replied, "but Sara, I do love you. I thought you understood that. Because I have told you. So it's not a passion—I'm sorry for both our sakes about that—but it is a feeling, one I do not have for any other person in this world."

She heard that. She heard that clearly. He was continuing to talk, but she could only hear what he had just said.

"You can't just come back, Stefan," she said softly but with finality. "You have to earn that right, or else nothing between us has or will change. Although it already has in many ways. I'm not the woman you left, Stefan. I know that sounds trite, but it's true, and frankly, no one is more surprised than I." She paused, catching her breath as she caught up with her thoughts. "You must move out of her house," she said suddenly. "You must take your own apartment. And you must see a therapist again," she added, her mind now working faster than the words could leave her mouth. "*We* must see a therapist . . . together. And I want that woman out of your life. I want her fired. When that's done we can talk again. But not before."

He looked at her with disbelief, which she, too, would have done if he had not been in the room and if a mirror had been near. "I can't do that, Sara," he said. "She has a child to support. What about her life, her livelihood?"

"What about it?" Sara said. "I don't remember her giving me that consideration, so frankly, Stefan, I don't feel I owe her a damn thing. And if that makes me hard and callous, good! It's about time. Now those are my demands. Take them or leave them. But if you and I are to have any kind of shot at making it again, I suggest you take them."

"You haven't said if you want that shot, Sara," Stefan said, looking at her closely.

"Well, I do, Stefan. I really do," Sara replied as she stood, a signal the meeting was at an end. "And I'd like us to get back together for the very same reasons you just expressed. But they are not enough. I need something more that maybe you can and maybe you can't give me. It's up to both of us, each in our own way, to find out."

She had maneuvered him to the door. He stood there, searching her face, looking for someone he suddenly realized was gone, undoubtedly forever. She closed the door behind him, standing quite still, waiting for the reaction she knew would come. But her only conscious feeling was that of hunger; her only thought that of the egg salad in the refrigerator. It was not the nurturance she required, but it was currently what was available. She took it.

SIXTEEN

THE woman sitting opposite her in the airport cocktail lounge was waiting patiently, smiling as she watched Joanna over the rim of a glass bubbling with club soda. As Elaine Winters nibbled at the dried nuts the waitress had served with their drinks, Joanna nibbled at her bottom lip, a nervous habit she suspected she had picked up from watching Sara.

Two hours ago she had been at Los Angeles International Airport, en route to her monthly IANDS meeting in Oakland. But at the boarding gate, the prospect of what she would face—another evening's talk about unaccepting husbands, hostile children and disbelieving families—caused her to balk. Such an exchange would only increase her anger and the fact that she was more than just a little bitter.

"Joanna," she heard Elaine begin, "since I'm fairly certain it wasn't a burning desire to see Fresno, California, in the spring that brought you here on the spur of the moment, why don't you talk?"

Joanna didn't quite understand how she happened to be in Fresno or what prompted her to call the Winters woman. But at the airport she had found Elaine's number where she had once placed it in her wallet, never thinking—or was it always knowing?—that one day she might use it. When she had called in somewhat of a controlled frenzy Elaine never hesitated but insisted she indeed fly up. She stared at the woman, so much the older image of Lilith, and after taking a deep breath, began.

"Elaine, has it ever occurred to you that maybe our near-death experiences are great big jokes, and since we're the butt of them we can't see their humor or think them funny?"

"What a relief!" Elaine replied as she faked mopping her brow. "And here I thought it was something serious you wanted to discuss." When Joanna's mood didn't lighten, Elaine added: "Yes, I once felt that way, but it was a very long time ago. You know it's no joke, so why do you ask?"

"For no particular reason, except maybe for the fact that my life has fallen apart ever since my supposedly wonderful NDE," Joanna said, barely disguising her bitterness.

"Your life, Joanna?" Elaine parried. "Or are we possibly talking about those parts of your life, or perhaps *world* is a better word, that have fallen apart?"

"Is there a difference?" Joanna asked.

"Stop. I hate melodrama. Particularly from intelligent women," Elaine admonished.

"Listen, I know I'm supposed to be terrifically grateful for having seen the Light, been given a second chance . . ."

"Damn straight!" Elaine interrupted.

"Right. It's a gift. But I think my life would be in much better shape had I just kept my mouth shut about it from the first," Joanna said, her bitterness again obvious.

"Do you really believe that?" Elaine asked, her head cocked to look at Joanna more carefully.

Joanna sighed. "No," she admitted, becoming even more morose. "It would be awful to pretend it never happened. That would really make me crazy."

"And it would be awful for the people in your life who need you to speak out about your experience," Elaine offered as she signaled for the waitress to bring some of the corn chips she saw being served at another table.

"I don't think my husband or daughter would find it so awful," Joanna replied, somewhat amused by what she thought was Elaine's naïveté. "Frankly, I think they would be thrilled if I went back into the closet and closed both its door and my mouth."

"That's just two people in your life. What about the others?" Elaine persisted.

"Others?" At first the question seemed ridiculous, but as Joanna thought, she realized there were others. Like Lileen, so hopeful now that there was something beyond her illness, beyond her present life. Something and Someone. And then those people—not many but enough—who had written or phoned after her *Los Angeles Woman* appearance. Many had been grateful, some curious, others even emotional, as they felt she had bolstered their hope for an eternal life or had validated something they, too, had in some way experienced but to which they could never give voice. She had been moved by the outpouring of feeling from strangers.

"Yes, there have been those who have profited by my speaking out," Joanna admitted, "but they're not my family," she added as if to say that negated the experience.

"So?" Elaine asked, her eyes carefully scrutinizing Joanna.

"So everything!" Joanna replied angrily. "That's the big joke to which I was referring, the joke that seemingly is on me. I had this incredible experience. I died. I stood before a magnificent presence in the form of Light, wanting nothing more than to remain in Its glow. But I left, or was banished—I can't remember which—and for a reason: that I had unfinished business here. So I came back. For Reynolds and Stacey."

"Are you so sure? Are you so sure it was for Reynolds and Stacey?" Elaine added when she saw the confused look on Joanna's face.

"For God's sake, Elaine, why else would I have returned?" Joanna demanded impatiently.

"For you, Joanna! Not for God's, Reynolds's or Stacey's sake, but for your own," Elaine replied as she put down her glass of club soda to confront Joanna.

"You never suggested that before," Joanna protested.

"You weren't ready to listen. And I wasn't certain. I'm still not. How could I be? I'm not God. I'm only suggesting that in that Light, before that presence, you understood your life wasn't yet complete, that there were things you needed to do for yourself, things you needed to make right, fix, which would then perhaps help to fix things for others. Like your family."

"My family," Joanna echoed, her voice heavy with ridicule. "I'm an embarrassment to them. I walk about my own home feeling like an intruder, and I'm sure they see me as one. They certainly treat me like one."

"Weren't you listening?" Elaine asked as she reached across the table to grab Joanna's hands. "Forget your family for the moment. Deal with what I suggested—that you returned for you, not them. Aren't you entitled to your life?"

"And what about my obligation as a wife and mother?" Joanna demanded.

"You have an obligation first and foremost to yourself. And you know that," Elaine said vehemently. "You're just not comfortable admitting it."

"It makes me crazy with guilt," Joanna replied.

"That's an old tape. Lose it," Elaine advised. "Look. I know how you feel. I've been in your shoes and I remember all too well how they pinched. I also remember how my husband and Lilith wanted to put me into that very same closet you mentioned. And for a while I went in. But I had to come out. And you know why, Joanna? Because it was killing me not to, killing me to deny not only who I was but to deny God. And that's our first obligation: not to deny either."

"So what do I do about my family?" Joanna asked angrily. "Leave them?"

The words had flown from her mouth without forethought or warning. She could not reclaim them, despite her urge to scoop them up and hide them from inspection.

Elaine looked directly into Joanna's eyes. "Only you can answer that question."

"You stayed," Joanna said, her reply more an accusation than a statement of fact.

"Yes, but not without much struggle," Elaine replied. "Actually, I was able to stay when I realized I could go—that Jack and Lilith would survive without me. Through months . . . no, years, of doubt and anguish, I finally learned that I had my growth to complete and that they had theirs. I felt that by staying all of us could grow by dealing with who I was. It became my family's choice, and I knew if they elected not to deal with who I was, then I would have to move on.

"Joanna," Elaine continued as she leaned forward, taking and holding Joanna's hands even more tightly in her own. "The lesson we must learn—hard as it is—is for us to take the people we love as far as they can go, and when they can go no further to just let go. And to understand as we release them that each person grows at his own speed. Joanna, you and I have had experiences that can further people's growth. We offer. They either accept or refuse. It's their choice, just as it is ours either to remain still or to continue to grow."

"Elaine, look at me. I'm past forty and I'm five foot six. How much more am I supposed to grow and into what?" Joanna asked pleadingly.

"From being just a spark to becoming part of the Light," Elaine replied softly. "Don't talk, Joanna. Just sit. Think. Somewhere deep within you've always known that to be true. Somewhere, you know, we have lived before; we will live again, until we become one. With ourselves, one another and God."

Joanna fought back her reaction to cry. With a little false laugh she said: "You know what Reynolds would say if he were here and heard you just now?"

Elaine cupped Joanna's chin in her hand. "Yes," she replied, her eyes searching Joanna's. "But does it matter?" It was a question, one of many, Joanna took twenty-three thousand feet into the air en route from Fresno to Los Angeles. The answers created more turbulence than the sudden spring thunderstorm that buffeted the plane throughout its one-hour flight.

In the week since her meeting with Elaine Joanna remained upset, often feeling but resisting the urge to cry. She was grieving, mourning, even though she could see life around her basically unchanged, here and not gone. She found herself busy, too busy, trying to be more people than it was humanly possible to be. But Lileen was failing, and suddenly it became terribly important that Lileen's foundation be properly administered. She ran between her own office and the halfway house in East Los Angeles, where she mothered girls who seemed happy for the attention. She talked with them as she had never talked with Stacey. And they listened as Stacey had never listened to her.

The foundation was financially sound, and when she told Lileen that, she could see the singer relax. Each day, it seemed to Joanna, Lileen was a little weaker, a little less there physically than when she had last seen her. Joanna did not offer false encouragement, although she never ceased hoping or praying, something she found herself doing more and more. Lileen seemed unafraid. Often she was like a child requesting a bedtime story. There was no end to the amount of times she could listen to Joanna recount her near-death experience.

It was still not an experience she could use in her on-the-job training at Cedars-Sinai, where she was now working the wards twice a week helping people to die in the most simple ways. The work was not yet satisfying, but Joanna was certain it would be one day. More satisfying than her work at the office, which she did well but without any spirit.

And so the days passed, and although she was aware there was activity about her, saw and heard the preparations, the arrangements, it seemed to her that the day she came home to find the mini moving van in her driveway, it had happened overnight. She stood looking at it uncomprehendingly. What had been just talk, just a day, a week, a month ago, was now a reality, and she felt unprepared. But then, Joanna wondered, was any parent ever really prepared for the day when her child moved out and into a world for which she seemed so unready?

She stood in the doorway to Stacey's bedroom, looking around at what had once been so familiar. Her eyes confronted the empty record cabinets, the stereo on the floor with its disconnected speakers nearby, the overstuffed cardboard boxes. The room seemed barren, devoid as it now was of those little things, like Stacey's penguin collection—she had always so loved penguins—and the pictures she had arranged for Stacey to take over the years with such personalities as Michael Jackson, Kiss and Olivia Newton-John.

She walked about the room, half empty, half filled with crates and cartons and "little things" yet to be packed. Like the photo albums, filled with pictures she couldn't remember them taking, let alone saving. She was surprised by their existence, surprised their memories were things Stacey wanted to preserve. She was even more surprised by the collection of postcards, sent from various cities and countries throughout the world. Sent by her, the day she arrived on some client's behalf, sent to Stacey to make her mother feel better, less guilty, about being away. It brought her closer to Stacey and now, as she thumbed through the cards, Joanna realized the same had been true for her daughter.

Joanna was sitting on the floor, poring over memories, over a lifetime that had only spanned eighteen years. She was sitting cross-legged, yoga fashion, much the way Stacey would sit when she was four and five . . . at her feet in the living room or in the kitchen, playing, making up nonsense songs, chattering or asking the endless questions children ask that take endless patience for a parent to answer.

She fingered the junk jewelry, the little grasshoppers and bumblebees a mother bought for her daughter before her daughter found fashion for herself. They were all saved, all preserved and prepared to make the trip to a new home, a new life. Including the cameo brooch she had bought for Stacey in New York, just after her release from the hospital and before she came home. Joanna clutched it in her hand before returning it to its place beside the other things that so obviously mattered to Stacey. She rose slowly, looked about the room and the things that remained to be packed. All spoke of relationships that must have mattered. Must have. Or why else were their memories being preserved?

"What are you doing in here?"

The question, spoken hostilely from the doorway, took her by surprise.

"The door was open, Stacey . . ."

"So you came in to pry."

"No. That's not it at all."

"Then why, Mother? Why did you come in?"

"I guess," Joanna replied as she gazed from her daughter's face to the things that had once made this her room, "just to say good-bye."

He could not see for the sun and for what felt like tears in his eyes. The day was dazzling, with white clouds moving like Sunday-in-the-park strollers across a boisterous blue sky. As he stood on the roof deck of the three-tiered house, Dean looked across the whitecapped waters of the bay. In the distance he could see the Long Island shoreline, and it seemed much too close.

He had not wanted to come to Fire Island. Now, at the end of their three-day weekend, he did not want to leave. On that distant shore were responsibilities, decisions and facts to be faced. Reality, something he had never really dealt with very well.

An arm slipped around his shoulders and rested there, its weight heavy. He felt Ralph standing next to him, his eyes also searching the shoreline. His reality had been faced, which was why he had come to the Pines—to escape it, at least for a little while.

The arm felt strange, resting as it was upon him. He was not used to being that kind of support for another. The weight of responsibility. The weight of friendship, of a relationship that was losing its definition. Which disturbed him, and had ever since their late Thursday night arrival.

It was beautiful atop the world, which was how the roof deck felt, nestled as it was among the trees on the highest spot in the Pines. Evenings at this very place they had watched a pink and orange sun in a blue and purple sky descend into a city they knew was there but couldn't see. Mornings, alone or together, they had watched the sun rising, bursting forth in whites and yellows that blinded. Never, however, had he watched with an arm, *this* arm, wrapped about his shoulders. Still, Dean didn't move, trying as he was to lock the moment in his mind forever.

It had been three days of moments, many of which his mind was still sifting through for definition. The ferry across the bay had put distance between one reality while establishing another. From the moment they had stepped ashore at the Pines they were different—still friends, but something less and yet more. The house on Shady Walk that Ralph had borrowed from friends for the weekend was steps from the bay, and once they had climbed the wooden ramp to pass through the wooden gates, they were in a world made private by sky-high fences, those man-made and those, like the towering pines, made by God.

He had stood in the entranceway, trying to believe that what was there before him was his for the weekend. The house rose above and around a pool, about which were pots and barrels of shrubs and flowers. Bees buzzed and birds chirped. This was no view that he had ever seen from the windows of Ninety-second Street. Looking out on the pool were the bedrooms. Above, up a circular wooden stairway, were the living quarters. And on the roof, this deck, this entry to moments in the sun and under the stars that were unlike others he had ever known. It was not a beach house or a crash pad, but a beautifully furnished and fully equipped home.

It had made him nervous. From the beginning it had felt like two people playing house. And what a wonderful house to play in. Except for the bedrooms. One, quite large, with its own bathroom, TV and a king-sized bed, obviously meant to be the master bedroom. The other, tiny, with but two single beds separated by a small chest of drawers, was for guests. He had sensed Ralph would have shared the one big bedroom happily. He had said as much, in a joke that made reference to the fact that the bed was big enough for a blond surfer, Mikhail Baryshnikov and the two of them. He had laughed and then taken the smaller of the two rooms. Ralph had said nothing. But then what was there to say? Hadn't he, Dean, by taking the smaller bedroom, said it all? And what had his sleeplessness said then to him . . . about them?

He felt Ralph's arm slip from his shoulder, heard him say as he patted his butt that they had best get a move on if they were to catch the two o'clock ferry. But he couldn't move, not yet. He was trying to freeze-frame the moment just as he had so many others that weekend. Like their jogs along the beach, four miles in all, late each afternoon as the sun was setting. He remembered the sudden whoop and holler and then his surprise when Ralph ended his run by whipping off his trunks and running naked into ocean waters whose temperatures were still in the fifties. He had watched as Ralph had flopped about like a seal, even making the appropriate noises. He had been surprised again when Ralph refused to put on his suit after his swim, preferring to walk the beach, as several did, with his Speedo wrapped about his neck.

He had been uncomfortable with Ralph's display and the glances they had received. He had never been daring, never had lived his own life. He had always been too frightened to do anything that might draw attention to who he really was. Between his living at home and then later with Chris, he had lived only at auditions or in the underground of bars and baths. He was then an invisible person. With Chris, that, too, had been an insulated life. No one and nothing came in. They seldom went out. Reality was of their own creation. Only it hadn't been real, just safe.

Appearances weren't important to Ralph. Not anymore and certainly not at Fire Island. He greeted strangers, engaging in small talk that actually seemed to bring him much pleasure. He had even accepted a couple's invitation for drinks. After much argument they had gone, Dean remaining fearful that the invitation was for something more than cocktails. It was. They had stayed to play Monopoly.

He could feel Ralph standing next to him again, and he hoped he wouldn't have to deal with yet another intimate gesture, a fear he had faced whenever Ralph entered his tiny, almost airless bedroom, and throughout the house, shared with a man he suddenly hardly knew, at least in terms of time. "Dean, we've got ten minutes to make the boat."

And still Dean couldn't hurry, wanted to stay in this house, on this island, to feel himself again awaken from his afternoon nap to hear the sound of water exploding as a body cannonballed into the pool just outside his bedroom. He could smell the burgers on the barbecue, the garlic rising to mingle with the salt air that dampened everything but spirits on the island. He could hear the churning of the washer-dryer just outside his bedroom in the pool shed, a sign their day was beginning, sheets and towels being made ready. And then there were the deer—a doe and her two fawns—that had wandered up the ramp looking for food, their eyes wary, their nostrils flaring. And he had somehow seen some part of himself in them and had been incredibly shaken and yet touched when they all took berries from Ralph's hand.

Nothing had happened and yet something had. Exactly what, Dean didn't know, but he could feel it and he was disturbed. He turned away from the view, from the moments, and took the steps to the ground floor slowly, methodically, as though he might trip, although he had always been surefooted. As he watched Ralph check the house to make sure all was shuttered and that nothing had been left behind, he felt incredibly sad. But again he didn't know why.

They heard the boat whistle and then saw the ferry moving slowly away from the dock just as they arrived. Dean checked the posted schedule. Another would be leaving in thirty minutes, which, if they stretched the speed limit, meant that he would just make his appointment.

Although prearranged, the schedules choreographed, it now seemed a rotten way to end the weekend. At a cemetery, at a ceremonial rite for his mother. With a father he hardly knew and had hardly known. And with a brother whose presence was a reminder of the reality he had chosen to leave even if only for a weekend.

He wondered what Ralph was feeling, returning as he would be to an empty apartment and one that would remain empty for quite a while if his children's persistent silence was any indication. He had hurt for Ralph that morning when he had called his kids in Houston—as he did every Sunday—only to learn they were "out." They had been "out" ever since his return and his disclosure. He had assured Ralph that one day, when they were older, they would be "in," and Ralph had nodded in agreement, more to reassure Dean than himself.

With time to kill they wandered into the Boatel, a restaurant-bar by the dock that was the hub of the Pines activity. Scores of men, with a sprinkle of women, were lunching late as they sat outdoors, some shielded from the sun by umbrellas, others with their faces purposely turned toward the afternoon rays. From the indoor bar, music, blaring loudly, made normal conversation impossible. As he ordered a burger and a Miller Lite, Dean turned his attention to the men who were dancing on a floor off the bar. Although he tried, he could not remember when he had last danced or if he had ever danced with Chris.

And yet he had once loved to dance. Prior to meeting Chris, when he was much younger, of course, he would arrive at Twelve West and the Flamingo at midnight and leave the discos five hours later, content that his only company was the rising sun. Those were the days when you could dance alone or with a stranger, several strangers simultaneously. No need to verbalize; the feet did the talking. And other parts of the body that gave off signals for interpretation. It was all very self-involved, safe, with its lack of touch on any level. But it had also been freeing, a certain tension release that was different, more creative and more rewarding than sex because it required more of him.

As he watched the men dancing he tried to recall exactly when his own dancing had stopped. And why. He assumed it was part and parcel of a lifestyle that had evolved when he and Chris had begun living together, a lifestyle in which he sacrificed and then denied major portions of himself he had thought then, without regret.

So engrossed had he been in his own thoughts that he wasn't certain when or how it had happened. But as he watched the dancers, Dean saw what seemed like a familiar form, a muscular man, moving if not gracefully then spiritedly. The man's face was smiling, beaming actually, as he followed the gyrations of a partner who moved considerably better than he did. Dean looked across his table to verify what he was seeing. Ralph's chair was indeed empty, and it was indeed Ralph dancing. And he was reminded suddenly of Chris, sprinting down a Manhattan street, a winged visored hat on his head, happy and unmindful of who was watching and what they thought.

Ralph was glowing, his face shiny from beads of sweat, when he returned to the table. Standing, he guzzled his beer, looking from the dance floor to Dean. "Well, what do you say, Di Nardo? Do you want to dance, big boy?"

His responses were many, but none were verbalized. Yes, he did; no, he didn't. What did it mean? What didn't it mean? Was he asking for just a dance or something more?"

"Dean," Ralph said, his eyes never leaving Dean's face. "If you don't dance now, then when?"

His father had danced. He had always danced. With women who would dance with him, perhaps because his wife wouldn't or couldn't.

His mother, the long-suffering woman whose husband had strayed. But who wouldn't have strayed from her unhappiness? She had been afraid of life and had lived it hidden safely behind her husband and family, seldom venturing into the world except through newspapers and television, both of which made her even more apprehensive.

As the car sped west toward the city Dean recalled the arguments. His father, wanting to visit Las Vegas. His mother, refusing, believing they needed the money more for other things. But in retrospect, what other things could have been more important than a trip that might have soothed, perhaps even saved, a marriage? His father had wanted to visit Italy. Why visit what their parents had rejected? she had argued. And successfully. They never went to Italy. Or anyplace else either. So just how successful had she been?

And so because she couldn't dance, his father had found someone, several someones, who could. He had danced with her and her until he finally met and remained with a woman who, Dean was astonished to realize, contemplating the reality of his thought and the fact for the first time, was his stepmother.

As they drove in silence, he thought about the cemetery he was about to visit and the plot where his mother was buried next to her mother and father, a sister nearby. It was on a hill overlooking Manhattan. He winced. As in life, so in death. His mother, looking at life as she had when she was alive—from a distance. A very great distance.

He was more his mother's son than his father's. His life, too, was dedicated to keeping himself safe, distant and deprived. Living on a hill. In a brownstone. But how safe was he if he felt so anxious? His house often felt now like a prison. Yet it was also a home, a refuge to be protected.

And he should protect it. For in doing so there just might come the protection he so sought. He must fight for the house. Not just because it was rightfully his but because of what the house was: evidence that two men had lived and loved there, of a marriage some would deny, refute. He couldn't allow that. If he gave up the house without a fight, he was giving up on himself.

He looked across at Ralph, intent on the Sunday traffic speeding toward Manhattan. Ralph had fought for himself with his children. He might have lost the battle but he had won the war, the one that mattered, the one within him. It might have seemed like a hollow victory, but Ralph knew that children change. They grow up, and some even mature. Circumstances change. But the one thing that remains constant is you: you and the relationship you establish to you, with you and for you.

He had never done that.

He could see the approach to the cemetery. The arrangements were for Ralph to drop him near the plot and then drive on to the city. It had seemed the most simple solution, particularly since he would be dining at Tony's that evening. At least that was what he had told both himself and Ralph. But it was an excuse, and a lie, he realized as Ralph stopped the car. It was his way of keeping Ralph separate—no, of keeping himself separate from his family, from their judgments. Or were they his own? He hadn't wanted to explain Ralph to anyone. Least of all to himself, he realized.

''Wait for me,'' he said suddenly.

''Don't go,'' he added as Ralph sat behind the wheel, a puzzled look on his face.

''Goddammit, Ralph. Come with me,'' he demanded as he stood by the car, not moving until Ralph nodded.

Janice was the first to greet him. She was standing next to a woman he did not recognize, although he knew who she had to be. She was not the cheap, gaudy blonde he imagined but a plump, well-dressed woman in her fifties, with strands of snow-white hair falling across her round and weathered face. She was smiling at him in recognition, although he was certain they had never met. He looked toward the grave site and saw Tony, his arm lent supportingly to a man Dean realized with surprise and difficulty was his father. He approached the two slowly, forgetting both the women and the man who had joined them.

Standing just to the left of the men, Dean stared at the tiny grave and headstone that stated the person lying there was his mother. He resisted the urge to throw stones, to beat up on the earth of her grave, to curse his mother for her stupidity. Which had only been the birthings of his own. He wanted to beat up on his father for all the years the man had beat up on him, emotionally and verbally. He wanted to hurt him as his father had hurt them all by dancing with everyone but him . . . but them. Instead, he stood with tears running down his face. He looked about. She was dead. His father, too, at least the father who had haunted his childhood and so much of his adult life was also dead, left behind so long ago. Only he had never left him.

He looked at his father and felt confused. Why were tears streaming down his face? And the face, not that of the father who lived in his mind but that of an old man.

He is seventy-three, Dean realized, surprised. His father's grief—or was it guilt, and did it matter?—was another surprise. His father was looking from the grave to the sky, and there was no mistaking the pain etched about his eyes and mouth. It was more than guilt, Dean realized. Guilt wouldn't bring a man to his wife's grave year after year. With flowers and wine. To toast the spirit, to wish it well.

Their eyes met. His father's face changed. It opened, and there was a hesitant, almost a shy smile. Dean approached and took the offered hand that held his, and not in a handshake. It was the touch of a child and not the grip of a man. His father was nodding, smiling and silent. He stood next to him, Tony at his other side, staring at the grave. He felt as if he were finally burying his mother and the marriage he had made in his mind between the father of his childhood and the boy he once was. As they turned away he saw his father's woman—no, he corrected, his wife—coming toward them with a scarf that she insisted his father wrap about his neck despite the fact it was June. She would not be refused. Dean felt her concern. He saw his father act with displeasure. But it was only acting.

"So," his father said as he offered Dean a plastic cup half filled with the ceremonial wine. "You look good. Suntanned. How's work? We see the commercials all the time.

"I think this thing with your house is very bad, very wrong," his father was saying. "It's your house. Fair and square. Tony tells me the facts. You'll see; you'll win."

For Tony to have told him the facts, he must have asked, Dean realized. And one usually asks because, on some level, one cares.

His father had turned, seemingly staring in Janice's direction, but it was not Janice he was looking at. Dean said nothing.

"You are coming to dinner?" Tony asked.

"Yes, and if you and Janice can handle it on short notice, there will be one more," Dean replied.

"We can handle it," Tony said softly. They stood together with neither speaking until Tony said: "Listen, this isn't the time to talk business, but time is running out. Have you given any further thought as to how you want me to handle Barbara's petition to proceed?"

Until that moment, whatever thought Dean had given to the question had ended in the confusion of two sides—both his—tearing at him. "I want to go for it. Now," he replied.

"Are you sure?" Tony asked as his hand reached out to grip Dean's shoulder.

His reaction was to pull away, but he didn't. He felt the warmth and the intensity of the physical touch, understood its intent, and answered: "Surer than I've ever been, but scared shitless nonetheless."

Tony nodded. As he again squeezed Dean's shoulder he said: "Let me tell Janice we've got one more for dinner."

Dean saw Ralph standing off to the side alone. He

walked toward him quickly, taking him by the arm and leading him to where his father was standing.

"Dad, I'd like you to meet Ralph Kayne."

His father squinted as he looked up. "Is this your friend?" he asked.

He didn't stop to think, didn't stop to measure the full ramifications of both the question and his response. He just replied, "Yes, Dad, he is. Ralph . . . this is my father, Carmine Di Nardo."

Sara looked at her youngest. "You guys certainly can pick your time to have a frank discussion. Can't you see I have some heavy decisions to make—like which earrings do I wear and what bracelet?—and you ask if your father is coming home? Honestly, Naomi, where are your priorities?" She saw her daughter's face fall and realized her attempt at humor had been lost on her youngest. "No, Naomi, your father will not be coming home with me." Again she saw the look, this time on all her children's faces. She could not decide if the pain in her gut was physical or emotional. If physical, perhaps it was the baby, she thought, fighting to get out. Maybe he or she would succeed within the next ten minutes and then she wouldn't have to wear this ugly dress to an awards dinner.

She would not be manipulated, would not allow the guilt she felt when looking at her children's expressions to decide her life. "Look, guys," she began abruptly. "I know you would like your father to come home and I know you've heard that he wants to come home, but it's just not that simple."

"Why not?" Robert demanded. "You either want him or you don't. Fish or cut bait. It's no big deal. Yes or no."

She stood there staring at him, trying not to flinch from the hostility.

"Lots of kids at school tell me," he continued, "that their parents have gotten it together after one or the other—and sometimes even both—have been caught screwing around."

She felt the girls' shock. And their hurt. She knew Robert was testing her, using words to hide and yet vent his anger.

"Girls, do me a favor while I get ready," she said calmly. "Go look for the taxi and let me know the minute it arrives. The longer it has to wait for me, the longer that meter runs and the more it costs."

They left, their questions basically unanswered. Well, so were hers, Sara thought. She turned toward Robert. "That sucked. If you're mad at me, say it. But don't use your anger to hurt me through your sisters. Now spit it out. What do you want from me?"

He shrugged and turned from her.

"You don't know, do you?" she said as she signaled for him to sit next to her on the bed. "Welcome to the club. I don't know what I want from me either. It's a confusing time." Her hand was stroking his hair as she spoke, trying to smooth the rough edges of her words as she did. "On the one hand you're mad at your father for leaving. Yet you're mad at me for not taking him back. And in between there are all kinds of feelings about why he left and where you fit in all of this. Am I right?"

Again he shrugged. She took his face in her hands and said: "Robert, if there was anything I could do to make your world right, I would. Unless it made my world wrong. And taking your father back right now might be the wrong thing for me to do."

"For *you* to do," Robert echoed.

"Yes. For me. As much as I love you and all my children, what concerns me most in this issue is me. 'Cause if it's not right and I'm not happy, believe me, you won't be happy either," Sara said.

"Don't you want Dad back, Mom?"

The voice was plaintive. It hurt. "I love your father, Robert, but we messed up," she explained. "Your father has hurt me. He says I've hurt him. Rob, I don't want to hurt anymore. So I don't know. I only understand that I can't go back, only ahead."

"Why can't you move ahead with Dad?"

"I'm not saying I can't. But I'm not saying I can. I'm just not certain your father can give me what I want and need." Sara laughed. "Particularly since I'm not even certain anymore what I want or need. And that adds to the problem."

"Then why are you going to that dumb dinner tonight?"

She considered the question and then gave Robert the same response she had given herself when she had asked the same question. "Because I belong there and because that award is as much mine as his," she added angrily. "And because he asked that I be there. And . . ." she faltered, "because I want to."

It was awkward. Stefan on the dais and she at a table of his colleagues, each of whom she was certain knew of their estrangement and the reason for it. And there was one empty seat, one person yet to arrive, although the soup had been served.

They were more solicitous than usual, taking pains to include her in the conversation, each nervous, fearing that someone might inadvertently say something that would create still more tension. From those she expected support, the wives, she received rejection, they seemingly threatened by both her presence and her position.

And still the seat remained empty.

The baby kicked, a sign that he was no more comfortable than she.

They asked about the baby, cautious questions about its obviously imminent arrival. She appreciated their awkwardness but was more concerned with her own. She mentioned she would soon be joining their ranks as a teacher, and they laughed, thinking she had meant potty training and such. When they learned she did not, they were surprised. Teaching did not seem to go with the image they had of her.

They finally left her, drifting off into their own world of research and shop talk. She amused herself, looking about the room for a face she hoped she would not see. She didn't. And still the seat across from her, between two of Stefan's colleagues, remained empty. Once *her* name was mentioned . . . *Denise,* and it was followed by a long silence before the discussion was resumed.

She looked to the dais, where Stefan's attention was diverted from his chicken by a bearded elderly man to his left. She could see the flush on Stefan's face. Her own also felt hot. It was warm in the glass-enclosed dining room, the air conditioning either not quite effective or not yet in effect this early in June. The surrounding gardens, however, looked cool in their summer colors. Sara felt an urge to walk among the blooms, even to lie and bathe in their presummer scent. She wondered if the near two hundred assembled at the dinner, now involved in their glacé, would notice. If they were like Stefan, scientists, they would not. Not unless she did it under a microscope or in some controlled lab setting or in the pages of some research journal.

The waiter took away the place setting before the empty seat at the table.

As she sipped her tea, Sara thought about the award Stefan was receiving. She remembered it was being given for . . . "commitment beyond the usual." She giggled. A few at the table stopped in their conversation to look at her. Well, it *is* funny, she wanted to say in her defense. Except maybe it wasn't, she decided. But then again, hadn't Stefan's commitment to her been beyond the usual? Again she laughed in spite of her efforts not to. The baby kicked, this time angrily. Sara stopped laughing. This was no laughing matter. She tensed and tried to listen to her body. Had it been a kick or a contraction?

The presentation began, with Sara half listening and half timing what could have been nothing more than gas. Dimly she heard Stefan extolled first by a member of his department, then a dean and now a departmental chairman. She breathed deeply, turning her attention solely to what others were saying about her husband. Stefan was indeed an admired and respected member of his academic community. He was being honored, and she felt honored in the process. She wished now that she was seated by his side, for that was where she had been all these years, even when he was not physically present.

He was standing, handsome in his tuxedo, thanking university officials for creating a climate in which someone like him and his excellent staff could work. He spoke of his colleagues, looking directly at her table, and thanked them for their professional and emotional help. And then he singled out Denise Wolfe.

She felt the sharp intake of breath, not her own but that

of others at her table. She felt the eyes look from the empty seat to her face, to Stefan and then back to her. She never took her eyes off his face, her own remaining inscrutable as she listened to him speak of Denise's devotion to her job, her contribution to his work.

She struggled to rise, thinking if he could so embarrass her then she could him by leaving. But she remained seated when she heard him say how sorry he was that Denise Wolfe wasn't here tonight and how even sorrier he was to accept her resignation.

She heard the murmurs at her table.

And he wished his colleague luck in Durham, North Carolina, where she had obtained a job as head of her own department at Duke University.

He continued to speak, but she hardly heard. He had fired her. Stefan had let Denise Wolfe go.

He was thanking one last person and once more sharing his award.

Who, this time? Sara wondered.

My wife, Stefan explained, who created the space and the climate at home that gave me the serenity and the stability and the nurturance that all academicians and scientists require.

Words. Just words, she decided. Many men had said similar words over the years when accepting their honors. But it didn't matter. None of the men had been Stefan, and none of the women about whom those words were spoken had been her. Again she heard the murmurs and felt the stares of those seated about her. This time she did not look away but smiled. To those skilled at reading facial expressions, it was obvious Stefan Schell's wife was saying: Every word my husband speaks is true.

Her heels clicked on the hardwood floors, reverberating throughout the empty house. The van, with whatever carpeting and furnishings that hadn't been sold and were making the move to the Truesdale estate, had already left. Walking about, mentally photographing corners and nooks, Joanna thought how much bigger the house now seemed without furniture and how very empty without people. But then the emptiness had been there even with people, she realized. Breathing deeply, Joanna tried to dispel her pervading uneasiness. A move was never simple. This one was particularly complicated, difficult and anxiety-producing—more than just a physical stretch.

She stood in the foyer, looking into the living room and then the dining room, remembering when she had stood in this very same spot almost twenty years ago and had thought how the house had "possibilities." Like their marriage and their lives together. But that was twenty years ago, yesterday and yet a lifetime.

She listened. She heard nothing but silence, which she discovered was different from quiet. The former was unnerving, actually disquieting, while the other was what one paid for when one paid taxes in Beverly Hills. Even the phones had been disconnected. Like everything else in the house, and soon, like everyone.

The sudden figure in the doorway frightened her until Lilith's face came into focus. Joanna nodded, acknowledging her presence. Lilith kept a distance, as if understanding that for the moment that was what Joanna needed. When she spoke it was, however, with some urgency. "We must leave in a few minutes if we're to be on time for the service." Again Joanna nodded. She understood. It would be the last professional service Stone and Bennett would render Lileen Lavery. Her own, so deeply personal, had ended two days ago at Lileen's bedside, holding her hand as she drifted in and out of coma and in and finally out of life. She had neither wept nor mourned but had silently rejoiced for a woman with whom she had shared more than with most. And when she had released Lileen's cold and limp hand, it had felt as if she had released something more. She had. Some part of her that had also been sick but that was now dead and needed burying.

Perhaps she had been wrong. Perhaps she should have told Reynolds then. But she had wanted to make each of their moving days as simple and unemotional as possible. She wondered now, as she wandered upstairs for a last time and a last look, if that were possible. At the head of the stairs was what had come to be known as the guest room. It became that when she had lost the baby and, later, her every hope of ever having another.

She smiled as she gazed into the room, thinking of Dean's ecstatic phone call. It had greeted her on her return from the hospital the day of Lileen's death. Sara had given birth to an eight-pound, three-ounce girl. To be named Rachel . . . after her mother. It was then that she had cried. For Sara's act of forgiveness and for her fear that Stacey would never reach so liberating a place. And at that moment she had known she was mourning and yet celebrating her lost-and-newfound lives, and that she had to act on both.

She should not have waited, Joanna again thought, chastising herself. She should have spoken to Reynolds then. What matter that they seldom spoke anymore? What matter that they never truly had? They must now, and they would as soon as she found him.

The door to what was once Stacey's room was open. Which hurt, as the door to Stacey's current room was not. Joanna had yet to receive an invitation to the house in West Los Angeles that Stacey now called home. She did not expect she would, not immediately. She had called, had tried to reach out, to touch, to hold, but it was like trying to touch or hold air. The relationship had no substance. It was there but invisible. Her daughter was happy living as and in her boyfriend's shadow. Joanna remembered when that had been true for her and wondered if that would ever change for Stacey. She looked about the empty room. The little girl she had so loved was nowhere to be found, and so she closed the door, knowing as she did that it was more than just the door to a room she was closing.

She was crying when she entered her bedroom, empty, silent except for the sound of water running in the bathroom, where Reynolds was showering away the sweat of the move. She stared at the space where their bed had been. It was just one of the many places where their marriage had failed. She remembered the first night they had made love in this room. The memory was not as hurtful as she had feared it might be as the experience had been unsatisfying . . . for her. And she recalled how then she had thought that was how it was meant to be and would always be because she was a woman. How that had changed! But only years later and with Barney Reardon.

She would not be denied that expression, or any other, any longer. That she had was more her fault than Reynolds's. She understood that and her responsibility now, which was, as many had maintained, to herself and not to others.

He came out of the bathroom holding her overnight bag. "I don't understand why you didn't have the movers take this with everything else to the new house," he said as he zipped up his fly and slipped into loafers he was wearing without socks.

"Because they're not going to the house," she said softly.

"Well, then, where the hell are they going?" he asked without looking at her, his focus on the hair he was now brushing in the still-covered-by-steam bathroom mirror.

"With me," she replied, wondering if this was the way to end a marriage. But what do you do—post banns, send an announcement, take time on the radio station your husband listens to during his drive time? And it was not a hasty decision or an unexpected one. Not really. Certainly he must have expected to hear the words she was about to say. Just as certainly he must have contemplated saying these very same words these many months of their estrangement.

"Are you going to explain?" he asked, his attention now focused on her rather than on his hair.

"Reyn, I'm going to live at Lileen's halfway house. It has a suite of rooms that's fairly private and I think I'll be happy there. At least for a while," she said softly.

She could see him trying to compute her words. His expression spoke of his difficulty.

"You certainly can pick your spots to make your decisions," he said angrily. "But it's typical, isn't it? Jesus, Joanna, don't you think you could have said something sooner?"

She shrugged. "I don't know. Either way, there's no winner and no winning combination," she replied. "But contrary to what you may think, I was actually trying to help us both. Maybe I didn't pick the right spot, but what was I to do, Reyn? Move with you and then pick up and move again? Sorry. I don't have that kind of stamina. This is painful enough. I've been raw from the pain all week. But I've packed you up and I'm seeing you off. I've taken care of things. Now I'm taking care of me."

"Well, I'm not going to say I'm all that surprised. Christ. Since that goddamn accident I've been living with some crazy woman," he replied as he stared out the window.

"The accident has nothing to do with this. Not really," Joanna said, fighting to control her anger.

"Oh, sure. You're living in the clouds, talking to God and the angels, running all over the country to discuss death rather than staying home and living, and you're going to tell me the accident has nothing to do with this. Come on, Jo. Be real."

"Our problems existed long before my near-death experience, and you know it," Joanna said calmly. "Your extramarital affairs didn't begin with my talking to God and the angels, as you put it. Nor did mine."

Her admission of infidelity caused him to turn from the window, his face ruddy, his expression disbelieving as he stared at her. "Who?" he asked.

She almost laughed, thinking how typically male the question was. "It doesn't matter who," she said, "any more than it matters who were the women with whom you were involved. What matters is that both of us went elsewhere for what we were not giving to or getting from the other."

"None of those women mattered," he said angrily.

"Which is sad. The man I was involved with did. Only I didn't know that then," she replied.

"So what now, Joanna? You going to take off and sit on some mountain contemplating your navel for the rest of your life? Or are you going to sit on some guy's dick and contemplate *his* navel for the rest of your life?"

"Reyn, don't be mean or ugly. Neither is really you," she said softly. "It's your pride that's hurt, but nothing more. Deep down you know you're really not unhappy about my leaving. In some way it must even be a relief."

His expression changed. His eyes softened first, then the rest of his face and finally his body. He didn't resist when she approached and took his hand. "Reyn, I love you.'' He looked at her oddly. She laughed. ''I know. It's a strange thing to say to someone you're leaving, but it's true.'' She was smiling as she gazed into his eyes. ''You'll always be my prince, Reyn, the boy who charged into and took over my life. But Reyn, unless it's Charles or Albert, princes aren't really real. Nor are princesses unless their names are Diana. Mine is Joanna. For the first time in my life, in my mind, I'm real. And so are you. But our realities are different. Reyn, you deserve someone who shares your sense of what's important, who shares your reality, and I deserve the same,'' she continued. ''I'm so very grateful for what we had together, as it brought me here, to this point, and although I'm sad to be leaving you—Stacey, too—the truth is you both left me a long time ago. We left one another, but we never said good-bye. Now I am.''

He did not respond. He simply took her hand, hugged her to him and then swept past her into the hallway and down the stairs. She followed, her overnight case in her hand. At the door he turned. She smiled. He blinked. She could see he tried to return her smile, but was close to crying. She watched from the doorway, seeing him leave her life. She then closed the door behind her, turned the keys in the locks and did not look back as she signaled to Lilith waiting in her car that she would trail her to the funeral home in the Isuzu she had purchased just the other day.

EPILOGUE

"I don't find this thrilling," Sara said as she bit into the chopped-liver-and-pastrami sandwich that had made the trek from the Carnegie Deli in Manhattan to Princeton with Joanna and Dean.

"You want thrilling, Sara? Try my corned beef," Dean said as he offered half his sandwich.

"That's not what I mean and you know it. Life is definitely not fair," Sara groused. "The one time when I really would have loved to lunch at Tavern on the Green and I have a legitimate excuse that prevents it."

As if on cue, the legitimate excuse began to cry, and Sara hurriedly pushed back from the kitchen table, her fingers already on the buttons of her blouse as she said: "Feeding time at the zoo. I'll be back in a minute."

"Why don't we come up when you're finished?" Joanna called. "I'd like to see my goddaughter."

"I'll holler when Miss Piggy has finished pigging out," Sara replied from the top of the stairs.

As Joanna returned to her own sandwich, a now soggy mass of white-meat turkey on white bread with Russian dressing, Dean hoisted his cream soda in her direction. "To being forty-one, if anyone cares," he said.

"It is a bit anticlimactic after the angst of forty," Joanna replied. "But then, what wouldn't be anticlimactic after the year we've all just had?"

"The Second Coming, a new movie from Garbo. But that's about it," Dean said.

"I don't care. I'm glad I came. I needed to see your faces. And," Joanna added almost with a sigh, "I needed you to see mine."

Dean looked at Joanna, still trying to reconcile that someone so beautiful and seemingly serene could be so troubled.

"I see you, Jo," he said. "More clearly actually than ever before."

"Good," Joanna replied, "as sometimes of late I feel as if I've disappeared or slipped away. It's been a terrific adjustment going from one life and one very certain identity to something totally new and unfamiliar. I find I'm often alone. But not lonely. Actually, I felt more alone and lonely before I left Reynolds. I guess I didn't know how unhappy I was until the situation was behind me and I didn't have to pretend to myself anymore."

He understood. Not that he had ever been unhappy with Chris, but he had been lonely. For something more major than a partner or mate: himself.

"The weekends are particularly difficult," he heard Joanna say. "It's then that I miss who I once was, miss being married, miss the relationship. But I never miss the man, and I find that so sad. To be with one person for so many years and not miss him at all is saying something, and I'm not sure I like what it says."

Dean thought about Joanna's words and the thoughts those words prompted in his own mind. Thoughts of Chris. Unlike Joanna, he didn't miss the relationship, but he did miss the man. There were not many like Chris. Yet he wondered, given who he was today and who Chris had been, whether they would still be able to make a go of it. So much had changed.

"You're happy, aren't you?" he heard Joanna asking, and he had to admit that, despite certain continuing anxieties, he was. With his decision to play the heavy in the new soap, his life was suddenly full. And complete. "You know," he mused, "you feel a helluva lot better when you begin to take the responsibility for your own life. Even as you hate it. Making decisions is so damn difficult. Not second-guessing yourself is even harder."

"You are sounding so wise," Joanna said, smiling.

"I think, Jo, I'm finally growing up," Dean said.

"Don't!" Joanna said softly as her eyes caressed his

face. "Stay and play with me for just a while longer. This time I'll let you use my pink pail and shovel."

He laughed, remembering the playground on Flatlands Avenue and the afternoon his mother and Joanna's mother had taken their children together to play in the sandbox. They might have been five, six at the most, and Joanna had a new pail and shovel that she wouldn't share with him.

"So I punched you," Dean said aloud.

"Yes, you exerted brute force, and although I cried, it was then, not that first day in kindergarten, that I really fell in love with you," Joanna replied. "Wouldn't I have made some caveman a wonderful woman? Belt me once and I'm yours." She was laughing, but her laughter stopped abruptly when she realized that today she was no longer anyone's punching bag, that no one—not even Stacey—could beat up on her physically or emotionally.

"What it it, Joanna?" Dean asked, picking up on Joanna's sudden change of mood.

"I was thinking about Stacey, who's angrier with me now than she's ever been," Joanna said. "She is absolutely furious that I've left Reynolds. She blames me for the breakup, but in some strange way I think she really blames herself. She has even accused me of leaving to punish her. So now she punishes me by rejecting me totally. It hurts me, but it also makes me so angry and I think that's good."

"She'll come around, Jo," Dean said softly. "Not that I'm any expert on kids, but I've seen how Ralph's daughter has surfaced and how she and Ralph are beginning a whole new relationship. I think it's only a matter of time before his son makes contact again, too."

"What is it with you two holding hands? Is it love or a seance?" Sara asked as she entered the kitchen, her fingers still working the buttons of her blouse. "I'm going to miss these," she said wistfully.

"What, the buttons?" Dean asked.

"No, dummy, these!" Sara said as she pointed her chin downward. "My boobs. They're so wonderful. I feel like Loni Parton."

"I think you either mean Loni Anderson or Dolly Parton," Joanna said dryly.

"Whatever," Sara said, unconcerned. "The point is, boobs are one of the great pluses of pregnancy and nursing for us flat-chested girls. God, I even turn myself on looking at my bod. But alas," Sara said mournfully as she picked up the remains of her sandwich, "they will soon be history, as deflated as my spirits when I wean Rachel at the end of the year."

"Why so soon," Joanna asked, "if you're enjoying it so?"

"Because I've informed the Board of Ed I'll be available for substitute teaching come the spring term," Sara replied as she added still more mustard to her sandwich.

"And just who is going to watch the baby?" Joanna asked.

"Details, details," Sara said, annoyed. "Maybe I'll get lucky and the kid will get married, or if marriage isn't her thing then live with some kid whose mommy will take care of both of them."

As Joanna laughed Dean said: "That's the problem with having a child late in life. It ties you down."

"Listen, gorgeous one," Sara said, her tone suddenly quite serious. "The only child that ever tied me down was me. Today, if I'm tied to anyone or anything it's by choice and necessity and not by neuroses. And the truth is: I don't feel tied. Not in the way you mean. Maybe that's because I know Rache is the last child I'll ever have. I'm not wishing the time away but savoring every moment, although if the truth be told, I'd be delighted if the child would clean up after herself. You'd think if man has learned how to make a self-cleaning oven, God, with all his practice, could have learned by now to do the same with a kid."

"This woman is high on chopped liver," Joanna said. "And speaking of high, weren't we supposed to meet you *up*stairs?"

"I thought Rachel needed some time alone," Sara explained as she began to crumb the table. "She likes to lie there and drool after she eats, letting go with an occasional fart here and there, which seems to pleasure her."

"Charming. You've convinced me I should just sit here and finish my lunch," Joanna said. "After all, if you've seen one baby, you've seen them all, even if none was ever quite so attractive as you make this one seem."

"I've got to get her up soon anyway," Sara said, laughing. "This is Stefan's afternoon to visit," she explained.

"How often does that happen?" Dean asked.

"Several times a week," Sara answered. "He dotes on Rachel. And why not, she flirts with him outrageously. She bats those baby blues and the man is a wimp around her."

"And how does Mama do with Papa?" Joanna asked.

Sara giggled. "We're dating. Isn't that sweet? A forty-one-year-old woman who gets herself all gussied up and then takes herself and her boobs over to her husband's apartment for an evening of fun and games."

"Oh, yeah? Just what kind of games and how much fun?" Dean asked.

"Well," Sara began, "first we have dinner. Usually take-out food from the Chinese restaurant. Maybe some moo shu pork or Hunan chicken . . ."

"Sara, we are not interested in what you and Stefan eat, for God's sake," Joanna said impatiently.

"And we talk," Sara continued, unperturbed and not about to be rushed. "Yes, folks. I know that comes as a big surprise, but . . . Stefan talks. And then—here's the good part—we sometimes go to bed. At least we have the last four times, which equals our entire sex life for the year 1984. And come to think of it, '85, too. And the sex is better than it ever was," Sara said in a conspiratorial whisper. "Stefan actually breathes hard now, which may not sound like much to you but to me it constitutes hot sex."

"Sara!" Joanna protested as she tried not to encourage Sara by laughing.

"Well, it's true," Sara said. "Stefan is a lousy lay and a bit of a bore, but I love him and I've given up trying to analyze why."

"So you'll get back together again," Dean said.

"Watch my mouth and read my lips if necessary," Sara said. "Because I already told you what's happening. We are dating. We are talking. To one another and a marriage counselor. He is trying; I am trying. And that's as far as it goes,'' Sara said emphatically. ''For now! I'm not rushing into anything. I'm having a wonderful time dating my husband, and that for the moment is sufficient.'' She giggled again. ''You know, I actually sneak into my own home after midnight and then go around the house the next day blushing, wondering if my kids know where I go at night and what I do once I get there. I tell you, it's wonderful.''

And it was. Joanna could see that on Sara's face, hear it in her every word.

''And what about you, Joanna?'' Sara asked, her face that of an innocent. ''You getting any these days?''

Joanna choked on the last bite of her sandwich. ''You sleaze! Am I getting any indeed! When? When am I supposed to be 'getting any,' as you so grossly put it? Do you forget I'm working at an office, a halfway house and a hospital?''

''Oh, just answer my question,'' Sara said, annoyed.

''What are we, back at school, and this is show-and-tell?'' Joanna demanded.

''If you got something to show, yes. Tell it,'' Sara replied.

''Sorry to disappoint you, but the answer is no. I'm celibate,'' Joanna said. ''In case you've forgotten, I'm still a married woman.''

''What has that to do with anything?'' Sara asked as she sipped the beer she had been told was good for nursing mothers. ''You're separated.''

''But not legally,'' Joanna responded, ''and that seems to matter to me, which is why I'm beginning that formal process next week. In part, Sara, so that I can be available. Which is such a nicer way of saying the same thing you just said ever so tackily.''

''Oh, puleeze,'' Sara groaned. ''This is me, remember? I've not forgotten my old childhood friend, Joanna Erlich. And once fast, always fast, I say.''

''Why a legal separation, Jo?'' Dean asked. ''Why not just a divorce?''

''Because one is faster than the other. Divorce in California can be very complicated, particularly when a couple has a lot of joint holdings,'' Joanna explained. ''It will take months before the lawyers will come to an agreement, and I want to be free sooner.''

''I don't understand,'' Sara said. ''What is a legal separation going to give you that you don't already have now?''

''A legal piece of paper that says I'm separated . . . separate,'' Joanna replied. ''Which means if I want to date, I can.''

''But you can do that now,'' Sara persisted.

''But I can't,'' Joanna corrected. ''I know it's archaic and that it doesn't even make much sense, but I find while I'm still legally married, I'm unable to function like a single woman. So in the meantime I am seeing—although I don't know that I would call it dating—someone I have known for years. But not in the way I'm getting to know him now.''

''I knew it,'' Sara said triumphantly. ''There is a man, and she's been holding out on us. Who is he, Joanna? And if you expect to see your goddaughter I suggest you cut the crap and talk straight and fast.''

''He's someone in my business, a contact, actually, who I recently met again on a press junket,'' Joanna said quietly. ''That he remembered I only drink dry sherry moved me, particularly since he had only heard me order it once before, and that was when I had told him I wouldn't be seeing him anymore.''

''Let me see if I've got this straight,'' Sara said, her mind reeling. ''You had a lover and you won't sleep with him now because you're not legally separated.''

Joanna nodded.

''I understand,'' Sara said. ''It makes perfect sense. Doesn't it, Dean? Please, God, let it make sense or else my brain is drying up faster than my milk.''

''Actually,'' Joanna continued, ''what's happening between this man and myself is rather nice. And like you, Sara, I haven't the vaguest idea where it's going—although I suspect you really do—and I don't care. I just know it's nice to be making a friend of a man instead of just making him. That's new for me.''

Dean was struggling under the weight of his reactions to Joanna's words. His situation, although different, felt similar to hers. Only less comfortable. It had been easier with Chris, so much more comfortable and with so much less to risk. Theirs had begun as a sexual relationship that then grew into intimacy. That had been usual in the gay lifestyle. With Ralph the situation was reversed, and now there was an obligation to sex, a commitment, that wasn't there with a stranger.

"And what about you there, Sphinx? What's happening in your life?"

"Dammit, Sara. What do you think this is, the sixties and some encounter or rap group where everyone has to talk *straight?*" Dean asked angrily.

"Oh, come on, Dean," Sara pressed. "*Share . . . relate . . .* give us your *gut feeling,*" she said, trying to suppress her laughter.

"You want my gut feeling? Hold on. I feel it coming on and in another moment I'm going to vomit all over you. Now how's that for a gut feeling?" Dean asked.

"Don't you think he's being very hostile, Joanna?" Sara said.

"Oh, no. Leave me out of it," Joanna replied. "If Dean wants to remain private, wants to keep himself *closeted,* that's solely his affair."

"I love your subtlety, Joanna. You have a real way with words—that stab you in the back," Dean said, pretending to be annoyed. "The truth is I don't know what to say because this thing with Ralph is totally unlike anything I've ever known before."

"What 'thing' with Ralph?" Sara demanded. "I think I missed a beat here. I went into the hospital, was in labor for four hours, and suddenly, while I'm busy birthing, one friend is dating a former lover while the other has a 'thing' going with a gorgeous man who obviously adores him."

"Sara, shut up. You're crazy," Dean said.

"I'm crazy? Oh, no. You're the one who's crazy if you let him get away," Sara said.

"Sara, unlike you and Stefan or Joanna with her man, Ralph and I are really friends. That's what makes it so difficult for me to move it to another level."

"So call in the Seven Santini Brothers, but move it," Sara said. "He's special. And if you need help in combining sex with intimacy I've got the name of a great shrink."

"It isn't only the sex, Sara. There are other problems . . . dangers for someone like me," Dean explained. "Ralph is a very strong man. He's a producer, and producers take charge. Of everything. It would be very easy for me to fall into the trap of letting him take charge of me. I think you of all people, Sara, can understand that danger."

She nodded. She did.

"Well, I don't want that, although there's still some part of me that does. I think that, too, you can understand. So no jokes, please. I'm hanging in, but it's hard. The only thing that makes it somewhat easier is, as Sara has said, he loves me and the truth is I love him."

His face changed. It relaxed. As did he. "You won't believe this, but that's the first time I've admitted that," he said, close to tears.

Sara blew her nose rather loudly. "Well," she said finally, "if Madam here is done with that WASPY sandwich of hers we can visit the miracle upstairs. I do hope you brought gifts, a little incense and myrrh."

"White-meat turkey and Russian dressing is not WASPY," Joanna protested as she followed Sara upstairs.

"Oh, shut up, Joanna, or admit it. You're a closet *goy,*" Sara said as she led them to Rachel's crib, which was just beside her own bed. "Behold the fairest of the fair . . . Princess Rachel."

They stared into the crib at a pink face whose light blue eyes stared back without fear at the two strange faces peering down at her.

"But this baby is gorgeous, absolutely gorgeous," Joanna said.

"I must say, Joanna. I do not find your surprise at such a fact a great vote of confidence," Sara said. "In case you haven't heard, the apple does not fall far from the tree."

"Sara, I think by now you should have noticed that the angel in that crib is not an apple but a little girl," Joanna countered.

"Do you want to hold her?" Sara asked as she picked up Rachel and placed her in Joanna's outstretched arms. Joanna struggled awkwardly until she found a position in which she and the baby felt comfortable. Sara watched, pleasured and proud, as Joanna cooed to Rachel, but she was keenly aware of the tears edging out of Joanna's eyes.

"One of my happiest times was when Stacey was a baby," Joanna explained, her voice cracking from emotion. "And I'm not fooling myself. I know working with the girls at the halfway house is me just trying to be the mother I feel I wasn't to Stacey when she was their age." She looked down at Rachel, whose fingers where toying with the necklace dangling provocatively just above her breasts. "Maybe I should adopt some little girl and try all over again. I have plenty of time, at least an hour a week that isn't claimed."

"You know, Chris often talked about our adopting a child after we bought the house," Dean said suddenly. "It was something he really wanted to do, but then I couldn't see myself with a little Vietnamese or any other kind of child for that matter. I was too much of a kid myself. I think Chris always felt cheated, and I didn't understand that until I heard Ralph say almost the same words Joanna just did: that the happiest times of his life were when his children were young. So maybe I made a mistake."

"You can always rectify it," Sara said. "There are thousands of unwanted children, regardless of what the Pro-Lifers say, that you could adopt. God knows you can afford it, plus the help you would need."

Dean laughed, but it was bitter rather than humorous. "Sure. I can see the agencies now just rushing to give away their babies, even the ones you so rightly say nobody wants, to an aging homosexual who might lose his home, not to mention his jobs, in a court scandal coming up very soon now."

"How soon, Dean?" Joanna asked, her voice reflecting her concern.

"We have a court date for the second week in November," Dean replied.

"That soon?" Sara said worriedly.

''Not soon enough,'' Dean replied. ''I wish it were tomorrow. I've lived with the uncertainty long enough.''

They were silent, each considering the dangers and the possibilities of what Dean was facing.

''What are your chances?'' Sara asked as she took Rachel from Joanna's arms.

''Depends on the judge,'' Dean replied. ''On our side we have legal right. Moral, too, in my opinion. On their side they have myth, popular prejudice and the legal fact that a woman who has not lived with a man in ten years can still claim to be his wife and therefore be entitled to all benefits. I'm prepared for the worst.''

Joanna looked at Dean, surprised at the calm with which he was speaking. ''You are going to fight?'' she asked, wondering if his calm was based on the path of least resistance or passive acceptance. ''It *is*, after all, your house.''

''I'm going to fight, Joanna,'' Dean said softly, ''but not for the house. Sure, I want to keep it, but that's not as important as it once was. It won't be my home much longer if Ralph and I decide to live together; neither my home nor his would be right for us. They're filled with memories and attachments that have nothing to do with who we are today.''

''Yes, I understand that,'' Joanna said, thinking of the home she had been so reluctant to leave on North Canon Drive.

''When we get to court,'' Dean continued, ''I'll be fighting for me. I'll be fighting because I'm really afraid to fight, to put myself out there for people's judgments and criticism. We're talking of job loss here and of giving up every chance of ever being thought of as a leading man should it reach the media that I am gay.''

Which it probably will, Joanna thought. Again she stared at Dean. He was right. He was growing up.

''What I now understand,'' Dean was saying, ''and what I can't run from is the fact that losing all—the house, my career—is nothing in comparison to losing me. And if I denied again who I was, what I am, that's what I would be doing. How could I live with myself if I did that? How could I live with Ralph, *be* with Ralph, if I negated who and what I was with Chris and what we were to one another?''

''You're going to win, Dean. I just know it,'' Sara said.

Joanna got by the lump in her throat to say: ''He's already won, Sara. No matter what the judge decides. I know. Nothing feels so good or so right as when you stand up and say to others, This is who I am and this is what I believe. And no house is a home. No,'' Joanna repeated. ''A home is what you carry inside you.''

And when she looked up at her friends, looked about, Joanna began to cry even as she laughed. For suddenly she saw not only who she was with but where she was . . . finally and at last in the one place she had never been and where she had always wanted to be . . . upstairs in Sara Rosen's bedroom. It was everything and more than she had thought it would be. In its own way it, too, was home.